THE HIDDEN LIBRARY

HEATHER LYONS

Cerulean
Books

PRAISE FOR THE COLLECTORS' SOCIETY

"The most unique, fascinating, wondrous book I've read in a very long time! I was glued to every page."–*Shelly Crane, New York Times bestselling author of Significance and Wide Awake*

"So unique and different, the first thing I thought when I finished . . . Man I wish I would have thought of that! Buy this book, you won't regret it!"–*#1 NYT bestselling author Rachel Van Dyken*

"This book should come with a handwritten tag that says 'Read Me.' And you should. Right now. One of my favorite reads of the year. Loved it! I want to live inside Heather's brain."–*Daisy Prescott, USA Today Bestselling author of Modern Love Stories*

"This fantasy was a breath of fresh air. It was unique, inspiring, and obviously a five-star read. If you enjoy romance, adventure, and traveling through worm holes go get this book ASAP!"—*Jennifer Foor, author of the Best Selling Mitchell Family Series, The Kin Series, The Bankshot Series, The Twisted Twin Series, Diary of a Male Maid, Hope's Chance and Love's Suicide*

"One of the most inventive stories I've ever read. Brimming with sexiness and romance, magic and lore, it's a modern-day fairytale adventure that is not to be missed."–*Vilma's Book Blog*

"THIS BOOK WAS EPIC! . . . I wanted to escape into a story that held not only romance, but also mystery. And that's exactly what I got when I read **The Collectors' Society**. I got a riveting, refreshing, and unique plot that was not only driven by a beautifully sweet romance, but also a thriving story filled with suspense and unbounded mystery."–*Angie and Jessica's Dreamy Reads*

"Alice is the new standard that I set for all heroines."–*BFF Book Blog*

"Deserving to be a new classic for the modern day, **The Collectors'**

Society should be on your must read list."—*The Paisley Reader*

"If you love classic literature, and you love fantasy and fairy tales, this is a must read book for you."—*Book Briefs*

"This is one of those books where you have to sit back and question an author's sanity because how the hell did they ever come up with this amazingly insane and totally unique idea if not for a bit of insanity on their parts. All I can say is thank goodness for Heather Lyons and her crazy thoughts, **Collectors' Society** is. . . . . . I can't even explain it, just know that it IS . . ."—*Reads All The Books*

" . . . A unique tale that will leave you breathless, enthralled and begging for more. If you thought you knew classic fairy tales, think again!"—*Resch Reads and Reviews*

"I'm finding it almost impossible to put down in words the love I feel for this story. It was nothing like I expected and yet everything I wanted."–*The Book Hookup*

The Hidden Library
Copyright © 2015 by Heather Lyons
http://www.heatherlyons.net

Cerulean Books
First Edition
ISBN: 978-0-9908436-3-4

Cover design by Whit And Ware
Editing by Kristina Circelli
Book formatting by Champagne Formats

To Jon,
true love, north star, and binary
all rolled in one.

INTERROGATION TECHNIQUES

ALICE

"**Y**OU AND I ARE due for a talk, don't you think? Lady to lady."
The cackles erupting from the woman before me would make the sorceresses of Wonderlandian lore proud. Or even the Red Queen, who often practiced perfecting such a laugh to be used during the Red Court's infamous bandersnatch arena games. Rage has turned Rosemary's eyes bloodshot yet glassy, and with her black hair dipped white and in a bird's-nest array around her head, she promises to be a fright to behold for many.

I am not afraid of Rosemary, though. Especially not when she is constrained as she is.

We are in one of the Institute's more secure rooms with a locked door behind me. The only piece of furniture within is the chair she's strapped to. Everything else was hastily removed prior to our entrance.

The Collectors' Society, the clandestine organization I work for, never saw fit for such a space prior to the last few days. While technologically advanced and cunning, their specialties have lain in the acquisition and preservation of catalysts from various Timelines, not the capture and interrogation of villains. But two such persons newly reside within the Institute's walls, and answers must be taken, whether willingly or through force.

As my partner is currently embroiled in important meetings, I am the woman to happily provide such coercion.

"What is your name?"

Spittle flies from between Rosemary's lips. "Go fuck yourself, you ugly bitch whore!" A frenzy overtakes her, much like the berserkers of yore. She shouts, she struggles against the straps binding her to the chair, she froths at the mouth. And then, just when it appears she might burst out of her skin and morph into a beast, she begins singing in a voice so beautiful, so rich and pure, a woman with a softer heart than mine might shed a tear over it.

Unfortunately for her, though, I am no such lady.

Carry on, beyond the skies,
beyond tumultuous sea,
to the heart of the mountain
lies wondrous future for ye.
Sing, sing, little children!
Spill blood graciously.
Rest assured, in the end,
treasure and glory await thee.

The villainess' head tilts back, her eyes close. Her voice lowers and begins anew.

Fear not the blade of death,
fear not the hole of time.
Come, come, little children!
Harken to beauteous sign.

The small earpiece I am wearing vibrates as Mary Lennox's voice says, "Well, if she isn't crazier than a bag of hungry opossums, then I don't know what's what."

I am unsure of what opossums are, but I feel it is safe to agree with my colleague's assessment. I have known and fought many a crazed lady in my life, but Rosemary is one of the most unsettling. The others—the Queens of Red, Hearts, and White—all had method and rationale behind their madnesses and were more than happy to wax eloquent on issues when queried. I may have rarely agreed with their actions, but I knew what made them tick. This woman, who has attacked me multiple times and is suspected to have destroyed numerous Timelines and thereby murdering countless souls, cannot willingly offer up any rhyme or reason for her actions.

She is an alien creature if there ever was one.

I cannot allow what she has done to continue, even though Rosemary is now in Society custody. A team of our agents captured her and an associate whilst several others and I were acquiring the Wonderlandian catalyst. Unfortunately for all, though, S. Todd, Rosemary's assumed paramour and partner, escaped after annihilating a catalyst and slashing Abraham Van Brunt's throat. The Society's leader is currently recovering in a nearby hospital and doing well, but the events have left our organization impatient to bring these fiends to justice.

I clap politely whilst Rosemary softly hums another stanza. Her eyes close in rapture, her head slumps forward. "What a pretty song. The time for such diversions is over, though. What is your full name?"

Rage overtakes her once more. This time, her fits send her and the chair she's strapped to toppling over onto the ground. From there, she lashes about like a fish out of water.

I step forward, crouching down over her sideways body until I have her pinned sufficiently below me. She gnashes her teeth, snarling like a rabid beast. I carefully take hold of her jaw, ensuring my fingers remain safe from her overly sharp-appearing teeth. "You are responsible for the deletion of numerous Timelines. True or false?"

Attempts to whip her head about are stymied by both my grip and the awkward angle of her body trapped beneath mine. "Eat shit," she hisses.

I am undeterred at her pathetic efforts. She no longer holds the upper hand, no matter what delusions she suffers under. "Where is S. Todd?"

"You're going to die, bitch!"

Further questions are answered with loudly voiced assurances of my upcoming albeit untimely demise. I am close to violence when a thought comes to me.

I release her face and stand up. Interestingly enough, my sudden retreat has left her momentarily stunned.

"Alice?" Mary's voice fills my ear. "Is everything okay?"

My colleague has been observing the interrogation via a security camera stationed in the corner of the room. To answer, I push on the small earpiece. "Have the door opened."

Rosemary resumes her cackling. She thinks she has bested me, and I allow her this piece of assumed yet false accomplishment.

When I exit the room and the door is locked behind me, I instruct the guard, "As she chose to fall to the ground, leave her be." And then I make my way to the nearby medical wing of the Institute.

"She's going through detox," Victor Frankenstein Van Brunt informs me minutes later. The Society's resident doctor has been overseeing Rosemary's so-called health for the last few days. "From what I can tell, she's been hooked on meth for ages. I warned you that getting straight answers out of her would be difficult."

Despite having gone through detoxification myself after leaving Wonderland and all of its drugging influences behind, I harbor no sympathy for Rosemary. Nor do I personally care what *meth* is or how difficult it may be for one to wean herself off of it either voluntarily or by force. I desire answers that will lead to solutions and nothing else will suffice. "What can be administered to compel her to answer my questions?"

Even after fighting alongside me just last week, somehow this statement from my lips surprises the doctor. He glances down at Rosemary's chart, brows furrowed. "You mean, like a drug?"

"Exactly."

His brows furrow even farther. "I think that she's—"

"One of two links we have to Todd. And most likely a murderous fiend herself."

A wry hint of a smile curls a corner of his mouth. "I was going to say that, coming off meth the way she is, I cannot vouch for the effectiveness of any such drugs."

"But do you possess them?"

He nods toward the door. "Lady's choice down in Mary's lab." Before I leave, he stays me with a gentle hand. "Did you ever interrogate suspects in Wonderland?"

I think that, given the chance, Dr. Frankenstein Van Brunt may be horrified at how many times I have done just such a thing. "War often requires a person to do whatever is necessary."

"But we aren't at war."

"Ah, but there you are wrong, Doctor. We most certainly are at war right now."

I march down the hallway to where Victor's love and partner, as well as my friend and colleague, awaits. Inside, I find Mary Lennox hunched over a microscope, swearing under her breath. I allow the door's slam to indicate my arrival. Never one for surprises, though, she doesn't even flinch. She simply motions to the tablet next to her, now showing a muted scene of Rosemary appearing as if she's howling herself hoarse whilst still lying on her side upon the floor. "Don't tell me you let that hag get to you."

I sigh irritably as I make my way over to where she is. "The so-called kid gloves I've been requested to utilize aren't working. It's time to switch tactics."

"That's Society policy for you, I suppose." She glances up from the microscope. "We're thieves, not interrogators. Nobody really knows what to do with all of this."

"Is the belief that, one morning, Rosemary and F.K. Jenkins will wake up and think to themselves, *'Goodness, the folks at the Society are upstanding gents and ladies. I think I'll tell them everything today,'?*"

An unladylike snort escapes her. "Maybe Jenkins. That toad might crack sooner or later. But Rosemary?" Her nose wrinkles. "That'll be the day. Coming down off meth is only making her even more batshit crazy."

Thankfully, Mary doesn't sound as if she pities Rosemary any more than I do. "When I was in recovery, I was placed in a straight jacket." After being exiled from Wonderland, I'd returned to England and immediately checked myself into an asylum. It took months to wean myself off of the natural yet addictive drugs found in Wonderlandian food and drink.

My comment makes my colleague smile. "Were you in a padded room?"

"After threatening to bite bits of their faces off and send my armies after them, the nurses and staff of the Pleasance Asylum felt it best I be restrained to just such a room for both their and my safety."

"Too bad we don't have a padded room," she says forlornly. "We ought to petition for one once Brom is up and running."

I survey the lab—multiple refrigerated cabinets with glass doors line the walls. Inside are bottles and vials of all shapes, sizes, and colors. "Are these all from different Timelines?"

She rises to her feet only to lean against the gleaming white counter. "Pretty much. There are some from here, though. The Society has been collecting samples as long as they've been visiting Timelines."

"What about the Wonderlandian ones you collected?"

"Over in refrigerator seven." She motions toward the far wall. "I hope to start working on them soon. The SleepMist that took me and Finn out is totally intriguing. Plus, I've still got to work on synthesizing the venom from your spider soldiers that came home with us. They are such sweet little things."

Intriguing is definitely not the word I would have chosen to describe what the Queen of Hearts' soldiers did to my colleagues at the Society. Infuriating is a bit closer, in my opinion. "And here I was thinking you were all about plants."

"Plants make drugs." She's smiling again. "You can thank my interest in botany for leading me to my degrees in chemistry and pharmaceutical sciences."

Ah, yes. As I've recently learned, Mary's purpose in the Collectors' Society is multifaceted. In addition to helping collect catalysts, she's sent to various Timelines to collect plants, medicines, and drugs for research. As she once informed me, "You never know when such things will come in handy on future assignments."

It's something I'm hoping holds true. "Do you have anything in here that might compel an unwilling person to loosen their tongue?"

She walks over to where I'm standing and places both hands on my shoulders. "You are a woman after my own heart. I most certainly do have something in here that will do as you request—several somethings, actually. And I will happily supply you with any and all of these concoctions."

"A few months back, I saw on a television program that there's something called a truth serum."

"Locally, you mean?" She waves a dismissive hand between us. "Sodium thiopental is unreliable. It's used to relax people, yet even relaxed, there are those who can lie, distort, or embellish with the best of them. Its reliability is movie stuff." A slim beaker is extracted with a clear fluid within. "Now this bad boy is *book* stuff. I nicked it from a recent yet futuristic Timeline, and it's bloody fantastic. The only problem is, I'm having trouble synthesizing it. There are certain chemical compounds found within that Timeline that I'm unable to reproduce yet. I suppose this will just give me a reason to go back and get more."

I take the vial from her. Its label reads: TRUTH SERUM. "This is not sodium thiopental?"

"Oh no. This does exactly what it says."

"I'm terribly disappointed it doesn't have a clever name."

She shrugs. "The people in the Timeline I collected it from are a bit literal. What can you do?"

"How many dosages does this contain?"

"I'm not sure, to be honest. I have two vials of the stuff. We can start small and adjust as needed. I ought to point out I've only ever read about its effects; I've yet to see them in action. Should I warn you that there's always the possibility of overdose?"

I hand her the vial and press the button on my ear. Someone other than Mary has also been listening in on my interrogation attempts. "Have Rosemary brought into the medical wing and strapped down upon a bed. I plan on resuming my questioning within the next hour."

A small hiss sounds before the A.D., otherwise known as Jack Dawkins or the Artful Dodger, answers. "Copy that, ARL." As Van Brunt's assistant, he's been overseeing the housing for our two prisoners of war.

I take out the earpiece and stuff it in my pocket.

"Will you tell Finn what we're doing?"

Victor's brother and my partner, Finn Van Brunt, has taken over the Society's day-to-day operations as his father recuperates from his horrific attack. I'm loathe to trouble Finn with anything right now, as he's carrying many heavy weights on his shoulders, but as we've recently begun to build a meaningful relationship between us, I don't want further secrets to be the norm, either. While both our pasts have skeletons not yet revealed, I firmly believe our present and our future have no room for such further deceptions.

"Of course." And then, more wryly, "If I can lure him away from those meetings he's been trapped in from morning to night these last few days, that is."

"Poor man. You couldn't pay me to deal with all those people."

Once word got out amongst Society members and liaisons, Finn's phone has rang constantly. Everyone has questions, even more have opinions. The task of putting out fires is not an easy one.

"Fortunately for Finn," Mary continues, "Brom is coming home today. Man has his throat slashed, and what does he do? Insist upon convalescing at home as quickly as possible so he can continue working. Personally, I'd find myself a nice manly nursemaid and enjoy a bit of R&R, if you know what I mean."

Once Victor determined their father was in stable condition, the Van Brunt brothers immediately drafted plans to bring him home to be tended to by specialists they hand selected from Timelines the Society has good diplomatic ties with. To bring in local doctors would risk Society secrets, something Van Brunt would never stand for.

Both my and Mary's phones beep. Upon each of their screens reads the following message from the Librarian: *Meeting in three hours to discuss latest wall findings.*

An immense collection of photographs, newspaper clippings, book pages, and drawings from key stories were found taped and tacked upon the attic wall of the Ex Libris bookstore. It was a terrifying, infuriating monstrosity to gaze upon, as it is now assumed to be the key to unraveling Todd and Rosemary's destructive plans toward catalysts and Timelines. Van Brunt contacted several people across various Timelines to crack its cyphers.

I motion to my phone, an object still so foreign to me. "I pray this is good news."

"You and me both." Mary checks the time. "Best go and inform Finn of what we're planning. I'll get the serum readied and meet up with you in about fifty minutes. Be prepared to kick some ass."

I always am.

COURTING

ALICE

FINN IS, AS MARY and I correctly assumed, entrenched in yet another meeting. Inside the Institute's conference room is a group of a dozen or so men and women from various Timelines, hammering away at the younger Van Brunt with the same questions he's fielded for days now: *Where is Todd? What is Rosemary saying? What is F.K. Jenkins saying? Why can't you find Todd? Are any Timelines currently in danger?*

My partner handles them deftly, though. He is a smooth talker and has an uncanny way of setting even the paranoid at ease. When he notices me standing in the back of the room, though, he wraps the meeting up in just a way that has members and liaisons filing out with relief on their faces.

I shut and lock the door behind the last straggler.

"You," Finn tells me, "are a welcome sight."

As is he. My heart flutters as I take in his handsome visage. Tall, sandy-haired, and with the most lovely blue-gray eyes I've ever seen, I have been painfully attracted to Finn Van Brunt since the day I arrived at the Institute. I resisted the burgeoning feelings growing within me for months, reluctant to reopen my heart after the prophecies of Wonderland tore me apart from the man I loved and planned on spending my life with. And yet, when finally forced to face the truth, I could not deny the strength of my feelings toward my new partner.

He is good and kind and honorable. He is my north star after being lost for too long.

I make my way around the table, to the front of the large room. "Perhaps not so welcome. Rosemary is resisting answering my questions."

This does not surprise him in the least. "Jenkins, too. Henry Flemming spent a good two hours earlier today beating his head against the wall. All Jenkins has to say is how he's going to sue every single one of us and that he's an American."

Flemming is an older former military man who, like me, was sorely disappointed in how Society members stymied us from proper interrogation techniques. Old habits die hard, because irritation rose within me during the meeting in which we were told this. *Me, the Queen of Diamonds, requiring permission to interrogate a prisoner of war the way I see fit?* But then I remembered I am in New York City, not Wonderland. My position in the Society is not elevated above the rest, nor are its members mine to command.

That said, there was no mention of a restriction upon drug-induced interrogation.

"Do you have a few minutes to spare?"

Finn Van Brunt has the most delicious of smiles. "For you? Always." He holds up a finger and then goes to turn off the light and to close the blinds on the windows facing toward the hallway.

I lift my eyebrows up in silent question. He has no shame, though. "It's the only way to guarantee privacy." To illustrate his point, his phone chirps until he places it on silent. "What's up?"

"I will shortly be utilizing a truth serum of Mary's to compel Rosemary to talk."

It is comforting that my statement does not faze him. "What do you need from me?"

I reach out and finger the softness of the plaid shirt he's wearing. I like these shirts of his. I like how they look both comfortable and inherently sexy on him. I like them even more on the floor of his bedroom. But this is not the time for such lascivious thoughts, not when there is so much else to be done. "Nothing. I just thought it best you know. I expect to have answers from her before the night is through."

It's his turn to reach for me. Exhaustion drips off of his lean body. While he slept in my bed last night, he arose before dawn and has been in constant meetings and status reports throughout the day. After years of such experiences in Wonderland, I know the feeling well and wish there is something I can do to shield him from such responsibilities.

"I trust you, Alice. I know you'll do what it takes to get the job done. I wish I could be there, too, but . . ." He sighs quietly. "My afternoon is booked straight until the meeting the Librarian just scheduled to discuss the wall findings."

I wonder what he would think of my old methods, cultivated when madness and I were close friends. I would not have hesitated to hang Rosemary by a foot upside down until she feared her leg would tear from her body and words spilled from her mouth. "Has there been a breakthrough?"

"I don't know if I'd call it a breakthrough, but there's been some movement." His hands settle on my hips. "Let's just say you and I will be leaving first thing in the morning for an assignment."

"Is that wise, considering how Todd is on the loose?"

He tells me it is, and as I trust him, too, I let it go at that. Business must go as normal, according to Society members. Whilst we must hunt the fugitive, members must also focus on our shared mission to protect all Timelines.

We are about to open the conference room door and enter the hallway when he stops. He turns to me, his lovely eyes achingly sincere. "I want to take you on a date when all of this craziness is over. A real one. We've kind of gone about this all backwards, haven't we?"

One corner of my mouth lifts up. "Are you saying you'd like to court me?"

There is no playfulness to his face, no quirk to his own lips. My heart flutters at his seriousness. "Yes."

He wants to court me.

Too many emotions rush around in a caucus race throughout my body. I have no doubts of Huckleberry Finn Van Brunt's feelings toward me. I understood them two minutes ago just as well as I did this morning when I woke up and from the night before and from the day in Wonderland where he said, in not so many words, that he was falling in love with me.

I told him he was my north star, and meant it. He countered we are binaries.

He and I . . . We've never said those words, though, not the ones that truly spell out fragile, deep secrets of a heart and soul. Words so easily and yet unfortunately uttered by many, be it to express their appreciation of fried bits of potatoes to sports teams on the television. Words offered so frivolously about a variety of subjects and yet can be the most difficult, most painful, most meaningful, most cherished syllables we gift another person.

I have said these words before, to another man. Another man I still love. One I know, in the deepest confines of my heart, that I will love until the last breath escapes my body. A man who courted me in secret and then publicly in the face of astonishment, disapproval, confusion, and, in the end, prophesies.

I have willingly given the man in front of me my heart, though, whether he knows it or not. He now holds it in his hands, and while I pray he is my future, there is still a part of me that bucks in conflicted confusion and delight by this declaration of his.

He wants to court me.

And yet, as sweet and romantic as such a gesture might be, I require no such formalities. My affections for Finn Van Brunt have already solidified into something real and wonderful and meaningful. I reach up and touch his cheek. There's neglected stubble there, and I rather like this, too. "What would we do on such a date?"

Before he can answers, pounding on the door brings with it the A.D. "There's a call for you in the HQ, Finn." And then, noticing how close we're standing together, in the dark to boot, his rubbery grin slips down several notches. "You two wankers are at it again?"

I cannot count how many times my hand has itched to smartly slap this man's impertinent face, but none perhaps as strongly as now.

My partner must feel the same, because his voice turns cold. "Your recent loss of money is making you into more of an asshole than usual, you know. How much did you have to pay Mary again?"

The A.D.'s beady eyes narrow toward Finn's obvious displeasure. "That would be none of your business."

"Except," Finn says flatly, "it is, isn't it? You made it mine."

The A.D. and Mary made a wager some months ago on whether or not Finn and I would ever give into the feelings building between us. Granted, it displeases me that such an inappropriate wager was made in the first place, even by Mary (who, I ought to point out, cares very little for propriety), but it is vaguely diverting to see just how hard the A.D. is taking his loss.

"A friendly word of advice," Finn continues. "My personal life is off-limits, as is Alice's. Is that clear?"

A small jerk of a bitter nod follows. "Wouldn't dare encroach upon the Queen and her boy toy's business now, would I?"

Finn takes a meaningful step toward the A.D.; the man bolts out of the room. To me, he says, "This is like the tenth transmission today. I want to track down whoever spilled the beans about our captures and strangle him or her."

"I would have never thought the Institute to be filled with such gossips."

"Everywhere is filled with gossips," he says dryly. "Except perhaps one of those monasteries where they've taken a vow of silence."

I close the door once more, and there, in the darkened conference room, I steal a kiss from the man I've fallen in love with. Live sparks flare throughout my body as we press up against the wood, and I wish, wish oh so very much, that there was time for more. But there isn't, of course. There are meetings to be had and villainesses to interrogate. There is still a fiend to bring to justice and a father and employer to welcome home. When we reluctantly pull apart, I like what I see, though. Finn's lips are swollen in just a way that makes me want to ensure they stay that way all day, even when we are apart.

The door is opened. We reenter into stark, brutal realm of reality.

"Oh!" He snaps his fingers. "Before I forget, there's this fundraiser the Society goes to every year at the New York Public Library in a couple weeks. There will be drinks, music, and dancing. I was wondering if you'd like to come with me?"

He is utterly adorable asking such a request, as if there was a chance I would reject him. "I would be honored to accompany you."

Wendy Darling, the Society's technology specialist, materializes before us, a pair of tablets in her hands, headphones ringing her neck, and a combined earpiece/mouthpiece upon her head. Her hazel eyes narrow as they track the slim length of space between our bodies. "The A.D. let you know about the transmission?"

Finn accepts one of the tablets she proffers. "Yeah. I'm on my way there now."

"Since you don't seem pissed, I take it he didn't tell you it was—" She quickly bites her lip. Shakes her head. Adds, more softly, "It's Tom."

Tom. I wrack my brain for the name, only to come up with a brief mention of a Tom from Van Brunt and Victor shortly before we left for Wonderland. A Tom had called then, hadn't he? Or at least contacted Van Brunt in some way. Finn wanted nothing to do with the matter, and when Van Brunt thought to persuade his son to speak to this Tom via his brother's influence, Victor smartly put their father in his place.

For a moment, the three of us stand in the hallway before the tech hub of the Institute, unfamiliar tension taking the place of words. But then Finn clears his throat. "I'll catch up with you at the meeting in a few hours. Good luck with Rosemary. If, by some miracle, I can escape these meetings, I'll come up to help." He leans forward and brushes a gentle kiss against my temple before heading into the hub.

As the door closes behind him, I ask Wendy, "When is Van Brunt scheduled to arrive?"

She taps on the tablet. "In about two hours. He's already sent a dozen emails out this morning. That man is a workhorse, if you know what I mean."

I do know. Being bedridden has not been easy for the Society's leader. Finn's phone has beeped incessantly with messages from his father during the last few days.

"Dr. Heidegger is with him," she continues. "As is . . . Crap. I always forget his name. The dude that's a surgeon but studies extraterrestrial microorganisms?"

I haven't the slightest clue who she's referring to.

She shrugs. "Dr. Watson wanted to come in, but he was delayed in his Timeline."

Fair enough, even though I have no idea who Dr. Watson is, either.

"Brom is in good hands." She utters this defensively, as if I've indicated otherwise, and it takes me aback. Before I can say anything, though, she mutters, "The A.D. wanted me to tell you that Rosemary's waiting in the medical wing," before walking away.

A CALL

FINN

MY FISTS ARE ITCHING to punch something, I'm so pissed off. Part of me wants to turn around and walk back through the door. The asshole would absolutely deserve it. Who the hell does he think he is? My message has never wavered. We are not friends. We do not talk. I will not forgive him, no matter how many times he may apologize or explain himself. His rationalizations are meaningless.

Anger, old and familiar, burns within my chest as I stare at the central screen in the hub room. It's black, indicating the transmission has been placed on hold. I'm tempted to tap the End Transmission button on the tablet Wendy just gave me and just get the hell out of here already, but Brom's voice sticks in my head.

"Sometimes, being a leader means doing things you don't particularly want to do."

Isn't that the truth. I've lived that for two days straight. And still, I can't help the outrage pounding against my rib cage. I have over two-dozen Society members and liaisons within the Institute walls, desperate for answers. The Janeites have been riding my ass over multiple transmissions. Brom is scheduled to arrive within the hour. The Librarian has called a meeting to go over some troubling findings. And in between putting out fires, I'm supposed to go and do a rush order on finding an important catalyst. So obviously, this is when the asshole tries to get ahold of me.

A beep sounds, indicating the caller is still waiting, and it reminds me I need to send somebody into 1876/96TWA-TS and reclaim and reassign Society property. He doesn't deserve it, and if he thinks it will somehow lesson my anger toward him, he'll have a lifetime of disappointment ahead of him. How many times do I have to say it? When is it going to sink in?

Why won't he let go?

I force myself to sit down in the chair facing the screen. I force myself to remember what my shrink used to tell me: *"Violence gets you nowhere. Neither does holding grudges."*

Yeah, well, they've served me just fine over the years, haven't they?

I finally tap on the button marked Resume Transmission. The picture wavers before his face comes into view.

Tom fucking Sawyer.

He blinks, his eyes filled with surprise. "Huck! I was worried you weren't gonna come talk to me!"

That familiar twang of his plucks my still raw nerves. "What do you want?"

Like the selfish moron he is, he's taken aback. "Huck, now—"

"Don't call me that."

"It's still your God-given name, whether you like it or not."

I made damn sure that my birth certificate—the only one that matters, the one that I have here, in New York City—reads *Finn Van Brunt* and nothing else. While my adoptive parents may have had idiotic sentimentality attached to Huckleberry, I sure as hell don't. That name? The one that ties me to this asshole in front of me? I'll be damned if I ever go by it again. "I repeat—what do you want?"

His mouth opens. Shuts. Has the audacity to appear wounded, and it's only fresh lemon juice on a paper cut that refuses to heal. "You can get off your high horse with me. Just because you went to those fancy New York schools—"

I let out a bark of a laugh. "Are you serious? You want to lecture me about my education? *That's* why you called?"

"I'm just sayin' you don't need to get all hoity-toity about your new smarts and fancy accent."

Part of me, a part I've worked hard to shove deep down, wants to mock him over such jealousy. He and I both know why he's on me about my education—he's bitter as all hell I'm smarter than he is nowadays. That my situation is better than his. That I'm no longer his poor, ignorant, charity case tag-a-long. *Tom Sawyer and Huckleberry Finn.* Two literary bros everybody sees as best friends, because they don't know the truth. "You called. Not me. I'd be more than happy to take the high horse and myself straight out of this room."

Frustration fills Tom's face. "Why won't you let it go?"

It's like a jab to the kidneys. Can he really just gloss over what he's done? Is he really that much of a dick? Christ. For the thousandth time, I can't believe I wasted a single second of my life on this waste of space.

"Huck, it's been—"

"Are you kidding me?"

But he keeps going, "A few years now, and you know I'm awfully sorry—"

If he were in front of me, I'd punch him in the face for that. Awfully sorry? What kind of piss-poor excuse is that? Who says that after what he's done? *Awfully sorry?!*

"And it's time to let bygones be bygones—"

Over my dead body.

"I just think it's a right shame how those people changed you. The Huck I know wouldn't be—"

"What are you not understanding, Tom? What part of *I don't ever want to speak to you again* is difficult to grasp? Or is my so-called fancy accent too much for you to comprehend?"

He finally shuts up. Blinks some more like the idiot he is. Damn right, I'm changed.

"What part of *I will never forgive you for what you've done* or *You and I are no longer friends* isn't sticking?"

"Jesus preaches about forgiveness."

I'm incredulous. Now he's trying to rationalize what he's done via religion? "We're done here."

I'm just about to tap End Transmission when he waves his hands like a madman. "Wait! I . . . I didn't get on this thing about that. I have news you need to hear."

Unless it's news that informs me I've been the victim of a cruel, practical joke for the past decade, and what happened really didn't, I don't give a damn what he has to say.

"The Widow Douglas is dying."

My finger hovers over the tablet.

"The doc says it's consumption. She's coughing up lots of blood and can't get outta her bed much more anymore. It's only a matter of days now, if even that."

I'm numb, I think, because all the anger fades into a lack of anything worth comprehending.

"Ever since her sister died all those years ago, she's been all alone in that there house of hers, remember?" He swallows. "Aunt Polly's been bringing her some meals, but she stopped eating a few days back. A bunch of us have been helping out, making sure someone is there with her at all times. Ain't right, going when you're all alone."

The Widow Douglas dying. It seems as if she's been old for ages now, only . . . only now she's actually dying. She's alone and she's dying.

"She's been asking about you, Huck. Been talkin' about you lots lately. Reminiscin' on how she feels like she coulda done more for you. Says she wants to see you one last time. You were the only child she ever had."

A buzzing fills my ears.

"Feel as you may about me, you ought to come and pay your respects. She took you in when she didn't have to. She got you educated, or at least a good start. Gave you a roof, food. She's a good Christian woman, Huck. And whether or not you deserve it, you've got a bit of her heart."

That's rich. He throws that in my face? After what he's done? Worries that *she* will die alone? Claims it ain't right?

Before he can say anything else, I tap End Transmission, both drained and worried I'll tear apart the hub.

I expected another round of pathetic apologies. Another round of Sawyer trying to reestablish whatever it is he thought we were to one another. I didn't expect this.

I stand up, sliding the tablet onto the control panel. And suddenly, I'm thirteen years old, and I'm on the Widow Douglas' couch listening to her and her spinster sister lecture me about everything under the sun.

"Sit up, dear. Slouchin' isn't proper."

Slouching was comfortable. Sitting up was a pain in the ass.

"Did you make sure you washed behind your ears?"

I scratched at the skin Miss Watson referenced; nope, I must've forgotten that one again. Bathing was a right pain. Swimming in the river could cure all this, couldn't it?

The widow asked, "I'm thinking about us having some pie made for after church on Sunday. You like pie, don't you?"

I did, actually. But any I'd ever eaten were stolen. Pies were luxuries far and few between.

They went on and on with their instructions of societal proprieties. Each time either issued a new one, or, heck, said one they'd spouted off before, I itched to run right through the door. I'd had over a dozen years mostly on my own; I'd done just fine, hadn't I?

I was suffocating in here. They were suffocating me with all their good intentions.

I didn't fit into that world of theirs. I didn't fit in anywhere.

TRUTH SERUM

ALICE

I N DIRECT CONTRAST WITH her frightful state, Rosemary's sweet voice fills the medical wing with the same melody from before. And still, the glass windows around us vibrate in fear. Her loudly offered melody grudgingly reminds me of the songs Wonderlandian soldiers sing before they march into battle, though. Perhaps Rosemary, as insane as she might be, understands what is to happen between us today, and how it is, in fact, war between us. This is a battle of wills, and I fully intend on emerging the victor.

The song ends as Mary wheels in a small metal cart filled with vials and syringes. But silence is not a gift given. The melody now morphs into the steady heartbeat of a clock.

Tick-tock, tick-tock.

Mary sticks a hypodermic needle into the top of the vial marked

TRUTH SERUM. "How she manages to keep that up and still breathe is beyond me."

The chanting grows louder. More fervent. Come to think of it, it is rather surprising the woman is able to draw breath and keep up the steady pace of her nonsense.

"I got word from Victor that he and Brom are en route back to the Institute," Mary says amiably.

The chanting stops; the silence draws both Mary's and my attention.

Ah. Interesting. It appears Rosemary did not know that Van Brunt survived Todd's attack, and hearing he has is most distressing for her. Excellent. I want her off balance. "Are you ready to have that conversation now?"

She screams a wide swath of obscenities toward our persons.

"You know, one almost could get bored by how few adjectives this one has in her arsenal. Sluts? Whores? Bitches?" Mary tsks whilst affording Rosemary a false yet sympathetic glance. "The charitable thing to do would be to supply her with a thesaurus."

This earns my colleague an, "I'm going to enjoy killing you, you fucking bitch whores!"

"See?" Mary flicks the hypodermic needle's chamber, ensuring any linger bubbles disappear. "No variety. How can we truly respect somebody who doesn't know what a synonym is?"

The villainess' body bucks wildly against the mattress, her wrist and ankle straps leaving her muscles straining and the springs below her squeaking in protest. "I'll show you a synonym, you ugly bitch whore!"

"Once more, my point is proven," Mary tells me forlornly. "I fear you and I will be forever *bitch whores.* Ugly ones, to boot. My ego is too fragile for this." She motions at our captive. "Shall we?"

Yes, we shall.

Without further notice, Mary jabs the needle straight into Rosemary's arm. Our prey howls in indignant yet curiously fearless fury at such an attack, but soon enough, she sags against the bed. A thin sheen of sweat lines her forehead and the fever in her eyes dulls.

There's the broken woman I've been waiting for.

Mary switches on a recorder as I take my place by the bed. "What is your full given name?"

Her dark eyes swing my way, and I'm surprised to see the rage bubbling beneath the glazed surface. Does she know she's unwillingly answering my questions? "Rosemary Nellie Lovett."

While quickly given, Mary and I share a meaningful yet equally troubled glance. Nellie Lovett was the infamous Sweeney Todd's reputed paramour and accomplice who perished due to poison.

"Where is Todd?"

"I don't know."

Mary simply shrugs when I lift a peeved brow. "I told you I've never used it before," she mouths.

More firmly, to Rosemary, "Where could he be?"

Now there's cruel pleasure reflecting out of her eyes. "The possibilities are endless."

I brush back my disappointment. There are still other pertinent questions to be answered, ones that could lead us forward. "What is Todd's full given name?"

Her rage and frustration is back, because she practically spits out, "Sweeney Patrick Todd."

S. Todd. *Sweeney Todd.* Rosemary Lovett. *Mrs. Lovett.* Logic is wrestled down and applied as I process this revelation. Words can be still be lies even if they are fervently and wholly believed. Names can be lies, too. Names are nothing but assignments. Names are nothing but costumes we wear.

Even still, I can't help but admit I'm disconcerted by her perceived truths. How can it be possible this woman is the Mrs. Lovett from the infamous penny dreadful *A String of Pearls?* The original Lovett died at the hands of Sweeney Todd himself in that storyline. Furthermore, the murderous barber expired when he was hanged for his crimes once the authorities captured him. The lives of Sweeney Todd and Mrs. Lovett of lore, the ones from 1846/47RYM/PEC-SP, have long been snuffed out. One of the concepts that has been hammered into me time and time again during my tenure at the Society is events which occur during the book associated with a Timeline are gospel. They cannot be changed.

And yet, conversely, both Finn and the Librarian have told me the authors of these books leave things open to interpretation. So . . .

I ask carefully, "Are you the Mrs. Lovett from *A String of Pearls?*"

The emotions within her eyes shift to something I cannot easily identify. "I don't know."

I don't know is far more worrying than a simple *no.* "Is your associate Sweeney Patrick Todd the Sweeney Todd from *A String of Pearls?*"

Once more, unidentifiable emotions consume her. "I don't know."

"Do you know what is meant by *A String of Pearls?*" Mary interjects.

The villainess seethes as she spits out her confirmation.

"Elaborate for us its significance then," I instruct.

Between clenched teeth, she snaps, "It's the story associated with our original Timeline."

"Our?" I query. "You mean yours and Todd's?"

Another reluctant confirmation follows.

I turn her answers over carefully. "What is your earliest memory?"

Surprise now reflects up at me. "Staring out of a window at an asylum, wondering why the sun hated England so much."

Very curious. "How old were you in this memory?"

Her jaw must be dreadfully sore from all her clenching. "Eight."

Curiouser and curiouser. "Was Sweeney Patrick Todd at the asylum alongside you?"

She is displeasured to provide me confirmation.

"Who are your parents?"

"I don't know."

I add, even though I sense I already know the answer, "Who are Sweeney Patrick Todd's parents?"

"I don't know."

"How do you know your names are your own, then?"

I've surprised her yet again. "The asylum told us so."

"Why do you destroy catalysts?"

She doesn't even blink or hesitate. "Because we are told to."

"By F.K. Jenkins?" Mary interjects.

Rosemary's scorn is evident. "That fat sack of shit only thinks he's in charge."

"You do not work for F.K. Jenkins?" I ask

"Fuck, no."

"Do you work for or with Todd?"

"With."

I plow forward, undeterred. "Whom do you work *for?*"

24

"I don't know."

"You never thought to ask who you were carrying orders out for?" I shake my head, disgusted. I ought to feel some sense of sympathy toward her, that she was foolish to go forth and carry out inexplicable deeds without reasoning and knowledge, but at the mild shrug against the mattress, all I can muster is repugnance.

Further questioning moves us ahead mere inches. Rosemary and Todd have been romantically attached since they were children. They were recruited as teenagers, although it is Todd who serves as link between the two and whoever they work for. They were brought out of their Timeline and educated locally. Jobs were held on and off for years—during these spans, little to no orders came through. Once they did, though, everything else was put on hold. Rosemary delights in the destruction left within her wake. To her, none of the people over the years were real. They were book people, she maddeningly claims, and never thought to draw the same distinction to herself despite her beginnings. Details are not her strong suit. She blindly follows and worships Todd (who she refers to as her soul mate), finds F.K. Jenkins to be just as abhorrent as we do, and has never possessed the inclination to search for any answers of her own. She is content with having no understanding of her past. To her, retrieving catalysts is a game, and their destruction merely another move she must make in order to win. She isn't a reader; she has never read from start to finish a single book associated with any of the Timelines she'd targeted. It is her assumption her paramour doesn't indulge in literary pursuits, either. They've shared a singular pen to edit with, but she has no idea where it came from or if it resembles Society property. Between her and Todd, they've collected nearly a dozen catalysts and personally destroyed half of those. As for the rest, she has no idea where they went. Todd gave them to Jenkins; Jenkins passed them to someone else (although she has no idea how). Jenkins is a reader, though. Jenkins always read the books before they went onto assignments, she tells us with disdain.

She and Todd, in her mind, are gods.

Eventually, Mary's truth serum runs its course and answers dry up. Screaming returns alongside threats. She will make us pay for what we've done. She will personally cut out our tongues and add them to her collection in her box.

I make a mental note to ask if a box filled with vile trophies has been located during any of the Society's many searches of the Ex Libris bookstore's attic.

Mary's phone beeps, reminding us we have a meeting to attend within the hour. As my colleague tidies up the needles and vials, I once more take hold of Rosemary's chin to steady her face and control her gnashing. I lean down, close enough that my words are for her ears and hers alone. I tell her, "You've been a very naughty girl, Rosemary Nellie Lovett. Please be assured that you will never walk out of this Institute alive."

She shows her hand by shrieking, "He'll come for me! He'll carve you up and I'll bake you into pies!"

I certainly hope he'll try. I am banking on it, actually.

FINN

I **PRAY YOU BE** sympathetic to our concerns, sir," Emma Knightley is saying.

Is it petty that I want to shove my father's perfectly sharpened pencils into my eyeballs and eardrums simply to drown out her unfailingly polite voice? Worse yet, sitting across the room, out of view of the monitor and thereby outside of Emma's range, my father offers me a smug smile as if to say, "See what I have to put up with on a daily basis?"

I resist the urge to flip him off.

"Of course I am," I lie to Emma, "but I hope that you can understand where we're coming from, too."

It's the same conversation she and I have been running through over the last three communiqués. Some asshole at the Society let slip to the Janeites shortly after Brom's attack that we have two suspects in custody, and for some ungodly reason, they feel as if they are entitled to whatever information I get before anyone else.

True to form, Emma glosses right over what I've just said and continues to push the Janeites' agenda. "We would be most amenable to sending someone to assist with questioning."

Imagining a Janeite interrogation leaves me fighting to hide my smile. "I appreciate that, but it's not necessary. As soon as we have anything, I promise we will share. But until—"

"Mr. Van Brunt, there is much . . . concern over whether or not the items collected are indeed the catalysts for our Timelines."

Even my father rolls his eyes at that one.

"Please be assured that all of the catalysts in the Museum are, in fact, genuine and have been verified by the Librarian. You have no reason to believe otherwise."

"There is still a villain afoot," she blurts out, gravely and yet timidly all at once, "and, as you know, the Janeite League Timelines are quite beloved."

She's fucking with us, right? Because it's not like any of the rest of the Society's members' books have never sold a copy before, right? Or be made into movies or TV shows? I fight back the urge to set her straight and say, instead, "Since the acquisition of 1814AUS-MP, all of the major Janeite Timeline catalysts have been acquired. Outside of breaking into the Institute and then the museum, there is no possible way the suspect can do any damage to your Timelines."

Whispering occurs off-screen. Emma keeps her eyes on me, though, a serene smile on her face. I'll give it to these Georgian ladies—their manners are impeccable, even when they're insulting the shit out of you. "We would be most grateful, Mr. Van Brunt, to be appraised of the security measures being taken to assure such protection."

"I hope you can understand I am not at liberty to fully describe our security systems to you as that would defeat the purposes of such things."

More whispering, sounding a lot like the buzzing of angry bees. Emma's face pales at the same time her cheeks splotch bright red with outrage. "Surely you are not accusing the League of . . . of . . . impropriety!"

"Of course not," I quickly assure her. Across the room, my father sighs in frustration for the both of us. "I'm just stating that Society policy states that only active field agents at the Institute are cleared for access to the Museum."

Again with the whispering off-camera. I try not to groan as I imagine which Janeite or Janeites are sitting just off-screen. Let's see . . . Elizabeth Bennett Darcy, most likely. She's clever and got a good head on her shoulders, but is stubborn as all hell. She's the real brain behind the Janeites. Anne Eliot Wentworth . . . No. Well, maybe. She's super soft spoken and doesn't tend to deal with Society matters much, but all her years with her husband have left her with a good understanding of military matters, too. There's a possibility she could have been called in. Marianne Dashwood Brandon . . . Very likely. Marianne is always one for proper outrage and action, and also had married a military man. Her sister Elinor? Probably not. Elinor is much, much more reserved than Marianne. Catherine Morland Tilney? Hmm . . . she's probably around, too, and the main instigator of this whole mess. She's got a wild imagination, and likely laid out her assumptions and fears to the others in vivid detail.

"Perhaps," Emma carefully murmurs, "we could designate a representative as an active field agent."

It isn't like Brom hasn't offered this option to them before when we had openings. The Janeites always rebuffed him, insisting nobody was willing to separate themselves from their Timeline long enough to work full time for the Society. So, I can't help but call their bluff. Chances are, they say this now but their tunes will change shortly. "You are more than welcome to submit an application for employment."

A gentle knock on the door sounds before cracking open. It's Alice, and she looks troubled. Just what did Rosemary tell her?

My father taps on his wrist. Shit—that's right. We've got a meeting to go to.

"We hear that an agent was recently conscripted without application," Emma is saying.

We hear. *We* think. *We* worry. *I'm* ready to kick the ass of the person giving the League this information. "Emma, I hate to cut this short, but I really need to take care of some important matters here."

The whispering off-screen is frenzied. "I am most keenly aware of your obligations, Mr. Van Brunt, but I pray you indulge us for just—"

I tried. I swear to all that's holy, I really did. It's time for firmness. "I'm sorry, but I refuse to discuss our hiring or recruiting situations for our current employees. Even here at the Society, we have rules about confidentiality. If the Janeite League wishes to have an active field agent on the team, they are more than welcome to submit an application, just like anyone else from any other Timeline would. Until then, I really need to go so I can ensure we track down the remaining suspect."

She blanches. The whispers turn to outrage. And I, no doubt being the dick Emma and the rest of the Janeites are pegging me for, end the transmission without further warning.

Alice slips inside the room, shutting the door behind her. "I apologize for interrupting your call." And then, to my father, "It is good to see you, Van Brunt."

He mock salutes her.

I lean back in my father's chair. "Actually, I'm glad you did. No doubt Emma Knightley could have gone on for another hour if given the chance."

Brom's look is disapproving. I point at him, saying, "You know she would."

Aha. He cracks a smile, because he knows I'm right.

Alice stares at me for a long moment in that calculating way of hers. It took me awhile to get used to it. She isn't one to blurt out her thoughts like so many of the people I know, but instead carefully chooses exactly what she says even if she's razzing you. She clutches her cards against her chest; she carries her past with her like a tattoo no laser surgery can erase.

She is a hedge maze I'm afraid I've lost myself within.

"Mary and I were successful in our usage of the truth serum, only . . ." A frustrated sigh is blown out as she holds a small recorder aloft. "I fear I've basically cut the head off of a Hydra."

I wrack my brain, trying to place the familiar-sounding name. What the hell is a hydra? It sounds like something from mythology, or possibly a fantasy or sci-fi based Timeline. Dammit, I hate feeling like an idiot. Familiar yet loathed insecurities resurface, and I force myself to remember I am not that kid anymore. I've got a lit degree from NYU, for crissakes. Magna cum laude, to boot.

Brom taps on his wrist again. As there's no time to listen to the recording in full, I ask her to give us the highlights.

By the end of Alice's recounting, I've finally remembered what a hydra is—some kind of monster that, when one head is cut off, many take its place. She's right to use that analogy, though, because these answers of Rosemary's leave us with more questions than ever before.

In related news, I'm left with a monstrous headache.

"How many catalysts does the museum have?"

"I don't know the exact number," I tell her. "But it's a lot. That said, there are millions of books, so it's also not enough."

"We need to question Jenkins next, and do it soon."

"Flemming will have to take over for you, as we're off on an assignment tomorrow, remember? Besides, he's already getting to know the proprietor of the Ex Libris bookstore pretty well these last few days."

She glances down at my father. His smile is rueful but in perfect agreement with what I've said.

A huff of air scatters stray hairs around her face. "Fine." And then, hesitantly, "It's hard sometimes to stand back and let others take charge. You would think I'd be resigned to that, what with the prophecies and all, but . . ." Bitterness reflects in her eyes.

"Old habits die hard," I fill in for her when she doesn't finish.

"They do indeed."

As I wheel my father out of his office and down the hall, I look at this woman, this beautiful, maddeningly secretive queen without a country, and all I can selfishly think is how damn glad I am for Wonderlandian prophecies.

Close to two-dozen people crowd around the wooden table spanning the length of the room by time we arrive in the conference room. Wendy already has a computer hooked up to project plenty of visuals of items found on the Ex Libris bookstore's attic walls. A standing ovation erupts the moment everyone sees Brom, and it leaves him more than a bit embarrassed. My father holds up his hand and then makes a slashing motion in front of his neck. Everyone in the room goes awkwardly still, their eyes wide.

Victor and I find Brom's sly way of poking fun at himself pretty damn funny, though. Our poor dad is beside himself, knowing that asshole Todd got the drop on him. I guarantee it'll be the last time, though. His ego won't ever allow it to happen again.

"Relax," my brother says as he lowers his lanky frame into a chair near the front. "He's just telling you blokes to shut up."

That's Victor for you.

Mary comes to sit next to him, pressing a quick kiss against his cheek. "Tact, my love. Remember? You're working on utilizing it."

The Librarian makes her way over to Brom, and if I'm not mistaken, there are tears in her eyes. "It is so good to see you back where you belong, old friend." And then, more formally to the crowd, "Thank you all for coming. While I wish I had the full extent of answers to give, tonight's meeting will be brief. Specialists are still working on decoding the riddles found upon the walls of the Ex Libris bookshop, but there are a few bits of information I would like to share." She extracts a small laser pointer and angles the red dot at the pictures on the screen hanging over the head of the table. "While dismantling the items to bring back to the Institute for study, Jack Dawkins discovered something we had missed before. Behind every sheet of paper, there is a carved set of numbers and letters."

This I already knew, having been briefed on it the morning after I returned from Wonderland. And carved is a generous term—most of the numbers and letters were barely scratches that cut into the wood's meat. Some are nearly impossible to read.

"At first, it appears as if the numbers and letters are random. None match Timeline designations, years of publication, titles, or authors. For example, found beneath a torn page from *Anna Karenina,* a Timeline verified to have been deleted, was the following code: *x7SpRn.*" A red dot hovers over a zoomed-in shot of the scene. "1877TOL-AK is affiliated with Leo Tolstoy. There are no As, Ks, Ls, or Ts within the coding. 7 might have matched 1877, but it was unlikely when considering other parameters. That said, the more we looked, the more we saw some slight commonalities. Most Timelines that have been deleted have Xs at the beginning. Their numbering makes no sense, though—none fall within order of deletions or go higher than ten. As for the letters—"

"They're initials," Alice interjects firmly. "At least, the ones to the right are."

All eyes turn toward her.

"*Sp* indicates Sweeney Patrick. *Rn* is Rosemary Nellie. If I had to guess, the letters are representative of who possibly found or destroyed particular catalysts associated with Timelines."

The Librarian says nothing, but I've known her long enough to see she's impressed by Alice's quick summation.

I am, too. Damn, Alice is hot when she gets all *know-it-all.*

"Did the suspects finally talk?" Professor Otto Lidenbrock asks from his place down the table. Lindenbrock is one of our best agents in the field despite his age, but he gets off on more adventures than paperwork.

Alice smiles coolly. "Rosemary did."

Surprised, pleased murmuring fills the room.

Victor asks, "Do all the codings have letters like these to the right?"

"No." The Librarian turns back toward the screen. "And many have various other letters assigned to the front. Of the twenty-six letters in the English alphabet, less than half are represented in some form or another." One of the pictures zooms in when she points to it. "Note how some are capitalized, and others are lower case. Some are upside down. There is no clear consistency. That said, our researchers have been focusing on the order of the most recent deletions, beginning with that of 1889TWA-CY." The pictures on the screen shift, dissolve, and reform to showcase a torn page illustrating a knight astride a winged alligator (although I suspect it might meant to have been a dragon), waving a banner that reads, "This horrible sky-towering monster."

It's *A Connecticut Yankee in King Arthur's Court* by Mark Twain.

The night we found out about the tragedy, Victor railed at me about the significance of Todd destroying 1889TWA-CY's catalyst. It was a message, he insisted. A clear memo Todd was sending to both me and the Society. He knows who we are, he knows who the authors associated with our Timelines are, and he has no qualms about taking us out, one by one.

My brother had a point. The only comfort is that most Society agents' Timelines are protected. Our catalysts all reside within the Museum below the Institute. And that's a shitty comfort to hold on to, when countless lives were destroyed all in the name of making a point.

"Beneath this page was the following inscription: /10SpRn. There was no letter at the beginning, just a slash." She flicks the red dot so it draws a quick line, finishing the X we all began in our minds. "There were two other Timelines which had slashes at the beginning of their designations." The pictures shift again, bringing into focus a mangled DVD cover insert and a dust jacket ripped in half. "Both have identical codings: /8SpP."

Wuthering Heights and *The Jungle Book.*

"If Sp indicates Todd, who is P?" one of our agents, named Mr. Holgrave, says.

The Librarian meaningfully looks to Alice, a hint of a smile touching her lips. When my partner says nothing, the Librarian adds, "Who, indeed?"

A distinct yet discreet grunt of exasperation escapes Alice's lips.

"Interestingly enough, neither of these Timelines' catalysts have been collected yet by the Society," the Librarian continues. "Furthermore, it has been strongly suggested to us by those researching these riddles that both 1847BRO-WH and 1894/95KP-JB are at immediate risk. Therefore, Brom and I have discussed the matter thoroughly and have decided that, despite the current quest to locate Todd, we must quickly send agents into both Timelines to collect these catalysts. While we already have several teams in the field on previously scheduled assignments, we cannot wait until they come back."

Translation: Alice and I, as well as Victor and Mary, are the lucky ones.

"Please be *Wuthering Heights,* please be *Wuthering Heights,*" my brother mutters under his breath.

"Victor and I will take 1894/95KP-JB," Mary says brightly. "I haven't been to India in ages."

Victor sighs heavily as he slumps down in his chair.

"To be fair," I point out, "you could just as easily end up in the Artic. Some of the stories take place there."

He proves his maturity by flipping me off in front of everyone. Mary indulgently pats his cheek.

The Librarian pays us no mind. "We cannot know for sure that Todd has yet to acquire these catalysts, but it is believed he has not."

As always, the question, *"Believed by who?"* rests on the tip of my tongue. But I learned long ago that asking the mercurial woman any such questions is pointless. She'll only tell you what she wants you to know exactly when she wants you to know it, and not a moment sooner.

Dossiers and copies of the books are passed out to the four of us. For the rest of the table, new files detailing the crazy coding unearthed beneath the items found in Todd's attic are sent to their work tablets. Within minutes, the only people left in the room are those of us who are scheduled to leave at the crack of dawn.

Victor's lips twist into a sour grimace as he stares down at the file he's been given. "You would think by now the infamous Sherlock Holmes would have cracked this case. He's had nearly two weeks with all the information. Some kind of bloody legend he is."

Brom had been the one to select whom to send photographs of everything found on the attic wall. Our father and Holmes may be on good terms (well, as good as one can be with a narcissistic egomaniac like the famed detective), but Victor is right. The best we've gotten from Holmes is that a slash might indicate a possible deletion? Hell, it took Alice all of ten seconds to figure out what the letters meant. Clearly Brom and the Librarian are relying more on celebrity than present effectiveness.

"Get up, lazybones." Mary drapes herself across my brother's shoulders. "We've got studying to do."

He twists his face away from her attempts to pinch his cheek. "You had to go and pick bloody India, didn't you?"

"India's good for the soul." She tugs him out of the chair. "See you two when you get back."

I have a feeling those two are going to do little studying tonight.

AN ODE TO POLARIS

FINN

HOURS LATER, AFTER SKIMMING the texts associated with 1847BRO-WH and overseeing the details with the catalyst location, Alice and I are on our way up to our apartments. Except, the moment the elevator doors slide shut, I have a change of heart about our destination. The last few days—hell, weeks—have been so intense and crazy that I'm selfish enough to want to spend some time with just her. No catalysts, no interrogations, no meetings, no battles, no anything but *her and me*.

I press the button for the top floor of the Institute and then tug her toward me. My hand cups the back of her head, my mouth meets hers. Her arms fold me close, and I'm no longer thinking about the Janeites or Todd or mysterious codes and bosses, because when Alice Liddell Reeve puts her mind to it, she can make you think of nothing at all and live, instead, in mere sensations. I'm kissing her, she's kissing me, and everything in me turns hot and fills with aching need.

Our ascent thankfully has no stops or interlopers. I'm still kissing her when the doors slide open, still kissing as I lead her out into the wide, open space. The top of the Institute is a ballroom: a gorgeous, oft-ignored area that has gleaming parquet floors, elaborate antique chandeliers, a painted ceiling, and gilded crown molding. The last party held in here, one celebrating my parents' anniversary just months before my mother's death, was magical. The NYC skyline glittered beyond the massive stained-glass-topped windows lining the room on all sides, and when the champagne flowed, it felt like you were floating above the city. There was so much love in this room that night. So much happiness. I remember standing there, my glass raised like everyone else's as we toasted Brom and Katrina, thinking: *There's no way that kind of love is real.* It was like something out of a damn book, which was saying something, considering.

Now, the furniture within the ballroom is pressed up against the walls, covered with white sheets. There's a morose kind of quiet within this space, like it's desperate for happiness to return. There have been no more parties—not because they've been banned or anything, but because life just kept moving on.

This room, once upon a time, was all about love. It needs to be again.

I fumble for the switch to illuminate the chandeliers. Original to the building, they're old and beautiful, the kind that splatter refracted, soft light in enchanting ways a disco ball can only ever dream about. I take Alice's face in my hands and whisper against her mouth. "I know we should be resting before we leave, but . . . maybe we can have that first date tonight. Here."

Her hands come to rest over mine. We're standing so close to one another that I can feel her heart racing against mine. She's trembling—just a little, but enough to make me think my parents were on to something after all.

She must hear me and all my crazy, jumbled thoughts, understand what I mean, because she murmurs, our lips still just a hair's breadth away, "I don't need courting, Finn. I just want you."

I kiss her again, long and slow until we're both panting. I pull away and it's then she sees the room for the first time.

Eyes wide, her lips curve upward in delighted surprise. Maintaining a hold on one hand, she pulls me to the middle of the room and then to the windows. Like the night of my parents' anniversary, NYC has brought its A-game with its city lights.

I dig into my pocket and tug out my phone. As she stares out at the vista, I quickly scroll through my song playlists until I find the right one. One I haven't heard in years, one I haven't been able to delete because I couldn't say goodbye.

Strains of music fill the air. The look of absolute delight on Alice's face is worth the ruthless reality of going on an assignment on little to no sleep. "You know how to waltz?"

I leave my phone on the window ledge, the speakers facing outward. "Katrina loved to dance. She would bring me and Victor up here, and then Brom would come, and we'd be laughing by the end, but damn, it was wonderful to see her so happy."

Her hands curve back around my face and she stares at me. My heart thumps painfully within my chest, because I swear she's not just looking at me, she's unraveling me. Her lips touch mine, and it somehow feels different from any of the others we've ever shared. It's almost as if she's trying to memorize this moment, like she's scared it will disappear or be taken away from her. Like I'll be taken away from her.

It's something I will never let happen.

"You told me once you liked to dance."

"You are mistaken. I love to dance." She pulls away from me and holds her arms out. Her eyes, those gorgeous blue eyes of hers, shine in the chandelier light, and it's then I know this room really is magical. Because how else can I explain what's happening between us? This pull, this understanding. It's the best kind of magic. It's the kind that makes me want to believe in fairy tales—the good kind. The kind where the endings have hope.

A hand curves around her waist. The other meets hers, and although she's not in a ball gown and I'm wearing jeans and a flannel shirt, I spin her across the parquet floors. It feels like I'm falling into that fairy tale, it's so right here between us.

She smiles at me as we dance. There are no words, but her smile tells me everything I need to know. There are a thousand words in that smile, and three that matter more than any of the rest. Because of that smile and what I feel toward this woman, my heart feels like it's going to beat straight out of my damn chest.

Dancing transitions to kissing. Kissing transitions to want and need. My shirt comes off. Her dress. My pants, her bra. My underwear, and then her panties. We're naked and on the floor, and the strains of waltzes drift softly throughout the room, and I'm worshipping her body, it's so fucking gorgeous. Her breasts, the curve of her hips. The slope of her neck, the way her clavicle forms an imperfectly perfect line. The tiny outie of a belly button, the small constellation of freckles that ring it. I trace it all with my hands and my mouth until she's writhing beneath me, hot and wet and hungry. My hand is between her leg, and I'm circling and rubbing her clit, one, then two fingers in, and wanting to see her come more than anything else right now, because it's the most fantastic sight in the entire universe. She arches her back, her hands going from my hair to my shoulders to my chest, and I'm sucking and licking as she moans and, damn, I'm so hard it's not even funny. I want nothing more than to bury myself in her, but there's this need to see her, hear her come. It's like a drug, I think. A high I can't resist. Finally, she explodes in my hands, her scream of pleasure ringing out across the empty floors and over the strains of Mozart, but before she's fully down from her high, she's already got me in her hand.

My breath is stolen. My eyes roll back, and it's my turn to groan, because *holy hell.* I have to fight back the urge to give into the orgasm already clamoring for release—I'm not ready for this to end. I'm kissing her again, kissing and sucking her breasts and neck and she's writhing once more, arching once more, this time even more frantically.

She says my name, says, "I need you in me. Now."

I slide in, but as soon as I've pushed all the way to the hilt, I have to stop. I'm on my elbows, above her, staring down at her sweaty, flushed face, and my heart contracts and expands so quickly that it's a miracle I'm even still alive.

I love her. I'm so crazy in love with this woman, I want to scream it from the rooftops.

She traces her hands up my back, so lightly goose bumps flare to life. She's got that look again, like she's so afraid that this isn't real. That it's a dream. Like somehow, I'm not in her, like somehow, we're not connected by more than just our bodies.

I wish I knew what to say to her to let her know that I'm not going anywhere. There isn't a single damn prophecy in any Timeline that would ever keep me from her. But I'm not good with words. I slowly start to pull in and out, my rhythm steady and strong. Her hips match mine, and we move to more than the music—we move to the sounds of one another's heartbeats. My mouth is on hers again, and I pray with each thrust, with each stroke of my tongue, with each beat of that muscle in my chest, she understands what she means to me. How she has stolen my heart in the months she's been here at the Institute, and how I don't ever want her to give it back. How she made me believe in love, made me believe it's real. That's it's worth fighting for. That it's worth holding onto with both hands.

Her body shudders as waves of ecstasy wash over her once more. I push more, thrust harder. Her hands curl around my face, like she's afraid I'm going to float away. We kiss, we kiss, and when I follow her into the undertow, when her name falls from my mouth like it's a wish, I hold on tight.

Later, when the sweat on our skin turns cool and the floor turns hard, she murmurs, "Someone should write a book about how Alice Liddell from Wonderland falls in love with Huckleberry Finn. I might rather want to read that book."

I bury my face in the curve of her neck. She smells so goddamn good right now. "What would it be called?"

She's quiet for a long moment. I run my hands along her body, memorizing the planes the best I can. A sigh of contentment floats between us, and I have no idea if it came from her or me.

I can't remember being so happy.

"It would be a love story," she finally says.

"That's the title? *A Love Story?*"

"No, no. It would be called *An Ode to Polaris.*" And then, "Polaris is the name of the North Star."

I kiss the hollow of her neck. "I know what Polaris is. We're binaries, remember. Can't it be *An Ode to Binaries?*"

"The point is, it would *be* a love story. And it would be my favorite."

The breath in my chest stills. Is she—is she saying what I think she's saying? I have to swallow before I can talk. I'm reminded of how my father looked at his wife when she was telling all the revelers at their anniversary ball of how he proposed to her. He looked at her like she was the most important thing in his world. Like she was the most precious. Like the sun rose and set on her.

As much as I loved them both, it was alien to me then. But I get it now. I absolutely get it.

When I answer her, my words will only come out as whispers, there's so much emotion in me. "It would be my favorite, too."

BITS OF THE PAST

ALICE

AFTER A QUICK SET of introductions, a woman with blonde curls motions to a pair of chairs nearby. "Please, come and make yourselves comfortable by the fire." Her vision flicks away from us to briefly settle on one of the windows in the room. It's blustery beyond the thin pane, the sky menacingly dark. A tiny sigh of pity stays trapped within my chest as I imagine Finn and myself going back out into such conditions. Our host agrees, as she adds earnestly, "It's not a good time to be out on the moors. You two must be chilled to the bone. Let me order you some hot tea."

Catherine Earnshaw is around my age and quite pretty, if not a bit guarded. Finn says to her, as she moves toward a bell, "We would appreciate that very much."

I'm startled to hear his voice alter from his American accent to something much more like his brother's or mine. And it isn't false, either, not like so many one hears in the movies or upon television. The lilt that spills from his lips sounds natural, like he's spent his entire life in England

Once her housekeeper has come and left, Mrs. Earnshaw sits down in a chair across from us, and Finn spins a yarn explaining our presence. Hailing from Oxford, we are recently married and honeymooning in the region. I'm shocked when she accepts his tale, especially since I myself would find two strangers on foot out in the isolated moors to be more than a bit suspicious. But our hostess is not so jaded as I, because she kindly insists we must stay the night at Thrushcross Grange as her guests.

"My husband will be home shortly. He's visiting tenants over at the Heights, but I am sure he would be just as delighted as I to wish you much joy on your union."

Truthfully, I am glad that we are here instead of at the foreboding Wuthering Heights estate. A brief overview of 1847BRO-WH's story the night before left me atypically apprehensive about our destination and assignment: death, obsession, ghosts, jealousy, and violence plagued the people within its pages. Jabberwockies and bandersnatches I can deal with; specters, in my opinion, are better left to tales told in the dark of night to those who have yet to witness true atrocities. Wonderlandian soldiers delight in spinning stories over campfires of ghosts of beasties and those whose lives were cut tragically short, and although most were spellbound by such suppositions, I nearly always found something better to do with my time. There was strategic planning, maps to pore over, and wounded who needed comfort.

I wonder if Mary and Victor are dealing with ghosts in India.

Finn peppers Mrs. Earnshaw with polite questions about the area, and a good three-fourths of an hour is spent on sly reconnaissance despite us already having an asset in place. Mr. Earnshaw arrives soon after, and we are invited to join the couple for supper. Hareton Earnshaw is a quiet man who is more than content to allow his wife to embrace the role of hostess. The hearty stew offered to us is oddly comforting: simple yet reminiscent of meals spent with my family during my youth. For a moment, pangs of *what if* and *what could have been* and *what once was* pluck at my insides. For all I know, my parents still assume I am safely housed within the walls of the Pleasance Asylum back in my Timeline. I can't help but wonder what they are doing right now, what my siblings are doing. Do they miss me? Or have the years spent in Wonderland left them accustomed to my absence from their lives?

"Mrs. Van Brunt?"

I blink rapidly, refocusing on the woman sitting near me. There are lines of concern decorating her forehead, and all eyes in the room are angled at me.

She called me Mrs. Van Brunt. My alias name, yes, and a married one, to boot, but with its vocalization, a slight flush tinges my cheeks. For the few hours I slept last night, I happily dreamed of a long life with this man. "Forgive me," I murmur. "I suppose I am more tired from our journey today than I previously thought."

"I will have our housekeeper show you to your room," Catherine Earnshaw says quickly. "My apologies for keeping you up when I ought to have known you would have been exhausted from the day's journey."

I smile and thank her. Would she still feel so generous toward me if she knew I was about to dig up her mother's grave this night?

Upstairs, Ellen Dean, who has off-and-on served as housekeeper, confidant, and maid to the Earnshaw and Linton women for decades, quietly closes and latches the door behind us once we are in the room. Her worn face eases into a small yet somewhat timid smile. "Mr. Van Brunt, it is a pleasure, and may I say, relief, to have you here tonight."

Finn turns to me. "Alice, this is Nelly Dean. She's been our liaison here in 1847BRO-WH for several years now and was instrumental in helping the Librarian identify the catalyst so quickly." His English accent is gone, reverting back to the warm, familiar American twang I'm accustomed to hearing from his lips. "Mrs. Dean, this is my partner, Alice Reeve."

Her curtsy is exceedingly proper, and it only solidifies the inopportune pangs of homesickness—not to England, as one might assume, but to the Courts of Wonderland. I give a gentle nod of my head in return. "I am most pleased to meet you, Mrs. Dean."

"You're not like Mr. Van Brunt here or his father, are you?" she asks. "From America, I mean. Are you from another Timeline, then?"

"The sun never sets on the British Empire—in any Timeline." I'd heard this phrase on a television program I'd watched about my homeland recently and found it both amusing and satisfying.

Finn rolls his eyes, and I can't help but shrug.

Mrs. Dean informs us she will be waiting in the kitchen in two hours. The Earnshaws will be in bed before then, and so will much of the rest of the staff save an elderly man named Joseph who will accompany us to the church graveyard in a nearby small town. When she leaves, I ask Finn, "Have you ever dug up a grave before?"

"No." He clears his throat. "But there have been a few other Society members who have."

How positively ghoulish. "Do you think your brother and Mary are robbing graves in India?"

He lets out a small laugh, one that is a warm balm for a cold, blustery night on the moors. "Uh, I doubt it."

"Catalysts are funny, aren't they? Ever so random, too. To go from carpetbags to play books to crowns to lockets. It would be much easier if it was a consistent item, wouldn't it?"

He nudges my shoulder with his. "Impractical, though. Something found in a book like *Wuthering Heights* would probably not be found in one like others in something like *The Sentinel*."

I lift my eyebrows up and he gifts me with another of his lovely chuckles.

"Sorry. *The Sentinel* is a short story by a science fiction writer that talks about an object found on the moon, presumably left by extraterrestrials. My point being, items in space wouldn't be found in the moors of Nineteenth Century England."

I nudge his shoulder in return. "Have you been to the moon?"

"I have not had that pleasure yet," he says with mock solemnity.

"And space? What about on a spacecraft? Or any of those," I flash air quotes with my fingers, "*science fiction* stories you're referencing?"

"Once. I had to get a piece of a super computer that was programmed to determine the meaning of life. It was surprisingly cooperative with my request once I told it my purpose, and seemed to run just fine without the small chip I took."

"The computer talked to you?"

"Actually, it did. We didn't chat long as, you know, I wasn't supposed to be there or anything, but it didn't even blink an eye when I told it there were many universes."

I hope he's being metaphorical when he talks about a computer blinking. Truthfully, modern technology mystifies and unnerves me; to know that there is a talking computer that searches to solve lofty questions that surely people of all Timelines have sought answers for? I shudder softly. "Did it ever find what it sought?"

His eyes sparkle in the dim candlelight. "You mean—to the meaning of life?" I nod, and he says, "Well, yeah, I guess. Only, it doesn't really make sense."

"To you, perhaps."

Once he explains that, according to this particular Timeline, the answer to the mysteries of life, the universe, and everything else comes down to an even number and nothing else, I find I must agree with him. Although, wouldn't Wonderland approve of that absurd yet mathematically attractive answer?

Once I'm done chuckling, I ask, "What was the catalyst for your Timeline? I don't think I've yet to learn what it is."

The humor we've just shared slowly eases from his face. "It wasn't anything exciting." He pauses, then says, almost as if I'm forcibly extracting the answer from him, "Just a needle."

I'm a bit disappointed. Finn's stories are, from what I can ascertain, quite popular—and the catalyst ends up being nothing more than a needle? "A sewing needle?"

He nods, but offers nothing else. Charged, uneasy silence fills the space between us. Manners dictate I let the subject rest. He is clearly uncomfortable with discussion of said needle, and it is not as if I am wholly unaware of his overall yet mysterious discomfort surrounding his past. He has been so forthcoming and generous with details of his life, all excepting his childhood. For a moment, I am ready to let the matter go, but then . . . then I remind myself that this is not just a colleague. This is not an acquaintance. This is a man I have let into my heart, and has allowed me access into his as well.

I want to know him, all of him: good and bad and all that lies in between. And in return, I want him to know and feel the same way toward me.

I want the life I dreamed of last night.

I prod softly. "What is the significance of such a catalyst?"

Long seconds tick by, leaving me sorely regretting how I blocked him at every turn for months, holding him at arms' length whenever he inquired about my past. I should have trusted him, known that he would hold my pain and past and fears and experiences gently in his hands and do nothing more than simply support me. I ache to do the same for him.

I am on the verge of offering a long-overdue apology when he once more clears his throat. "It was used to make a pact. You know, the kind that requires blood?"

My hand slips to his knee and squeezes. "Your blood?"

His sigh is barely voiced. "Mine and another's."

I think back to the call he took yesterday, the one that left him on edge and distant for much of the day. "Tom's?"

He doesn't look at me when he answers in the affirmative. And I'm taken aback, because there's anger there, and, if I'm not mistaken, disillusionment, too.

"Alice, I . . ." He shakes his head and focuses instead on our hands rather than my face. "I don't know how much you know about my history with Sawyer, but—"

"Nothing," I quickly assure him. "And, Finn, I apologize if I am overstepping my bounds. I was just curious about—"

He takes my hand. There's a vulnerability clouding his eyes that until today I had yet to see before on this normally confident man. "No. It's fine. You have every right to ask me these things. All I meant was . . ." He swallows, as if the words he's saying are difficult. "Sorry. It's just, talking about my fucked-up childhood isn't my favorite of topics."

"We do not have to talk about it then."

He nods, and yet words slowly trickle out anyway. "Sawyer and I used to be . . . I guess you could say we were good friends. Three of the books for my Timeline focus on that relationship and our adventures together, actually. And I guess some of the fourth does, too. Just not as much, thank God."

There is no misinterpretation concerning his scorn toward this Tom Sawyer. I lift our conjoined hands and press my lips against the back of his knuckles. And then, more meaningfully, his mouth.

Little steps, I tell myself. He and I, we have the rest of our lives to reveal such small, intimate details to one another.

A LOVER'S LOCKET

FINN

B Y THE TIME WE reach the graveyard, I'm in a weird place mentally. For one, I know I was dodgy when I balked at Alice's questions. I mean, shit—I've seen her past in vivid color, haven't I? I was in it, and felt its blood on my hands. She knows me, yes, but she knows the me of now. She knows the me I want her to know.

I tell myself, as a highly pious man named Joseph lectures us on how God will most likely look down upon us for the sins and atrocities we're about to commit and yet still willingly hands me a shovel he carried for a not-so-short distance in blustery conditions, it's not like Alice willingly offered up her past, either. I had to actually go to Wonderland to get answers out of her, and I think if I hadn't, she would have gone right on keeping them inside her. Honestly, though, her refusal to talk about it was one of the things that really attracted me to her in the first place. She obviously had a painful past and knew how to hold onto it like it was both a lifesaver and concrete boots molded to feet. It was something I could understand, something that made me feel less like the odd man out in the Society. Brom's was checked, but he fully embraced it. "The past makes us who we are," he often told Victor and me. "It lets us mold the future. I would not be the same man sitting before you, had I not been who I was in my youth."

Victor's past is easy, despite the seemingly never-ending slew of shitty genetics his biological father saddled him with. I mean, he was found when he was so young that he doesn't even have concrete memories of his Timeline. Katrina and Brom raised him in such a way he never knew real hardships. He went to elite schools, had British tutors who refused to allow him even the slightest bit of an American accent, and had parents, friends, and family who loved and respected him. He had shrinks and treatments. His life has been charmed—he went from the son of a whore, living on the streets, to becoming a very rich, influential doctor.

Mary isn't much different. While she grew up in India (okay, well, she was a rotten kid back then, from what she tells us, and was trapped in a building when everyone else died around her) and England (where nobody died and she learned to garden and miraculously coax bedridden cousins to walk again), she's all about embracing her checkered history. It's something she pulls out and hugs like a goddamn teddy bear.

Nobody else seems to wish that they could just take an eraser to it all. I mean, hell, the A.D. brags about his jail time like he was in Tahiti, on a beach with a bunch of hot girls in bikinis rather than a flea- and rat-infested hellhole riddled with criminals who would think nothing of sticking a shank in your side for a scrap of bread. And Wendy, who lived in an orphanage most of her childhood, sees it all as a magical experience as she waited for Peter Pan to come and whisk her away.

But me? I wish I could go back and erase Tom Sawyer's entire existence from my life and my original Timeline. I'd erase our adventures and the fact that my biological father was the town drunkard and that, if I was lucky, I found welcome barns in shitty weather or even have people give me the time of day. I'd even erase going on the lam with Jim and the sweet taste of freedom we both finally got to savor. And maybe that would mean I wouldn't be here, doing what I'm doing, but part of me viciously thinks it would all be worth it.

But I can't go back and change any of it. That sonofabitch still claims a large influence over a decade of my life, and he's still done what he's done. And I'm here and he's there, and now I'm about to dig up some lady's grave all so I can take a piece of jewelry away from her. For a good reason and all, but still.

A fine mist coats our skin and clothes as we come to stand before a trio of graves: two men and one woman. I suppose it could be worse: at least it isn't straight-up raining. Damp is preferable to soaked. "Do you know their story?" Nelly Dean is asking us.

"Only a little." Alice takes the second shovel from Joseph. "We perused a bit of the book to get the lay of the land."

"Surely, miss," the man exclaims, "you are not thinking of digging, are you?"

I can tell she's fighting back the urge to put him in his place. "Unless you are willing to help us," she says tightly, "I certainly will be."

He makes the sign of the cross. "Grave robbing is a sin."

I mutter, "So is murder and mass extinction."

Joseph has, according to Nelly Dean, been in the know about the Society nearly from the first week we made contact with her. Apparently, he spent much time in church praying for all our souls, and for Mrs. Dean's, too, as he initially accused her of devil-inspired insanity. But he came around for one of her status checks, and I guess, outside of the witchcraft he initially accused her of, also came around to believing we were legit. That hasn't stopped him from reminding us every so many minutes that what we're about to do is pretty damn awful.

Look, I'm not arguing with him. Does he think I want to be out in these godforsaken, damp moors, digging up some woman who locals claim is a ghost that haunts the area to this day? Hell, no. But I also don't want to find out that a popular book like *Wuthering Heights* has its Timeline destroyed because the Society was too squeamish to get their hands dirty.

Joseph prays loudly as Alice and I tear into the grass covering Catherine Earnshaw Linton's grave. The Librarian told us a little about what to expect once we uncover her coffin. One side will already be open, so the body will most likely be in poor condition. Apparently one of these dudes wanted his coffin open, too, so they could, what, stretch their dead hands out to one another or something? To this day, some people think crap like this is romantic. FYI: it's not. For all we know, the ghosts of both Cathy and her lover (brother?) Heathcliff will come and scare the shit out of us for daring to desecrate their resting place. But I'll give it to Alice—she's right here with me, digging into the grass and dirt, acting like she's having tea in her palace back in Wonderland rather than sweating and freezing all at once in a graveyard. It takes us longer than I thought it would before our shovels hit wood, though, and even then, we both pause and look up at Mrs. Dean and Joseph.

"Last chance," I say kindly, even though I'll be pissed if Alice and I did this all for nothing. Alice, for her part, is breathing hard but doesn't complain once.

God, I am so taken with this woman. I mean, she didn't even blink when she found out what we had to do. Well, she mentioned it was ghoulish, but it wasn't like she said no or even had doubts. And that's another thing that is so crazy attractive about her—she does what has to be done.

Dean and Joseph exchange anxious looks; there is anguish and fear on both their faces. They're spooked, I realize, and have spent the better part of the last half hour glancing around the graveyard like they expect ghosts to pop up, too. Hell, I've been in some crazy Timelines before, but never actually encountered a ghost before, so this is all pretty damn unnerving and their behavior isn't helping matters. But after a long, meaningful moment during which nothing is said, they both nod. "Yes," Nelly Dean says softly. "If it means our . . . Timeline, as it is, will be spared the horrors others have had to face, then yes. Catherine would not wish us all to go to hell."

Joseph glances around fervently. "Heathcliff would."

Mrs. Dean does not argue with him.

Alice and I carefully scrape the rest of the dirt off the top of the grave, leaving the side the Librarian referenced untouched and still covered as best as possible. Then I take out a small crowbar I brought along with us to 1847BRO-WH and gently pry up a couple of the planks on the other side. The last thing I want is for an unstable coffin to collapse.

Beneath me lies a dirty skeleton and scraps of a dress. More importantly, a necklace peeps up at us.

Thank God we got to it before Todd.

Mrs. Dean gasps as she peers down into the hole Alice and I are wedged into, a trembling hand covering her mouth. Joseph prays louder and harder. Even though I already know the answer, I ask them anyway if they want to be the ones to extract the locket ringing the skeleton's neck.

Joseph doesn't stop praying to answer me. Mrs. Dean chokes out a definitive no. And I'm not going to let Alice do it, even though I have no doubts she would if asked. So I awkwardly squat down and fight to unclasp the fragile necklace and not break out in the shudders threatening to overtake me. The bones that my fingers brush against my skin are cold and now damp, thanks to the mist, and all I can think is: *Holy shit, those ghosts better not show up right now or I might actually vomit all over this grave.*

Which would be super manly and all.

Once the necklace is free, I pass the locket over to Alice. She glances up at the housekeeper. "Would you like to see it one last time, Mrs. Dean?"

The woman shakes her head. "No, miss."

Alice carefully wraps the necklace in a handkerchief and stuffs it into her coat. "I wonder what's in it."

"Hair," Mrs. Dean says. "Hair from the gentlemen whose graves surround poor Cathy's. She loved them both, see."

I situate the planks to their former positions and ask Joseph to pass down the nails and hammer he's brought. A few quick pounds and soon, Alice and I are filling the hole back up. As we lay the sod back into place, carefully so that no one will be able to tell we'd been there, I realized I'm exhausted both physically and mentally. So is Alice, but damn, if she isn't acting like she's not.

It makes me want to kiss her, but I've just been desecrating somebody's resting place, so maybe I ought to at least wash my hands first.

Jesus, my priorities are so screwed up.

But then I look at the trio of graves before us, and then at all of the others peppering the graveyard, illuminated by the pale candlelight of the lanterns we've brought. Thoughts of kissing disappear. Even though I've tried so hard to hold it back, to ignore it, to pretend this isn't a thing, it hits me anyway like a sucker punch.

I sit down, hard, on the damp grass that I just replaced.

Without missing a beat, Alice says in that regal voice of hers, "A moment, please? We just want to catch our breaths." Mrs. Dean and Joseph quickly wander off to the entrance to the graveyard.

Alice sits down next to me. Her dirty hand reaches and wraps around mine. I can feel fresh blisters on her palm.

She never complained. Not once.

I stare at the plot before me, at the name of the woman whose body I just manhandled. I think about graves and of bodies and of death and of how absolutely, brutally unfair life can be. It hurts to think these things. It hurts like hell.

I think them anyway.

The wind picks up, whistling and howling through the branches of the trees nearby. "Finn?" She squeezes my hand, not even seeming to care that I was just manhandling a skeleton. "Are you all right?"

No, I want to tell her. No, I'm not all right. I'm about to tell her I am fine, though, when different words fall out.

I tell her, "Someone I know is dying." Someone who, no doubt, will have a grave just like one of these. But before Alice can finish her condolences, I keep going. "Katrina doesn't have a grave."

The back of my eyes burn, and it's not from exhaustion, although I'd like to claim otherwise. My adoptive mother, the only one who has ever counted in this pathetic life of mine, does not have a grave we can visit. Her life was cut short when Todd or one of his cronies destroyed the catalyst for her Timeline and there is no body to mourn over, no grave to visit, no proof outside of photographs and memories to highlight how bright she burned in my life and others.' Brom put up a memorial to her at the Institute, but it's a small plaque decorating some hideous statue that he thinks she would have approved of. She wouldn't have, by the way. Her taste was way more refined than his. And the thing is, how many people walk by that thing and never think twice about the person who it's dedicated to? Too many.

I do, though.

My mother deserved better than she got, and I'm going to track down the motherfucker who did that to her and exact justice, whether Katrina would have wanted that for me or not.

"I'm so sorry," Alice is whispering. She shifts my hand to her other, so an arm can wrap around me. "I'm so sorry, Finn."

Graves are funny. They're actually incredibly selfish things. Dead people don't give a shit whether or not they're buried in a grave or cremated or frozen or sent into space or scattered to the winds. The dead are dead. They're beyond caring. But we who remain, the greedy survivors, we need something like this. We selfishly take a body and put it in a plot of land that could be, I don't know, used for a variety of other things other than letting skin and bones rot within, and we selfishly put up a slab of marble or concrete and we then use all these things to let us cling to the past.

Katrina doesn't have a grave, though. And that's acid in the pit of my stomach. I loved my mother. I still love her.

And yet, the absence of my mother's grave isn't the only one that cuts deeply. So does Jim's. One of my oldest, truest friends, one of the very few who treated me with respect and as an equal when I was a kid, doesn't have a grave, either. So, yeah. Sweeney Todd is going to pay for what he's done to my mother and countless others. And when I'm done doling out that bit of justice, I'm finally going to go avenge Jim, just like I should have all those years ago.

Tom Sawyer is going to pay for what's he's done.

GHOST STORIES & SELFIES

ALICE

FINN HAS GONE TO speak with his father, so I am the one who
must deliver our latest acquisition to the Librarian. It takes me a
good ten minutes to pass through all of the security measures before
I enter the Museum, a cavernous yet elegant holding room buried deep
beneath the Institute. Instrumental music that Finn informs me is called
elevator music fills the space, and no matter how many times I've heard
it in this room or her office upstairs in the library, I still cannot seem to
succinctly draw the line connecting such peppy tones to the inscrutable
woman who calls herself the heart of the Society.

She loves it so, though.

I find the Librarian dusting books on shelves within a small office
that consists of little more than a pair of overstuffed chairs, a turquoise
telephone, and a coffee table that is made from a large slab of raw rock

and quartz, cut open and polished until it shines like glass. "Ah," she says, not even bothering to turn away from her cleaning duties, "I was wondering when you'd come."

I suppose this is less insulting than her frequent charges of my tardiness.

"Was there any difficulty in obtaining 1847BRO-WH's catalyst?"

I'm annoyed she asks such a thing, when I'm confident she already knows the answer. "Outside of the labor, none at all."

She finally turns around and offers me a wide smile. She is truly beautiful, with thick dark hair and bright eyes more shrewd than kind. "Why, Alice. You and I both know you are no stranger to getting your hands dirty."

"Contrary to what your crystal ball must tell you, until last night, I had never robbed a grave before."

Her laugh fills the small room. "Could you relate to Cathy, though?"

It's a challenge to hold back my irritation. "Dead and possibly a specter?"

"Torn between two loves."

Honestly, the gall of this woman. I drop the handkerchief-wrapped locket in her outstretched palm, refusing to rise to her bait.

The Librarian unwraps the catalyst and pulls it up by its chain. The small locket is dirty, yet manages to glint in the bright light anyway. "Catalysts are always symbolic," she muses. "This, for example, represents the enduring struggle between two lovers its owner was torn between during both life and death." She picks up a small cloth conveniently sitting on her desk and begins to polish the stolen jewelry. "Did you see her ghost, perhaps?"

My answer is clipped. "No."

"Some people believe that beloved objects such as this can be haunted by their owners." She flashes me an indulgent smile. "Do you think that possible?"

"If it is," I say tightly, "Mrs. Linton will be haunting you down here in the Museum."

Another laugh. "She would have much company then."

I am mortified to admit the hairs on the back of my neck rise at her throwaway comment, but I refuse to glance around me to verify whether or not the Librarian is telling the truth.

"I have another assignment for you today."

I temper my impatience. "I intended on spending my day further questioning Rosemary and Jenkins."

"Unfortunately, Henry Flemming misjudged how much truth serum to administer to F.K. Jenkins," she says, "and our stock is depleted. I sent word to Victor and Mary. They will be en route to obtain more by morning. Until then, I have an assignment for you."

Frabjous.

"I'll need you to go to the New York Public Library and fetch several books for me."

Fetch, as if I am a canine?!

"They'll be waiting with a young but enthusiastic librarian named Bianca Jones. She is a local contact of ours, and a valuable one, to boot. Please ensure you show her your best side." The infuriating woman wraps the locket in a clean cloth from her desk. "You need to get out more, after all."

So people keep saying to me. I know they mean well, but honestly, nearly a year in modern-day New York City has not found me as acclimatized as one might assume. Everything is so fast and big and loud. Cars race by, people shout into their phones, planes roar overhead, and everyone is in a hurry. There is little leisure remaining in today's society, it seems. And rather than embracing the sensation of a breath of fresh air on my outings, I am more apt to wonder if I'm in a fishbowl, trapped by tall buildings and choking on polluted air.

"Your consideration toward my welfare is much appreciated." My words are cool, though.

"Also, I need you and Finn to head upstate to purchase a pair of books for me tomorrow, ones associated with stories mentioned upon the Ex Libris wall. I mentioned the acquisition to Finn a few weeks back, but . . ." Her lips press together ruefully. "Things have been chaotic around here. He may have forgotten. I'll have all the details sent to you within the hour so you can better acquaint yourself with them."

I stifle the urge to curtsy in the most mocking of ways. I've gone from Queen to page, apparently. "I am sure there are much more imperative things to be done here in the pursuit of Todd and the mysterious boss or bosses behind the Timeline deletions."

"We have people working on it." Her tone remains friendly, although now laced with steel. "These matters are crucial to the workings of the Society. I would not send you and Finn if I did not think it essential."

She's utterly maddening.

Minutes later, we have woven our way through rows of catalysts until we reach the locket's latest resting place. The glass-faced security box is already open and waiting, its golden light focused on a small velvet-covered necklace display situated in the middle. As she arranges the chain around the stand, she says lightly, "Ghosts are not always white-robbed specters, howling or weeping in misery. And yet, all of us are haunted by ghosts, Alice. Even you."

She says this like I am not painfully aware of how my past haunts me on a daily basis. "What or who are your ghosts?" I challenge.

When she shuts the door to the case and locks it with both metal key and key card, it appears as if she might answer my query. There is sadness on her lovely face, regret that I've not seen before. But like the ghosts we are discussing, the emotion vanishes quickly without lingering trace. "I hope, in the coming weeks, you will trust your instincts. Ghosts cannot always be rationalized with, unfortunately."

Her about face is most peculiar and exasperating all at once.

"Be careful on the way out." She taps the side of her chin thoughtfully. "One might worry we've roused the dead with all of our talk."

Midway through an uncouth eye roll, a hint of gut-wrenching crying surfaces somewhere deep within the Museum, followed by a few notes of giggles that rise slightly above the strain of the Librarian's beloved elevator music.

I stare at the woman in front of me. She simply studies me in return. I turn and leave without another word.

Immense and beautiful, the New York Public Library stretches wide and lovingly down its street. Lions guard the stairs leading up to the doors and people mill about. It is a stately structure, one that cannot help but demand notice on a day as fine as this one.

Inside, I make my way through a gleaming hall to the main reading room. Chandeliers dangle over rows of tables with brass lamps lining the sides. Above soars a painted cloud ceiling surrounded by gilded, carved designs. The walls are lined in marble and books, and rather than the room feeling small and crowded, I'm left in awe of its expansive nature. Dozens of people are reading and circulating about in the quiet yet warm atmosphere.

In a world riddled with technology, it does my heart good to see value still placed in words and pages. Although, I might not inform the Librarian of this, considering she might just lord it over me in that supercilious yet cryptic way of hers.

I wander throughout the library until I locate an information desk. A helpful man sends me back into the main reading room, toward the far end. There, with a cart of books at her side, is the person I'm looking for.

I stroll up to her and clear my throat. "Forgive me for interrupting your work, Ms. Jones, but my name is Alice Reeve. I've been sent on behalf of—"

The petite, lovely woman before me, her hair a gorgeous riot that stands tall and wide around her head, drops the book she's holding. She whispers, "Oh. My. God." And then, faster, *"Ohmygod."*

I glance around us to see if there is a commotion I am unaware of.

One of her slim, brown hands latches onto my arm, startling me. "I am your biggest fan. *Seriously."*

I have no idea what is happening right now.

She lets go, as if she's just realized she's possibly left bruises, she was holding onto me so tightly. The book on the floor is quickly reclaimed and shoved onto a shelf. And then, whispering, "I've probably read your stories like a hundred times apiece. I've seen all the movies. Was first in line to see the last one—you know, the one that was all crazy and dark and featured the Mad Hatter as the hero?"

Well, now I've heard it all. The Hatter a hero? What utter rubbish.

Nonetheless, she's still talking. "I was totally hoping you two would hook up in the movie—"

As I've finally learned what *hooking up* means, I'm appropriately and fully disgusted.

"I'm babbling, aren't I? I am so sorry. It's just . . . I'm obsessed with all things Wonderland. You are—" Her hands flap between us. "God, you're like a thousand times more beautiful than the girl who played you in the movie." She points to her flat belly. "My husband and I want to name our baby Alice."

I am speechless. How in the bloody hell does she know who I am?

"Here, let's go to my office. I have what you need." And then, as I trail after her, completely oblivious as to what in the blazes is happening right now, she adds, "I hope you don't mind, but . . . I'd love it if you could sign one of my books for me. And maybe take a selfie?"

I clear my throat again. "I'm sorry, Miss Jones—"

"Please call me Bianca."

More gently, "Bianca, I'm afraid I haven't the foggiest idea what a selfie is."

She finds this hilarious.

Minutes later, we are ensconced within her small office. Before I can ask about the volumes I've been send for, she's digging through her desk, prattling on about a series based on Wonderland she'd read a few years back that were apparently *awesome* in their reimaginings. "The Mad Hatter was an assassin!"

I nearly choke on this absurd bit of information.

"Your love interest in that series was . . ." Bianca extracts a book out of the bottom drawer of the desk. "Some guy. I remember wishing it were the Mad Hatter, though. He was hot in that one. All gritty and manly."

Honestly, now. *Gritty?* What is with the modern yet absurd romanticizing of the Hatter?

It's then I notice she's got a framed picture above her desk of a girl sitting at a long table with a man in a hat, a hare wearing clothes, and a mouse peeping out of a teapot. A sinking feeling tells me that this is supposed to me.

The book is laid open on the desk. A pen is offered. I'm even more perplexed.

"You said you'd sign my copy?"

I stare down at the abhorrent text in horror. Did I agree to such a thing?

"Obviously I promise not to show it to anyone! Or sell it." She titters nervously. "You can just sign it with your first name. *Ohmygod.* Alice in Wonderland is sitting in my office."

Oh, for goodness' sake. Has anyone else from the Society had to go through such a surreal event as this?

The book is removed once my name is hastily scrawled within. Bianca sidles up behind me, leaning down and placing her head next to mine. Her phone is stuck out in front of us, a picture is taken.

As she made it so we could see the screen during the process, I can attest she looks as she's about to scream in joy. I appear as if I am, as Mary would say, confused as all hell.

"Okay. Now that we've gotten my fangirling out of the way, let's get down to business." She drops into the chair behind her desk. "The Librarian has requested five books, but I was only able to track down three. The other two were checked out a few weeks back and have yet to be returned."

The woman in front of me is a librarian, and yet she still refers to my colleague by the title and not name?

"That said," Bianca continues, "I will let her know as soon as they're in." She tugs over a tote bag. "I've placed these on an extended checkout, considering I don't know how long you all will need them. If you need to renew, please make sure you either call or come to me directly rather than do it online or at the desk."

She passes over the cloth bag. Inside are three books, just as she said.

I thank her and stand up. She's immediately on her feet, rushing for the door. "Do you like working for the Society?"

She really is all over the place, isn't she? "I do."

"I have to be honest, I would kill to work with you guys. I mean, outside of what I'm asked to do here and all. I know I've only been affiliated with the organization a few years now, but I've put in an application. Did you have to apply?"

"No," I say simply. "Miss Jones, I thank you for obtaining these books for me. But I'm afraid I must depart now."

"Oh!" Her face falls but she quickly pastes on a smile. "Of course. You have worlds to save, after all."

A telephone in her room chirps, preventing her from following me. Telling myself it isn't cowardly at all, I make a break for it whilst she is distracted.

I've just exited the library when a nearby voice exclaims, "Well, well. If it isn't the elusive Alice who is new to New York."

Standing next to one of the lions guarding the stairs is a man I never expected to see again. A number of months back, I'd met him at a dance club Mary had taken me to. We'd danced together, and at the end of the night, he'd asked to see me again.

I'd politely declined. The evening concluded on several more important notes—that of a Rosemary sighting and of a quarrel between Victor and Mary. My dance partner was quickly forgotten.

Yet now here he is, in the bright sunlight gracing the steps to the library, grinning at me as if he's discovered something he's lost. Tall, raven-haired, and distinguished, he's dressed in a smart suit. A gold and cobalt ring glitters on his pinky finger.

"Hello, Mr.—"

"Gabe." He smiles even wider and takes a few steps toward me. "Gabe Lygari."

Ah. That's right.

He sticks out a hand. I offer mine, but rather than indulging in a quick handshake, he flips my hand over and kisses the back of my knuckles. I bristle at this inappropriate sense of unearned familiarity. One night at a club and drinks shared does not equate an attachment, let alone a friendship.

"I have to admit, I've been searching for you. I was worried you might have tumbled down another rabbit hole."

I lift my eyebrows up, unamused at both his tenacity and poor joking.

He chuckles quietly. "Sorry. I'd forgotten you weren't into the typical Alice in Wonderland jokes."

"It was nice seeing you again," I murmur, taking a step down on the stairs, but he comes to stand before me.

"Let's go get some coffee. My treat. We can catch up."

"I'm sorry, Mr. Lygari, but—"

"Gabe, remember?" He flashes another smile, like we are old friends. He really is quite handsome, but looks are never enough.

"I'm sorry, Gabe, but I must be getting home now."

He slips on a pair of mirrored sunglasses, but does not move out of my way. "I'm surprised to see you here, to be honest."

"At the library?"

"I suppose," he says, "I didn't take you as a reader. No—don't take that the wrong way. I meant no offense. You just struck me as more of a take action woman rather than a reader."

I ask coolly, "Who says a woman can't be both?"

He chuckles again. "Let's go get that coffee. Or, hell, an early dinner. You can explain to me how you are one of those take-action-readers."

I step around him. "My apologies, Mr. Lygari, but I really must be going. Good day to you."

This time, he does not stop me. But when I slip into a cab at the base of the library, I discover he is still watching me. A hand is raised in farewell as I drive away.

I do not raise mine in return.

FAIRY TALES

FINN

CLICK OFF THE recorder and lean back in my chair, sighing.

"He's a right prick," Victor says. "I thought Mary was going to bloody castrate him right before my very eyes the last time we went in to ask him some questions."

Apparently, that is not an uncommon reaction from women toward F.K. Jenkins. I can't blame them, though. He's pretty much the standard definition of a misogynistic dick. "Would you have stopped the bleeding?"

My brother spins his empty paper coffee cup like a top, much to the displeasure of our father. "Shite, no. That said, I don't like where this is all going."

That makes two of us. Or, three, considering Brom is just as baffled as the rest of us. I rub my throbbing temples and wonder what in the hell we're going to do. "I find it hard to believe that both Jenkins and Rosemary don't seem to know the name of who they're working for." Except, they genuinely don't, or at least that's what they claim under the influence of truth serum. During his interrogation, Jenkins mentioned all of his correspondence with said mysterious boss was done via email and the occasional courier package containing books that served as targets. Wendy is doing her best to determine where the email address originated from, but claims she's getting stonewalled at every turn. The address is heavily encrypted and sent through a variety of servers across the world, so it could really be coming from just about anyone, anywhere, as far as we know. Our tech guru hasn't given up, though. She's still hammering away at it and swearing up a storm while doing so.

These fools had no phone calls with whatever psychopath was sending these order. No face-to-faces, at least with Jenkins and Rosemary. They took their orders blindly and killed without second thoughts. Well, Rosemary killed. Jenkins told them where to find people and catalysts.

It makes me crazy.

"Look," Victor is saying, "people are scared. They thought that Todd was the big get, you know? And we don't even have that sonofabitch yet."

I'm going to have to see a dentist, I've been grinding my teeth together so much lately. "I know."

"You have to promise me something. No matter what, we're still going to get that arsehole. We're still going to make him pay for what he's done to our family and countless others." He slams a fist down against the table. "They all will."

"You think I don't want that too?" I lean forward, dropping my elbows against the wood spanning the length between us. "You think—"

"No, I know you do," he says quickly. Brom reaches over and lays a hand on his shoulder, and my brother smiles sheepishly. "We all do, obviously. I'm just saying, none of us can lose that objective. Someday, I want to be the one to shoot his bloody bollocks off."

Brom sighs meaningfully.

I think that, given the chance after such a shooting, my brother would happily use Todd, Rosemary, and Jenkins for parts to reenact his birth father's experiments in a bloody blaze of vengeance. Truth is, I wouldn't stand in his way. Hell, I would happily pass him whatever limb he wanted.

Suddenly, I'm reminded of a time long ago, one I haven't thought of in ages.

The book was big and heavy and seemed to take up the width of the love seat we were crammed onto, two teenagers and their mother, but Katrina didn't mind. For such a beautiful, fragile-looking woman, she was strong. Brom would tease her about it, but that's all it was—teasing. Everyone at the Institute knew that Katrina was the backbone of everything. Katrina had nerves of steel, and a stare that could cut down the densest forest. Her heart was massive and her belief in doing the right thing was astounding. She was strong, both physically and emotionally, and it was one of the things that I loved best about my mother.

She tried so hard with me. So, so hard. She never let me run, and the truth was, because of her, I eventually stopped wanting to. She's the one who taught me that settling down was an okay thing. She's the one who taught me I could let my defenses go and rely upon family. That opening up my heart didn't mean losing myself like I once feared.

"Why is this book important?" she asked us that afternoon.

Victor looked across the space and met my eyes. He rolled his and I fought back the urge to laugh. I liked Victor. He was smart—smarter than Sawyer, but he never lorded it over me. He sounded so smart, too, and for the first few weeks I was at the Institute, I was too embarrassed to speak around him. Some of the kids in the neighborhood told me I spoke like some hillbilly hick on TV, one that should have all their teeth missing and live in the swamps with gators or have fleas or something equally horrifying and yet all too painfully realistic. I nearly got my ass kicked a number of times and a few black eyes when I did talk to those kids because language changed over the years. Attitudes and society had changed for the better. Words I grew up with were no longer okay to use, and it scared the shit out of me that I never knew that before coming to New York. I wasn't smart like any of the rest of them. I didn't have the schooling or upbringing they all did. It didn't take long to realize I was that hick they said I was. But Victor, smart, clean, cultured Victor, never got on me about any of those things. Granted, Katrina would have verbally tanned his hide had he, but still.

I let Victor answer Katrina's question, because I was afraid to say something stupid. Hell, even with all the tutors they'd hired for me, reading was still something I struggled with at that point, so it wasn't like I could even tell either of them what the title was.

"It's a book of fairy tales," he said. "Popular ones."

It wasn't the answer she wanted, but she didn't belittle him for it. "Why do we need fairy tales?" But before he could answer, she said, "Huck?"

Katrina was the last person I ever allowed to call me Huck, but even she stopped when I changed my name permanently.

My tongue felt thick, and I think I may have even started to sweat as they waited for my answer. I debated not answering, actually. But then I looked into her eyes and understood that she genuinely wanted to hear what I had to say.

So I told her, "They give people hope for happy endings."

"You are so right." She'd smiled. It was so beautiful, like that of one of the princesses' pictured within the thick volume. I loved those smiles of hers, and she was so generous with them. "It's funny, so many of the stories within this book are actually dark and rather violent, and yet, over time, we have come to associate fairy tales with the happiest endings we could ever imagine. This book represents the undying belief in good that people have. That's the power of books, boys. Stories such as these endure because of hope."

Children's and Household Tales, *otherwise known as* Grimm's Fairy Tales, *was the first book I voluntarily ever read once I knew how. And it was all because my mother taught me to hold on to hope.*

My mother did not get a happy ending.

"They'll pay for what they did." My vow is quiet. Angry. "Make no mistake about that."

Victor slumps back into his chair. "Where do we go from here, though? How do we find somebody whose name even their employees don't know?"

Todd is still a big get, our father writes on his whiteboard.

I nod. "Our picture has expanded, yes, but let's narrow our focus back onto Todd. We'll find him and then go from there. I think that neither Rosemary nor Jenkins told us everything they know."

"You think the truth serum was ineffective? You might want to mention that to the Librarian—she's requested Mary and I go get more in the morning."

I shake my head. "I think it's more like a genie granting wishes, where you have to be specific with your questions. And I think Rosemary and Jenkins figured that out pretty fast. We need to question them again. Repeatedly if necessary."

Victor nods and then moves as if to stand up. But just as quickly, he sits back down. "Before I leave . . . rumor has it Sawyer called this week."

Brom perks up at this.

Dammit. "And?"

They both wait patiently, and yet I add nothing. So my brother says, "And I had words with Wendy and the A.D., reminding them that all of those arsehole's calls go through me."

"I am going to reassign liaisons," I tell my father. And like a dick, I'm glad he can't argue with me about it right now.

Victor smacks the table again. "Good. Not everybody deserves a second chance."

Sawyer sure as hell doesn't. He needs to rot in hell for what he's done—at the very least, prison. Fuck him. Fuck St. Petersburg for being such a shithole. Fuck the whole lot of assholes who thought what he did wasn't wrong in the least. Fuck the whole region and their fucked-up mentalities about what constitutes a person. Fuck my entire Timeline.

I have to take a deep breath. Center myself, because I feel like I'm going to break something again.

I remember the day I found out about what Sawyer had done. I pretty much destroyed my room and then broke some kid in the neighborhood's nose simply because he *looked* like Tom Sawyer. The police were called. I was arrested. As I sat in the back of the cop car, I laughed so hard until I sobbed. Because I got arrested for breaking somebody's nose. Sawyer got to go his merry way when there was blood staining his hands.

Jesus, life was unfair.

I'd threatened to go back and make him pay, but in those early days, Katrina and Brom wouldn't let me. I think they were scared about what I'd do. I was scared, too. I'd never felt such rage before.

"Look," Victor is saying, "let me go into 1876/96TWA-TS, reclaim the liaison materials, and personally hand them off to whomever you choose."

My brother's trying to protect me. I get that. Or maybe he fears, much like our parents had, I'll beat the shit out of Sawyer and get myself arrested again.

"I appreciate the offer," I say dryly, "but I might have to go there anyway in the next few days, so I'll take care of it myself."

Brom's eyebrows lift once more. My brother knocks over his empty cup of coffee. "What in the bloody hell for?"

He makes a good point, considering I'd vowed multiple times to never step foot in my original Timeline again once our parents calmed me down from threats of extreme violence. "The Widow Douglas is dying and has asked to see me."

"Shite."

Yeah, shite all right.

"You can't be thinking of going alone?"

He knows me well. Hell, I haven't even decided if I *am* going. "I don't know."

"I'll—"

"Go with Mary to get the serum."

"You must be joking. Why—"

I glare at him. It's enough to cut that sentence off, but unfortunately allows the next. "Get Alice to go with you."

And he asks if I'm the one joking.

"Or Dad. Wheel his arse into St. Petersburg with you."

Our father has the audacity to actually nod, as if this is a good idea.

To him, I say, "I am not wheeling you into 1876/96TWA-TS." To my brother, "You're a doctor, man. You really think that's a good idea for me to do to our father?"

"Fine. It's a bloody awful idea. I just . . . I don't want you going alone."

That pisses me off. "Are you saying I need a babysitter?"

He's like a dog with a bone, though. "Finn—"

I lift up my eyebrows in challenge.

"Fine. What does Alice have to say about this?"

"Not a damn thing," I say coolly.

"Because you haven't told her, right?"

I'm done with this. I stand up, but he grabs my arm. Brom scribbles away on his board.

"You can't keep hiding your past from her. You know it's going to come and bite you on the arse sooner or later."

"Says the man who has an incredibly screwed-up relationship himself."

It's a low blow, one I immediately regret. As if he can help it.

Our father flips his board around. *Stop this idiocy at once!!!*

Victor blocks the door. "Which makes me a bit of an expert on how messed-up relationships go, right?"

"Speaking of, have you been taking the protocol regularly?"

Brom shoves the board out farther. Both of us ignore him.

"You're changing the subject."

"I can't inquire about your welfare? Oh, wait—that's something only you're allowed to do?"

I'm pretty sure he wants to take a swing at me.

"Finn—"

"Are you?"

"Yes, I'm taking the bloody protocol!"

But we all know he's lying. That's the way it always goes. He takes it until he feels better or gets distracted, and then it goes by the wayside and he backslides and shit gets real again. The highs and lows of Victor Frankenstein Van Brunt.

I reach past him, my hand curling around the door handle.

"Finn—"

It isn't the first time I've shoved my brother to get out of a door. I'm sure it won't be the last. The moment I'm in the hallway, though, I immediately wish myself back in, arguing pointlessly with Victor. Because standing in front of me is none other than Marianne Dashwood Brandon.

Damn, I need a drink.

"Finn, we're not—" Victor stops the moment he sees Marianne. And then he grins like a total fool—only it's not a genuine smile. It's his *get me the bloody hell out of here immediately* smile. Well, shit. Maybe he *has* been taking the protocol after all.

"Marianne," he chokes out.

"Mr. Van Brunt." She lifts her chin and then says to me, "Mr. Van Brunt." And then, farther behind us, "Mr. Van Brunt."

Victor and I nearly get frost burns from the greeting.

"Mrs. Brandon," I say, and her shoulders jerk back almost as if I'd punched her. Her eyes widen and yet zero in on Victor.

Thank God Mary isn't here.

"I didn't know you were coming," my brother says. "When did you—"

"I am here on Janeite business." She takes a deep breath and focuses on me and Brom rather than Victor. "I believe Mrs. Knightley has discussed our concerns with you?"

Stupidly, Victor doesn't take the cut like he ought to and run as fast as he can in the opposite direction. Instead, he blurts out, "You're wearing black."

I have to bite back my groan.

"As I was saying, Mr. Van Brunt, we—"

Victor doesn't let it go. "You weren't wearing black last time."

Forget a drink. I need a whole damn bottle of booze to deal with all this.

Marianne is outraged. "I am in mourning, sir!"

"Your husband has been dead five years!" Victor counters. Scratch my previous assumption. He's obviously not taking the protocol, because what kind of levelheaded person keeps up with this shitty line of questioning? "The last time I saw you, you were wearing some kind of yellow—"

"How dare you!" She slaps him straight across the face and then, realizing what she's done, takes a step back. A gloved hand covers her mouth, but I have to be honest—she looks more pissed then horrified.

Brom is, and appropriately so, exasperated yet unsurprised at his elder son's actions.

"Victor?"

My brother, also holding a hand to his now pink face, tears his eyes away from Marianne.

"Take Dad to his checkup. And while you're there, take the protocol."

He wheels our father away, but not before giving Marianne one last pointed look. And then, because today hasn't had enough excitement, Mary Lennox rounds the hallway corner and halts in her tracks when she sees Marianne and me.

I swear to God, it's like the Institute has suddenly turned into one of those Western movies, where one gunslinger stands off against the other on a dusty road. Mary's eyes narrow sharply; Marianne's widen and then do the same.

Part of me wants to defend my dumbass brother. Mary had dumped him a week before he and Marianne hooked up, and it wasn't until a few weeks later did they reconcile. The drama between these two is unbelievable. But most of me just wants to throw up my hands and remind everyone that we're not in fucking high school anymore. Not that I think either Mary or Marianne's schooling experiences were like mine, but still.

Marianne stands up a bit straighter. Frost fills the hallway when she says, "Hello, Mary."

Mary matches her pose and tone. "Fancy seeing you here, Marianne."

I reopen the door to the office I've inhabited this week. "Shall we?"

Marianne skirts around me and through the entryway, her silk dress swishing softly. Once the door shuts behind her, she murmurs, "I am sorry for all of that."

"Are you talking about slapping Victor or nearly getting into a cat fight with Mary?" I shake my head. "You always knew how to make an entrance."

She folds her hands primly in her lap. "I cannot seem to keep my wits around your brother, Finn. As for Mary . . ." She offers me a very modern shrug. "She and I have yet to see eye to eye on things. Someday, perhaps."

Finn is better than Mr. Van Brunt. I motion toward the small wet bar the A.D. keeps stocked regularly for my father. "Tea? Wine? Or . . ."

"Whiskey, please. I fear I am in great need of it this afternoon."

"Whiskey it is." I pour us both some from one of Brom's finer bottles, given to him by a Scot grateful his Timeline was safe, thanks to the Society. Once I'm seated next to her, I hold mine aloft. "To old friends."

A hint of a smile curves her full mouth. "To old friends. And to whiskey. How I've missed whiskey." Her glass clinks against mine before we sip the smooth, amber liquid.

I pull no punches. "I have to ask why the hell are you here, Marianne."

She grimaces. "It is as I said. Janeite business."

I sigh loudly. Does she really want to play this game with me?

"I am well aware of just how ridiculous this is," she says slowly, "and yet, I thought perhaps the Society would be best served by a League member who might not . . ."

"Focus on making matches rather than the big picture?"

She laughs quietly. "Just so."

"And," I say gently, "because you're the only widow and therefore assumed to have the time on your hands to get involved."

She sets the crystal glass down on the desk. "I had almost forgotten how much of a charmer you are, Finn Van Brunt."

"You look well." And she does. The last time I saw Marianne Brandon—what has it been, two years ago now?—she was much thinner and much more somber.

A tiny smile surfaces. "Let us just say that, when the opportunity arose to find myself useful, I did not hesitate to avail myself to coming here."

"Marianne . . ." I cut to the chase. "You need to know that Victor and Mary are . . ." I root around for the right word or at least description to describe just what in the hell my brother and his partner are. Eventually, I shrug. "Together."

"I am most grateful for your concern, but I assure you that I am long past whatever attachments your brother and I may have had in the past."

I lift up an eyebrow. Granted, it was more like a one-night stand (something Victor favors when he and Mary break up), but still.

"I realize that it must not appear as so," she quickly asserts, "but I would not have come, had I not felt I could be an effective member of the Society."

"You know I told Emma we required an application."

"Then let me fill out an application," she says mildly, "and we may get on with my employment." When I hesitate, she leans forward, her face earnest. "Finn, I fear I must . . ." She shakes her head. "Allow me this chance to make good use of myself here. Surely there is something within the Institute I may be assigned."

It's hard to deny her such a request, even though I know I ought to. Marianne Brandon is a loose cannon whose unfortunate *whatever* with my brother will almost certainly come back to bite me on the ass.

But, she and I have been friends for a number of years now. Of all the Janeites, she's the one I've been able to relate to.

"Times are tough right now. People are scared."

Determination shines in her eyes. "I wish to help."

What the hell. I stick out my hand. "Let me officially welcome you to the Society, then."

After pumping my hand vigorously, she sags back in her chair, clearly relieved.

CONFESSIONS

FINN

AN HOUR INTO THE drive upstate, Alice turns down the radio. "New York is quite pretty, isn't it?" Her smile is naughty. "Once you're out of the concrete, of course. Granted, we ought to be back at the Institute right now, figuring out Todd's location, but I suppose there is that."

I actually agree with her and had words with both the Librarian and Brom over the ill-advised timing of this trip. All the woman would tell me was, "I cannot trust anyone else to go, Finn."

Ugh.

"London has concrete," I point out. "Even in the Nineteenth Century." But the elephant in the car reminds me Wonderland isn't paved and smoothed like the modern day. All the roads they had there were either brick or cobblestone, which I can only imagine make long-distance travel a total bitch in a carriage or on horseback.

I like cars. And planes. And helicopters. And the Twenty-First Century in general, thank you very much.

"What about where you grew up? Was there much concrete there?"

My fingers curl tighter around the steering wheel as I stare forward. "No."

She doesn't push. Instead, she turns back toward the window and stares out at the trees and buildings flashing past us. And I end up feeling like a jackass, because Victor's stupid words keep coming back at me.

Damn my brother.

"I grew up in Missouri, along the Mississippi River," I finally say. When that gets no response, I add, "It's in the South. Well, it was considered the South when I lived there. Or even the West. It's more of the Midwest today."

Her head tilts back toward me. "Cowboys, correct?"

I can't help but laugh a little. "I guess."

"Were you a cowboy?"

It's actually cute that she looks so hopeful. "Uh, no."

"Ah well." She rotates her body, curling up within the leather seats of the car. "I might have imagined you as one as a child, upon a stead, wrangling . . . what do they call them? Horn doggies?"

I burst out laughing. "You mean wrangling *cattle?*"

She shrugs, but she's smiling wryly. "I was under the impression there was a special cowboy term for such things."

"Again, I hate to disappoint, but I never was a cowboy. My life wasn't nearly so glamorous."

"I didn't imagine it to be glamorous." A smirk curves her lips. "I just imagined you looking delectable upon a horse."

"You've seen me on one, remember?"

Her nose screws up, and it's fricking adorable. "That's different. I've seen plenty of men on horseback in Wonderland. I haven't seen a true-life cowboy."

I shrug, as if to insinuate she'll just have to keep on waiting to see one, and she giggles. Something in me shifts, though, and I find myself telling her something I don't talk about anymore. "I did do a lot of pretending when I was a kid," I admit quietly. "I liked to imagine I was anybody but who I was."

She's thoughtful as she studies me. "Most children do."

For the next half hour, I say nothing further. I just keep driving until well after the sun sets and night wraps around us. But all of the past is like an itch I can't help but scratch, and maybe Victor has a point after all.

I pull off to the side of the road. Turn off the car and the lights. Unbuckle myself and turn to face her. Somehow, the darkness helps me pluck at the truth.

"Alice, I'm going to be honest here. My childhood sucked. I can't really put it any other way than that. I grew up dirt poor, the son of the town drunk. It's not like I had a house to live in—I was lucky to find barns to sleep in in shitty weather. Most kids would have nothing to do with me, or at least their parents told them they couldn't. My most significant friend was a freed slave, and spent a good deal of time on the lam. I didn't go to school or church. To say I was ignorant and stupid would be putting it mildly. I got into more trouble than a kid really ought to. Several people tried their best to," I flash air quotes, "civilize me, only to come away sorely disappointed. It wasn't until Brom and Katrina took me in did I . . ."

I look away. It's started to rain, and fat drops splatter across the windows. I feel like I've been skinned and left raw and exposed, like I'd been all those years I sat on a shrink's couch and laid myself bare.

It's idiotic. I know it is. I'm nearly thirty years old. I have not one but two college degrees. I am not that ignorant, illiterate kid anymore from one of the worst, most racist time periods in American history possible. And yet, I still feel that person inside me, clawing around, searching for some kind of asinine adventure to go on, and it scares the shit out of me.

A click signals her seatbelt has been unlatched. The next thing I know, Alice has crawled across the console and is straddling my lap. Her hands go to either side of my face as she stares down, her eyes serious as they take me in. I can't help but wonder what she sees. Is she no longer imagining a cowboy, but a stupid, dirty kid?

She's a queen. And me . . . I'm . . .

"I—"

She puts a finger against my mouth and then kisses the space just to the left. Another kiss follows, this time to the right. And then she moves her finger so her lips can meet mine.

Goddamn, can Alice kiss.

My hands wrap around her upper arms and tug her closer. Forget truth time. This is way better. Her tongue is in my mouth, and when it touches mine, I can't help but moan like some kind of sixteen-year-old punk who can't control himself. But Alice doesn't seem to mind, because slowly, slowly, she runs her tongue alongside mine and forces another moan out of me.

We're in a car, on the side of the road, on the way to acquire some ridiculously expensive books for the Institute, and I'm already debating how far I can go with this woman without getting us arrested for public indecency.

She sinks down against me, rocking back and forth, her fingers curling in my hair. My hands drop to her waist, and then lower still, to trail up her bare legs and just under the hem of the one of those boho dresses she favors. I like these dresses of hers. They're incredibly hot on her, especially since she's got legs for miles.

She bites my lip. I just about lose my mind.

We somehow make it to the backseat. We really are like those six-teen-year-old kids, aren't we? My hand is up her dress, fingers sliding beneath the waistband of her panties, and she's unbuttoning my shirt. Every so often, headlights flash by us, slashing through the rivulets lin-ing the windows. I ought to put a stop to this now, get us back on the road and wait until we get to the bed and breakfast we've got booked by the dealer's, but like that itch I can't help but scratch, I need her right now.

I tug her panties to the side at the same moment she gets my shirt open.

She presses a kiss against my chest. Her fingers move to my pants, and I swear, when they brush up against my dick—already hard—I have to bite my lip to stop from finishing this before we even get started. "Slow down," I whisper. I slide a finger in, my thumb finds her clit; she's wet and warm and feels like a goddamn dream.

The buttons undone, she pulls me out and squeezes gently. I can't help but buck when she begins to stroke me. We match each other's pace, me pleasuring her, her pleasuring me, and before long, the win-dows fog up. She says, voice husky, "We can go slow later tonight."

The stroking stops so she can tug my pants down a bit farther. And then, before I can say—do—anything else, she positions herself over me and thrusts downward.

She gets her wish. I couldn't slow down if I tried. Together, we thrust and push and find the perfect rhythm that leaves her writhing above me and me in heaven below her. I cup one of her breasts through the thin fabric of her dress, running my thumb across the nipple and resume stroking her clit with my other thumb. It's her turn to moan, and it's fantastic, just so fucking gorgeous to listen to. When she comes, and it's soon, she throws her head back, shouting my name as yet another pair of cars sends their lights crisscrossing across ours.

She's the most beautiful thing I've ever seen in my entire life.

I push one, two, three more times and follow her over that edge, her name now on my lips. I think it's the fastest I've ever orgasmed.

Afterward, she leans down and kisses me slowly, taking her time to trace my lips with her tongue. She says quietly, "I love you, Huckleberry Finn Van Brunt. I love *all* of you. You are my north star, remember?"

I stare up into her eyes, my breath caught in my throat. I manage, I gasp, "Binaries. We're binaries."

In the darkness, I can still make out her wry smile. "Indeed we are." And then, before I can say anything else—like how absolutely crazy in love I am with her—she puts another finger against my mouth.

She kisses the space just to the left again. And then the space to the right. "I already know, Finn." And then she opens the door and exits the backseat, only to reenter the passenger seat up front, leaving me lying there on black leather with my pants down and my dick out and wet and satisfied and my heart ready to burst.

DOUBLE IDENTITY

ALICE

A S WE DRIVE UP the long stretch of rough, winding road that leads to the rare book dealer's property, I ask Finn, "Do most of the dealers the Society works with live in such secluded locations?"

He turns down the music we've been listening to—something he refers to as indie rock, and claims I will learn to love if I can only admit there is more to music than the classics. "Some. Antiquities dealers and collectors can be eccentric, if you know what I mean."

The collectors I knew in Wonderland were most definitely eccentric. I'm reminded of the White Queen and of her expansive array of morbid dolls that often serve more as hunting trophies than actual playthings. No doubt she would delight at adding me to such a collection.

The house we've traveled to is quite large and beautiful in a sleek, alien, yet modern way. Made of roughened wood, frosted glass, and burnished metal, it's surrounded by neat hedges forming a maze. Farther back, dense trees beyond what I assume to be a field populate the distance, leaving the scope of visibility minuscule amidst the velvety blackness.

"Have you met this dealer before?"

Finn shakes his head as I stare down at the dossier file on my phone. *Gabriel Pfeifer,* it reads, *specializes in first-edition books and objects associated with authors.*

Knowing what I know now, it all seems rather distasteful. What does that even mean, *objects associated with authors?*

"We are here solely for the pair of books, correct?"

Finn turns off the car. "Yes, ma'am."

"Do you do this often?"

"You mean, do I travel distances to fetch books for the Librarian?"

I nod. There's that word again. *Fetch.*

He shrugs. "Not a lot. We typically rotate through who is going to go get what she needs since she never leaves the Institute."

I shrug into a coat, as the air is brisk with the scent of snow. Finn also slips his on, and I surreptitiously ogle him in it as we walk up the brick path toward the frosted glass door of the house. As shallow as it is, I cannot help but continually admire his physique, whether it be in well-fitting coats such as the one he's currently wearing, or in nothing at all.

Thank goodness for detours.

As if he knows what I am thinking, he lifts his eyebrows up right as he presses a small white button off to the side of the door.

I simply smile lasciviously in return.

The door swings open, bringing with it a surprise. Gabriel Pfeifer is none other than Gabe Lygari.

Frabjous. Simply frabjous. What are the odds?

The blasted man's eyes light up. "Has the rabbit hole finally brought the elusive Alice to my doorstep?"

Well, if this isn't patently awkward and irritating. And also confusing, considering.

"I believe we are here to see a Gabriel Pfeifer," I say coolly. "And yet a Gabe Lygari stands in his place."

The enigmatic man chuckles. "As are many of us, I am a man of many names. But rest assured, both are applicable. I take it you two are from the Literary Preservation Institute? What a delightful coincidence."

"We are." Finn matches my coolness. His memory, apparently, is quite good even after a number of cocktails and excitement over fights. Even still, introductions are made; bland pleasantries are offered.

Lygari—or is it Pfeifer?—opens the door wider and steps to the side. "Please, come in from the cold. Reports say it will snow tonight. The roads leading into Bücherei can be treacherous if one doesn't know them well."

Once inside, he takes our coats and carefully hangs them up before leading us down a short hallway just off the side of the foyer. At the end is a set of large, ornately carved and painted doors decorated with golden knobs.

"Bücherei is German for library, right?" Finn asks. I know him well enough to hear the faint trace of suspicion in his voice at seeing this man here, although I doubt Lygari does.

Our host's smile is indulgent as he extracts a large, old-fashioned skeleton key out of his pants' pocket. "Good catch. When I first bought this expanse of land many years ago, I knew it could go by no other name. Here, let me show you why."

As he slides the key into the keyhole, I gaze up at the carvings. Gruesome in image, they depict people of long ago in a variety of seemingly terrible situations. There is a wolf dressed as a woman, eating a girl in a red cloak. Another scene showcases two ladies slicing bits of their feet off, a translucent slipper nearby. There is another with a witch shoving children into an oven, and yet another with a woman sitting at a spinning wheel, her pricked finger dripping blood. Scene after scene run the lengths of the doors.

I do not favor them one bit.

A number of clicks and whirls sound before Lygari removes his key. The doors open silently, as if invisible hands lead their way. "This," he tells us, "is the heart of Bücherei."

It strikes me that the bulk of Lygari's house is just as he calls it—a library. Countless rows of books line the walls from floor to ceiling in an immense, three-story-high gallery. Sitting upon mosaicked floors depicting more monstrous scenes like those upon the doors are glass cases filled with more books and a variety of seemingly unrelated objects.

"I've been collecting books my entire life," Lygari is saying as Finn and I take in our surroundings. "You could say that my entire life revolves around them. As does, I would assume, yours." He pauses, then add, "Being part of a preservation organization and all."

Above us is a painted fresco depicting a dark forest, violent waves crashing upon cliffs, and a mountain complete with a cave. Glowing eyes stare forbiddingly down upon us.

"I house my entire collection here at Bücherei," he continues. "Or at least, the only one that matters. There are some books and paintings in my Manhattan apartment and offices, but they are nothing more than second-rate offerings."

I repress stark uneasiness as I glance away from a tiled scene several feet from us that illustrates a crone offering an apple dripping with what appears to be poison to a young woman. To say the room is unsettling would be putting it mildly. What kind of person would surround themselves with such images?

A hospitable one, I'm loath to admit. Lygari offers us mulled wine already waiting upon a silver cart off to one side, alongside a variety of canapés. "Forgive my poor service." His smile turns apologetic. "I'd given my housekeeper the night off before I knew the Institute would be sending representatives out." And then, boldly, "Imagine my delight at our running into one another not once, but twice in two days, Alice. And after a good couple of months of me trying to find you, to no avail. How interesting is it that both times have been in libraries?"

Did I say hospitable? Surely, I meant unbearably boorish and more than a wee bit stalkerish. I turn to Finn and say flatly, even though I already know he does, "Perhaps you remember Mr. Lygari from a dance club we both found ourselves in earlier in the year?"

Lygari chuckles, his blush insincere at best in the face of my rigid reminder that I am wholly uninterested in pursuing anything between us.

Finn sets his glass down upon the rolling tray. "We truly appreciate your hospitality, but as you pointed out, it's forecasted to snow, so we'd like to get on the road as soon as possible. Are the books in question still up for sale?"

Lygari sips his wine as he studies Finn. "Of course." He lowers the glass and motions toward a nearby glass display case. "I'm afraid I'm a bit of a hoarder. There are some stories I have multiple first editions of, and not because I've forgotten I've acquired one already. Such as this one." He moves toward the exhibit. "At last count, there are five first editions of *The Old Man and the Sea* by Ernest Hemingway within Bücherei's walls. And that was after I gave away several to employees."

I peer into the case. There is a black typewriter posing next to a pair of books—one closed, its bright blue and brown cover facing us, and another propped open, its yellowed pages filled with ramblings about sharks.

"It's Hemingway's." Lygari taps on the glass. "If I'm not mistaken, he wrote *The Old Man and the Sea* on this very one."

Finn says nothing as he stares at the typewriter, but his eyes narrow significantly.

"I—" Lygari chuckles once more. "Forgive me. I know you two are eager to get on the road, but I have so few visitors here at Bücherei. I'd love to show you some of my more impressive acquisitions if you don't mind? I promise not to keep you too long. It's just . . . this is part of my lifelong work."

I fully expect Finn to refuse him, but the suspicion on my partner's face morphs into what can only be described as carefully constructed interest. "We can spare a few minutes."

We'd like to frankly get out of this ghastly so-called library, but I suppose I can grudgingly understand why Finn wants us to look around. Bücherei isn't what we were led to believe it was based on the Librarian's report on Lygari.

Over the course of the next half hour, Lygari tours us around his personal library. It is, according to him, nearly six thousand square feet and houses roughly a quarter of a million first- and second-edition books. It's only for what he calls truly significant stories does he go out of his way to hunt down author artifacts. There are multiple typewriters, pens, journals, writing tables, chairs, and various odd documents and books found in cases throughout the gallery. For an author named Charlotte Brontë, he has a tiny manuscript in booklet form he claims was written when she was a mere fourteen years of age. For a man named Leo Tolstoy (*Leon,* he sniffs, is the correct name), there is a pencil with electric lighting. For another named F. Scott Fitzgerald, there is an inscribed flask. When we stand in front of a large case with a drop-leaf table in it, two books with familiar names stand upon it: *The Adventures of Tom Sawyer* and *Adventures of Huckleberry Finn.* Both are by a Mark Twain.

My attention swerves sharply back to Lygari.

Finn stares silently at the books as our host delightedly prattles on about how difficult it'd been to acquire the table—it'd been gifted by the author's daughter to a museum that didn't really want to let go of it. But apparently everything has a price in this modern age, because here the table sits, inside a glass case in none other than Gabe Lygari's house, and much of me wants to smash through the barrier and break the table into kindling.

I watch Lygari's mouth as he tells us about it, to suss out a hidden agenda. Coincidences, at least those I've experienced in Wonderland, have never been things to trust.

"You know," Lygari says, "I have something you might like to see, Alice."

Considering this unpleasant surprise, I rather doubt that.

He leads the way toward a case on the far side of the room, and based on the red covers with golden pictures, I have no doubt which books lay within. Now it is my turn to view which items he scrounged from a long-dead author, only now I can succinctly understand how Finn must have felt moments before. My stomach cramps as if a strong fist was shoved against my belly.

There are photographs decorating the area around the books. At least a dozen, and all of extremely young girls in varying poses that seen more lurid than innocent.

"Some people think Lewis Carroll was a pedophile," Lygari muses as we stand before the case. "I'm not so sure, though. There's a certain charm to the photographs, don't you think?"

A sour taste fills my mouth; anger fills my veins as I take in the images. *Coincidences,* the Caterpillar often told me, *are never really coincidental at all.*

"How very curious," is my flatly stated response. Is he playing a game with us?

"Your collection seems well curated," Finn says in a deceptively light yet inquisitive voice. "Do you allow the public to view it often?"

Lygari, for his part, seems less than devious as he talks about these abhorrent items. There is no hint of specificity, no clue that he has any inkling as to who we are when he informs us that the collection is a personal one. There is merely a sincere joy in his tone indicating that, to him at least, artifacts such as these in this room are to be cherished.

I study him as he talks, search for some tic that illuminates proof of subterfuge, that there is more to all of this than mere coincidence. And yet, I can detect none. His eyes do not shift. His attention does not waver. He does not stammer out well-rehearsed prompts. What he does say flows easily, and with great ease.

I sorely regret dancing with him.

Eventually, Finn offers a yawn I suspect is manufactured. And I am frustrated that I can tell this about him—a smooth-talking liar when necessary—and yet cannot ascertain the slightest bit of *off-ness* from our host. "It appears it's finally started to snow," my partner says, his attention lingering on a darkened window nearby. "We really should be on our way now."

Although clearly disappointed, Lygari goes to fetch the books we'd been sent to retrieve. I turn to Finn, troubled.

"Do you—"

His head angles to the side. A surreptitious glance shows a security camera in one corner. A few more perusals show more cameras. The eyes above me, glowing softly in the fresco, appear to track our every move in the room.

Lygari, it seems, takes no risks with his possessions.

The next few minutes are tense. Neither of us talks. Neither of us peruses the room further. We stand there, surrounded by objects belonging to those who may have crafted our lives without our permission or knowledge. It does not feel like a place of worship, though, not like Lygari surely means it to be.

It feels like a mausoleum.

Finally, Lygari returns. Gloved hands present us with two books. While obviously old, neither is in poor condition. In fact, I'd hazard to suggest neither has even been fully read before.

Finn extracts a cashier's check; books and money are exchanged. At the front door, Lygari murmurs, "It was a pleasure seeing you again, Alice. May our next meeting not be so far into the future."

It most assuredly will, if I have anything to say about it.

In the car, silence reigns until we've made our way back to the main road. Lygari was right—the route to his home is difficult to maneuver in dark and icy conditions, even for a driver as good as Finn. But once we are officially off Bücherei lands, with our GSP telling us how to get to a nearby bed and breakfast we've reserved, Finn mutters, "What an asshole."

It is a kind assessment. "How did the Society become affiliated with such a man?"

He fiddles with the heat settings without taking his eyes off the road. "The Librarian seeks out different buyers for books she needs, and this guy has been on her radar for some time. Only, he's never been willing to sell anything before. It hasn't stopped her from trying, though. Apparently, he's got one of the best private first-edition collections in the country, if not the world."

"He has two names."

This makes Finn laugh, although there is not much humor in it. "One could say most of the people you know have two names."

"Society members, yes," I allow. "People from different Timelines than this, yes. But how many people native to here utilize multiple names? Is this a common occurrence?"

Lygari's reasoning why he had two quite distinct surnames wasn't valid reasoning at all. *As are many of us, I am a man of many names. Be rest assured, both are applicable.*

"A lot of artists are like that. Actors, actresses, authors . . . Pseudonyms allow anonymity in an increasingly small world that doesn't tolerate much privacy."

"He is a book collector," I point out. "Not an artist. Do people such as he require much privacy?"

"Pseudonyms aren't uncommon in the auction world. Identities are often withheld. When a lot of money is at stake, privacy is desirable."

It still does not sit well with me. "You believe Lygari's collection is worth much."

"Alice," he says softly, "I wouldn't hesitate to claim he has nearly fifty-million dollars of books and collectibles in there. And that's a conservative number. Some of the items he has are considered priceless. He had handwritten letters from some of the most famous authors in the world. Pieces of furniture associated with the writing of classics.

Typewriters. Pens. Coupled with first-edition books, all in amazing condition?" He shakes his head. "A lot of first editions look exactly as you expect them to, especially if they're classics. The covers aren't in the best of conditions, the pages are worn and possibly torn, and a lot of times, people have scribbled their names within or used bookplates or stamps. Each one of those things can depreciate the value of a book. His collection, though . . . I'm not going to lie. I've seen a lot of book collections, but I don't think I've ever seen one in such good condition. It's almost like he got them from people who bought the books on release day and then put them immediately into storage. The Librarian's collection isn't as good. She'd kill for that library, to be honest."

I just bet she would.

"It was strange how obsessed he seems to be with fairy tales, though, wasn't it?"

The suspicion in his voice is obvious.

"What do you mean?"

"The doors. The floors. The ceiling. They all depicted scenes from fairy tales, which was weird considering I didn't see a single case highlighting any of the books they come from. Even we have first editions of *Children's and Household Tales* by the Grimm Brothers and the three booklets that comprise Hans Christian Anderson's *Fairy Tales for Children. New Collection,* as well as the compiled version he put out a year after the last booklet." And then, his wry smile visible in a passing car's headlights, "Surely even you had fairy tales in your Timeline."

"You mean in my England? Of course," I admit. "But I never read or heard them. My father, being a learned man, preferred me reading Greek and Roman philosophers. My mother found children's tales to be too dark for proper families. I suppose, having now viewed such images in Lygari's library, I can see why."

"Are you serious?" His head briefly tilts toward me. "You honestly don't know who people like Cinderella or Snow White or Rapunzel are? What about the phrase *once upon a time?"*

I shrug. "Some of the names are familiar, but as I grew up surrounded by mostly my siblings, who were raised in the same way I was, and those children whose fathers also worked at the University, we did not spend much time talking about such things. And then I left England for Wonderland at eighteen, and all of those sorts of tales became irrelevant, anyway. Wonderlandian fairy tales are much different from those I believe we just viewed. I have read many of those."

"So you never imagined yourself to be a princess when you were a kid?" He's amused. "Never imagined some prince came to save you or you saved him?"

My fingers twist tightly in the fabric of my dress. "I am a Queen. I was crowned during my second trip to Wonderland, when I was nearly eight. To pretend I was anything less than would have been ridiculous. And I quickly learned I could save myself."

"Right." He sighs quietly. "Sorry."

I place my hand on his knee. "Why are you apologizing?"

He bites his lip and stares ahead, saying nothing. And still, I interject before he can answer. I know it is unbearably rude, but I cannot allow him to assume anything otherwise. "Finn. You must surely know that my Wonderlandian status has nothing to do with my role in the Society. Or with us."

One of his hands lies upon mine and squeezes.

"I am not *your* Queen," I say quietly. Meaningfully. "I am simply your Alice."

And that, to me, makes all the difference.

A WHITEBOARD

FINN

WHEN WE GET BACK to the Institute, my father and Victor corral me in Brom's office. Sawyer has called again. The Widow Douglas, the town doc says, has two, three days tops—if even that.

Brom writes on the little whiteboard he carries around with him everywhere lately: *You need to go immediately.*

"Are you crazy?" I can't even believe I have to bring this up to them. "There are interrogations to continue! We still haven't found Todd!"

We will hold down the fort until then.

They won't let this go, will they? I switch subjects. "Avery mentioned to me a book she'd read recently that had some kind of futuristic medicines that heal people right away."

Brom sighs, but this perks Victor's attention. "Elaborate."

I shrug. One of our shared friends from our university days, Avery Lincoln, is always reading popular young adult novels. "It's like I said. I think they're sprays or shots—she wasn't too clear, and I haven't gotten hold of a copy of the book yet—but whatever they are, they heal somebody immediately. I think it would be a good idea if we get us some in light of. . . ." I try to phrase it kindly. "Todd's abilities with a knife."

Poor Brom. He's still utterly mortified he let some guy get the drop on him and slash his throat.

Thankfully, my urging does exactly what I wanted it to. Victor is all abuzz about this possible wonder drug, and before long, I've given him the name of the book and he's out the door in search for a copy.

Brom frowns at me.

"Look, do you want to get back to work or what? This way, we'll have all hands on deck in our search."

He sighs again as he scribbles: *Nonetheless, u need 2 go & pay ur respects. It will help u move on.*

"Since when do you write like an illiterate teenager?"

He rolls his eyes. Erases the shortened words and replaces them with: *You need to go and pay your respects. It will help you move on.* And then he adds: *I'm tired. Forgive me my poor grammar.*

"You should be resting."

My throat was affected, not my legs! I don't need this BLASTED CHAIR.

He probably doesn't, but Victor and I also know he'll pretend he didn't just go through a horrific attack and overdo it if we don't get him to take it easy. "Mom would make you rest."

Sadness fills his eyes. *She would also tell you to get your ass to 1876/96TWA-TS.*

"I was kidding about the text lingo. Feel free to shorten your words. Or, you know, not cuss out your son."

Stop avoiding.

I drop down into the chair across from his wheelchair and really take in my father. My strong, smart, learned father is mostly out of commission, his head propped up and his throat still bandaged. And it infuriates me to see him like this and know that the psychopath who did it is still on the loose.

I'm fine, he writes, like he's reading my mind. And then: *Go. It's hard to move on when your past is unsettled.*

"I don't see you going and apologizing to Ichabod Crane for scaring the shit out of him." Honestly, though, it always has cracked me up that my father was actually the Headless Horseman from *The Legend of Sleepy Hollow.*

He died before I was mature enough to do so. I regret that. You can also stop cussing out your old man.

"He and I will never be friends."

Brom knows I'm talking about Sawyer. *No one said you had to be.*

"I won't forgive him."

Jim would want you to.

My words are venomous. "Jim's *dead* because of that asshole!"

My father is dogged as he writes faster. *Jim loved you. He wouldn't want this to eat at you your whole life.*

Well, we won't ever know for sure if that's the truth or not, will we? Because Jim is dead and Sawyer isn't, and no apologies can ever bring back my friend or rationalize how or why his family didn't even have a body to mourn over. "The situation was beyond my control," Sawyer had the nerve to say when I called to confront him. "What would you have done in my place?"

That selfish justification only highlighted the difference between Sawyer and me. He saved his own skin by allowing an innocent man to be lynched and then burned. I would have rather died than betray somebody who gave me his or her trust.

Jim was, for a long time, the only person who treated me like their equal. The kindness and love he showed me kept me afloat.

I miss my friend. Desperately.

My stomach churns. Old, familiar anger sears my veins. And yet, my father continues to sit there, watching me expectantly. I'm pissed off he had to go and bring up how Katrina would have wanted me to go, or that Jim would somehow believe I should forgive the person behind his death.

Regret, Katrina once said, *means nothing to the dead. But to the living? It's the worst of demons, because it takes up residence inside your head and heart and whispers gleefully about your darkest pains.* Victor and I never really paid much attention to this, because what would Katrina have to regret? She was a good woman with a huge heart. She held nothing against anyone, at least, not like the rest of us do.

My biological father regretted not figuring out how to steal all my money before he died.

My adoptive father regrets dressing up like some headless ghost and scaring some schoolteacher so bad, he left town and became a recluse (a rich one, but still).

My brother regrets that he's let biology trump love and happiness time and time again, and that for some asinine reason, he cannot symbolically overcome his biological father's genes and reputation enough to take hold of what he wants most.

And my regrets are so vast sometimes I wonder if they're going to swallow me whole. If only I'd been there to stop what happened. If only I knew ahead of time. If only I'd thought to suggest Jim and his family move to New York City and get the hell out of a racist, antebellum South. If only I'd told him what he'd meant to me, what he still means. If only I'd kicked Sawyer's ass. If only I knew my mother's Timeline was being targeted. If only she had stayed here, instead of going to visit her ailing father. If only I got to see her one last time, so I could tell her how much I love her and how that love changed my life.

She was right, though. *If only* is a beast.

Sawyer is in St. Petersburg. But so is the widow. And she took me in when I was nothing and did her best when pretty much nobody else gave two shits about my welfare. I may have loathed living with her, and resented the hell out of what she was trying to do to me, but years removed have allowed me to understand the expanse of her heart.

I can't let another *if only* rot away my insides.

"I'll leave in the morning," I tell my father, only to clarify quickly that I'll be gone, at the most, one night. "There's stuff to be done around here. I've already been gone too much."

He gives me a thumb's up.

"First text lingo, now thumb's up?" I round the wheelchair. "Dad, I'm worried that Todd did more to you than cut your throat. Is this like when some coma patients wake up, they can speak in a foreign language they never knew before?"

Har har.

It isn't until we're in the elevator do I tell him, "I'm worried about Victor. I don't think he's taking his protocol regularly. I'm afraid there's going to be a whopper of a high before the crash comes."

I'm worried, too.

"Maybe," I say quietly, "whatever this miracle drug is can also help him."

Brom's quiet sigh fills the elevator. His scrawl across the whiteboard is something we Van Brunts are all too familiar with when it comes to Victor.

He writes: *Genetics.*

CO-OPTING

ALICE

I N BETWEEN THE MANY meetings he's been resigned to over the course of the day, my partner reminds me that tonight will be the first time an official status report with 1865/71CAR-AWLG is logged.

As if I could forget.

We are once more in the ballroom, indulging in a small picnic I hastily put together when I learned he'd have forty unaccounted for minutes between meetings. I've spread out a blanket, and with warm, golden sunlight filtering in through the windows, the specks of dust in the air around us sparkle like diamonds.

I like these moments when it is just him and me.

"I was thinking you might want to be the one to take the report?"

The cup of tea I'd been set to drink from pauses halfway to my lips. And yet, although conflicted, I calmly confirm my acceptance. The following minutes are spent on clinically stated details and a preview of what to expect. The report is done via video, and both the caller and the receiver will be able to see one another. It will be recorded and possibly viewed by other members of the Society who are working on 1865/71CAR-AWLG's case files.

Status reports are typically short. The Society, he reminds me, has no say, influence, or an official/unofficial position in political or global matters in Timelines. The Society is at all times neutral to such things but will record events in status reports to inform agents who possibly travel to these locations. He points out I am an exception, one that both Brom and the Librarian agreed does not fall within normal restrictions due to my Queenly status. Most agents within the Society are given a caseload of Timelines they are responsible for working with. Many agree to work with their own worlds, although there are some within active duty who refuse to.

I pick at the buttery, chocolate-filled croissant sitting on a gleaming white plate before me. "Who shuns their original Timeline?"

Finn wraps his hands around the cup of coffee I've just poured him. "Victor, for one. Brom oversees 1818SHE-F."

Interesting. "Has he even stepped foot in it since he was originally brought here?"

"Once. We went as a family one holiday and it was terrible planning on our parents' behalves." His smile is bittersweet. "None of us have been back since."

"Do you oversee yours?"

The smile slips off his face. He busies himself with adding sugar to his coffee—a sure sign something is amiss, as I've yet to see Finn enjoy the beverage as anything but black. "Brom oversees that one, too."

For a moment, he looks away, through the large pane of glass nearby, out at the white clouds lining the sky. Even still, I can see the emotions raging in his eyes and tensing all of his muscles. Finn, who has been so forthcoming over my tenure in the Society, so generous with his trust, is hiding something from me.

Once more, my inclination is to leave him to his privacy. But then I remind myself that we are a team. *The nice thing about partners,* he once told me, *is that two are always stronger than one.*

He is not alone. I am here for him, good or bad.

I scoot across the blanket until I am pressed up against him. My fingers find his and lace tightly until they feel like one. I cannot imagine he is upset about my fielding the call from Wonderland. After all, he was the architect to allow me such a privilege in the first place.

His generosity, I think, is a beautiful thing.

"Talk to me, my star," I murmur.

Quiet seconds tick by; his fingers have tightened around mine. I lean in and press my mouth against the curve of his jaw, just below his ear.

He says flatly, "I'm going to 1876/96TWA-TS in the morning."

The jolt of surprise is unpleasant. Another assignment? At this rate, Todd will never be found.

"Someone I know is dying, and I need to go pay my respects."

Wait—he mentioned this before, hadn't he? When we were in 1847BRO-WH. He'd said nearly the same thing: *Someone I know is dying.* And then he'd changed direction and spoke of his mother, and here we are, nearly a week later, and I have somehow let his painful confession go.

1876/96TWA-TS is *his* original Timeline.

I lay my head against his shoulder. "I am coming with you."

I am charting new waters here, for even though this is neither my first relationship nor my first love, things feel different with Finn. Maybe it is because we were friends first. Maybe it's because he found his way into my trust and my heart in the kindest, gentlest way possible. Maybe it's because when we touch, prophecies, consorts, Courts, or shuffling decks are not worries. I only feel sparks. Maybe it's because he has seen my past, seen the ugliness and pain associated with it, and he is still here, holding my hand.

For months after I'd left Wonderland, I had given up hope that a meaningful life was within my grasp. I foolishly yet voluntarily wallowed in the belief my destiny had been stripped away from me, my purpose torn asunder. I was wrong, though. My destiny, my purpose, evolved. I met this man, and rather than chastise me for being blind to all the possibilities life still has for me, his kindness and tenacity coaxed me out of the darkness. I attempted to foolishly push him away, yet he dug his heels in.

He did not give up on me, even when I warned him he could die in

Wonderland. He came with me anyway. I will not give up on him, either.

Finn murmurs, "It won't be pretty."

"I imagine you thought the same thing of Wonderland, especially when witnessing an orgy and a vicious attack, all within the span of a pair of hours. Not to mention you were attacked yourself, with Sleep-Mist." An event that still eats at me.

A breath of amusement escapes him. Yet still, he has not rejected my statement. Several more minutes crawl by in the elegant silence of the ballroom. And then he says, "Okay."

I shift my head to run my nose the length of his jawline and then back up to place another kiss where the previous lay before. "I was afraid I was going to have to bully you into seeing the wisdom of my plan."

"You, bully? *Never.*"

It's my turn to release a ghost of a laugh.

"Also, what plan?"

"It's not really my plan, per se. I believe it was yours. I'm just co-opting it."

"Listen to you, sounding all Twenty-First Century with your *co-opting* threats."

I reach up my free hand to pat his face. "Nonetheless, my point stands."

"What was *my* plan, then?"

"You told me two are always stronger than one."

He's quiet for another long moment. "Will you stop me from beating the shit out of someone?"

"Would you want me to?"

"I don't know," he admits.

"Is this the person who is dying?"

I feel rather than see the shake of his head. And then he pulls out his phone and checks the time. "I have yet another meeting to get to. Holmes messaged to say he wants to brief us on the latest updates on his code cracking. And you've got a status report to get ready for."

"How does one get ready for such a thing?" I muse. "Is there a special suit of armor one must wear?"

"Unfortunately, no. You looked hot in armor, by the way."

"Sweet talker. I bet you say that to all the women you ride into battle with."

"Only you." When he presses a kiss against my temple, I close my eyes and savor the way delicious tingles skip merrily up and down my skin and spine. Softly, so only I can hear, Finn whispers, "My past isn't like yours, Alice. St. Petersburg isn't like Wonderland."

I tell him I know this. That it does not matter one bit.

As we tidy up, he tells me of the widow who took him in long ago. He words come slowly at first, and then steadily as the past urges its way out. He talks of the widow's kindness and generosity, but of how he didn't feel like he fit in there and feared she would smother him. And then he tells me of how society shunned and yet found him fascinating all at once, considering he was witness to a murder and helped prevent another. As a result, he earned himself more wealth than most children ever dreamed of. He was a free spirit then, abhorring fancy clothes, schools, and churches. He despised being forced to abide by society and regularity. Education was not a priority then, and he ran away often. He spent a great deal of time going up and down the Mississippi River with a former slave named Jim. It is obvious this man means much to him, just by the tone in his voice. Furthermore, he was, Finn admits to me emotionlessly, the worst kind of troublemaker a kid could be and that I would have run the opposite direction if I'd happened upon him then.

The unfortunate truth is my parents would never have allowed me near him as a child in the first place.

As he tells me these things, I try to wrap my mind around his past and his present. Finn Van Brunt is a leader—an intelligent, thoughtful, funny, trustworthy man whose hidden talents are continually a delight to discover. Huckleberry Finn, he insists, is someone he prefers to stay in the past.

I think, had I met Huckleberry Finn as a child, though, I would have been just as taken with him then as I am now.

As we step into the elevator, I press a kiss against the corner of his mouth. "None of that matters to me. The only thing that does is that *this* still means something to you."

He smiles at my further co-opting of words he's uttered to me before, ones I cherish deeply. "I think it always will."

It is exactly what I hoped he'd say. I think it is my truth, too.

STATUS REPORT

ALICE

"**D**ESTINIES," THE SAGE SAID, "*are like roads.*"

My fingers curled inward as I rose from my seat. I was in no frame of mind for riddles, not when my doomsday date was nearly upon me. But the eyeless woman turned her head toward me and said calmly, "Sit down, Your Majesty."

And then she actually waited until I did before she droned on as if we had all the time in the world. "Relationships are much like destinies."

Anger within flared as hot and bright as the overbearing sun baking us from the skylight above.

"Therefore," the Sage continued, "relationships are like roads."

I literally bit my tongue until it bled to keep my ballooning opinions within my mouth.

"Some roads are circular. They start at one spot and end in the same. Some roads fork and force their travelers to choose which way to go. Some roads go great distances. And then there are those that end abruptly."

The rebuttals clamoring inside of me were filled with desperate rage.

The rock in the Sage's hands rolled across her palms, onto her knees, and then back into her fingers. "Who is to say that a short road is less meaningful than a long?"

No, I thought. No. She cannot be telling me this. My—our—last resort cannot be saying such a thing.

She placed the rock upon the ornate stand next to her ratty chair. Its dull thud echoed within the cave. And then she stood up, curtseyed, and wandered into the black depths lingering beyond.

I fought against the impulse to throw her rock after her, but I could not restrain myself from yanking strands of my hair out, one at a time, until the sting of my scalp barely tempered my impotent wrath. Finally, when there was a much-too-large pile of hair upon my lap, the bell that allowed my departure sounded.

Hours later, in our home within the tulgey woods, I found Jace pouring over documents alongside the Cheshire-Cat and the Caterpillar. He looked exhausted—they all did—but the moment I crossed the threshold leading into the library, shared fatigue morphed into burning curiosity and hope.

I bit my lip. Willed myself not to rage. And that was when all their faces fell, too.

"Your Sage," I informed the Caterpillar, "is just as maddening as you are."

For once, he did not have a derisive comment to lobby at me. All I got in return was bleakness.

Jace steered me out of the library and into the downstairs washroom. I sat down as he poured a bowl of water and rummaged around the cabinet for soft cloths. No questions were asked, no admonishments given. When he gently dabbed at my the tiny scabs decorating an all-too-large section of my scalp, I thought: How can this not be right? How can these feelings that consume us be wrong?

"Destinies are like roads," I told him bitterly, "and relationships *are like destinies. And some roads end abruptly but are meaningful nonetheless."*

"We found nothing pertinent." His own bitterness matched mine. "We went over anything and everything that is even remotely related to our situation, but there was not even an inch of wiggle room to be found."

Three days were all that were left. Three days before I was to leave this man behind, leave behind my crown, my throne, my friends, my work, and my life in Wonderland.

A choking noise filled the room and my ears, one that originated deep within my chest. Jace held me tightly, and I him in return. He felt right to me, this felt right. And yet Wonderland insisted this was not true, that everything he and I felt for one another was, in fact, not beautiful and right, but poisonous and wrong.

How could that be?

I was supposed to marry this man. Together, we were to combine our thrones and stretch our influence between both the White and Diamond courts. There were schools to build, universities to christen. Farm subsidies to enforce, trade pacts to craft. We were going to embark on these changes hand in hand, our wills unified as we ushered Wonderland into a golden age. We were going to have children, possibly many, and our beloved heirs would continue doing what was best for Wonderland even if they were not chosen by the land to rule in our stead.

But our desires were nothing more than dreams. I was to go to England and be nothing more than Alice Liddell and live a life that did not feel like mine and eventually marry some man I could never possibly love. Jace was to stay in Wonderland and stay the course and eventually marry some woman who was not me and to think of it was excruciating.

I stare down at the tablet below me, marveling at how sharp the pain of such memories still are.

"Are you okay?"

Wendy hovers nearby, a hint of concern reflecting from her eyes as her green hair drifts messily about her head. "Of course." I click the tablet off and swivel in the chair to fully face her. "Is there something I can do for you?"

The concern disappears. "Thought I'd just check in before my meeting to make sure you understood how the status reports go."

"As technologically inept as I may be at times," I say, "I'm fairly certain there is little to botch up here, especially as both you and the A.D. have written out instructions for me." My tap upon a pair of notes nearby is meaningful. As soon as Finn went into a teleconference with Brom, the Librarian, and Sherlock Holmes, I was conscripted into a status report training that left me irritable and once more loathing modern technology.

Wendy flushes at my words yet does not leave for her daily department meeting she chairs. "All status reports are recorded."

"I am well aware of that."

The look she gives me is comically yet gently accusatory. I refuse to encourage or elaborate upon any of the gossip I'm certain she's been privy to, though.

My chair swivels back toward the large series of screens on the wall. There are two minutes left until the communiqué goes through. "I am sure you do not want to be late for your meeting."

She hovers for an additional silent minute before relenting and exiting the room. When the door clicks shut behind her, I open the app on my tablet that controls status reports. Already logged in are the following bits of information:

Nickname: Alice in Wonderland
Official title(s): Alice's Adventures in Wonderland
Through the Looking-Glass, and What Alice Found There
Author: Lewis Carroll
Timeline origin: 1865 and 1871 respectively
Designation: 1865/71CAR-AWLG
Current liaison(s): The White King of Wonderland
Catalyst: The Queen of Diamonds' crown
Location: Room 1508 [notation: override by L-1 / AL-AWLG—0150R monitoring switched to system XPU-11; encryption CLASSIFIED]
Status: LIVE

My heart nearly jumps into my throat when a chirping sound fills the office. Upon my tablet, a message flashes across the screen: *Status update transmission from 1865/71CAR-AWLG*. A green button declaring *Accept* and another, red in color and saying

Decline, sit beneath the brightly colored words.

It's a shaky finger that taps upon **Accept**.

The largest of the screens before me flares to life. There upon it, his face just as dear to me now as it always has been, is the White King of Wonderland.

A button on my tablet blinks, indicating the session has begun recording.

For a moment, neither of us says anything, but then, on cue, we both let out a shaky yet quiet chuckle. "This." He motions to what is no doubt a matching tablet to mine. "Is possibly the most surreal invention ever made."

"Were there any difficulties using it?" I ask.

"None at all. I was given detailed instructions I memorized before destroying. I must have read them a dozen times before doing so."

I can't help but smile; he does the same. He is in his room in the white pavilion, in the middle of his army's encampment. The sight is a most welcome one. He is alive, he looks well albeit exhausted as ever, and here we are, worlds apart, and yet still able to talk with one another.

I have not lost him after all.

"How terribly boring that must have been."

"It was a good distraction from the battlefield, to be honest."

My smile dims. How could I have forgotten, even for a moment, to ask about what is important? "Were you able to recover the Cheshire-Cat?"

"I am happy to report," he says, the ghost of relief haunting his words, "that he is now here at the White encampment."

A massive breath of relief escapes me. "Was he harmed?"

Regret flashes across the all-too-familiar planes of his handsome face. "He is shorter in the tail and prone to nightmares he will vigorously deny, but you know the Cheshire. It would take much to break his spirit. He is already ordering me about and overseeing all war meetings."

"Callou, callay." If only I could claim the same about the Caterpillar. I would welcome his high-handedness even here in New York.

Jace leans forward, his nearly colorless eyes serious. "There is more you must hear. I was unable to locate your Grand Advisor's body, but his head graces the Hearts' Castle no longer. None do. We struck down and burned all pikes and crosses decorating the roads leading in."

What makes my eyes sting even more is the assured knowledge that the Caterpillar would disapprove of the twining strands of both relief and grief urging me to cry.

"It is not safe now to travel, not with the Red forces looming, but I will ensure he has a proper burial at your castle at the earliest chance I can get. The people will not forget his sacrifice."

"Thank you." My voice wobbles as I fight to get myself under control. "I will be forever grateful to you and your brave soldiers for what you have done."

"He meant much to me as well."

We have veered dangerously toward paths too emotional and painful to tread across whilst communicating through screens. I right our conversation. "How is the war going?"

"It is a hardship that is affecting too many Wonderlanders." Jace rubs at his dark hair, leaving it askew. "Homes are being destroyed at alarming rates. Kidnappings, murders, crops being burned . . ." He shakes his head. "All of this in addition to plagues and droughts in parts of the country. Vast numbers of refugees are fleeing toward the fragile safety of our combined borders. Our soldiers are burning candles at both ends, and yet I must ask more of them every single day." And then, more quietly, "I have often wondered just how much truly worse things would have been had you not left. It is a terrible time for Wonderland, my lady."

The turmoil my people must be going through is acid in my veins.

"That said, I have come to an agreement with the White Queen. We are to put our differences aside to ensure that the White and Diamond regions will be jointly protected by our three armies."

I'm stunned. "She is willing to protect my people and their lands, to acknowledge my continued sovereignty?"

Somebody calls out, "Your Majesty, you are needed."

The White King sighs quietly, his eyes falling briefly shut. When they open once more, I press *End Record* on the tablet below me.

"Promise me you did not give too much to ensure the White Queen's cooperation on my behalf."

He does not answer me, but he does not need to. I see the truth in his eyes, and it's a brutal punch to my gut.

Wonderland, as beautiful as it is, continues to demand too much of the two of us.

Horns blare in the distance, their sounds so bitterly familiar to my ears. "When?"

"I don't know," he murmurs. "Perhaps soon, if the White Queen has her way. She feels it will be a thumb in the other Courts' faces, and will turn the tides in our favors. It is a good plan when you give time to consider it. While our alliance has been tentative over the last number of years, it is still the only one the people can hold onto during this time of unrest. A strengthened White Court can only benefit the land in general. This way, half of the Courts will be unified. Any further cemented alliances between us will be discussed upon a later date."

I am loath to agree, but he is right. It is sound logic. The people of Wonderland would rally behind a strongly unified pair of Courts, especially as the others are splintered or struck completely asunder. Mine is, as it was the day I left, under his oversight, and if his cooperation with his counterpart assures their safety, I cannot allow my personal feelings to otherwise derail such matters. "Please inform the White Queen she has my gratitude."

Bleak resignation shines from his pale eyes when he tells me he will.

Wonderland asks much of its monarchs. Sometimes too much, and yet . . . we still give until we have nothing left, and even then, we give some more.

"I must go now. I'm to check in with you every month, correct?"

Helplessness claws at my insides. There is so much I wish to say, and yet know I cannot. "Yes."

"Then I will talk to you in two fortnight's time." He pauses, then says my name softly.

I wait.

But after a quick shake of the head, he crosses an arm over his chest, so that his hand touches his heart. I mimic the action, and the sentimentality burns strongly within the confines of my heart.

Nightrider Quigley, the King's second-in-command, calls out once more before the screen goes black.

The urge to pluck strands of hair out is nearly overwhelming. I am different now, though. I have left behind the woman who gave into such madness. I sit for long minutes, fighting this urge, listening to the whirls and beeps of machines I can't pinpoint. No matter how much we might have wished differently, Jace and I are on different roads now. Our shared journey abruptly ended. I am in love with another man, and not reluctantly so. And yet, it makes me want to wreak the most terrible of havocs with my vorpal blade when I consider how unfair it is that Jace has not been afforded the same opportunities as myself.

He deserves to fall in love again, to find somebody who will steady him in the crazy world he inhabits. Even though our shared dreams of a life together died, Jace deserves to still have everything we hoped for: companionship, family, happiness. Wonderland will not afford him such a luxury, though. His crown and duty come before his personal wants and needs.

Somehow, whether I wanted it or not, I escaped the same fate.

The door behind me opens and shuts. I'm too numb to even turn to look. But there's no need, not when I already know who it is.

Finn sits down in a nearby chair and scoots it closer to where I rest. "How did the status check go?"

"I thought you were in a meeting?"

"According to his business partner, Holmes is delayed shortly. I have my suspicion he's still asleep. While we wait, I thought I'd come in and check on you."

His gesture is unbearably sweet in light of the latest news. My fingers tighten in the soft fabric of my dress as I tell him, my voice deceptively light, "The Cheshire-Cat was recovered. He has officially resumed his duties at the White King's encampment."

"That's great."

"The Caterpillar's head was also liberated."

I like this about Finn—he does not pressure, even though I know his curiosity must be white hot. And why wouldn't it? While I am certain he is confident in the strength and certainty of my feelings toward him, he is only human.

I tell my partner, "Your modern technology is amazing. To think I can see and speak to people in Wonderland whilst sitting in New York City, nearly a hundred and forty years in the future, and to hear firsthand of how badly the war is going. War here, war there. There is too much warfare in all worlds."

His touch is gentle. "I'm so sorry, Alice."

Much of me wants to compartmentalize before turning inward. When we stand up, I nearly allow this to happen. After all, it's easier, less messy to hold it all in and assume responsibility for such confusing, bitter feelings. But when we reach the door and he puts his hand on the knob, I finish the tale. "The White King will officially join into a political union with the White Queen that will solidify their Court's influence and stability during the war."

Finn's hand falls away from the door as he turns to face me. He's shocked but is trying to hide it best he can from me. "You mean like . . . marriage?"

I shake my head. "No. Or at least . . . not yet. But such a political union is not as common as you would think it to be. Remember, Kings and Queens of Wonderland may rule jointly over their lands, but it does not mean they are romantically or even socially attached. Many despise one another. Many strike at the other politically. Official unions guaranteeing cooperation can be powerful weapons in Wonderlandian governments." I lick my lips. "It was honestly the only way to ensure her cooperation with defending the Diamonds' lands, as well as moving forward as a cohesive unit. His soldiers, and mine, are spread too thin to assure the safety of the refugees pouring in from all over Wonderland and fight against the other Courts at the same time. Plus, the people will find relief in this, to know that there is at least one Court in the land that they can trust upon. In this regard, both monarchs in the White Court will champion the Diamonds' lands and peoples. Refugees are pouring in at alarming rates."

Finn doesn't say anything, though. He merely pulls me into his arms and holds me tight. I listen to the steady thump of his heartbeat and think, once more, how unfair it is that I have Finn and Jace has no one. Love, as wonderful as it can be, is a brutal mistress.

SILENCE

FINN

I T'S COLD IN ST. PETERSBURG, colder even than New York City. Light snow dusts the muddy ground while a train whistle pierces the air. Union soldiers mingle around the small station, many drowsy as they wait to board their next train.

The United States is in the middle of its bloodiest war. Death is in the air. Death, it seems, is everywhere I go lately. Wasn't Alice so right when she talked about how there is too much warfare throughout all the Timelines.

When I brought up the current state of affairs to Alice, minutes before we edited into my original Timeline, she simply scoffed. "You came to Wonderland in the midst of its civil war, did you not? This is no different."

It feels different, though. Missouri, while officially torn between both the South and the North, is a place of unrest. Both abolitionists and pro-slavery groups have moved into the area, pumping their propaganda to anyone who will listen. There is heat here, and cowardly people sitting on fences.

My skin crawls in anger.

Marianne Brandon requested to take on the role of costumer during her residence in the Society, which was fine by Brom and me. Truth be told, I worried about her being in the field. Alice jokes about Victor having a soft heart, but it's Marianne who truly does. By serving her role in researching different Timeline clothing and eras alongside the Librarian, she'll be able to effectively do her job for the Janeites and report back what's going on.

"Besides," she informed us, "I rather like to sew nowadays." And then she clarified, patting one of the many sewing machines littering the Institute's wardrobe rooms, "Even more so with these beauteous inventions. It's rather soothing, isn't it?"

Who was I to disagree?

She spent all night tailoring old Civil War-era pieces we'd confiscated during various assignments to Alice's measurements, and then a coat and pair of pants to mine. Alice and I appear just as if we belong here in St. Petersburg, even though I want nothing more than to turn around and leave.

Before I left, Brom reminded me to take money I'd long ignored, money I'd found once upon a time and money that made me a target for a drunken father. Money I barely ever touched, viewing it more of a curse and a symbol of society's attempts to conform me into something I wasn't. And now, here I am, using it after swearing I never would, and the resentment in me only intensifies.

I can only pray I don't land in jail today. Holy hell, I do not need that, not when there's so much waiting for me back on my desk at the Institute.

Alice adjusts both her hat and coat before smoothing her hands down her hoop skirt. I won't lie—she looks beautiful, but alien, too. I know we are from a similar time period, but to see her in such a tight corset and such a wide skirt is jarring.

I need a drink already. Hell, even a whole bottle.

"Will we go straight to Mrs. Douglas' home?"

A nearby horse, desperate to escape its master, rears up. There is a child close to its angry hooves, one that can't be more than two or three. I dart forward, snatching the boy as the owner tries to get his horse under control.

A woman runs forward, screaming the child's name. As I pass him off to her eager arms, she nearly burns holes through me, she's staring so hard.

Well, hell. I'm not here ten minutes and I've already run into Amy Lawrence. As kids, she and Sawyer were a thing off and on for years while he and Becky tortured each other. What are the odds that I'd have to save her kid of all people?

"Well, I'll be." Her eyes go wide. "Huckleberry Finn! It's been years since we last saw you! Thank you for saving my boy."

Alice slips her hand through the crook of my elbow as she catches up with me. I tip my hat reluctantly. "Hello, Amy." To the boy, I say softly, "You need to be careful of horses, okay? They're awfully big and sometimes forget to look down at those of us who are smaller."

He nods solemnly, looking as if he knows he's going to be in trouble as soon as he gets home. "You ain't small, mister."

I was though, once upon a time. I remember standing next to Jim on the banks of the Mississippi, and it felt like he towered over me.

Amy completely ignores her son, though. "Aren't you right handsome nowadays, Huck? We girls in school used to whisper about how, once you allowed yourself to embrace civility, what a fellow you'd turn out to be. And here you are, looking well. Is this your wife?"

Before I can answer, or, hell, stop from gritting my teeth, Alice says in that regal voice of hers, "Yes."

Thank God she's wearing gloves so Amy can't verify whether or not that's a fact.

Amy blinks, no doubt unnerved at how little details either of us are willing to provide. She shifts the boy to her other hip. "Tom will be thrilled to see you, no doubt. He's at home right now—Becky's due any day, I suspect, and he's been a right mess, waiting to see if he finally gets a son."

I neglect to tell her that I had no idea Sawyer's wife was expecting, nor do I care.

Another familiar face appears, only to make my jaw ache from the amount of grinding that's going on. It's Sid, Tom's brother. And . . . apparently Amy's husband, as he takes the boy from her.

I never liked Sid much, but even I find this to be a strange match. Sawyer's former flame and his brother? I wonder how much that has stuck in his craw over the years. Pettily, I hope a whole damn lot.

Sid offers me his hand; I reluctantly shake it. And now we're officially forced into introductions, which Alice bears with her normal aloof grace. A story is spun of how she and I met when I moved to London for work, and after several months of travel here, we're set to go back within the week.

I leave no wiggle room. Sid, once an annoying tattletale and probably a consummate gossiper nowadays, will hopefully ensure people understand that I am not officially back, and most likely will never return again.

Sid parrots his wife's belief that Sawyer will be over the moon to hear I'm back in town. Fuck that. I turn and leave without saying another word.

"How long," Alice murmurs, "do you feel it will be before we see this Tom Sawyer?"

I dip my head as yet another person stops and stares as we walk by. "Not long enough." And then, quietly, "You should probably know that he and I had a falling out."

When I opened up to her yesterday about my past, I neglected to mention anything about Sawyer.

And still, she simply smiles that wry smile of hers. "I would have never guessed. Would you like me to stop you from beating the shit out of him? Or shall I help? Gentleman's choice."

A bubble of surprised laughter escapes me. But then, just seconds later, I'm scowling once more. On the street corner ahead, somebody is preaching about how Abraham Lincoln is a demon come to earth. A group surrounds him, rapt as they nod in agreement.

All of my amusement fades away until disgust roils around in the pit of my stomach.

"Lincoln was one of your presidents, was he not?"

I tear my eyes away from the mob. "Yeah. He'll be assassinated in a few years. If, you know, this Timeline follows all the rest."

"I feel for him. I myself have had multiple attempts on my person, and it can be exhausting, constantly wondering if the next time will take."

We round a corner, and memories long repressed wash over me. I ran down this street many times, my bare feet thick with mud. The last time I walked down it, it was to leave this place behind. Brom and Katrina had made me an offer I couldn't refuse—a life of adventure that also had purpose. And now here I am, making my way to the large house up on a hill I once resided in, and I honestly don't even know how to feel about it all.

The porch creaks just as it did sixteen years before. The paint is peeling, though, and there's a quiet to the property I don't quite remember. A knock to the door brings a young woman whose face is unfamiliar.

I take my hat off. "I'm here to see Mrs. Douglas."

I never called her Mrs. Douglas. She was always the widow to me—or rather, the widder, considering my poor vocabulary and lack of education. But I'm not that kid anymore, and the woman who took me in for a small span of time deserves more than that.

"I'm sorry," the girl says. "But the miss is not doing too well for visitors."

She's a maid, I realize. A really, really young one, too. Maybe fourteen? I was thirteen or fourteen when the widow took me in, a hopeless charity case that proved to be a massive failure. Maybe this girl has done better than me.

"I think she'll want to see me." I clear my throat. "Will you tell her that Huckleberry Finn is here to visit?"

"Well, you shoulda said that first!" The door groans as she opens it wider. "The miss has been talkin' about you. She'd want me to make an exception for you."

Inside, everything is nearly as it was years before. The house is clean, the furniture worn. The maid takes my hat and overcoat alongside Alice's. "Can I get you nice folk some tea? It's might chilly outside. My pa says it'll snow hard soon."

As she hangs up our coats and hats, Alice mutters, "How nice it would be for us to go somewhere tropical and away from all this blasted snow. Everywhere we go seems to be on the verge on snow." To the maid, she says, "Tea would be lovely, thank you."

The girl curtseys and scurries out of the room. Alice sits down upon a threadbare chair, but I'm too antsy to follow.

Somewhere, upstairs, a woman is dying.

Footsteps sound, and soon enough, the town doc emerges, his black bag in hand. "Daisy, can you—" He stops as he takes me in. "Son, I am right glad to see you."

Daisy reappears with a tray in her hand. "Doc, this is the nice boy the miss has been asking for."

"Not so much a boy anymore, are you?" the doc asks me. He sticks out his hand. "It's good to see you, Huck. You look as if you've done well for yourself."

The backhanded compliments just keep a'coming. "Thank you, sir."

"She's close now," he tells me. "I wouldn't be surprised if she didn't last the night."

Alice asks, "What ails Mrs. Douglas, if you don't mind me inquiring?"

"Consumption." He wipes his face. "It'll be best to not get too close."

Daisy passes out cups of tea. The doc sits down across from Alice, sipping his tea wearily. "Go now, son. She's been in and out of consciousness today, and talking is a might difficult. Keep that in mind."

Alice makes a move to stand up, but I hold out a hand. She nods, her eyes filled with understanding and concern.

I make my way up the stairs, my boots echoing against the wood and paint. Miss Watson used to snap about how I apparently walked too loudly, and how it wasn't what polite folk do. One afternoon, she had me practice going up and down the stairs for what felt like forever, a book on my head to help me stop slouching. My thighs burned afterward, and yet she still found me a disappointment. I'd wanted to run away that night, but the widow caught me as I was sneaking out the window.

And here I am, near sixteen years later, stomping once more. Miss Watson is long dead, the widow nearly so.

Her room looks the same. The same quilt upon her bed, the same wooden frame. The same pictures and needlepoint upon the walls, the same dresser off to the side. A chair now sits by the bed, a bowl of water on a nearby stand. The moment I cross the threshold, her eyes creak open.

She sighs. Coughs. "If I live or die, Huckleberry Finn is once more in my house."

I sit down on the chair. "I'm sorry for taking so long to come see you."

A frail hand reaches for me. "You are so handsome. You look like a right, proper gentleman."

Her intentions are good, and yet I can't help remembering being that kid who wasn't a gentleman.

A coughing fit overcomes her, and when she pulls away her handkerchief, it is spotted with bright red blood. "I wanted to know life has done right by you before I go to meet our maker."

I feel like an impersonator answering this question, but I do so anyway. She coughs again, the sounds rattling her thin chest and shaking the bed.

"What can I get you?" I glance around the room. If only I'd let Victor come.

"Nothing." She gasps. "The Lord will see me soon enough and will take care of me then. Tell me about your life, Huck."

The room smells like sickness, and her skin is sallow. Memories nearly suffocate me. "I work for my father in New York."

A smile has just enough time to emerge before another round of coughing leaves her even weaker. I don't let her ask anything further—I just tell her about my life. I tell her how I went to two different universities, and that I can speak three languages. I tell her about traveling all over the world and of discovering new cultures and peoples. I tell her that the family I left her for, the one that I allowed in after years of her trying, were good people and that I love them deeply. I tell her that I found the woman of my dreams, and that she sits downstairs in her parlor.

The widow smiles the whole time, her coughs punctuating my story like commas and periods. Her handkerchief is nearly scarlet, there's so much blood. By the time I'm done, she whispers, "You always was the charmer, Huck."

Doctor's orders be damned, I lean over and kiss her paper-thin cheek.

She reluctantly nods off to sleep, her breath shallow and rattling. Beyond the curtains and glass, it's started to snow harder. Soon, the rattling stops and there's nothing but bone-aching silence.

I make my way back down the stairs, my boots finally soft in their meetings between rubber and wood. Alice and the doc are still in the parlor, but neither is talking. It's all so quiet.

Alice stands up the moment she sees me. Within seconds, her arms are around me, and mine around her. I bury my face against her neck, not even knowing how to feel. Her fingers twine in my hair, holding me tightly like once more, she's afraid I'll float away.

Eventually, the sound of new boots on the stairs emerges. Unable to help it, a bitter smile curves my lips at the thought of what Miss Watson would have said to the town doc. Would she have forced him to walk up and down with a book on his head?

A door opens and closes. A loud, familiar voice fills my ears. I kiss Alice's cheek and let her go. And then I turn around to face Tom Sawyer in person for the first time in over a decade.

The sonofabitch has the audacity to look happy.

"Huck! Sid said you was here, but I didn't quite believe him. But here you are, an'—"

I punch him so hard he hits the ground, out like a light.

CONFRONTATION

ALICE

I T TAKES MUCH PRODDING, but Finn finally allows me to examine his hand. We are safely ensconced within a local inn, in a snug yet sparse room that at least has a proper fire. Upon arrival, I'd immediately requested water and bandages, which only made my partner's already questionable mood turn darker.

"Well." I peer down at the tender flesh. "I do not think you broke anything. At least on your end, that is."

He sighs.

An extraordinarily pregnant woman who accompanied Sawyer to Mrs. Douglas' home screamed once her husband hit the ground, and I'd unfortunately been tempted to smack her myself. In any case, I'd hissed, "Show some proper respect. There is a woman dead in this home, and your histrionics will serve no purpose."

"Huck!" She tumbled awkwardly to her knees and grappled at the unconscious man's chest. "How could you?"

Finn promptly stalked out of the house and I calmly followed. Daisy, the little maid, ran after us and stood on the porch until we'd reached the bottom of the hill, almost as if she couldn't believe what she'd seen.

Once I caught up with him, I said mildly, "I suppose you decided you wanted to beat the shit out of him after all, didn't you?"

Finn did not respond, nor did he say anything else until we reached the inn. At that point, everything was clinical and to the point: we wished to have a room for precisely one night. Money exchanged hands, and then furtive glances as a few of the employees whispered amongst themselves how we traveled with no luggage and that they were positive Huckleberry Finn had returned home.

He wanted to go back to New York but I'd let him know that while he had been upstairs, the doctor informed me Mrs. Douglas had requested Finn to take care of her funeral arrangements. We are to stay until he can do so in the morning and then promptly depart.

I've just finished wrapping Finn's hand when a knock sounds on our door. It's tentative, yet neither of us gets up to answer it.

The tension in Finn's body rouses internal alarms. I have seen him angry before, I have seen him focused and in a fight, but I've never seen him quite like this.

"Huck?" Another round of pounding, louder now, echoes throughout the small room. "I know you're in there! Open the door. You—you need to hear me out. Huck?"

I gently place Finn's hand back into his lap. "He's a tenacious one."

All I get out of Finn is a grunt.

The alarms within me ring louder.

The door handle jiggles, the pounding turns deafening. "If you think I'm goin' to go away, why, you got another thing comin.' You hear me, Huck Finn? I am not leavin' before I say my piece! You owe me that!"

Finn explodes out of his chair and nearly tears the door off its hinges. Sawyer, now sprouting a red-and-purple-welted face, nearly trips over the threshold.

"I don't owe you shit," Finn barks. "Now get the hell out of here before I finish what you deserve."

As I make my way to the door, Sawyer pulls himself upright,

straightening his coat. "Now, see here—"

Finn punches him once more in the jaw. Sawyer slams up against the wall beyond our door, and hysterical wailings sound. Frabjous. The pregnant woman has come along for the show.

Miraculously, Sawyer teeters forward, undeterred. A hand rubs his chin, which, truthfully, I'm more than a bit suspicious might be broken. "Huck—"

Finn's fist pulls back, ready for a third punch, but the pregnant woman slides between their bodies. "Stop it! For the love of God, you two must stop this fighting!"

"I warned you," Finn snaps. Instead of a punch, he juts out a finger, past the woman at the wobbly man.

A crowd swells the hallway. Curious eyes all angle toward the two men and the sobbing lady.

"Do something!" she shouts at me.

If I was not so concerned she might immediately go into labor from her histrionics, I just very well might have laughed. But while her tear-streaked face produces no pity within me, I also know that a burgeoning crowd in a town already on edge thanks to war is not the most favorable of places to air grievances. "If you truly want this to cease, then persuade Sawyer to depart at once."

She is shocked by my ambivalence. She clearly would not last a full day in Wonderland.

A hand grabs hold of Finn's shirt. "Please, Huck. I know you're mad. But—"

He jerks away, leaving her stumbling. "Are you fucking serious, Becky? *Mad?* You think I'm just *mad* at this sack of shit?"

Sawyer's eye has swollen shut. He is a pitiful-looking thing if there ever was one.

Becky breaks into heaving sobs again. I sigh and push my way into the hallway. A quick scan locates the innkeeper. "You there. Come and take this woman to somewhere more discreet. And be quick about it, lest you wish to have a babe born upon your floors."

The heavyset man with a handlebar mustache rumbles forward. "You come with me, Mrs. Sawyer. I'll get you a nice cup o' tea."

She resists, though. Sobs some more. "Don't you dare kill him. Do you hear me Huck Finn? Don't you dare! He's got a family!"

Finn's words rattle the walls. "Jim didn't? What about his kids?"

The murmuring crowd goes silent. Even Becky has finally gone quiet, albeit hiccupping.

Jim was the name of Finn's friend, the freed slave he said was the only from childhood he ever felt a true kinship with. And now . . . is Finn saying Jim is dead?

"You act as if I was the one to pull the noose," Sawyer garbles, and Finn pushes past Becky and punches him again so hard, the man slumps once more to the ground. He is still conscious, though. Barely, but his dazed eyes look up at Finn, blinking in shock.

Becky resumes her hysteria.

"Take her," I order the innkeeper.

He jabbers, "This is a peaceful establishment! I won't put up with this kind of—"

"But you'll stand back and watch innocent people lynched," Finn rages. "Right? Or, is the only kind of violence you accept the kind against people you don't even consider people, because they're nothing more than property to you? Because their skin isn't the same color as ours?"

Frenzied whispering of Northern sympathies surface.

"He's been dead going on ten years now," Sawyer mumbles. "It ain't like—"

Finn rounds on him, his hand closing around Sawyer's throat as he shoves the man up against the wall. "Say it," he hisses. "Go ahead and try to justify, once more, what you've done. And I don't care if it's been ten years or ten minutes. Jim was my friend."

The innkeeper finally pulls Becky away, with threats of fetching the sheriff.

Tears leak out of Sawyer's eyes. "You don' understand, you—"

"You're right." Finn's fingers tighten, leaving Sawyer gasping. "Because here's the thing: Jim was good to you. He risked *everything* to ensure you were okay after you got shot. Remember that? When you were an idiot and went and got shot? Hell, of course you do. You still wear the damn bullet around your neck like a badge of honor! But Jim risked his freedom to get you help. And what for? You knew he'd been freed by Miss Watson. *You knew.* And yet, you nearly allowed him to get killed all so you could chase your fucking high."

Sawyer's eyes roll back in his head. The pieces of Finn's puzzle begin to slide into place. Suddenly, I am reminded of a framed photograph in Finn's bedroom, of a dark-skinned man with eyes crinkled and a warm smile. A younger Finn stands beside him, his arm around the older man's shoulder.

"How does it feel?" Finn's voice is filled with fury. "Knowing the life is being choked out of you? Wondering if your last breath is almost here? Did you ever wonder what it was like for *him* that night?"

The crowd is so thick, I would not be able to traverse down either side of the hallway if I even desired to. I touch his shoulder, and immediately, Finn lets go of the swine. "You killed him anyway," he spits out. "You fucking *led* them to him."

Sawyer coughs gasps, his hands instinctively, protectively, going to his own throat.

"He was my friend, and you led a group of murderers straight to him. You stood back while they beat him and then hung him from a tree. You did nothing to stop them! You were there, weren't you? I bet you watched the whole damn thing!"

My blood turns cold. Any shred of pity I might have for Sawyer dies a quick death.

But Finn isn't done. "You then stood by while they cut him down and then burned his body. You did all this to a man who was warm and gentle and generous, a man who had a family and whose heart was wasted on a piece of trash like you."

Sawyer cries silently, still slumped on the ground. The crowd moves closer, disgustingly eager for every word.

"Becky says I shouldn't kill you because you have a family." Finn squats down. "Did that stop you from letting your slave-loving buddies know where Jim was hiding?"

Sawyer says nothing as he stares at his former friend.

"What the hell happened to you, Tom? I knew you were a selfish bastard, but I didn't think you were so evil. Jesus, I was blind, wasn't I? What kind of person are you? You sell out your friends, you buy your way out of the war . . ." He shakes his head. "You're a coward."

"H-h-huck," Sawyer mumbles, as if words are physically painful to utter. "Y-you—"

"Don't you dare apologize. Your apologies are worthless. *You're* the one who chose to get involved with Southern sympathizers. You are the one who fell in with anti-abolitionists."

"I didn't know at first! They were just—"

Finn refuses to let him finish. "Your excuses mean nothing."

"I did my best to separate myself from them once I saw what they were up to!"

Finn is not swayed one bit.

"You don't understand, they threatened Becky when I told them I—"

"I. Don't. Care." Finn stands back up, his hands curling into fists. And then, "I have a lot of regrets about my fucked-up childhood. But you're the biggest of all."

Fat tears streak down Sawyer's face. "Don't say that, Huck. We can—"

Finn is merciless. "Don't ever contact me again. Is that clear?"

"But . . . I'm the liaison for—"

"We are going to go to your house," Finn continues, "and I am going to collect every last piece of equipment. And I swear to God, if you say one thing to me during the handover, I will not hesitate to finish what I should have started all those years ago. The only reason you're even breathing right now is because my parents physically restrained me from coming the day you told me about Jim."

A murmur ripples through the crowd. A singular word sticks out like a sore thumb, and it has me immediately on the defense. I touch Finn's shoulder again. I murmur, "We need to go."

Sawyer has begun babbling. His words are hard to understand, coming from such swollen lips and a bruised jaw, and it only further enrages my partner.

In any normal situation, I would not hesitate to stand back and allow Finn to extract whatever bits of justice he feels necessary. His compass has not steered us wrong before. But if the crowd is correct, his reluctant visit to 1876/96TWA-TS will become much longer than the singular day he'd hoped for.

"Finn." My grip on his arm is firmer. "This coward is not worth any further time. We need to go. Now."

The crowd's murmurings intensify just as Finn stands back up. And then Sawyer says, "If you just listen to reason—"

Finn's fist first meets Sawyer's stomach and then his bloody face once more. The man finally slumps to the ground, unconscious. And still, Finn hits him again. Kicks him.

A harsh voice yells out, "Put your hands up, or I'll shoot."

There is a gun pointed our way, and a badge on a coat. Finn's hands slowly rise, and when his eyes meet mine, there is no regret in them.

The next few minutes are a flurry of confusion. The town's doctor has been summoned, and I am agog when the crowd sympathizes more with Sawyer than Finn. My partner is placed into rudimentary handcuffs, and the whole while, the only thing he says is, "It'll be okay, Alice."

I immediately go for my dagger, hidden beneath the folds of this massive dress I'm trapped within. Finn shakes his head when he recognizes my intent, as if he knows even I cannot fight our way out of so many people in this tiny hallway.

Helplessness, the worst of all emotions, clamors just under my skin. Arguing with the sheriff does no good. And when I move to follow them, the grizzled man puts a hand out. "Ma'am, I'm requesting you stay behind. Jails ain't a place for ladies such as yourself."

Finn mouths, "Get the equipment."

My blood boils when the sheriff roughly shoves Finn down the hallway. The crowd is scandalized my partner would dare to put his hands on an upstanding citizen like Sawyer. Those who recognize him shout about how they knew he'd never grow up good. One elderly lady says something along the lines of, "He was a devil of a child, and all of his godlessness has come home to roost."

It takes supreme will to not to knock her down on her arse.

The crowd surges behind the sheriff and Finn, jeering and calling for blood, and I do my best to push through. The moment I reach the door, though, there is a pair of men who must have heard the sheriff's inane order, because they remind me that it would be best I go back upstairs and rest.

One dares to put his hands on me. I inform him that if he does so again, he will most assuredly lose said hand. And I am close to following through when I force myself to remember that getting myself incarcerated is not the best way to free Finn. That said . . .

Sobbing makes its way out of the inn, informing me that Sawyer's wife must still be inside.

A decision is made.

I make my way back in and follow the weeping. Sure enough, Becky Sawyer sits inside a small sitting room, a cup of tea clattering in her hands as she acts as if Armageddon has descended upon us. A woman I do not recognize waits with her.

"Get out," I tell the woman.

She scurries away. I shut the door behind her, lock it, and then for good measure, drag over a nearby chair and wedge it beneath the knob. The insipid woman upon the couch shrieks, and I have no other choice than to slap her smartly across the face—not hard by any means, but just enough to focus her attention.

"My God, woman," I snap. "Will you pull yourself together? This cannot be good for you or the babe."

She gapes at me, but luckily, her outrage supplants weeping.

I pry the cup and saucer from her hands and sit down in a chair across from the couch she's draped across. "Now that you have ceased your ridiculousness, we will have a talk, you and I."

"Is-is Tom—"

"A doctor is tending him as we speak. No doubt, despite his revolting cowardice and highly despicable morality, he will recover with little more than a concussion, a few broken bones, and undoubtedly much wounded pride."

"You don't understand," she whispers, and I hold up a hand.

She and Sawyer have said this far too often tonight. "Then make me understand."

Her eyes flit to the doorway and then back to me. I calmly pour a fresh cup of tea from the pot sitting on a nearby tray. "Have no fear, Mrs. Sawyer. You are in no danger of physical harm from me, at least on this night. I merely have questions that require answers."

She swallows, yet accepts the drink I offer her.

"Now," I say, pouring myself a cup as well. "Let us discuss what it is I do not understand."

"Huck is being unreasonable," she whispers. "He's hurt Tom so much all these years by refusing to listen."

"Forgive me for being so blunt, but am I wrong in assuming your husband had something to do with the murder of a man named Jim?"

Becky blinks at me, dumbfounded. "Well, now, it ain't as easy as that."

"Was the man in question lynched?"

She blinks some more. "Yes, but . . ."

"Was he guilty of any crime? Jim, I mean?"

More blinking.

"Theft, perhaps? Murder? Rape? Robbery? Something that would even remotely justify such a heinous punishment?"

Stammering occurs, with very little substance behind it. Becky Sawyer is nothing but a mimsy, I realize.

"Mrs. Sawyer, where I come from, lynching is a despicable crime that requires the most severe of punishments. It is one I have no tolerance for in any circumstance. Now, perhaps you can explain instead what it is you think Finn is not understanding about this situation."

Over the course of the next quarter of an hour, Becky informs me of how Tom met up with anti-abolitionists prior to their marriage when he moved to Southern Missouri to work for a few years. They were, she claimed, charming and convincing about their beliefs, and Tom—whom she insists is good-hearted and far too trusting—fell prey to their ideology. This was before the war, when Missouri was newly flooded with both abolitionists and pro-slavery groups, each eager to sway others to their causes when it came to the beating of the war drums. Always up for an adventure, Tom was keen to get involved somehow with the furor gripping the area, but went about it, in Becky's mind at least, all wrong.

"His friends ended up being affiliated with anti-abolitionists." Her voice trembles. "When Tom figured this out, he thought it best to leave. They weren't having none of it, though. Said they had to ensure Missouri aligned with the Confederacy instead of the North."

I have no patience for Tom if his stupidity was truly so strong he could not see his acquaintances for who they really were. "How does this tie to Jim's lynching?"

Her lower lip quivers as she stares down at her cold cup of tea. "They wanted a show, and started to flush out freed slaves. They didn't think it was right, that blacks be free."

From the tone of her voice, it seems that Mrs. Sawyer may hold the same reviling belief. "And your husband went along with this?"

"He tried to leave," she whispers. "He realized it wasn't fun no more—"

"Fun?" My voice is a shot in the room. "Brutalizing human beings, treating them as if they are inferior and pieces of property, is *fun?*"

"No, no," she quickly corrects. "It's just . . . Tom has always been one for adventures, and—"

"Lynching human beings is an *adventure?*"

She pales at my vitriol. "It wasn't like Tom was the one to hang Jim! All he did was . . . *tell* them where to find him."

My scorn could set the room ablaze. "Your husband did this willingly?"

"Of course not! They told him that if he didn't, they'd make him pay. That he'd be sorry for betraying them."

"Did they give specifics?"

She blinks again. I will myself not to shake her.

"Did they say what they would specifically do to, and I quote, 'Make him pay,' had he refused?"

"I . . . I don't know. They said they'd make him sorry. He was scared, rightfully so."

I hold up another hand. "Mrs. Sawyer, I fail to see what it is you believe Finn should understand. So far, from what I can tell, it is as I said at the beginning. Your husband is a coward and of highly questionable morals, not to mention someone of poor intellect. He—"

"He loves Huck," she interjects. "They were like brothers. He's felt like his arm has been cut off, not having Huck in his life."

I think of that photograph in Finn's room again, of who I assume is Jim. Tom is not in that scene. Jim meant something to Finn, though. For him to keep that photograph, to allow the rage and despair over his death for so many years to consume him and eat away at him only confirms this to me.

If Jim meant something to Finn, then he means something to me.

"Mrs. Sawyer, we do not have much time to waste. Finn is currently in jail, which is an entirely unacceptable situation for me. I require you to persuade the sheriff to free him immediately."

She gapes at me. "But . . . But . . ."

"Let us not mince words. Your husband was instrumental in the death of another human being. One, whom I believe, sacrificed much to save him years ago and was an innocent. Am I wrong in this assumption?"

She mutely shakes her head.

"He was instrumental in the death of somebody my partner valued very much."

"Well," she murmurs shakily, "Jim and Huck did have all those adventures when they ran off together . . ." In a much smaller voice, "Tom was always jealous of how close they were. He didn't think it right."

It takes everything in me to not to slap her again. There is no remorse in her voice over what has happen. There is just indignation and sadness over a loss of friendship rather than life.

No wonder Finn abhors his Timeline and these people.

"You must do the right thing and insist upon Finn being released from custody."

"But—"

"You and I do not know one another, Mrs. Sawyer. So let me be frank with you. I am not like those that your insipid husband once associated himself with. I do not make baseless, non-specific threats. Let me assure you that if Finn is not released from prison, or if even one hair on his head is harmed whilst he is incarcerated in this Godforsaken town, I will do everything in my power to destroy your husband. This means I will utilize every measure within my vast means to bankrupt him, to strip away your home, to render him undesirable to employers. And then, when he feels he has hit rock bottom, I will push harder. I will not stop, Mrs. Sawyer. And if you think I am making hollow threats, I entreat you to look within my eyes and realize I am not the kind of woman to do so."

This time, when she gapes at me, she does not blink.

"Do you know of your husband's association with the Society?"

She nods, her mouth quivering as it snaps shut.

I set my cup and saucer down on the small table that rests between us. "I am a member with many resources at my disposal. I am also not the sort of woman you should ever cross."

Her words are barely voiced. "You're not from here, are you?"

I slowly shake my head, maintaining eye contact the entire time.

She lets out a shuddery breath. And then she says, her voice little more than a squeak, "I will do my best."

"Excellent. But first, we need to stop by your home. There are some items I must retrieve."

"Are you two—is he your beau?" she asks me timidly. "Huck, I mean? I know someone called you his wife, but since you two work together in the Society, I paid it no mind, but . . ."

She doesn't finish, so I do for her. I say firmly, "He is my partner, yes. We work together at the Society. But in addition to that, he is the man I love. Mrs. Sawyer, if you doubt I will not do everything in my power to assure his wellbeing and freedom, this town will have a brutal surprise coming."

She swallows. "Understood."

When I finally open the door, the innkeeper is hovering nearby, a gun in his hands. "Mrs. Sawyer? You okay in there?"

I very nearly roll my eyes. He is a toad of a man, and clearly arthritic. I could sweep him off his feet and place him in a chokehold before he even aimed properly at me.

The mimsy I'm with offers a wan smile. "I am fine, Mr. Scruggs." Her eyes slide toward me briefly before she adds, "This fine lady was helping calm me down."

Scruggs frowns deeply, his bushy mustache enveloping his lips.

Becky takes a deep breath and straightens her spine. Good girl. "Where is Tom?"

"The doc is examining him upstairs right now, and the last I heard, he's fine. Doc has him awake and answering questions best he can. I suspect he'll have a headache tomorrow, though. It was a nasty beating. I can take you up there if you like."

Her lips quiver as she shakes her head. She turns to me instead. "Might you accompany me home?"

"Now, Mrs. Sawyer," the innkeeper stutters, but one look from me silences him.

The Sawyer house isn't too far away. Becky chatters on about the two children they already have—although both are currently in residence with her father at his nearby home. Her father, she clarifies, is a judge.

Excellent.

"I'll talk to him tonight," she vows. "He's always had a soft spot for Huck."

Even more excellent.

Our stay at the Sawyer household is brief. Becky knows exactly where Tom keeps his liaison supplies, and brings them to me within mere minutes of our arrival. As she hands them over, I take note of a sketch hanging on the wall of the sitting room we're in, one that features a very familiar face.

I imagine that picture might be taken down shortly.

"It is best you stay at your father's tonight alongside your children," I tell her.

Her eyes widen in confusion.

I sigh irritably. "I highly doubt your husband will be sent home tonight. If he has any sense, the doctor will keep him for observation until the morning. You've had a stressful evening, and it would behoove you to stay where someone could keep a watchful eye on you. How far along are you?"

Frankly, I'm getting tired of the blank looks she offers me. "I'm past due," she admits. "My babies always take a little longer than normal, the doc says."

"All the more reason to stay at your father's."

I escort her there whilst visions of delivering a babe upon dirty, slush-covered roads try to take root. Thankfully, her family's home is close by, and welcoming lights fill the windows. As we approach the path leading to the front door, a sob hiccups out of her.

"You heard the innkeeper," I say more gently than I feel. "Your husband will be fine."

"Huck truly hates Tom, doesn't he?"

I do not sugarcoat the truth. "It appears he has good reason to."

"You don't know what they were like when we were kids. They were so close. They were always getting into trouble. I mean, they even went off to Africa together." And then, more quietly, "Jim went, too."

Her mimsiness is unbearable. And the fact that she is childish enough to resent Finn's friendship with Jim for Sawyer's sake? Despicable. "Ensure your father has Finn released as quickly as possible. It is my goal we depart St. Petersburg in the early morning."

"Do you think . . . now that Huck got his punches in, they might be able to put this behind them?"

Confident I already know Finn's choice, I slowly shake my head.

She heaves in a fractured breath. "He really thought, if he could just get Huck to listen . . ."

"If he thought Finn could ever understand such a thing," I say coldly, "then your husband never truly knew him."

Becky Sawyer looks broken, bereft even. "Tom thinks it's because once Huck left, he fell in with the wrong people. Northerners who brainwashed him into becoming somebody he isn't."

I am done with this woman and her small-minded cretinism. "The moment you have word of your father assuring Finn's release, send me notice at the inn."

And then I turn around and head back toward the inn. The sun is just now setting, leaving the gray sky to darken, yet the roads are still filled with plenty of people bustling about in carriages and upon the boarded strips lining the stores.

Step after step, my anger and helplessness inflate until I do not know what to do with them. St. Petersburg has its fair share of soldiers milling about. Finn is no doubt behind bars at this very minute, and just the thought of it has me seething. I ought to wait, to see my plan through, but something in me insists Becky Sawyer, like her husband, cannot be trusted.

My feet change direction, back toward the center of town. I have two daggers upon me. If I am not mistaken, the jail will not be overly crowded with personnel. I wrack my mind, trying to remember what I'd learned about American jails, especially in less than cosmopolitan areas such as this. There is a sheriff, and not much else, perhaps. If that is the case, I could easily subdue the lawman and get the cell open myself.

I must ensure Finn is fine. I—

Something sharp pierces my back. Hands grab my shoulders and then wrap around me. My muscles go limp, my eyes sag. An acrid smell stings my nose, like the distinct lack of bathing and proper tooth care have left a person on the verge of disintegrating.

Fight, I tell myself, but my knees give way.

"Hello, Alice," an all-too-familiar voice coos, and then darkness rushes at me.

HORIZONS

FINN

The sheriff is outside, yelling at the crowd gathered. I can't exactly make out his words, but I wouldn't be surprised if they were along the lines of: *you need to disperse, go home, this is a peaceful town, we'll hang this sonofabitch tomorrow.*

Ah, mob justice at its finest.

I lie back on the small bench in the cell and stare up at the flaking ceiling, honestly not giving two shits about whether or not Sawyer is doing okay right now. All I feel right now is numb. My hand ought to be throbbing—shit, the knuckles are bloody and three times their normal size. I think I might have even broken one, I hit that asshole so hard with that last punch. But my hand doesn't hurt. Neither do my wrists that are already turning purple from the rudimentary handcuffs this sheriff used. None of it hurts except for a knot in my chest every time I imagine Jim, scared out of his mind, being strung up on some tree.

My friend—my kind, big-hearted friend—died because of the color of his skin.

Katrina was pissed. Well—sad and pissed all at once. "What will you do?"

We'd just gotten back from the police station. She and Brom, not for the first time, had to come down in the middle of the night to bail me out. Victor hovered in the background as our mother questioned me, his eyes wide and almost frightened as he stared at the person he called brother.

I'd told them I wanted to go straight to 1876/96TWA-TS. I needed—hell, I didn't know what I needed. It wasn't like I could go see Jim's body, considering it'd been burned after the hanging. I had no idea where his kids were, so it wasn't like I could go and find them and bring them here and away from the sickening world we were born into. It wasn't like there was a funeral to attend, either. People were scared. Jim wasn't the first lynching, and I was terrified he wasn't going to be the last.

But I told my adoptive parents I wanted to go to 1876/96TWA-TS, and now Katrina was calling me out on what I'd do once I got there.

"I don't know," I told her. "Something. Anything. I can't stand back and let his death mean nothing!"

So far, Brom hadn't said much. He simply stood near the door, blocking it while crossing his arms, looking like a goddamn bear while he let Katrina try to reason with me.

It wasn't going so well.

"Finn, holding on to rage and the past does no one any good."

I hated that she often seemed like she could read my mind. "The past! He just fucking died two days ago!"

Brom rumbled, "Do not speak to your mother like that."

Katrina ignored him just as easily as she did my outburst. "Violence rarely solves anything."

"Who said I was going to do anything violent?"

"Sweetheart, were you not arrested tonight for beating up an innocent boy?" When I said nothing, she added, "We are obviously quite aware of who he resembles."

One of my tutors had told me about some guy called Hammurabi. An eye for an eye, he said. I liked that, because Sawyer needed to pay for what he had done. And since Sawyer wasn't in front of me, and some punk kid who was picking on some small-for-his-age kid simply because he was black was, my fists wanted justice.

"You're not going," Katrina eventually insisted. "It will solve nothing."

The Institute was put on lockdown for the following month. My parents took no chances with me—I was never left in the position to edit anywhere. Instead, I got to visit my shrink on an every-other-day basis. He asked me even more questions about my childhood, my good-for-nothing Pap, about Tom Sawyer and all the illusions and pedestals I assigned him, and about Jim. At first I said nothing, because he kept asking stupid questions like, "How does Jim's death make you feel?"

In the end, he told me I suffered from survivors' guilt, whatever the hell that meant.

1876/96TWA-TS became something poisonous to me, much to the confusion of my parents. Instead of accepting my past, it became repugnant. Everything about it felt wrong. The people. The racism. The slavery. The backwater mentality. The forced morality and civility that thinly veiled prejudice, misogyny, and snobbery. The longer I lived in New York City, the more I despised everything about my childhood. I resented I was born into such a place. Loathed that I even associated myself with anyone who lived there, especially those who lived in their misguided, blissed-out existences that thought it was okay to devalue the life of somebody as wonderful as Jim. I came to hate Twain and his goddamn books.

I hated that he put those things in print.

I thought of all that time Jim and I spent together, when we both ran away from a society that persecuted the both of us. He was kind, and funny, and loyal, and his heart was too big for those assholes.

Katrina won in the end. Eventually, I lost any kind of urge to go back to 1876/96TWA-TS. I wanted nothing more to do with it, even when Brom eventually came to believe it would do more good than harm to set this all behind me.

And yet, here I am. In a jail cell, no less, having done exactly what my mother feared I would have done all those years before.

I swear, Katrina, I did my best to forget 1876/96TWA-TS. I really did.

I force myself to think about other things, lest everything turns red once more. I think about things that will most likely not matter to me soon. Things like finding Todd and extracting payment for what he's done to my family. I think about who could be in charge, and why they are deleting Timelines. I hope my brother has found whatever miracle drugs I told him about, and that my father will be healed. That my brother might be healed. I think about how funny it is that, after years of searching for her, I actually found Alice—only to fall in love with her.

"Son?"

I tilt my head toward the bars, expecting to see the sheriff but find Judge Thatcher instead.

I nearly laugh. Justice is a funny thing, especially here in the South. People are always complaining about justice in the modern-day world, but they don't know how good they really have it. And now here is Becky's father, Sawyer's father-in-law, and he's going to make sure I pay for what I did.

I can beat the shit out of a man like Tom Sawyer, and the town goes crazy. Jim is horrifically murdered for no reason other than the color of his skin and nobody says a peep. What the hell kind of world is this?

Purgatory, I think. Hell.

"Son," he says again, "I've had a talk with the sheriff."

I'm not your son, I want to tell him.

"We've agreed it's best if you are on your way and leave town immediately."

That gets my attention. I roll to my side and sit up.

"Becky says it was all a big misunderstanding—"

A big misunderstanding?!

"And Tom has been beating himself up pretty bad all these years, knowing he done wrong by you."

By me?!

"Neither of them want this to be a sore spot between you all anymore. I'm just gonna need you to promise me, son, that when you leave, you won't be coming back. I know you're probably worried about following through on the widow's wishes, but be rest assured I'll personally take care of it all for you."

A sore spot?!

I stand up and make my way over to where he's standing, just beyond the bars. Through the windows on the far side of town, I can see that the sun is rising. There's no snow, but I can only imagine how cold it is.

"A man died," I say quietly. Angrily. "More than that, many men died—and are still dying."

"War is brutal. No doubt about that. We've got families who have been gutted, fighting on both sides. People are fighting right now and dying to set these things right. But this anger you have toward Tom—none of this is gonna bring Jim back, son. None of it. All it brings about is sadness and the past and a lifetime of regret."

He could be my fucking shrink. "You think I should just forget what he's done?"

The Judge looks tired. "Now, I never said that. Huck, one of the things I've always admired about you is that you always knew who you were, and you believed in what you believed and you came to those decisions on your own. Tom ain't like that. You left, and it's obvious you got yourself an education. From what I hear, you got yourself a good job and a good lady. You expanded your horizons, son. Tom hasn't." He sighs. "Tom is, in many ways, still that boy you once knew. His horizons have remained limited. He's . . ." The Judge shakes his head. "Now, I love my daughter, and I love her husband, but even I can admit that he ain't the most selfless creature out there. What he did was wrong. He knows what he did was wrong. Your fists ain't gonna bring Jim back, Huck. All they're gonna do is keep you angry and miserable. Moving on will, though. Moving forward and making damn sure things change."

Before I can say anything, he removes the sheriff's keys and unlocks the cell.

"I think a wind of change is coming," he says quietly. "War changes everything." Glancing down at my hands, he adds, "You'll want to get that checked out whenever you go to where you're goin'."

A coat is passed over to me, alongside my gun and a hat. "People are still angry. You'll want to keep the hat on." He extracts a golden pocket watch. "There's a train leaving, heading north in a little over an hour. Make sure you and your lady friend are on it."

I shrug into the coat, wincing slightly as my knuckles brush against the wool. Just before I get to the door, he says, "Huck?"

I turn around.

"Keep expanding those horizons."

I tip my hat and make my way outside. This early, there aren't many people milling about. Wagons trundle up and down the road, their drivers lethargic as they make their deliveries. I take the Judge's advice and tilt the hat, keeping my head lowered as I make my way through town. The inn itself is fairly quiet, a man dozing behind the counter that I don't recognize.

I need to get the hell out of here already.

Upstairs, though, our room is empty. The bed is still made, as if nobody slept in it. Bandages and a bowl of water rest near a dead fire, untouched from the night before.

Alice is nowhere to be found.

Would she have edited back to the Institute? Perhaps she did as I requested and reclaimed Sawyer's equipment and then took it back. But . . . no. Alice isn't the sort who would leave anyone behind, even if it were the smart thing to do. Alice doesn't run away from fights.

Alice pushes herself straight into the middle of them.

I'm halfway down the hallway when I hear a voice coming from one of the rooms. "I think it's time we had a chat, Huckleberry Finn Van Brunt, don't you?"

PARALYSIS

ALICE

WOKE UP IN a room I did not recognize to S. Todd's face leering over me. When he whispered, his rancid breath left me literally gagging. "Good morning! Are you ready to play?"

I attempted to shove him off, to retrieve my daggers, but I couldn't move.

He'd giggled when he saw my panicked understanding. And then he laid his body on top of mine, belly to belly, hips to hips, legs on legs until breathing became laborious.

"Don't try to move, gel." And then he laughed and laughed, and I did my best to bite off his nose or ear, but I was unable to even move my mouth much.

Dread I'd never felt before consumed me.

He pressed his cracked and peeling lips against my cheek, and I gagged some more. This only served to amuse the fiend. He kissed the other cheek, and for a moment, I wanted to cry, I felt such utter and desolate frustration. In all my years, in all my battles and struggles, I had never been at such a disadvantage.

Why couldn't I move?

But then a name came to me. One that left me astoundingly even more alarmed than before.

Finn.

I fought harder, willed myself to move, struggled under the weights Todd had somehow trapped me beneath, and yet still couldn't shift a singular inch. Panic turned me wild—every last nerve ending in my body was on alert, every muscle was ordered to move, and all that resulted was more of Todd's laughter and a shortness of breath that had me gasping beneath his weight.

I could only pray Becky had followed through and convinced her father to free Finn. If something were to happen to him, whilst I was trapped in here with his mother's murderer . . .

The more I struggled, though, the greater he delighted in my plight. Eventually, the sharp, disgusting stab against my hip of arousal left me as emotionally paralyzed as I was physically.

The cad dropped his head, his nose digging into the base of my neck. "I can see why he favors you so."

This cannot be real. This cannot be real.

Todd shifted his body so that it spooned the side of mine, leaving me gasping for air. A dirty hand drifted across my cheek and then across my still lips.

Rage, beautiful, searing rage exploded within me.

The rough hand took its time drifting lower and then lower still. I imagined in fervent detail the joy and painstaking time I'd take carving him into little pieces and then gutting him.

My hoop skirt, I discovered, had already been removed, as had the voluminous amounts of clothing excepting my chemise.

I imagined slicing his penis the way a mother would cut up sausages for her children.

As he dragged the chemise higher and higher up my legs, Todd gleefully took his time informing me I'd been drugged, yet conveniently left out naming said drug. It was no use to fight the effects, he claimed.

Each struggle would only hasten the inevitable—which, naturally, he did not see fit to elaborate upon, either.

His fingers brushed the skin just above my knee. I thought about how I'd feed him the small slices of his penis shortly before I allowed him to die. "You're not so dangerous now, are you, Miss Alice in Wonderland?"

But then he'd sighed regretfully and rolled himself to his back. My eyelids I could move, thank God, and when he began pleasuring himself next to me, his grunts and groans only heightening the fury pulsing within me, I closed my eyes tight and visualized even more ways I would make him suffer. And suffer he would, for all of the heinousness he has inflicted upon so many.

Once sated, he stood and pulled his pants up. "I have it on good authority your partner will be out of jail shortly."

I'd wanted to cry again—but this time from relief. What made him stop? Not that I was complaining—far from it—but a fiend such as this does not seem to have the best of impulse control.

He buttoned his vest and slipped on a filthy coat. "We shall have a meeting with him." Several switchblades were tucked into various pockets. "That was quite a show he put on yesterday, was it not? I rather enjoyed seeing the infamous Finn Van Brunt losing his temper like that."

Todd had been there, watching? And then: *he knows Finn's name?*

"I imagine he'll lose his temper today, don't you think? Should I tell him I took some peeks underneath that chemise while you slept?" Todd came over and lifted me up like I was a rag doll. Somewhere down the hall, a door slammed. "Ah. Perhaps he's already been released! Are you ready for some fun, Alice?"

My damn head lolled and fell upon his shoulder as he hoisted me next to him.

Footsteps sounded in the hallway. Todd called out, "I think it's time we had a chat, Huckleberry Finn Van Brunt, don't you?"

And now here I am, my breath shallow from more than the constant struggle to move as I wait for the door to open.

No further footsteps sound. All I can hear is my heartbeat, loud and strong and fast.

Todd slips out one of his switchblades, and in one of his grandiose yet pathetic shows, twirls it until it opens. The tip is pressed against my jugular. Thoughts of Van Brunt in the hospital fill my mind, and it only adds fuel to my bonfire of rage.

Suddenly, the door explodes into the room in a hail of splinters and broken bits. Standing there, wearing a coat I do not recognize, is Finn.

He appears fine. His right hand is scabbed and mangled, but other than that he is fine. I allow myself a small bit of relief at the welcome sight before transitioning to bloodthirsty wishes for retribution and violence.

"Welcome, welcome!" Todd digs the switchblade's tip just enough into my throat that I am assured blood drips down my neck. "We were wondering when you'd appear, weren't we, luv?"

Finn doesn't look at him when he speaks, though. His focus is squarely on me. There's surprise in his blue-gray eyes; rage, too. But what gets me the most is the fear, because he knows there is something wrong with me. If there weren't, this revolting villain's hands would no longer be attached to his arms.

And yet here I am, molded to Todd's side, my head resting on his despicable shoulder, standing in a thin chemise.

"Looks like you found me," is what Finn finally says. A muscle in his arm twitches, like he's ready to go for his gun, but Todd is quick with his response.

"Now, now. You wouldn't want to do something that you can't take back before you hear what I have to say, would you? Besides, our time here is limited. I cannot imagine that fellow patrons have not heard the ruckus you've caused." His high, thin giggle shakes the both of our bodies.

"You want to talk? Fine. Let her go first."

Finn's harshly voiced order only leads to more giggling.

I wish I could say something to him. Wish I could throw my head back and knock Todd out. Wish I could snap his arm and then take the blade he's slowing digging into me and slide it across his neck, just like he'd done to Van Brunt. Like he's trying to do to me. Only I would not be so clumsy to leave him alive.

I wish so very many things.

It's comical, in a sad way, to ruminate on how many times I've faced assassination attempts over the years. I cannot even count the number, to be honest. And still, I managed to consistently turn the tide in my favor and emerge victorious. The Caterpillar berated me afterward, charging me with reckless luck that would sooner rather than later dissipate. *No person is invincible,* he would insist. *No person is charmed.* And I believed him. Frequent visions of my lifeless body on a Wonderlandian battlefield haunted my dreams. And yet, now he is dead at the hands of the Queen of Hearts and I am drugged and unable to control my muscles, clutched to the side of a man who I easily bested before.

I will my arms to work. My mouth. My head. Even just my fingers. Move, I command my muscles. *Move.*

"Are you sure this is what you want me to do?" Todd is saying to Finn.

My partner's silent questions are the worst. *Why is she just standing there,* I can practically hear him wonder. *Why hasn't she eviscerated this sonofabitch already?* He directs several at me. *Give me a clue, any clue as to what's the matter with you.*

I wish I could say I can speak effectively with my eyes, but I am so livid I'm positive all that emanates from me is fury. This situation is entirely intolerable.

"Let her go," Finn says, in the most terrifying voice I've yet to hear from him, "and maybe, just maybe, when the time comes, I'll show mercy when I kill you."

Todd slowly pulls the blade back and away from my neck. "If that is what you wish . . ." And then, quick as lightning, he jams it into my side and lets go of his hold on me.

Naturally, I slump immediately to the ground. For crying out loud, will the indignities of the day ever cease?

Apparently not, because I land at just the right angle that the blade digs deeper into my side. When a spontaneous cry escapes my lips, I have to struggle to get the pain under control.

Finn is across the room, his bloody fist meeting Todd's face and then stomach. The two men grapple for several minutes, fists flying and furniture giving way until the room is in ruins. "What the fuck did you do to her?" Finn shouts. "Did you drug her? Why is she like that? Alice! Are you okay?"

For his part, Todd nonsensically chants threats and rhymes about pies and barbers and crows and rats, giggling the entire time. Crunching transitions to wet, soft sounds. Finn's questions continue to go coherent-ly unanswered until the barber's ravings cease altogether and the fiend falls onto the ground next to me.

If I wasn't in so much pain, and if I could talk, I very well might tease Finn about how he feared he would beat the stuffing out of one person on this trip, only to come away with having done it twice.

My love is on the floor with me, my head now in his lap. Relief leaves me exhausted. "Oh, Jesus . . . Alice. Are you okay?" When I don't answer, his face lowers until it's just above mine. "Can you hear me?"

I let out a tiny huff of annoyance. What a patently stupid question. Slowly, I blink once.

Thankfully, he's quick on the uptake, remembering how, when he'd been dosed with SleepMist in Wonderland, I'd asked him to blink once for yes, twice for no. He presses a kiss first upon my forehead and then one against my lips. There is a slight splatter of blood on his own fore-head, one I sadistically yet gleefully attribute to Todd getting, as Mary would say, his ass handed to him.

"Can you talk?"

Two blinks.

"Are you in pain?"

I'm tempted to lie and he knows it, because he immediately quali-fies, "The truth."

I blink once, hating that I'm unable to compartmentalize the pain as easily as normal.

"I'm going to pull the knife out. I'm sorry, it's going to—"

I blink once, hoping he knows I want him to do this for me. When he does, blinding pain electrocutes me; another strangled cry escapes my lips. Finn has something pressed against my side, stemming the blood flow.

"I'm so sorry, love. Can you move?"

Two blinks. Black spots dance above me, ones that want to take me away from Finn. And still, there is warmth in my heart. *He called me love.*

"Did he drug you?"

One blink. At least, I hope I blink. The spots are growing larger and yet turning darker all at once.

"Do you know what it was?"

Two slow blinks.

Finn lets out a shaky sigh and drags a phone out of his pocket. "Can you believe they didn't confiscate this? Didn't confiscate anything other than my gun. Not my books, not my pen, not my phone. Didn't even ask me about them."

I think it's been well established we're surrounded by a bunch of idiots in Finn's original Timeline. How he managed to rise above all of this and become the wonderful man he is is beyond me, but I am ever so grateful he has.

With one hand, he punches in a message. "We're going to get you back to the Institute, okay?"

I wish I could just tell him to get a bloody move on things already. Son of a jabberwocky, I am tired. Tired and outraged and . . . and . . .

"I'm so sorry, Alice." His voice breaks. "God, I'm so sorry. I wish—I shouldn't have let you come."

Men and their ability to turn overly dramatic in such situations. Honestly now, does he not recall how, when he accompanied me to Wonderland, he was drugged and captured himself?

Now that I think about it, I'm a bit done with the drugging and capturing bits. This is getting a bit ridiculous—first him, with the Queen of Hearts' poisons, and now me, with Sweeney Patrick Todd?

Coincidences are never really coincidental at all.

There has to be a connection between these similarly unfolding events . . . doesn't there? My brain feels as fuzzy as the leaves in the tulgey woods. Tired. It's hard to cleanly place the pieces of the puzzle together.

Finn struggles to take out his pen and the miniature Institute book each team is required to carry on assignments from his pants' pocket while an arm still curves around me, applying pressure on my wound. His body trembles against mine. Mine matches, if not exceeds, his trembling. I'm glad he's here with me, though. His arms feel safe when nothing else does.

Voices sound downstairs. Angry and yet scared ones all at once. Finn's pen quickly scrawls across the page indicating Victor's medical wing. "I'm going to have to lift you up," he says quietly. "I'll try to be gentle, but I can't guarantee it won't hurt."

I'm tempted to roll my eyes again, but one glance at the fear and worry in his has me blinking once instead. My heart expands and contracts in the face of the tortured, worried love shining from his eyes. I am so lucky. So, so lucky to have this man. And then my own eyes sag. Tiredness like I've never felt wraps around me and sinks into my motionless bones.

It does hurt when he stands up. The sharp stab wicks my breath clean away as he hauls me over his shoulder. And then, amazingly, he bends down and grabs Todd's foot. Just as the voices in the inn grow closer, Finn carries us through the glowing door he's written us, leading us back into the Institute.

TRUE LOVE'S KISS

FINN

T HE INSTITUTE IS IN an uproar. Worse yet, Victor isn't back from
the Timeline I sent him and Mary to.

I'd brought us directly to the medical wing. I sounded an alarm
and Brom and the A.D. came in mere minutes after the door closed
behind us. I let my father's assistant take care of the sack of shit I'd
dragged with us. Undoubtedly woken up by my cursing, Rosemary, the
medical wing's latest resident thanks to withdrawals, took one look at
her boyfriend and promptly began screaming like a banshee. More than
once, she threatened to kill us all, although I seemed to be her favorite
target of the moment.

Like I care.

Alice wasn't answering me anymore. Her eyes were closed by the
time I got her onto a bed, and I'll admit I legitimately freaked the fuck

out. So, between me and Rosemary, I'm pretty sure my father was desperate to find some sedatives to pass out like candy. But, all the while trying to persuade me not to tear Todd apart with my bare hands (and physically blocking me from doing so—all via his whiteboard) and ordering via the A.D. to strap the asshole to a bed on the other end of the room, away from Rosemary, Brom managed to send a flurry of messages about how I've brought back Todd.

Conveniently, all this also happened not twenty minutes from one of his regularly scheduled checkups. His doctor is now examining Alice, and all I can think as he peels open her eyes and peers down into them, flashing his little light and making small *mmm-hmm* noises, is: *She cannot die. I cannot lose her.*

I cannot lose another person I love.

My father's old friend is from a Timeline that had an outbreak triggered by an extraterrestrial organism, and since then, has dedicated his life to studying bizarre illnesses. He's a trained surgeon, though, and has worked extensively with the Society for nearly three decades on various cases. Although he claims the stabbing didn't seem to hit any major organs, he rushes Alice into a small surgery room Victor crafted but rarely uses. For the next hour, as he meticulously cleans out and fixes what Todd has done with his blade, I just about lose my mind.

The bastard has deleted far too many Timelines. He killed my mother. My grandfather. He slashed my father's throat. He drugged Alice and stabbed her.

S. Todd's time is nearing an end.

Blood and cultures are collected once the surgery is finished. Before he leaves for Mary's lab for analysis, the aging doctor informs me he has no idea what's wrong with the woman I love.

All I can do is sit here with her. Hold her hand. Tell her I love her, over and over. And then come close to hysterically laughing because I should have had the balls to say these words earlier, when she wasn't unconscious and apparently paralyzed.

"Finn?"

Marianne Brandon is standing in the doorway of the small room just off the medical wing I've had Alice taken to. There's no way in hell I was going to let her be in there with those fucking lunatics.

"Just wanted to let you know that Victor sent a communiqué. There have been some difficulties in procuring the medicines they're searching for. They're probably still a day out, at the very least."

I can't be mad at my brother, though. He's been informed of what's going on. More importantly, Victor knows there's something wrong with Alice. He won't come home until he's got her a cure.

"Furthermore, Brom and the Librarian want to talk to you."

I'm reluctant to leave, but Marianne assures me she'll send word if Alice rouses.

Minutes later, I'm in my father's office, pissed off and wanting to punch something again. Scratch that. I want to punch a specific someone again. And it'd be like shooting fish in a barrel, because he's currently immobilized back in the medical wing.

The Librarian pours herself a glass of wine. "We need you to go collect a new book."

"Fuck that," I tell them. Are they insane? "I'm not going."

My father sighs quietly.

"We would not ask," she continues, "if it were not imperative."

I mince no words. "You keep saying that. Send someone else this time."

Half of her mouth curves upward. "Well, in a way, we are. You'd be going with Marianne Brandon. In addition to working with the costumes, she'll also be assisting me with library duties. This is her first assignment outside of the Institute. She is nervous as it is."

I try to make my words as clear as possible. "I am not going anywhere."

"Marianne does not yet know how to drive."

Is this some kind of show where there's a hidden camera, and some asshole who jumps out and shouts, *"Surprise!"*?

My father turns to his colleague and gives the sharpest kind of nod a man whose throat is still tender can offer. She's immediately out of her chair, ensuring the door is locked. A recorder is extracted from her pocket; when she pushes a button, a conversation begins. One that I realize quickly occurred between her and me some time ago, one about book acquisitions for the quarter.

Brom clicks the end of the pen he's been fiddling with. Green laser beams silently scan the room from top to bottom. Before I can say a thing, he angles his whiteboard so I might see it. *We have reason to believe the Institute may be bugged.*

What. The. *Hell?*

On the Librarian's recorder, I'm arguing with her about the cost of certain books she wants to acquire. I remember this conversation. One of the books, coming from a collector in New Jersey, cost close to a quarter of a million dollars and was in truly shitty condition. There was no way I was okaying that purchase. And here we are, listening to my arguments again, and she's smiling ruefully as she sits back down, like some kind of ghost because she makes no sound. A piece of paper is carefully, quietly extracted from her pocket. There is a message there, already written out: *We have reason to believe Gabriel Pfeifer has a catalyst in his collection, albeit unknowingly. Pfeifer is currently in the city, attending a series of fundraisers throughout the week, including one tonight. You have been in his collection before. Marianne will not accompany you. She will stay with Alice. Wendy and Jack will run logistics. Bring it home.*

I look up from the note, stunned. On the recorder, the Librarian is telling me about how Marianne needs to get her feet wet. She's spliced new dialogue in amongst the old.

Brom points to the paper and twirls his finger. I flip it over and find a timetable and a sketch of the item in question. *Jack and Wendy are waiting for you at the helipad. Be back by dawn. Do not speak of this until you are in the air.*

My bodiless voice insists, "Fine. I'll go. I hate New Jersey, though."

I nearly start out of my chair. I can't ever remember saying such a thing.

The paper is reclaimed. In seconds, the words melt off the page, and then the paper itself disintegrates. Brom clicks the end of his pen, and the green light ceases scanning the room. The Librarian follows by turning off the recording.

"Don't worry," she says smoothly. "We will ensure Alice is taken care of while you are gone."

I find Marianne sitting next to Alice's bed. She's doing needlework, humming to herself. I ask, "Anything?"

She shakes her head. Since coming to the Institute, she's begun to wear her hair like anyone else in the Twenty-First Century. Currently, it's wild and free, with just a hint of waves. And she's wearing skinny jeans and an oversized sweater of sorts, and even I have to admit it's bizarre to see Marianne Brandon dressed like any other woman I'd see in New York. "The doctor came in shortly after you left, though. He conducted a thorough examination of her body and frowned the entire time. It was most unsettling."

It feels wrong to leave. So wrong. And yet . . . I can't just leave a catalyst out there, especially an unsuspecting one. Katrina told me once, when I asked why we risked so much to collect catalysts, that we always had to ensure the welfare of many over the few. It made good sense. While I always did my best to bring my partners and I back in one piece from our assignments, the risk was worth it to me. I've been shot at with both bullets and arrows. Stabbed. Burned. I've had to wiggle my way out of captures and fight my way out of tight situations. Each time, though, my thoughts were on those catalysts. Most people in Timelines have no idea that something so small, something so seemingly unimportant, can be the difference between existence and the void. I prefer that they don't know. I hope most continue to live that way. Nobody wants to fall into an existential crisis and wonder if some asshole of an author made him or her up or if they're even real at all.

Pfeifer has a catalyst? How, I have no idea. But if he's got one, I need to do what I do best and go and protect the people it represents. Alice would understand this. Hell, she'd be the first in line to argue that a person's individual needs come after that of a whole. She did it for Wonderland, didn't she? Gave up everything so her people would have a chance.

God, she's an amazing woman.

I smooth back her hair and kiss her gently. If only real life was like those fairy tales Katrina read me. If only true love's kiss woke the queen up and we lived happily ever after.

I whisper in her ear that I love her. That I have never loved anyone else the way I love her. I remind her that she's my north star, too. That, as binaries, I need her to fight. My gravitational pull needs her.

And then her eyelids flutter. A sigh, a beautiful, small, contented sigh escapes her lips.

True love's kiss. I'll be damned.

Hope bursts inside me. Our story isn't over, not by a long shot. Our story is just getting started, and no damn author is going to write it. We will. Together. We're going to write that book she wants.

Our ending is ours to find.

I kiss Alice again. Promise her I'll be back very soon. Walking away from the woman I love right now feels like probably the hardest damn thing I've ever had to do in a long list of impossible things. And yet, I do it anyway.

GONE

FINN

I N THE HELICOPTER, WENDY goes over the mission specs as the A.D. steers us north. Thanks to my and Alice's recent visit, and coupled with public land documents, builder's permits, and architectural plans, she's created a 3-D construct of Bücherei to help us break our way in.

I'm still wondering how in the hell I'm going to get past those massive doors, though.

"Interestingly enough," Wendy is saying as I go over the scans, "none of the plans we found indicate any part of the house was built explicitly for library or museum use."

Huh. "Honestly, it seemed *exclusively* used for the library. I think there was a little to the left of the main foyer that might not have been, but from the tour we took, Bücherei was pretty much a library and nothing else. I mean, the bookshelves stretched up several floors, all rimming the central exhibit hall. It spread the entire length of the back of the house and then some up toward the front."

She taps on her tablet's screen and brings up the original architectural blueprints. "I get what you're saying, but according to these, this is your standard three-story house with a large kitchen, dining room, six bedrooms, five baths, indoor pool that feeds to a larger one outside . . ."

The A.D. voice within our headsets crackles. "Standard, Wen? Standard to whom? Dunno about you two, but I don't know too many gents and ladies who have themselves a fancy indoor pool, let alone one that connects to another outside."

He has an extremely valid point.

The more I look at the plans, the more confused I am. "None of this is what I saw. These staircases?" I point to the scan. "Not there. These bathrooms? They were bookshelves. This bedroom, connected with a master bath?" I shake my head. "That's almost exactly where he had a Hemingway exhibit."

Her nose wrinkles as she peers down at the blueprints. "Are you sure?"

I tap on the screen, expanding the image. "This is supposed to be the pool room, right?"

"Yeah. It has sliding glass windows that open the pool into a more elaborate one beyond. See?" She flips the page to another, of an architectural painting showing what the finalized project would look like. Straddling both land and house is a massive pool that would make the ritziest of hotels jealous.

"That's not there." Or anything else on these blueprints except the front door and the hedge mazes.

What the hell?

"Are you sure you found the right blueprints?"

Her hackles rise immediately. "Of course I got the right ones." She expands the information at the bottom. The address matches the coordinates we're en route to, but none of it makes sense. "Is this or is this not the house you went to?"

I don't get it. The outside looks the same, yes. The same roughened wood and frosted glass, the same burnished metal. Altogether, the enormous house looks confused about what time period it was from.

She changes the image again, this time to something from one of those satellite programs that take photographs of every road and house. She punches in the address. There, amongst massive hedge mazes, is Bücherei. "The coordinates match, Finn."

I'm tired. That's it, right? I haven't sleep in . . . I don't know. Not even in jail. "I'm going to be honest," I admit after a long moment. "I have no fucking idea how to get us in then. This isn't—it looks like it from the outside, but the inside? It's not the house I've been in. And . . . the lock on the library door was pretty elaborate. It sounded like it had a number of locking mechanisms."

She stares at me like I've lost my mind. I'm thinking she may be right. "You always know how to get us in."

I don't know what to say. Can this day get any more surreal? I mean, I started out in a St. Petersburg jail, only to find, after searching for him for some time, Todd waiting for me after attacking Alice. My father says somebody has bugged the Institute. I'm going to a house I've been to before, but it's also not the same house I remember.

When I don't answer, Wendy swipes back to the blueprints. "I figure the weakest link is through the pools. No doubt there will be security cameras in this back area, but if we can enter via the gap between the pools—"

"We?" the A.D. pipes up. "Is the great Gwendolyn going to step away from her machines long enough to play with the big boys?"

She flips him off, but that only leaves the A.D. cackling. "Fine. You two will be going in via the pool's gap. As it's winter, the glass panes will be in place, alongside what look like storm window coverings." She expands the image to highlight a pair of metal shutters. "There will be a water trail, but I'm hoping that since Pfeifer's scheduled to stay in the city all week, by the time he comes back, it'll be dried up." Another swipe takes us back to the 3-D construct. "From your report, I've pinpointed several of the cameras at these locations." She points to what appear to be various bedrooms along with a sitting room of sorts, set just off the kitchen. "Based on your description, I think I've figured out the make and model. The inner cameras will be no problem at all to jam for five minutes. The outer ones, though . . . according to docs I hacked, Pfeifer's got the crème de la crème protecting his property. I'll be blitzing the satellite signals long enough for you two to get in and then trigger another blitz for your departure. " She grins. "I'm rather excited to try them out. They act like solar flare distortions. They can't be traced back to a source."

"What's our timeframe, Wen?" the A.D. asks.

"You'll have sixty seconds to get into the house before they resume. The same on the way out." She rifles through a nearby pack. "I've got a waterproof bag for you to carry back the veil."

That reminds me . . .

Brom and the Librarian have sent me to Pfeifer's to collect none other than Scheherazade's veil from *One Thousand and One Nights*. Historically, the Society has always had a great deal of trouble with this, well, collections of stories because there isn't a cohesive original text we can source from. That Timeline is still a mystery to us—we've had no contact, no way in, no way to even prove it exists. There are dozens and dozens of versions ranging from the Ninth Century to the Nineteenth Century, and each has varying stories from the others. People know the famous stories and characters—Aladdin, Sinbad, Ali Baba—but those didn't even come into play until some Europeans translated and created their own versions in the Nineteenth Century. So for us to get sent in to retrieve a catalyst from a wildcard Timeline we don't even know fully exists, one that somehow a book collector in modern day has obtained?

The uneasy feeling in the pit of my stomach expands. Something is off here. Something is wrong.

Pfeifer collects author artifacts. Everything in his collection, at least what I saw (and Alice and I were subjected to a lot of it), belonged to people who wrote the books. So, what in the hell is he doing with an allegedly ancient veil a vizier's daughter would have worn on her wedding day to a sultan? The same woman who tricked her murderous husband to not kill her by spinning some of the most fantastical, edge-of-your-seat tales that made him desperate to listen to more?

"Alice's report doesn't refer to Pfeifer correctly," Wendy is saying. "Why does it say Lygari?"

I refocus on the photo of the man she'd brought up on her tablet. It shows him shaking hands with the mayor of New York after a hefty donation to the city's arts programs. Hell, he even looks smug and handsome in the photo. "She said they met before and he told her his name was Gabe Lygari."

Wendy's nose scrunches again. "Weird. Dude is really well known in the literary and arts circles. I wonder why he would tell her a different name?"

"Maybe he was afraid she'd only want to bone him for his money," the A.D. interjects. "Gave her a nice lil' free-fuck alias instead."

I smack him on the back of his head. He yelps and mutters out an insincere apology.

Wendy shakes her head. "Why do I feel like you've done that before, Jack?"

"A player's gotta play," he says mournfully.

"Pfeifer is a German name," Wendy muses. "I don't think Lygari is, though. Which is bizarre, when you think his estate is also a German word."

Bizarre doesn't even begin to cover all of this shit.

For the rest of the ride, Wendy goes over the plan multiple times. Each time she points out the cameras and reminds us of the layout, the uneasier I get. It's not the house I saw. It's not the house I entered. I'm going in blind, and it seems like there's nothing I can do about it.

Alice is back at the Institute. She can't move. I need to question Todd and then break every finger in his hands before ramming his own switchblade into his side.

"You look really tired, Finn."

That's a kind way of putting it. Exhausted is closer to the truth, but even that's too gentle of a word. "Contrary to popular belief, beds inside jail cells aren't too comfortable."

Wendy twists large chunks of her green hair around her fingers. "How's the hand doing?"

Honestly? It aches. I didn't even think to have the doctor check it out, what with all the stuff going on with Alice. And I'm pretty sure I broke a knuckle or two. Fantastic. But I cleaned it when I took a quick shower and wrapped it before hopping on the helicopter, and that'll have to do for now.

But I shrug, refusing to tell Wendy any of this. I'll have Victor look at it when he gets back.

She's wearing sunglasses, so it's hard to see the emotion in Wendy's eyes when she puts a hand out. "I heard about what happened. I'm sorry."

The knot in my stomach hasn't loosened. If anything, it's tightened.

We land in a large field not too far from Bücherei that has no buildings nearby. The A.D. and I quickly change into our wetsuits and gear up with our visors and earpieces. Wendy assures us they're all waterproof, so there shouldn't be any difficulty with connectivity during the mission.

It doesn't take long to reach the edge of the hedge mazes surrounding the property. Wendy pulls out her surveying device and calculates the best way through to get us to the pool. "Make sure you let me know when you're through. I'll trigger the override blast. From there, you'll have sixty seconds."

"How do you know the hedges don't have cameras?" the A.D. asks.

Sometimes, I don't give the punk enough credit.

"I found the landscaping permits for that, too. There are floodlights in certain sectors and cameras, but none on this path." She glances down at her tablet. "This is a secretive back entrance, according to plans. A straight shot in. Why Pfeifer felt he needed it, I have no idea."

And secretive it is. Wendy sticks her hand into the bushes, winces, and suddenly a small panel toward the bottom more suitable for Wonderland than New York slides open.

The A.D., nearly as tall as myself, must be thinking the same thing I am. "You want us to crawl through that wee hole?"

She has no pity for us. "Get moving."

Both of us have to slither in on our bellies, and even then, I'm positive the wetsuit gets ripped up from the sharp branches we're barreling through. There isn't a spare inch of wiggle room to be found.

"Blimey hell," the A.D. chokes out from behind me.

The path we emerge onto is extremely narrow, only wide enough for one person at a time, and even then, it has to be traversed walking sideways while sucking your stomach in. Getting up from the ground is no easy feat, and I'm regretting not seeing the doctor before I left because I think I've done even more damage to my hand just in standing up. The A.D. struggles in his efforts, so I basically have to squat down and haul him up. He yelps a few times, only going quiet once I elbow him in the ribs. We slowly make our way forward, each crunch beneath our feet and snap of twigs from above leaving our heartbeats racing faster.

Finally, after what feels like nearly a half hour, we make our way to the pool on Wendy's blueprints. It's massive, with a pair of waterfalls. Just like Wen said, it feeds straight into the house.

I feel like the biggest idiot as I take it in. This isn't right. This—this can't be here. Have I hit my head and just don't remember doing so?

"WD, we're in position," the A.D. says on his comm.

Wendy's voice fills our ears. "Copy that, JD. Sixty seconds on my count, beginning now. Three . . . Two . . . One . You are clear for transition."

We spring from the tiny slit in the maze, barrel forward the twenty or so feet, and dive into the pool. Long, powerful strokes pull us forward quickly, and soon enough, we're beneath the metal and glass barrier and emerging inside the house.

"Outside security cameras resuming in three, two, one," Wendy says. "Triangulating scramble for inside feed. You have ten minutes to complete the retrieval."

I want to laugh. Ten minutes. Ten minutes to find, what? A veil inside a massive library that houses hundreds of objects, spanning three floors? We'll be damned lucky if I can figure out the weird mechanism Pfeifer used for his doors in such a tiny timeframe. He had a key, and those things had to be one, two feet thick.

We're out of the pool, winding our way through an empty kitchen. There aren't even appliances. We find a sitting room with a threadbare couch and nothing else. A bathroom. I spin around, trying to get my bearings. I track myself to the front door and then to the right, toward the imposing fairy-tale-inspired wooden doors, only to find . . .

A bedroom.

I wrench open the standard, cream-colored door to find the entire room to be empty. There isn't one damn piece of furniture within. A ceiling hovers directly above me, also cream in color, featuring a fan.

I'm out of the bedroom and down the hallway. A hallway I don't remember seeing. Another empty bedroom. Another bathroom. I sprint back up the hallway, toward the front door. Maybe I had it wrong. Maybe . . . Maybe we went to the left? But going down that short hallway leads me back to the kitchen.

There are no looming, carved doors anywhere. There is no library. There is—shit, Wendy was right. This is just a *house.*

Wendy's voice crackles. "Five minutes."

"Where the hell is this library?" the A.D. whispers. "I thought you guys said it was big?"

I'm up a sprawling staircase just off the sitting room, a staircase that I never saw on my first visit. There are more rooms up here, sitting upon carpeted floor. There are no mosaics of fairy tales scenes. The ceiling above is flat and filled with fans. No eyes hidden in the forest are watching me.

WHAT. THE. FUCK?!?!

I head up another set of stairs. The same setup is on the third floor as well.

I'm back down the stairs, nearly colliding right into the A.D. He's just as frustrated as me. "Finn! Where is it?"

"Two minutes," Wendy informs us.

Everywhere I look is just rooms. Regular floors. Regular ceilings. Regular doors. There is no library, no . . . This is a house. This is just a house and nothing more. What is going on here? What—

"Sixty seconds."

The A.D. knocks my shoulder, pretending to tap on an imaginary watch. And then, when I don't move, he physically yanks on my arm.

"Forty seconds."

He jumps in the pool first. I'm just about to jump in after him when I see something on the ground, near the entrance to the room. It's—it's a photo? How did I miss this the first time through?

My blood runs cold when I stare at the small, glossy paper in my hands. It's a photo of Alice and me. Together, in the coffee shop we like to go to. I'm—I'm going crazy, right? Because how in the hell is this here? This was taken . . . *Jesus.* Was this from the first time we ever went? That dress. I recognize the dress. How could I forget? She—

"Ten seconds. Switching to blitz. Remember, sixty seconds once you're through the pools."

I stuff the photo into the bag that was supposed to hold Scheherazade's veil and dive into the pool. I swim faster than I think I've ever swum before. And then, my hand aching like a sonofabitch, I pull myself out of the pool and launch myself into the barely noticeable crack in the hedge, scraping the shit out of my face while doing so. The A.D. is already there and also bleeding, his breath coming in hard bursts.

We look at each other, but I have no answers to give. Not one single goddamn answer.

"Victory, gentlemen?" Wendy asks once we've belly crawled our way back through what would make a better dog door than anything for humans to traverse.

"Wen," the A.D. says quietly, "there was nothing there."

"You couldn't find the veil?"

"No, Wen." He's uncharacteristically serious. "You misunderstand. There wasn't *anything* there. That house ain't lived in, luv. There's a shitty couch better suited for the gutter and nothing more. Not even toilet paper in the bathrooms, let alone a fancy library and collections. No furniture, no appliances. *Nothing.*"

We stand there, in that cold field, with the hint of snow in the air, none of us knowing what to say. In all our combined years in the Society, in all the various and fantastical and technologically advanced Timelines we've ever been in, nothing has even come close to what we've just experienced.

Just who in the hell is Gabriel Pfeifer? And why is his library now missing—or hidden?

HE KNOWS

ALICE

I AM CHILLED, AND I cannot tell anyone of this.

The kindly doctor—whose name I keep forgetting, but I suppose does not matter, since he is apparently on good terms with Van Brunt—is once more examining me. Marianne is in the room, scandalized probably more than she has ever been in her entire life, as the doctor peruses my semi-nude body garbed in one of those dreadful backless gowns they've forced upon me. One would think that, in such situations, especially in winter, the heat would be turned up to increase a patient's comfort, but alas, neither Marianne nor the doctor have thought of such comforts. My goose pimples, which I know must have risen to their stiffest peaks, failed to alert the doctor as well.

This is the second examination in, well, I don't know how long exactly. Several hours, I would imagine. Each time the doctor comes in,

mumbling about tests and results and inconsistencies, he requires another perusal and yet neglects to inform me exactly what he is searching
for. It's tiny, whatever it is, because his face is extremely close to my
skin whilst using a magnifying glass.

He makes a small grunting sound. "Help me turn her over, Mrs.
Brandon."

Marianne springs out of her chair, toward the bed I'm on. I like
her—she's passionate about her beliefs and yet compassionate, too.
She's read to me, discussed a variety of things (albeit one-sidedly), and
ensured I am given every comfort a person who cannot move an inch of
her body can be afforded.

"Gently now," he murmurs. "We must be careful of her stitches."

They roll me so that Marianne bears my weight as I rest on my side,
allowing the doctor full view of my back. She pets my hair, as if I am
a dog—and I know she means well, but honestly. The indignities are
frightfully too much, especially as something cold runs along my spine,
perilously close to my bare buttocks.

Marianne peeps her head up and over my torso. "Have you found
anything yet, Doctor?"

The doctor says nothing. A click sounds, as if he's taking a photograph with a cell phone. Another series of clicks, and then, as if having
a man I do not know hover above my buttocks wasn't bad enough, the
door swings open.

A sigh of relief heaves out of me. It's Finn. Son of a jabberwocky,
being paralyzed has made me overtly emotional, because seeing him
now has my vision blurring.

When he notices the doctor's position, his eyes narrow. "What the
hell is going on here?"

"I'm examining the patient," the doctor mutters. "What the hell
does it look like?"

And then, nearly immediately, Marianne says, "I have been present
the entire time, Finn. No improprieties have occurred."

It must be enough for Finn, because he wiggles his way around
Marianne so that he is now holding onto me rather than our colleague.
"You're awake." A kiss is pressed against my mouth, and the urge to cry
intensifies. "Are you in pain?"

Two blinks. And then, wondering how many blinks it would take to indicate how cold I am, I unleash a flurry of them.

He kisses me again, this time on the forehead. And then, blast it all, my eyes do well up with bloody tears when my north star quickly drags a blanket over. Because somehow, he knows. *He knows what I need.*

"Finn," the doctor says, his voice low and creaky from age, "have you talked with your father or the Librarian yet?"

"I just got back." Frustration colors his words, though, and in a way that makes me distinctly uneasy. "I wanted to come and check in on Alice first. But I plan on going to see them in a few minutes. Why?"

More coldness spreads across the base of my spine. "Can I confirm that you were in 1876/96TWA-TS when Ms. Reeve was attacked?"

When Finn runs his hands through my hair, it feels more loving and less like petting than when Marianne attempted her kindness. "Yes, but the asshole who did this is not from 1876/96TWA-TS. It's assumed he's from 1846/47RYM/PEC-SP, although I ought to note he's been in multiple Timelines over the past few years. Why?"

The doctor sighs so loudly that I feel his breath spread across my bare skin. "I'm not able to identify whatever is in her system. I'm working on breaking down the compounds, but . . ." He blows out another breath. "Whatever it is seems to be organic in origin, although from what I cannot identify." There's a bleakness to his voice that has me shivering from more than just cold. "I also have reason to believe there's a parasite in her system."

. . . *What?!*

"I'd like to do some scans to verify, but it doesn't appear Victor has the necessary materials here at the Institute. Here, let's get her comfortable again. I'll take these cultures back home with me and use my own machines. Maybe that will help."

When the doctor leaves, Finn asks Marianne to step outside for a few minutes. Once she's gone, too, he sits down in her chair next to my bed. My hand is in his, and his forehead comes to rest on our conjoined fingers.

The other hand, I can tell, is still a bloody mess. "We're going to fix this," he tells me quietly. "I'm going to question Todd tonight with the truth serum. This is going to be fixed. You're going to be okay."

Oddly, I am not as worried about my situation as I ought to be simply because I believe in him. He will not give up on me, just like I will never give up on him. I have nothing concrete to base this overwhelming yet wonderful piece of faith on, but it's curling throughout me like sips from a cup of cocoa on a frigid day: comforting and warm and perfect.

Gravity is a beautiful thing, I think.

I want to ask him how he is. How he's feeling. Yesterday was a raw day for him, in ways I fear came from years of pent-up anger and grief. I want to comfort him, hold him. I want to tell him that it's going to be okay, too. That I'm here for him. That, together, we will work through all of this tomorrow.

And that, maybe, just maybe, if I ever see Tom Sawyer again, I'll kick his arse, too.

But all I can do is just stare at him, hoping he can somehow sense all of this and know the depths of my love for him.

Bloody paralysis having to go muck everything up.

"I have a lot to tell you." He kisses my hand again. "But I need to go talk to my dad and the Librarian about some shit that's just gone down." He pulls back so he can see my face. "Do you want to be present tonight when I question Todd?"

I give him the firmest blink I can. Hell yes, I want to be there to hear what's going on.

He reluctantly stands up, placing my hand back on the bed like it's the most priceless thing in the world to him. And then I unleash another flurry of blinks.

He says, "I promise that as soon as Victor gets here, I'll have him look at my hand."

My eyes fill with tears again. *He knows.*

Finn's at the door, his hand on the knob, when he stops. He turns around, rare vulnerability on his face. "Before I go, there's something I need to let you know. Something that's taken far too long to be said."

The thing is, I know, too. Actions, I want to tell him, speak louder than words most times.

"Somehow, in the last half year, you've become my best friend. I've fallen in love with your laugh and the way you roll your eyes, but do it surreptitiously, because you think it's rude but you do it anyway. I've fallen in love with how you always have a comeback, especially when you're feeling exposed. I fallen in love with how you sink like a stone once you hit your pillow, faster than anyone I've ever met, and then snore like a lumberjack sawing trees."

It's enough to make me gasp in mock consternation. But also to turn to mush, which is an altogether inconvenient situation when a person cannot wipe their own eyes or sniffly nose or burst out the feelings of their heart.

"I've fallen in love with how you make the worst places incredibly romantic. And with the fact that, even though it doesn't seem like it, we're so damn alike. You get me when most people don't." More softly, "You stood by me in St. Petersburg. You didn't even bat an eye when I hit that asshole. You—you trusted me, even though you had no idea what was going on. I know you have trust issues, but God, Alice. Your trust means the world to me."

This man. How I love this man.

"I love you. I've never felt this way about anyone before. It's the best damn feeling in the entire world."

I unleash another flurry of blinks. He lets go of the knob and comes back to exactly where I want him. When he kisses me, slowly yet gently, I feel it in every numb cell of my body. His touch is like those sparklers I saw people using on the Fourth of July this last year here in New York: beautiful, bright, and fizzy, so magical their light left lingering pictures in the air.

They'd enchanted me. This man here? He enchants me more. He kisses me, because *he knows.* He knows me. He knows my heart.

He has become part of my heart.

My gravity pulls at his. His pulls at mine. We orbit one another, me and my north star, and I will be damned if anyone will ever tear us apart.

SURVEILLANCE FOOTAGE

FINN

"FINN, HOLD UP!"

Victor jogs through the mess littering the basement to catch up with me. Thank God he's back.

"I'm gone three days, and everything goes to hell!" He's not smiling, though. His voice is projecting, and there's a level of irritability and anxiety to it that leaves me more worried than anything else. He's on edge and so hopped up that I wonder if he's slept at all lately, either. "I'm sorry it took me so long. It wasn't the easiest to get hold of these supplies. There were a few times I was certain Mary and I were going to be captured." He shudders, yet lifts a bag. "I come bearing many treats, though. And Mary's bag is even more full than mine. She was like a kid in a candy store."

I could hug him, I'm so relieved. I know I ought to be busting his balls about taking his meds, but first things first.

We make our way through the elaborate security measures that allow authorized Society members to access the Museum. If there's anywhere in the building that is safe to talk about all the shit that's gone down, it's there. Brom and the Librarian are already below, getting briefed by Wendy and the A.D. I fill Victor in on the basics, and by the time the last set of doors slide open, he's on board with what I've got planned for tonight. He's also ranting and talking a million miles a minute.

I'm surprised, to be honest. Mary is usually on him about his meds like white on rice.

We find everyone crowded in the Librarian's tiny office. Folding chairs have been squeezed in, and in between those and the chairs and table already present, knees are practically touching when we all sit down.

"First," I say, "explain to me what you meant about the Society being bugged."

Brom holds up a hand, getting his whiteboard ready. Victor pops out of his chair, though. "First," he says, "let's get Dad all fixed up so he doesn't have to take ages writing this stuff out. From what I saw, the application is simple."

A slim bottle is extracted from his bag. Can it really could be as easy as just spraying something from a bottle on a wound to heal it? And yet, it is, because after Victor removes our father's bandaging and sprays the stuff, the angry red line across my father's throat fades away until all that's left is smooth skin.

Holy. Shit.

"Try saying something!" Victor's bouncing on his heels, he's so pumped.

Our father, our stodgy, cultured father, says in his distinguished voice, "Holy shit."

The Librarian claps her hands and then covers her mouth. The A.D. whoops; Wendy is agog.

"Take care of your brother's hand while you're at it." Brom is clearly uncomfortable with all eyes on him. "He's been too stubborn to have it looked at."

"Bloody hell," Victor yells as he stares down at the mangled mess that I call a hand. "What did you do? Punch a brick wall?"

"Two—named Tom Sawyer and Sweeney Todd."

Brom clears his throat. "And got himself arrested. Let's not forget that."

I kind of love my father's voice, even when he's giving me shit.

"Fine. I got myself arrested. I'm not sorry about it, though."

He sighs. "I only want what was best for you. I hardly think I ought to be stoned for such wishes."

What's best for me is getting back upstairs and figuring out what's wrong with Alice. What's also best for me is to stuff all this shit back into the box I've kept it in. I just—I can't process it all right now. I just can't.

Victor's got my hand fixed in no time. It's insane—it's like my hand was never hurt in the first place. Damn, that Timeline has something good going. Okay, well, not the alien invasion or anything, but man. With drugs like this, our assignments will go a lot more smoothly.

But, as fascinating as all that is, we've got much more important business to attend to. "Now, about the Society being bugged? Let's make this fast. I need to get upstairs and interrogate Todd so we can try out Victor's new medicine on Alice."

Wendy takes great offense to this. "My security system is unrivaled. I've cobbled together pieces of coding and technology we've gotten from various Timelines, making it impossible to crack. There is no way for anybody to have broken through it. *No way.*"

Brom exchanges meaningful looks with the Librarian. "You are very right, Ms. Darling. We have no indication that anybody has broken in from the outside. See, it has come to our attention that there might be a mole—or moles—*within* our midst, working from the inside out."

That's—no. *No.* No way.

The Librarian opens the laptop sitting on her geode of a coffee table while Wendy's eyebrows form a V. "I would know if there were any transmissions coming out of the Institute. All calls, even personal ones, are logged. My team goes over them at night to ensure nothing is off."

Before Brom can continue, she cuts him off. "We've also got video surveillance all over the building. All editing and retrieval information is downloaded off of pens after every assignment. If there's a mole, he or she shouldn't be too hard to find. I'll get my team to start combing through our records." She pulls out her phone. "Is there anything concrete you've found so far? Something we can maybe use as a spring-board?"

"Yes, Gwendolyn," the Librarian says softly. "We have, in fact, found something quite troubling."

On the laptop screen is security footage of Wendy's lab. She's in there, tinkering with what looks to be a pen prototype. The timestamp says it's nearly two-thirty in the morning. Wendy is a well-known night owl here at the Institute who rarely requires more than three, four hours of sleep at night.

The footage glitches, wavy gray and black zigzags bend the picture. And then Wendy gets up and heads over to a window, punching in the code to still the alarms attached. Suddenly, she drops down to the ground, her back to us.

In the room we're in now, down inside the Museum, she whispers, "What—?"

On the video, somebody comes through the window. Somebody lean and young and whose feet do not touch the floor. He has pipes pressed to his lips, and Wendy's head tilts back in awe as she gazes upward.

"Oh my god," the Wendy sitting in this room murmurs. "I—what?"

Still playing his pipes, the boy drifts down, circling Wendy. His gaze is adoring, and within seconds, they head over to her laptop. Many minutes are spent with him looking at whatever she shows him before he finally sets down the pipes. Something is whispered in her ear; Wendy nods and smiles dreamily. Papers are printed and handed over. Another few minutes are spent talking. He nods often, eyes serious, as he takes in whatever she has to say.

They head back over to the open window, and within seconds, the boy is gone. Wendy carefully shuts it, ensuring to punch in the security codes and reactivating the alarms. And then, as if nothing strange has just happened, she wanders back over to her laptop and types furiously for a good minute.

The picture glitches again before the Librarian presses pause. All eyes now shift to Wendy. She's still staring at the paused footage, like she can't believe what she's just seen. And then she says something that is absolutely the wrong thing in a moment like this. She says, her voice soft in disbelief, "He came. He finally came for me."

The A.D. explodes out of his chair. "What in the blimey hell is that, Wen? *He came for me?* You were just obviously fucking around with some guy, some *kid* who—who broke into the Institute, from the looks of it! And you gave him God knows what, told him even more, and all you can say is: *He came for me?"*

The A.D. and I don't often agree on everything, but I'm going to have to concur with him on this one.

Wendy's unfazed by the hostility rolling off him, though. Unfazed at how everyone is now staring at her like she's some kind of stranger. She stands up, whispers, "Pan came," and then promptly faints.

No—not faints. Victor's immediately on the ground with her as she convulses. Her eyes roll back and her arms twitch. "She's having a seizure," he tells us.

We all just sit there, not knowing what in the fuck is going on. Because, *Wendy* is the mole? Wendy is giving out information to Peter Pan of all people, if that's, in fact, what she was even doing?

Maybe I really am going crazy. I'm going into empty houses looking for libraries that don't exist, for catalysts for books with Timelines I don't know exist, and one of my oldest, dearest friends looks like she's been sharing secrets with Peter fucking Pan of all people.

Quiet horror fills the room as we wait until Wendy's body slows its shaking. Tiny choking noises escape her; there's white spittle ringing her lips. Victor is calling her name, but she's not answering.

"Use the spray!" the A.D. yells.

Victor doesn't even look up from her body. "From what I can tell, the spray is more for things like cuts or physical injuries, not internal ones. We don't know what's causing the seizure, or what could happen if we try to use the spray on something other than a physical wound."

"How did you find this?" I round on my father and the Librarian. "What even made you suspect this was happening?"

"They're editing." Brom is utterly unapologetic. "When I tried to take him down, before he attacked me, I saw Todd with a pen that appears far too similar to our own. That cannot be coincidence, Finn."

Why is this the first I'm hearing of this?

"It wasn't easy to find proof." The Librarian says this like she's talking about the weather. "But once we discussed the situation, I was able to locate a number of discrepancies with documents. I contracted a discreet liaison from another Timeline to look into the matters for me. Time jumps and corrections in surveillance videos were difficult to detect until we knew what to look for. Edited call logs, whose keystrokes traced back to Gwendolyn, had to be hacked. Society equipment that the registers show are in storage, gone without any indication where."

"This is bloody bullshit." The A.D. looks just as blown away as I am. "Wen—she's one of us!"

"What liaison?" I demand. When my father and the Librarian merely look at one another, I'm firmer in my request.

Eventually, my father says flatly, "Marianne Brandon."

What? "Marianne is a Janeite! She's from Georgian England where the biggest inventions in technology had to do with—shit, I don't know! Probably something to do with carriages!"

"We've been discreetly training Mrs. Brandon for years." He doesn't break eye contact. "She's been a field agent for some time now, and her technological know-how rivals, if not supersedes, that of Ms. Darling's."

My brother is just as startled as I. Even more so. Marianne has . . . Jesus. Where the hell does she hone this skill? It's not like the early 1800s in rural England had the Internet!

"I know this is a lot to take it—"

I don't let my father finish. "Is it your assumption that Peter Pan is a suspect in the Timeline attacks?"

"We don't know. This is the only video Marianne was able to recover. All the rest were successfully scrubbed, and all that's left is a series of timestamp jumps to indicate anything amiss. If our suspicions are right, there are a dozen such jumps. Who knows what could have happened during any of those time periods? Some lasted not more than sixty seconds. Some lasted upward of sixty minutes."

Victor finally looks up from Wendy. "No matter what she has or has not done is irrelevant right now. I need to get her upstairs and in the medical wing."

"You didn't tell me." My words ring in the small office. "You put me in charge of the Society while you were out, and *you never told me any of this.* What the hell?"

"I'll help," the A.D. is telling Victor.

"I'm supposed to be the great successor. You've groomed me to run this fucking place from day one. And you couldn't tell me any of this? You kept me in the dark about your suspicions?"

He opens his mouth to speak, but I cut him off.

"You sent Wendy with me earlier. To Pfeifer's. Why would you do that if you thought she was the mole?"

"We needed to see if there were any communiqués sent out indicating the change of location. There is fear that our whereabouts have been passed out ahead of time, enabling our foes to catch us off-guard. How else could Todd have found you in not one, but two different Timelines?"

I stare at the Librarian and wonder how she can just say something so flatly, so . . . I don't know. So clinically, when there is a woman we've known for years on the floor, having a seizure, and another upstairs, paralyzed.

Fuck it. Fuck them. I'm—I need to get out of here. My brother and the A.D. are already carrying Wen through the door, and I'm here, arguing with two people I always looked up to about how they've being keeping secrets from me.

The Librarian tries to block me as I leave. "We have yet to discuss the failed retrieval."

Is she kidding? "You try stealing something from a library that doesn't exist. Hell, maybe it's hidden," I snap. "I don't know. More power to you if you're able to do what I can't. Or—wait. Did you already know that that was going to happen to me today? Maybe you can tell me why the only thing in that damn house was this." I pull out the photo I'd found in Pfeifer's house and fling it on the table.

My father picks it up, surprise flickering in his bright eyes. "Finn, I know you are upset, but there is much to discuss. We—"

Now he wants to talk? "I'm going to help get Wendy upstairs. And then I'm going to interrogate Todd and figure out what the hell is wrong with Alice."

The Librarian gently touches my arm. "You may not like what you hear."

I let out a bark of laughter. "It wouldn't be the first thing today that's sucked, would it? This whole day has been filled with a bunch of shit I wish I'd never heard."

She actually looks hurt. Forget her, then.

"My mother is dead," I say in a low voice. "The woman I love is upstairs, paralyzed. My friend just had a seizure, right before our eyes. And the guy behind it—at least one of them—willingly let me capture him today."

They simply stare at me. But I'm right. Todd avoided the Society for months. He allowed himself to be cornered in a small room, and although he fought back, it was nothing like our previous struggle in the attic of Ex Libris.

I want to know why.

I'm out the door and running my security card through the scanner to get the hell out of the Museum when the Librarian calls out, "Some secrets are hidden for a reason, Finn."

Then maybe it's time to blow them open sky high.

WEE BEASTIE

ALICE

INN IS IN A state. Wendy has just been brought in and strapped (strapped!) down to one of the beds in the medical wing. The tiny area is now crowded with so many patients.

Marianne has rolled me into the room, considering she knew I wanted to be present during Todd's questioning, but the moment Finn sees her, she shrinks back in the face of his vehemence.

Her voice is steady when she speaks, though. "You know, don't you?"

"Not now, Marianne," he snaps.

"But—"

"He said *not now!*" Victor barks. He rounds on the kind woman who has been taking care of me since my arrival. "Honestly, though, he's right! How in the bloody hell could you keep this from us?"

Something is off with Victor. He's—he's manic, almost. And what has Marianne failed to admit?

She steps to the side of my wheelchair, so I can just see her out of the corner of my eye. "I would think—"

"Marianne, a word of advice." Mary says as she leans against the wall by the door, uncharacteristically serious. "Shut up right now."

And then, from Todd as he lays in his bed at the other end of the room, sung in a high-strung, warble-y voice:

"Second star to the right,
and then, 'till morning, straight on.
Bonfires alight,
we'll dance until dawn,
burning pages and worlds to ashes,
odes of wreckage, set to song."

Rosemary takes over, her voice, crystal clear and as beautiful as before, her eyes closed:

"Come, little children,
harken to true home,
lost no more,
forever scribed in wise tome.
Chaos is fleeting,
significance understood within poem.
Embrace the truths of eyes,
past the fires and gloam."

A good five seconds of stunned silence from the rest of us settles the room, but Finn breaks it. "Speaking of shutting someone up, sedate her."

"Gladly." Victor digs in a bag Finn has brought and extracts several vials and a pair of syringes.

A door opens behind me. Finn barely looks up from the vial he's picked up. "Don't get in my way."

"I wouldn't dream of it," Van Brunt says. Says!

Finn injects a hypodermic needle into the rubber end of the vial. "Mary, record the interrogation."

She's quick with her answer. "Naturally." Her phone is slipped out and turned on.

After rummaging around several drawers and cabinets, Victor

dumps a number of items onto a rolling silver cart. Rosemary screeches bloody murder as she watches him approach. Without prompting, Mary helps pin down the raving woman while the doctor sticks a needle into her arm.

Soon enough, her fight leaves her. Her eyes droop. The screeching ceases.

"Did your girlfriend tell you about this?" Finn holds up a syringe for Todd's viewing. Victor has already moved to his bed and is now in the process of holding Todd down for Finn. But the villainous barber doesn't struggle against the doctor one bit. He calmly lies there, as if nothing was amiss with this picture.

"You mean your little truth potion?" Todd's blackened teeth flash. "I know lots about it." And yet, he doesn't seem bothered by this, either. "Which little world did you find it in?"

Mary wanders back over to where I am. "Too bad we don't have popcorn." And then, leaning down so I can see her smirk, "Although, popcorn might be dangerous for you, seeing as you can't really chew."

Oh, ha ha.

Finn doesn't answer any of Todd's questions. He merely plunges the needle into Todd's chest, right into his heart. The villain gasps; his body spasms up into an arc. As if she knows I need a better view, Mary pushes the wheelchair I'm confined within closer to where he's now convulsing.

It's a pretty, pretty sight.

"How much dosage did you administer?" Mary inquires as the fiend's eyes turn white.

My partner merely shrugs.

"I'm just kidding. I really don't give a flying fig. Overdose away."

It doesn't take much time before Todd's body slumps back down upon the mattress. Spittle decorates his mustache, and he appears as if he'd just run a thousand kilometers and wasn't given any chance for rest. But his glazed eyes are open, wearily so.

Finn stands next to the bed, arms crossed. "Tell me your name."

"Sweeney Todd," the man slurs.

"Tell me your real name. The one you had at birth."

"'S my name." Dulled laughter burbles out of him, adding to the froth already decorating his whiskers. "Sweeney Patrick Todd."

"Bullshit." It's Victor. His voice is unnaturally loud in the room. "Sweeney Todd was hanged."

Glazed, dark eyes swing toward the doctor. In the same warbling, off-key voice from before, he singsongs nonsensical words about shaving, pies, and gallows. And try as they might, no line of questioning leads Todd to reveal any other answer than this one.

His name, as he knows it, is truly Sweeney Todd.

"What specifically did you do to Alice to make it so she can't speak or move on her own? Drugs? Injections?"

I'm surprised that Finn has switched to this so quickly. He has an excellent opportunity to grill this brute on his heinous actions, and instead, he's asking about me.

There's no hesitation. "Gave 'er a nice injection, I did. A nice li'l concoction that made 'er fall asleep." Slurred as it is, his Cockney accent, which I'd previously assumed was fake, fully emerges. Back in Ex Libris' attic, his accent sounded almost American. But now? Now I can see it was the other way around. "And then I took 'er back to the room an' had a nice little time, cuttin' her soft, soft skin an' puttin' the wee beastie 'n her. Tiny little bugger it 'twas. Pretty, too." He chortles quietly when his eyes find mine.

Revulsion comes at the thought of something—a beastie?—harboring within me. Hadn't the doctor mentioned a parasite? Is that it? Did Todd infect me with a parasite? Desperately pushing that terrifying thought aside for the moment, lest I go insane with all the *what ifs,* fury flames to life. And it does so in Finn, too, although I must admit I'm impressed he does not unleash his balled fists to beat the stars out of Todd once more. Instead, he asks about the specifics of the injection.

"Now," Todd says amiably, "that I don' know. I was given the supplies an' told to be careful, as there was no more beasties and drugs to be had."

"Who gave them to you?"

Todd looks up at Finn, his glazed eyes bright in the harsh lights shining down upon them. "The lady. She was the one to give 'em to me, an' she was the one to tell me how to use 'em right."

It's not hard to see that what little of Finn's patience he still has is rapidly wavering. And yet, Todd is giving details—lots of details, and without prompting.

He *wants* us to know these things.

"What lady?"

"Well, you see, she never tol' me 'er name. But she was a lady, all right. Held 'erself like she was the Queen of England, she did."

"What did this lady look like? Do you know her name?"

"She din' see fit to me 'er name, nor did I ask. Not my concern, see? She was tall for a lady, with all this dark hair piled up high on top of 'er head, like a tower. An' every time I ever saw 'er, she was wearin' red and black. Said she an' Alice 'ere go way back." Gleaming eyes fall upon me. "Said this was a little present, just for you. To remin' you of your place. To finish what she started long ago."

Had somebody tossed a bucket of ice water upon me, I couldn't be more surprised.

"Alice?" It's Finn. He's squatting down in front of my chair, his hands curling around my maddeningly limp ones. "Do you know who he's talking about?"

Of course I bloody know whom Todd's talking about.

Finn stares at me for a long moment after my singular yet assuredly angry blink before saying, "Is this someone from New York?"

I'm annoyed with his daftness until I realize he is being careful with his answers. Knowing Finn Van Brunt as I do, he will be out the door with a gun in his hand the moment he knows a name. It warms yet frustrates and terrifies me all at once, because I am the one who needs to be out the door, hunting down the Queen of Hearts.

Still, I force myself to take a breath. Issue two clear blinks.

"Your Timeline?"

One blink.

"England?"

Two blinks.

"Wonderland?"

One blink.

A loud snore originates from Todd's direction, yet everyone else is silent as they watch me communicate via ridiculous eye movements.

"Do you know what kind of drug he gave you?" Finn finally asks.

Two blinks—and then . . . and then his eyes widen, too.

"Do you think—"

One very firm blink.

"SleepMist," he murmurs.

Another very firm blink.

"It was a spray, though." He looks up. "Mary, go check your stock of SleepMist, please."

She doesn't have to be asked twice.

"Do you know what he means by the beastie?"

Two very frustrated blinks. Hearts has used a number of horrid drugs to torture people, but I have yet to hear about any parasitic kind.

For a moment, Finn says nothing. He doesn't even move. But then he takes a deep breath and squeezes my hands. "Victor? Can we try the new medicine on Alice?"

Medicine? What new medicine?

Victor digs a small canister out of one of the bags on a nearby counter. "I don't know if this will work. Your injuries . . . Brom's . . . They were different from hers."

Finn stands up, but does not leave my side. "Try anyway."

The Society's resident doctor comes over, the bottle in hand. "I haven't read her chart yet." To Todd, he barks, "Where did you inject this beastie?"

The villain's eyes barely creak open. Burbles, "Spine. Pretty, pretty spine."

Mary returns. "All of my samples of SleepMist are still accounted for."

She and Finn haul me out of the chair. I'm forced to go down the path of indignancy once more when my bum, albeit clad this time, is visible to all.

Something cold is sprayed on my back. I am settled back into the chair. Tension coats the air. Everyone in the room watches me as if I'm the most fascinating thing in the world.

A minute ticks slowly by. Finn asks, a ghost of hope in his voice, "Can you move anything?"

I try ever so hard, but alas, I am still merely a lump of frustration and rage in a chair.

He squats back down next to me, once more claiming my hands. "I'm sorry," his brother whispers. And then, to me, "I'm sorry."

Finn presses his forehead against our joined hands, and for a good half minute, nobody in the room speaks. Not even Todd, who is awake and watching us with great interest.

Finally, Finn lifts his head. "I love you."

The determination in his eyes leaves me breathless. No. *No.* He cannot think—

"I'm going to fix this," he continues.

A flurry of blinks is unleashed. And yet, he ignores my protestations, because he bends down and kisses me gently. Then he stands up, and no matter how many times I blink, he refuses to acknowledge my pleas.

He cannot think of taking on the Queen of Hearts. Not by himself.

"Brom," he says quietly, "I haven't yet had the chance to fill Alice in on everything that's happened. She deserves to know, even though none of it makes sense. She stays for the interrogation as long as she wants."

I cannot see his father's face to see if he agrees to this or not.

"Victor, I want you to interrogate this bastard and then, when the drugs wear out, question him again. Question them all. I'm tired of all the secrets. And take care of Wen. Then go take your protocol."

Victor does a little mock salute.

"Mary, don't let Alice out of your sight, okay? And . . . be nice to Marianne."

"We'll have girl time." Mary pats the top of my head, and it's a good thing I'm paralyzed, because I just might cringe. Oh, frabjous. *More girl time.*

"And you." He turns to Todd. "I'll be back for you. We've got a score to settle."

I'm blinking furiously. His smile is sad. He gifts me one more kiss, whispers in my ear that he loves me, and then he's gone, out the door, leaving behind a drooling pseudo-barber and a roomful of people who haven't the slightest clue what to say to me.

LITERAL CREATURES

FINN

WASTE NO TIME. I head directly to my apartment. I grab my pen, the Institute book, and a miniature-combined edition of *Alice's Adventures in Wonderland* and *Through the Looking Glass* that I've had in the drawer of my nightstand for nearly three years. I strap on a holster and then shrug into a warm coat. I put on steel-toed boots. I load my gun and screw on the silencer. I grab two extra clips. I select a switchblade Katrina gifted me for my eighteenth birthday and stuff it into one of my inside pockets. I grab a handful of energy bars and a bottle of water, filling my outer pockets until they bulge.

And then I write myself into Alice's story.

Wales is bleak this time of year, and cold as hell. It's nearly nightfall, and winds whip across the bluff I'm on. But I remember how to get to the rabbit hole, and I pray those guarding it remember me.

A fat spider dangles from a web atop the hole. I clear my throat, feeling more than a little stupid addressing an arachnid, but at this point, I'll do anything. I've failed so many people in my life. I've lost even more. I cannot fail nor lose Alice. "I come on behalf of the Queen of Diamonds."

It doesn't even move.

I elaborate my request. "I was here with the Queen several months ago and it is imperative I make my way into Wonderland so I might obtain her help."

The web twitches, as if I've finally got its attention.

"I regret to inform you that the Queen of Diamonds has been poisoned. I—"

"Poisoned!" The spider sounds pissed. "Who dared to poison our glorious and magnificent Queen?"

"I have my theories," I assure it, "but I can do nothing if I am here and Wonderland is beyond this hole. I ask of you to please grant me passage, so that I might find something of assistance for Her Majesty."

The spider springs from the web and lands directly on my face. It takes all of my will power and courage not to squash it and let loose some ungodly, unmanly scream. These spiders, if I remember correctly, are poisonous, and there is no anti-venom that will counteract their effects.

It creeps up my face, into my hair. I am statue still as it examines one ear to the other. And then it runs down my face, its tiny legs tickling the whiskers I haven't had time to shave off recently before stopping next to my mouth. Something light brushes my bottom lip. "You smell of the Queen."

I hope that's a good thing.

"What is your name?" I tell it, and it adds, "We know this name. You may pass, but you will be required to have one of our Guards accompany you, in case your words are lies. If they are, your death will be painful and slow."

I heave out a sigh of relief. "That's fine. You're more than welcome to come with."

"Oh, no," it says, springing back onto the web. "I am the Guardian. I do not leave." It plucks its web, and ringing peels sound. "You will have a different Guard. May you have success in your quest, Sir Finn."

Sir Finn?

I incline my head and then duck into the hole. I won't lie—it's a bit terrifying to launch oneself into a hole filled with who-the-hell-knows how many poisonous spiders, just waiting to attack, but I remind myself that Alice is waiting back at the Institute.

I can't fail her. I won't.

I throw myself down the rabbit hole.

Spiders scuttle up and down the walls, plucking thick, white webs lining their paths. Murmurings I cannot distinguish trail my descent, and when I hit the ground, grow louder. The walls drip arachnids; they dangle perilously close to the top of my head from above. Glinting black bodies encroach on my space in a thick circle—so wide that, even if jumped, I could not get past their battlements. A small path parts before me, and a spider the size of my handle trundles forward. I stay perfectly still as it crawls up my boot, up my leg, and partially up my chest. It has fangs—large ones, too.

This is no *Charlotte's Web.*

"I am Grymsdyke."

Jesus. Its voice alone is the stuff of nightmares. "I am Finn Van Brunt."

"You ally yourself with the Queen of Diamonds." It's not a question, though.

"I do."

"You claim she has been poisoned."

"She has. We don't know what it wrong with her, other than the poisons came from Wonderland. I am here to find her help."

The spiders break into quiet murmurings.

Grymsdyke's legs dig into my chest. "Where is the Queen now?"

"Back at our home. She is paralyzed and cannot move. I must hurry on this quest if I am to save her."

The spider scuttles across my chest and onto my shoulder. One of its legs paws at my face; the course hairs brushing against my skin feel like flames.

Fantastic. Fangs *and* leg hairs that cause irritation. This arachnid is a winner.

"I will accompany you." It lets out a weird grunting combined with a trill, and the spiders part before us.

Grymsdyke settles on my shoulder, just below the collar of my pea coat. Thankfully, it keeps its hairy legs away from my face. As we make our way into Nobbytown, it makes a weird coughing sound. "Your dress is strange."

I let out a quiet laugh. Even in the dark, I can see my breath, it's so brisk.

Neither of us speaks as I weave through the teetering buildings toward The Land That Time Forgot. By the time we arrive, my teeth are chattering. Exhaustion threatens to pull me under. And still, I knock, because there are many miles yet to go.

A small slat in the door, positioned somewhere in my kneecap region, slides open. "Password?"

Shit, I have no idea. I didn't actually pay much attention to what Alice said last time. "I need to see the Hatter."

The slat shuts with a thunk.

I take in the knotted wood before us. "How thick do you think these doors are?"

"As thick as most," Grymsdyke says, "and not a bit thicker."

Gee, thanks. I smooth my hands across and around the door, testing it. Beyond the wood, the thump of loud music beats. I'm close to knocking again when—there. I find what I need: a thin hairline crack.

I nudge my shoulder up a bit. "You better hold on."

It makes that weird coughing sound again. "You mistake me for one who has hands."

Spiders, apparently, have very little sense of humor.

I kick the door as hard as I can, against the hairline crack, and then kick it once more with equal pressure. It splinters, collapsing inward and past a startled rabbit in a purple waistcoat and a knit hat.

"That's my password," I tell it. "Now, which way to the Hatter?"

It rubs its paws together, trembling. "Sir—good sir, our illustrious, benevolent—"

"Cut the bullshit. I need to see him, and I'm not down with waiting." And then, because I figure what the hell, "I've got myself a nice venomous spider here who would be happy to persuade you."

The rabbit's pink eyes shift to my shoulder. Grymsdyke crawls a bit forward, so that his front legs dangle in just a way he looks like he's ready to leap. Its fangs are bared and a chilling hissing comes from, well, I'd say lips, but do spiders have lips?

The rabbit juts a trembling paw toward the left.

Left I go.

The club isn't as full as it was the last time I was here, not even by half. But the music is loud, the smell of sweet smoke is strong in the air, and the people writhing on the dance floor seem deliriously happy to be present.

We weave past a pair of couples fully getting it on (albeit separately), right there in the middle of the dance floor. And suddenly I'm remembering the time not so long ago, when Alice and I danced and then made love in the middle of a ballroom floor.

I will do anything, everything to make sure she can dance again.

"Do spiders party?"

"Of course." Grymsdyke sounds offended. "We have grand parties before the hive mothers eat their concubines. It is a splendid celebration for all."

Lesson learned: stop making small talk with the spider.

Luckily for me, though, I don't have to hunt down the Hatter this time. He's in plain view, sprawled across an ornate throne at the head of the room. Stark naked, his body striped in blue and mustard-colored paint, as he puffs away on a monstrously large hookah. A man wearing a donkey's mask sits at his feet, jerking him off.

Well, I guess this is better than crashing an orgy, right? I climb up the dais, my boots stomping against the delicate, webbed tiles. "We need to talk, Hatter."

He cracks open a glazed eye. "Aren't you a pretty thing. Let us not talk, pretty thing. Let us fuck instead."

I mutter, "I seriously don't have time for this." The donkey man is shoved to the side; I've got the Hatter by his throat. Several people nearby gasp. "Let me say it one more time, more clear. We need to talk, Hatter."

He smiles languidly, as if I'm not this close to choking him out. "Ah! You want to play games!"

"Let me bite him." Grymsdyke taps my shoulder. "He reeks of too much smoke and juice."

The Hatter reaches forward, past my arm. "An adorable pet!" But the moment he touches the spider, he yelps, recoiling into his throne.

"Bad pookie!"

Grymsdyke springs off my shoulder and onto the Hatter's bare chest. The man squeals but does as the spider says when it tells him to shut up.

Not caring that half of the eyes in the room are trained on us, I shove the Hatter back into his seat. I've got my switchblade out, angling toward a part I'm positive he doesn't want to lose. "Do you remember me?"

The Hatter squints past Grymsdyke. "Now that you ask, good sir, you do look a bit familiar. Have we had some fun before?"

The spider slashes out a leg, striking the Hatter on the face. "This is Sir Finn, and he is one who protects the Queen of Diamonds."

Clarity fights its way into the Hatter's glazed eyes. "Yes, yes. You belong to Her Majesty! I remember now. Most assuredly." He looks me up and down. "You are just as delicious as I remember."

And . . . he's at full staff again. Fantastic. What is it going to take to focus this guy? "I need to know where the White King is."

"His Majesty?" The Hatter titters. "Fighting, of course. The war is going badly, all around. Wonderland is in dark times, Sir Finn. Very dark times. The light has abandoned us."

How Alice dealt with this knucklehead for as long as she did is beyond me. "Do you know where the King is right now?"

"Is it teatime? If it is teatime, he is taking tea. He prefers my special blend, just as Her Majesty does. Or he could be on the battlefield. His Majesty is a most busy sire."

Grymsdyke slashes him across the face again, clearly just as frustrated as I. "How much juice have you had?"

"All of it." The Hatter leers. "Every last drop I could."

"What is this juice?" I ask the spider. "I get that he's stoned, but—"

"Oh no, Sir Finn. He has not had the beating punishment of rocks, although he most likely deserves it. He has consumed much juice, and it rots the insides out until all that's left *is* juice. It is a most destructive drink. I have seen a person or two in my time disintegrate right before my very eyes. But I will admit it is tasty, and makes ones like this have little cares except those of pleasure and fornication."

I rub at my forehead. Fatigue beats at every muscle within me. It's been—I don't even know how long it's been since I last slept. And I'm now supposed to somehow find the White King all by myself, in the middle of a war, because this fool is so drugged out he's going to some-day literally liquidate?

"I can take you to His Majesty."

My eyes fly back to the Hatter.

He stands up slowly, careful (as one can be, I guess, all juiced up) to not jostle Grymsdyke. "I will take you to him."

And then he salutes me with more than just his hand.

A quarter of an hour later, we're on horseback and headed out of Nobbytown. The Hatter is clothed, thank goodness, with hair already frosty in this frigid air from the ice water dunkings he suffered through to help sober up.

The ride is unbearable. The Hatter never stops talking. He tells us about, well, everything. His latest orgy. How the March Hare tried to dupe him with inferior thistlepoppy for his hookah, and that it left him more flaccid than rowdy (his words, not mine). How the Dormouse continues to be a bore. How he's on edge, because he hasn't had tea in the last hour. How he met a *sweet treat* whose mouth was (and here he laughed himself stupid) a *wonderland*.

"Please let me bite him," Grymsdyke quietly begs me.

We're attacked in the middle of the night. What appear to be four card soldiers, their uniforms ragged, bear down on us with pikes and swords. They are no pikemen, though, and their use of the devastating weapon is shoddy. I'm off my horse, my gun out, and I'm able to take two down in short time. Grymsdyke leaps off my shoulder and bites an-other; the soldier screams as large blisters form all over his body (which has now turned what appears to be purple). The fourth soldier manages to knock me off my feet. My gun skids just out of reach. We fight in the mud and grass, and soon, I'm able to reach his fallen sword.

His last breath, at the hands of both steel and a spider's fangs, is a gasp.

The Hatter peeks out of nearby bushes. "Is it done?"

Grymsdyke scuttles off of the still-dying soldier. "That one is a coward."

If I could high five a spider, I think I would right now. As I can't, I instead watch in fascinated horror as the blisters on his barely living first victim pop open. Each wet burst brings about a gurgle of a scream.

I bend down and put my arm out so Grymsdyke can climb up more easily. "Is this what you all can do?" I think of the spiders in Mary's lab. She somehow persuaded a pair to come back with her to the Institute after our last Wonderland visit, but I've never checked to see what she's discovered about their venom.

It resumes its perch on my shoulder. "This is what *I* can do." And then, upon reflection, "I am an assassin, and am good at my job."

No shit.

I'm reclaiming my gun and wiping it off on one of the dead soldier's tunics when the Hatter makes his way over to us. "War is bad," he whispers. All of his frivolity from earlier in the evening is gone. "It makes people do bad, bad things."

It's close to daybreak when white tents appear the distance. I kid you not, the Hatter is still talking. About an hour after the attack, he regained the wind in his sails. I don't think he's let a single minute go by without saying something ridiculous. I've tuned him out the best I can for my own sanity, though, and instead focused on trying to decipher all the shit that's gone down in the last day at the Institute: Todd, Pfeifer's hidden library, Wendy, Pan, Brom and the Librarian's secrets. My head hurts from it all. I refuse to waste time on anything to do with Sawyer, though. Grymsdyke, the coward, has burrowed himself inside my coat so he didn't have to listen any longer and is now snoring something fierce. I'm a bit jealous, actually.

When we are about two hundred yards away, the Hatter perks up. "Hally-ho!" His breath steams around him like smoke as he waves his hands in the air. "Gangan!"

Several card soldiers and knights pull away from the encampment and ride out to meet us. I recognize one of them right away. It's the Five of Diamonds, and thankfully, he recognizes me, too.

"Sir Finn." His pike tilts toward me.

Again with the Sir? "I need to see the White King immediately. Is he at camp?"

"His Majesty has just returned from a campaign to suss out the Red King's hunting parties. Allow me take you to him."

He stares at me as he waits for my response, and I can't help but stare back for a moment. The thing about Wonderlanders is that all their eyes are strange. Like this guy's. There's a sheen to them, a darkness that has nothing to do with pigment. Staring into them too long leaves me feeling as if I ought to keep one hand on my gun the whole time. Instead, I fall into step next to him. "How is the war going?"

Never much for talk anyway, all the Five of Diamonds will tell me is that war is good for the dead.

The camp is bleaker than the last time I was here—and then, it was pretty damn bleak. Soldiers are clearly weary and many frighteningly thin, showcasing multiple scars and/or wrappings. The smell of meat wafts off campfires, and men, women, and animals huddle around, clutching cups of warm tea. They watch us silently as we ride in, the slightest bit distrustful and overly curious all at once.

The Hatter falls asleep on his horse just moments before we reach the massive pavilion in the middle of the encampment. He twitches and smiles as he dreams—no doubt of happy orgies and better hookahs. I leave him behind with the card soldiers and follow the Five of Diamonds inside.

"His Majesty is in the strategy room," the pikeman says. "I will announce you."

The Five of Diamonds slips between the tent flaps, and I linger outside, wondering if I've done the right thing. I've taken a chance right now, a selfish one. The White King is in the middle of a war, and he's not only overseeing his own people's welfares, but those of Alice's, too.

I'll beg him if I have to.

The flap opens. Ferz Eponi, one of the King's advisors that resembles a less egg-like Humpty Dumpty, stands before me. "We did not think we would see you in our borders again, Sir Finn. Please, come in."

I'm getting the *Sir* bit even from him? "Thanks. I know this is probably a bad time—"

"All times are bad in war, lad. This time is just less bad than others."

Inside, I find a small gathering around a large table filled with miniature figurines. Ferz Eponi's twin, Ferz Epona is there, alongside the Nightrider, a stately unicorn that serves as the King's second-in-command. At the head of the table is the White King of Wonderland, looking even more tired than me, if that's even possible.

I go to bow, but he holds up a hand. "I would say it is good to see you, Sir Finn, but this is a surprise. Is the Queen of Diamonds with you?"

He's good. If I didn't know the depth of his emotions for Alice, I'd never have guessed them now. "No. But she's why I'm here. I need your help. *She* needs your help."

A large brown-and-black-striped cat slowly materializes on a chair nearby. Its yellow, unblinking eyes bore into me as it sniffs the air, tail twitching.

To the card soldiers at the tent flaps, the King says quietly, "Leave us." Once they're gone, his nearly colorless eyes flash. "Is Her Majesty in trouble?"

I lay it all out there for him to hear, from the attack to her paralysis, and then to the confession Todd gave about both a drug and a beastie. And then I describe the woman Todd marked as his supplier, and the already cold air in the tent drops another ten degrees.

The King shakes with rage. "She dares to attack the Queen of Diamonds?"

The cat's wide eyes narrow. "You are foolish if you ever thought she would not."

Alice's former lover throws an arm out, scattering the pieces on the table. And then the table is broken clean in half. None of his people move, though. The cat doesn't even twitch its tail. Which, come to think of it, is a bit stubby.

Of course. My exhaustion is leaving me dumb, isn't it? This has to be the infamous Cheshire-Cat.

I get the King's rage, though. Shit, I'm filled with it, too. But I need us to focus here. "Alice wasn't exactly able to tell me who we're talking about, so maybe you all can. Exactly who ordered this hit on her?"

They all turn to me, brows furrowed. The Cat's ears flatten as its stubby tail whips back and forth. "You said the Queen was paralyzed, not struck. Was she also beaten?"

"I will kill her," the White King snarls, and for the first time in our acquaintance, I can finally see the crazy in him, because he looks like he's about to go ballistic right here and now. His eyes have even changed color—no longer nearly colorless, they've now got a red sheen to them.

It's creepy as fuck, to be honest.

"No—not beaten. Look. I don't have a lot of time. First, if you know who did this, can you share with the class?"

Confusion reflects back at me. Who knew Wonderlanders were so fucking literal? It's my turn to break something. I smash my fist down against one of the larger intact pieces of the table. "TELL ME WHO DID THIS TO ALICE."

Nobody blinks at my vehemence. The Nightrider says, "Lad, from your description, the Queen's assailant could be no one other than the Queen of Hearts herself."

The Queen of Hearts . . . with Sweeney Todd? And there's Peter Pan floating around, stealing secrets . . . ? What the hell is going on? What—

Something touches my elbow. It's the King, and suddenly, there's a chair behind me, and I'm in it.

"When was the last time you slept?" His eyes are back to normal, thank God.

"I could ask you the same thing."

Bitter laughter curls out of him. "There is sleep when death comes to claim us. For now, let us fight through it together. What is it you need from me? How can I help the Queen in your New York City, while I am here in Wonderland? I will do anything. All you need is to ask."

"I think maybe the first drug Todd gave her was SleepMist, although he said he injected it in her. Is that a thing now?"

A brief discussion leads nowhere. According to their spies and experiences, SleepMist is still used with sprayers. It is rare, I'm told, for any drug to be injected in Wonderland. Drugs are consumed via food, drink, or smoke, which is why SleepMist is such a big deal. But then, it is argued, as it was the Queen of Hearts to develop such a weapon, who is to say she hasn't modified it into a concentrated liquid that could be injected?

Okay, fine. It may or may not be SleepMist. It's the *beastie* that has me really worried. "One of our doctors who specializes in extraterrestrial microorganisms—"

The Cat bounds off the chair and comes closer. "Extraterrestrial?"

"Alien," I correct, but he asks for clarification on that one, too.

"From space." I point upward. "People who live in space are extraterrestrials."

Everyone in the tent actually seems confused and potentially terrified of this possibility. Of all the crazy things in Wonderland, *this* is what freaks them out? Aliens?

I'm tired. I'm stressed. I'm going fucking crazy, because I lose it again. "Can we all just *focus?* What the hell is this beastie that our doctor thinks is a parasite? Todd admits to cutting open her lower back and sticking something in. Claimed it was pretty. Whatever it is, it's making it impossible for Alice to move and *I want to know what the fuck it is so I can get it out of her!"*

The Cat looks up at the White King, dawning filling its bright eyes. "If she is . . ." Its growl fills the tent. "Does she dare?"

The King runs his hands through his hair. He's pacing, muttering things I can't understand. Finally, "It has not been done for ages. The accords forbid it." And then, "If it is so—"

"We have not much time." Although the Cat stretches, it is clearly on edge. "Sir Finn, when did you say the Queen was attacked?"

"I don't know the exact time, but I'm going to say close to forty-eight hours now."

The King pushes his way out of the flaps, bellowing for the camp physicians. The look on his face scares the shit out of me, because he looks like it's been scared straight out of him.

He knows something I don't.

"What's in Alice?"

The Cat tilts its head. "A boojum."

All of the soldiers and advisors in the tent shudder and kiss their fingers.

"What is a boojum?"

"It is a type of snark. The nastiest."

My fists ball up. "What is a snark?"

"A beastie, of course."

I just cannot anymore. I'm close to violence. "Look! Do any of you know how to fix this? Because I'm wondering if this was a colossal waste of time!"

The Cat shakes itself until its hair puffs around it. "The Queen of Diamonds does not have much time. If we do not remove the boojum before it molts, she will surely die. Come, lad. Let us find the King. He is collecting what we require to purge the beastie from Her Majesty's body. It appears we will be visiting your New York City after all. What a turn of events this is." He faces the rest of the advisors. "You will hold our lines and our positions until His Majesty returns. Speak not a word of this to anyone."

They all bow to the Cat. As for me, I'm not sure I even have legs anymore. All I can think is that I have to get back to Alice and get that—that—whatever the hell it is out of her body before it's too late. "You can do it, though? Get this boojam—"

"Boojum," the Cat corrects.

"Fine. *Boojum.* But can you get it out?"

"I cannot," it says. "But you and His Majesty might be able to, Sir Finn."

"Everyone keeps calling me that. You know I'm not a knight, right?"

The oversized Cat leaps up into my arms. And then, amazingly, it shrinks down into a normal-sized cat. "You are the Queen's chosen consort. There has been some discussion about this, as it is an unprecedented occurrence. The general consensus holds your title to be Prince Finn, but . . ." It yawns a fishy-smelling yawn. "There wasn't time to have the heralds announce. You will have to suffer with Sir until then."

I don't even know what to say, let alone think of that.

The Cat grooms itself as I make our way through the camp. Grymsdyke crawls out of my coat and assumes his perch on my shoulder. Forget Wonderland. I've obviously edited into *The Story of Dr. Doolittle.*

MADNESS

ALICE

VICTOR RESUMES GRILLING TODD as soon as his brother departs, tweaking his questions for specific answers. Three doses of truth serum are administered, and by the start of the third, Todd is effectively drugged to the point he isn't able to evade concise answers as his comrades had. Victor, on the other hand, appears as if he can go for hours and hours. His eyes shine with a light I know all too well. A mad one that leaves me concerned.

"Whom do you work for?"

"Now," Todd slurs, "tha'll depen' on how you look at it. I work for who I am tol' to work for. For example, I worked for tha' angry lady who din't feel too kind t'ward li'l Miss Wonderland."

Victor knocks a rough hand against Todd's face, rousing his eyes open. "Rosemary and Jenkins claim they have never spoken to anyone else. Rosemary got her orders from you; Jenkins got his from email and courier. How did you get your orders?"

Todd's nose bunches up, as if he, even as drugged upon truth serum as he is, cannot quite remember. "I jus' knew sometimes. Woke up knowin' about where to go an' what to get. Sometimes I got meself a nice book or a piece o' newsprint, o' a pretty package . . . But there was the calls." His eyes, glazed now to the point his pupils were wide and eclipsed the irises, shine.

Upon his capture, Todd had no phone on him. No search of Ex Libris recovered one, either.

"Who called you? Did you know a name?"

"Name?" Todd's confusion grows. "Wha' is a name? There was names. Plenty o' 'em. Kop—Koppen—Koppenberg? Koppelberg? Somethin' like that. It changed, see. And 'e liked Buntin,' although I only 'eard tha' once o' twice. Got right mad at me for rememmering." The fiend lazily taps his forehead, but mistakingly pokes himself in the eye. Ha! "I remmemmer, though. I remmemmer 'is voice. Sweet as an angel's, it 'twas, and sometimes a devil, too."

"Did you meet this Koppenberg? Koppelberg? Bunting? In person, I mean?"

I think if he had the strength of mind to do so, Todd might very well roll his eyes. "You don' meet your maker, do ya? 'E speaks to you with signs and messages."

Victor grills him on Rosemary. On Jenkins. On all their relationships. On my attack again, and who ordered it. On why his accent changes (to which I am grateful, considering I wondered myself)—he is, according to Todd, a "man of many tongues and worlds." Victor queries how Todd knew Finn and I were in 1876/96TWA-TS, or even 1814AUS-MP earlier in the year.

A flying man bearing secrets told him, the pseudo-barber claims.

"Who is the flying man? What's his name?"

"'E don' see fit to tell me that. 'E's a creepy thing, though. I cut him once, to see if 'e bleeds red. We 'ave an understandin' between us, though."

Victor keeps at it for hours. Some questions are asked repeatedly, reworded each time to attempt a different, more concise response. And yet, the more serum Todd has, and despite the better his answers, he's now slurring his words together so strongly it has become difficult to discern proper meanings.

Just when my own eyelids are drooping, and I've begun fantasizing about all the ways I ~~will~~ may Todd pay for what he's done to me, Van Brunt pulls his son aside. Calls Mary over, asking her to go prepare something. Victor argues, eventually turning belligerent, but in the end, he departs with Mary. In his place, the father sits on a stool by the barber's bed. He holds out a photograph for Todd to view. "Do you know where Finn found this?"

It takes a good twenty-seconds of squinting before Todd's eyes light up. "Rose, they 'ave one o' your pretty photographs."

Rose does not answer him, having been sedated several times herself in the last several hours. Victor had no mercy for her, and it's questionable as to whether or not she's actually still breathing. As for me, I cannot obtain a decent look at the photograph. Van Brunt has it angled just right so that all I get is a glare of gloss.

Eventually, the Society's leader tucks it back into his pocket. "Do you know anything about Bücherei?"

Wait—Bücherei? Is he talking about Gabriel Lygari's home Finn and I went to awhile back?

Todd's head lolls back and forth. "What's Boosh—Boosher . . ." He snorts. "I don' know any Boosh."

"Do you know why the library was hidden from my team?"

Todd's giggles are closer to gurgles, but he has nothing to share concerning any hidden libraries. What does Van Brunt mean, the library was hidden? The one at Bücherei? How does a library *hide?*

The next few minutes are spent on the flying man and whether his name was perhaps Peter Pan. And if so, did he, Todd, ever work with Wendy?

This only leads to more giggles but no concrete confirmations.

Pan . . . That is the name of the boy who kidnaps members of Wendy's family, is it not? And—what does Van Brunt mean, did Todd conspire with Wendy?

Argh. Son of a jabberwocky, it is highly inconvenient not being able to speak.

Now awake, the green-haired beauty in question has laid strapped to her bed, quiet for hours. She has not argued, she has not questioned as to why she's restrained. She has simply lain there, listening like the rest of us. I do not like the way her eyes look, though. They're dull, almost as if a spark has been extinguished within her.

Eventually, the villain ceases responding. His eyes remain propped half open, as does his mouth. Drool spills out, and it's an unpleasant sight if there ever was one.

"Show's over," Mary says. She's returned, Victorless. "Alice is nearly asleep here."

While it's the truth, I also am desperate for answers that Todd cannot give us. For example, Finn has been gone for what I believe is over a full day. Nobody has bothered to inform me of his whereabouts, and as I am unable to ask myself, I am left moodily stewing in resentment and curiosity as Mary pushes me out of the main room and back into my smaller one. One would think they would offer me such information, yet none apparently think I have a right to know.

He said he was going to fix this. And then he left to destinations unknown.

The thought of him going up against the Queen of Hearts is terrifying. It's not that I don't believe in his talent with weaponry or his ability in a fight, it's just . . . If Hearts was to know what he means to me, she would do everything in her power to tear him apart in the most vicious of ways in her quest to send me a message.

Of course, she already has sent me several, hasn't she? The Caterpillar, the drugs . . . Still. The image of Hearts with her giant battle-axe, hacking away at Finn, is more than I can bear.

Marianne slips into the room, ensuring the door is closed firmly behind her.

"Want to share why Finn and Victor were furious with you?"

For the love of God, please do not let these two ladies go at it again. They've been politely yet insidiously snipping at one another for weeks now.

The woman who has played nursemaid to me comes over and helps Mary get me into the bed. "I am assuming they have been informed of the full extent of my role here at the Institute."

Mary pulls up the blankets and tucks them around me. A nearby cup filled with vile, thick, so-called nutritious liquid is readied for me to sip via a straw. I may not be able to move much, but at least I can swallow.

She asks Marianne, "Which is?"

"I was contracted to come in and search all of the Society's security systems, databases, and record logs for discrepancies."

This surprises both Mary and me. Mary asks, her voice decidedly less hostile than of late, "Isn't that kind of technology beyond a woman from a Janeite Timeline?"

I turn my head away from the cup and straw. I have no appetite of late.

Marianne sighs quietly. "When my husband, the Colonel, was still alive, we discussed our desire to participate more in the Society. He, being of military background, found a sense of genteel duty in it. I found it an exciting prospect, as it would give me purpose. I was a bit lost then. Our second baby had died, and I feared I would never hold one in my arms that could breathe. Brandon contacted Brom, and we discussed several roles I might find fulfilling here at the Institute." Her smile is bittersweet. "During a visit, I became enamored with the technology associated with the Twenty-First Century. It felt . . . magical, in a way. I saw it as one might see music—there were patterns and rhythms to be decoded, and lines to be played. And then, when Brandon died . . ." She reaches down and tucks the blankets around my legs. "I could not stand to be at home any longer, rattling alone in that great big house all by myself. My sister and her family were nearby, as was my mother and younger sister, but I needed something of my own. I dug out Brandon's equipment he used to communicate with the Society and contacted Brom. I spoke of my wishes, and he was pleasant enough to accommodate me. I was sent to several various Timelines to hone my skills, and have spent the better part of three years now living anywhere that is not home."

For a moment, nothing is said. Mary simply stares at Marianne. And then, miraculously, she reaches across my bed and lays a hand on Marianne's arm. "You go, girl."

Marianne's relief is noticeable. "Several weeks ago, the Librarian contacted me and inquired if I could come in and surreptitiously have a look around to determine if anything was amiss. She revealed nothing other than the Society was having difficulties finding the culprit or culprits behind the Timeline deletions. Conveniently, at the same time, the Janeites were in a state over not standing on the sidelines with Society matters. I volunteered to come and do both. Only, the Librarian urged me to remain quiet about my secondary mission, even from Finn. I loathed keeping him in the dark, but I did as asked. Victor was equally unaware."

"Men." Mary rolls her eyes. "Their feelings get hurt over the stupidest things."

A sharp pain in my lower back erupts. Could I arch off the bed, I would, but as it is, I simply release a keening cry that's impossible to contain. Blinding pain tears through me, unlike anything I have ever felt before. Colors swirl my vision until I am consumed; ringing fills my ears. Breathing turns laborious.

Pain saturates every inch of my body.

I think—I think people are in the room. Hands might be upon me. I fear I'm crying or screaming or both. I cannot see, cannot do anything but sink into pain.

Madness is a funny thing. One can live with it for ages: embrace it, fall into it, lose their inhibitions with it. Priorities shift. Realities change. Understandings transition. Madness, in a lot of ways, is a comfort. Madness allows soft footing past harsh truths we yearn to flinch away from.

Since my surfacing from madness, I've embraced logic. I've craved reality. And in return, I was handed a new kind of existence that asked me to let go of everything I ever knew and accept my world, and that of others, is not what was thought. That life was, in fact, *more.* That the surface we walked upon was thin and the depth below vast.

And now, ironically, madness is here to claim me again. Pain, blistering, consuming pain, is its own form of madness. And it has come for me, at long last, from the hands of one of my greatest foes.

The Queen of Hearts has found her way to slay me, and I am no longer even in Wonderland for her victory to take place.

THE BOOJUM

FINN

GUESS THE GOOD thing about traveling with people who are technically insane is that they don't really question things. Alice was different once she settled into the Society and began to trust me. Alice asked about the mechanics of everything. How do pens work? How does editing work? Why these books? Where does the door come from? Where does it go when it disappears? What about catalysts? Why are certain things picked for catalysts and not others? Why does a Timeline disappear when a catalyst is destroyed? Do we have, in fact, proof that the people are gone?

She's asked me all of these things over the last year. I did my best to answer her based on what I know, but I kind of loved that she never seemed satisfied with just the bare bones. She always wants to know *more*.

But she is not with me right now. She's back at the Institute, and I am instead trudging across a windswept bluff in Wales with a Wonderlandian King, a talking cat and spider, and a lethal pikeman, none of whom is asking me any details other than how long it will take us to get back to this New York City I hail from. Our journey from the encampment back to the rabbit hole wasn't exactly filled with a lot of talk, either. Attacked twice, once by a squadron of Hearts soldiers three times our numbers, we've all pretty much hit our limits. Bloody, bruised, and a pair of us running on nothing more than fumes, it's a miracle we came through as we did.

"It seems," the Cat said after the last fight, licking blood off its paws, "you can't throw a stone and not hit a Heart nowadays."

Let us hope that is true, because I've got a bone to pick with a very specific Heart.

I write us directly into the medical wing. We have no time to lose, according to the Cat. And the moment we all step through and the door vanishes behind me, screaming reaches my ears.

It's Alice.

I'm immediately pushing myself into the small room she's been staying in off the wing, fighting past the people already crowded around her bed. She's screaming, her eyes rolled back so far all I can see are the whites. My brother looks up and says, "Thank God you're back! Alice started screaming about an hour ago, and now she's not even responding to any of us anymore. I have no idea what's happening. I was just about to call an ambulance."

The Cat jumps up on the bed. Its amber eyes impossibly widen even more. "Pray we are not too late. Clear this room."

I don't stop for the questions people are throwing out at me, the ones wondering about why in the hell there's an oversized, talking cat on the bed or why a spider has just climbed out of my coat. I say, clearly and firmly, "Everyone but Victor and the people I've just brought with me, get the hell out of here."

This pisses Mary off big time, but I don't care.

The Five of Diamonds stations himself at the door. Victor notices him and frowns. "What in the bloody hell did you go and get that wanker for?" But I ignore him, too.

"Help me turn her over," the White King says. He looks just as close as I am to losing his shit, listening to the woman we love scream like this. She's stiff as a board, every muscle in her body elongated and tightened to the fullest, and all I'm thinking as we're doing our best to carefully roll her over is: *I can't lose her.*

"You won't," the King says quietly. "I will not allow it."

Did I say it out loud?

"You there," the Cat says to Victor. "Fetch us a sharp knife, a bowl of water, some towels, bandages, and a jar with a lid. Be quick about it."

Thankfully, Victor doesn't give any crap to being ordered around by a cat. He's out the door, rummaging through cabinets and drawers.

The King spreads open the back of Alice's medical gown. He traces a long, pale finger down her equally pale back until he comes to a bulge at the base of her spine. It pulses gently, glowing silver.

The King looks up at his advisor, his pale eyes wide with terror.

"I don't not think it has fully molted," the Cat says. "Her Majesty is not yet showing signs of such. But we must be quick of it." It looks up and through the window; Victor is running water in the bowl. "Sire, do you have what is necessary?"

The King digs into a small bag he's brought along. "Yes."

"Then begin the poultice. It must be ready to go as soon as we pull the boojum out, and must not have cooled past inefficiency."

Victor comes back into the room with all the supplies loaded onto a rolling cart. "Shut the door," the King orders the pikeman standing guard. "Allow none in."

The pikeman steps outside and shuts the door behind him.

As he extracts the items from his bag, the King looks up at me. "Snarks are nasty beasties, but the worst of all the species are the boojums. Many ages ago, these beasties were used to torture and terrify my kind. Inserted into the spine, they paralyze their hosts until they molt. At that point, they snap the host's spine and then proceed to devour them as a first meal. In essence, they cause their victim to disappear. The boojum then grows to its host size and often will molt once more and assume the host's shape. They could not talk, though. They only could eat. And eat they did—villages were ravaged by these beasties, families torn apart. The only way to kill an adult boojum was to burn it alive. The Courts banded together and forbid their use. Anyone caught using one would be put to death. The beasties were eradicated as best as possible. We have not had a case of boojum infestation in hundreds of years. To think that Hearts tracked one down, cultivated it to the point it was viable . . ." He cracks open a small, bright-blue egg and dumps it into a silver-lined bowl. "It is unspeakable." His voice wavers. "The Queen must be in unconceivable pain right now."

The Cat is standing on Alice's back, hissing and swatting at the bulge. "You, physician." It flicks its stubby tail toward Victor. "Are you good with cutting?"

"Very," my brother says firmly. He's a bit calmer, thank God, but it's obvious he's still take aback by a talking cat who can't seem to decide what size it ought to be, or what transparency.

"Be prepared to slice above this mound at my command."

The King sprinkles gray powder into the egg mixture. "Your hand, Finn. Please present it to the Cheshire-Cat."

I do so, and it immediately slashes me so strong, blood drips down upon Alice's body. And then the Cat calmly licks the remnants off its paw like it's nothing more than spilt milk.

The King grabs my hand and squeezes more than a fair amount of blood into the bowl. "I do not know if our tulgey leaves are fresh enough," he murmurs to his advisor. "I fear they are not."

"Make them be, if you must."

Two velvety, dried leaves are crushed into the mixture. "Part of the problem with boojum infestations is that it took the blood of a monarch for the poultices," he tells me quietly. "Many monarchs were not willing to provide their life blood to save those who were of lesser means in these early stages." He holds his hand out for the Cat to slash him just as deeply as it had me. He doesn't even flinch or seem grossed out that his advisor is lapping up his stray blood, either. "As I said, boojums, once adult, must be burned. In its larvae stage, it can carefully be removed and a poultice applied to the site of its infection."

Alice's screams turn hoarse, muffled by her new position. Grymsdyke, sitting on the pillow next to her head coughs that weird cough of his. "I do not like the way her eyes look, Your Majesty. You must hurry."

The King adds a crushed flower to the mixture and then mashes it together with a pedestal stone. The Cat growls. "Now, Dr. Frankenstein. Make sure you do not cut the boojum's body. If its blood spills inside the Queen, all will be lost."

Victor does exactly as asked. A thin line is cut over the mass until a silvery, mottled body appears. Two tiny eyes shift our way and stare up at us. Incredibly, the little fucker hisses.

The King shoves the bowl into my hands. He leaps onto the bed, straddling Alice's legs as he bends down to face the beastie. In between two fingers is a thimble.

What the hell? He's going to fight that thing with a . . . a *thimble?!*

The boojum's scream matches Alice's in strength despite being no larger than two, three inches across. It scampers out of her back, recoiling at the sight of the thimble. The King shoves the jar that Victor brought in over its body. Once upright, he tosses the thimble inside and screws the lid on.

He climbs back off the bed. "Quickly, Finn. Spread the poultice upon her back. Make it thick, and if possible, spread it below the edges, across every spot you think the boojum could have touched or infected. Use your finger, the one the Cat cut."

I do exactly as he asks. In my cut, the poultice burns like a motherfucker. But I spread and spread some more, even digging my finger underneath the flap of skin until the entire area is one large, right mess. And then, miraculously, Alice stops screaming. Her body goes limp beneath my hands.

"Her eyes have closed, Sire," Grymsdyke reports. And I think it's the first time Victor has really taken notice of the enormous spider, because he takes a giant step away from the bed.

"You must sew her up now," the Cat tells me. "Make each stitch count." It nods its head toward the King. In his hands are a needle and golden thread.

I have no idea how to sew. None. But this is Alice, and if I had to lay my life down for her right now to live, I would.

I climb onto the bed and straddle her just as the King did, ensuring my weight does not bear down upon her legs. The King and Cat chant something in a language I cannot understand, but the tones they use leave the hairs on my arms standing on end. Slowly, slowly, I lace the needle in and out, in and out, making the ugliest set of stitches ever across her beautiful back. But, by the end, the hole is closed nice and tight.

"Now," the King says softly, "apply the rest of the poultice."

I glob it on until it forms a mound on her skin. From there I'm instructed on how to place the bandages over it, covering the entire area.

"We'll need to make more poultice, enough for several days' worth of treatments. Just in case."

I crawl off the bed. The King is holding the boojum up for me to see. It has either passed out or died of fright, its body pressed up against the side of the jar and as far away from the thimble as it could possibly get.

Its face looks almost like one of those cats with a smushed-in nose. Pretty, my ass. This is the stuff of nightmares. Ones apparently terrified of thimbles, though.

"What happens now?"

"Now," the Cheshire-Cat says, "we wait. If the treatment takes, Her Majesty will recover fully within a few hours. If not . . ."

I wait, but he does not finish. Instead, he licks the area around the bandaging on Alice's back.

I round the bed and sit next to Alice, my chair so close my knees bump up against the bed. A tiny snore wrinkles her nose, and for some dumbass reason, it makes me want to both laugh and cry. *She's snoring, just like normal.*

Victor touches my shoulder. "I'm going to go call Dad to tell him what's happened. Would you like me to take a look at those cuts you two got?"

I shake my head. It doesn't even hurt that much anymore. The White King does the same.

"Call me if you need me." And then, my brother lays it true. "You look like shite, Finn."

I let out a small laugh.

"I'm probably talking to a wall here, but get some rest. You'll be of no use to Alice when she wakes up if you're on the brink of passing out."

The Cat jumps off the bed and follows Victor out the door, vanishing as it passes the Five of Diamonds in the hallway.

I take hold of Alice's hand. It's warm, thank God. I want to kiss her so badly, even just right here on her forehead, but I hold myself back.

I look up at the White King of Wonderland. "Thank you for believing me and for coming."

He rounds the bed to the other side, choosing to sit down in Marianne's chair. Now that the excitement and immediacy has passed, I can see the fear he's been carrying with him. "Finn . . ." He leans back and stares up at the ceiling. "You must understand that my heart will always desire the Queen of Diamonds. Always."

"I know." My words are just as quiet as his.

"When we learned of the prophecy, it felt as if all of my dreams died." His head drops so his eyes can meet mine. "Rather—all of *our* dreams died. It is a painful thing, having to let go of dreams and loved ones that are so cherished."

I can only imagine.

"The shared path we traveled came to an abrupt end." A bittersweet smile tugs up one corner of his mouth. "Her direction leads this way," a hand angles to the left, "and mine this way." The other hand angles right. "You know this, though. Even still, I feel it is important to impart upon you that you must never hesitate if you need my assistance. I will always believe you, Finn, because *Alice* believes in you."

All I can do is thank him again.

"Now, there is one more thing we must do before I insist upon you resting. Give me several minutes to arrange it. Grymsdyke, perhaps you could accompany me out the door, so that Sir Finn may have a moment alone with the Queen?"

The spider scuttles off the pillow. The King holds out an arm, and it makes its way to his shoulder.

When the door closes behind them, I can't help myself. I'm fucking exhausted. It's been two—three?—straight days of hell and insanity.

I cry.

Okay, not cry. Because, hell no. But my eyes definitely blur when I lean my forehead down against her cheek. "You're going to be okay." I press that kiss I wanted to give her earlier against her exposed cheek and then her lips. "Everything is going to be okay now."

The corners of her mouth tilt upward—just a little, but enough that it feels like somebody just punched a hole into my chest. And then her fingers curl around mine as a soft sigh of contentment is breathed out.

The door opens. I'm surprised to find Mary there. "I'm going to sit with Alice, okay? You're needed in the lab for a few minutes."

"I'm not leaving."

"Don't be a baby. Besides, His Royal Hotness has requested you."

When I brush past her, she says, "You look like shit."

"So people keep saying." I turn to the Five of Diamonds, still stationed at the entrance. "Don't leave this spot."

Grymsdyke pops its head out from the pikeman's shoulder. "I will go inside and guard the Queen, Sir Finn."

"Don't bite Mary," I warn it. "Not even if she tries to persuade you to live here forever."

"She does not have to convince me. The Cheshire-Cat and I have discussed this already. The Queen will see reason when I inform her of my decision to remain as her personal guard."

Well, then.

Down the hall, in Mary's lab, I find my brother taking blood samples from the White King. He doesn't look up when I come in. "Have a seat. I'll get your IV port ready in a minute."

"What the hell for?"

Victor pulls the last needle out of the King. "It is for a small bit of Wonderlandian blood magic. That is all."

That is all?

"The Queen is a monarch in her own right," the King says to me, "but it wasn't until her last visit did I come to realize she is not . . . protected, for lack of a better word, against some of the Wonderlandian ailments the way a native might be."

"I thought monarchs weren't dynastic. That they could be anyone from anywhere, as long as Wonderland chooses them."

The King smiles wryly at my observation. "While this is true, from what I can tell, she is still our first and only non-native monarch. She is susceptible to our land in ways that I am not, just as you are. Do not think I had not noticed how you munched on your native foods during our travels."

To be fair, I'd offered him an energy bar, only to have him tell me it tasted like the worst kind of *frumious* he'd ever put in his mouth.

Whatever that meant.

"So you think that by, what? Injecting your blood into our bloodstreams, we'll be less susceptible?"

The King lets out a voiced breath of relief. "Exactly. This is the best protection for the two of you we have come up with. Now that I am here,

I cannot let the chance go by, especially as Alice will want her revenge against Hearts."

I'm shocked, to be honest. Not that he would want to protect Alice from any future trips to Wonderland, but that he'd think to include me. *Especially* me.

"I cannot know for sure that this will work." He picks at the cotton ball and tape Victor places over the puncture site. "It is my hope, though. The Cheshire seems to think it will. I have provided your brother several vials for the both of you, but they are to be staggered out over the course of the coming weeks. If, by any means, you do return, we will do another round there. Tonight, you can start with your first dose. Be rest assured that I am perfectly healthy right now and my blood is clean."

In minutes, Victor has an IV port in my arm. I watch as the White King's blood sluices through the tiny plastic tubing, wondering just what in the hell I'm going to say to any of this.

I can see why she loves him. His heart is just as big as hers.

"I will go and sit with her, if that is all right."

I look up at the King. He is . . . not asking. He's more telling. Gently, though.

"I hazard to guess that, if we were to compare our hours of lack of sleep, you might win. Dr. Frankenstein is right. You will be of no use to Alice if you have not first taken care of yourself. Rest for the next hour or so. It cannot hurt and chances are, Her Majesty will sleep throughout it all. I imagine boojum extractions are taxing to a body."

"I don't think—"

"Listen to him, Finn," Victor says. "Besides. You know she'll see you looking the right mess you are, and she'll order you back to bed herself. Get the rest in now. Don't forget we have the New York Public Library fundraiser gala tomorrow night."

I'd completely forgotten about all of that. "I'm not going." Is he nuts? A fundraiser? When Alice is recuperating, Todd is here in the Institute, there's the Queen of Hearts to track down, and we need to figure out if Peter Pan is infiltrating the Society?

"You're going to go," Victor says calmly, "just as I am. Just as the Van Brunts have gone every single year, because of Society ties. You, as the incumbent leader, will be required."

"I'm—"

"Going. Besides, don't you remember? Mary says Alice was looking forward to it."

"Alice," I point out angrily, "is in a bed down the hall, having just had some kind of weird-ass bug cut out of her back!"

He ignores my protestations. "Get the sleep. Two hours. What can it hurt?"

"But—"

"He's already gone, Finn."

I look toward the door. The White King is no longer standing there.

Victor also glances toward the door. "The King was saying all these weird things I couldn't understand when I was taking his blood." His voice lowers. "And that talking cat creeps me out. He appeared out of nowhere and asked if he could have a look inside me. What the hell does that even mean?" Before I can answer him, he adds, "And you brought that wanker back with you, too. Did you see the look the Five of Diamonds gave me? I wouldn't be surprised if we woke up and everyone was dead."

"You're being overly dramatic," I say tiredly. But he's totally right. The Five of Diamonds is a loose cannon if there ever was one.

"Tell you what. Mary's got a bed in back for the nights she's working overtime. Sleep in there. I'll be out here working, anyway. I swear, little brother, I'll wake you the first minute I hear she's even moved her head to the other side. Although, you may want to shower before going back in there, too. Bloody hell, Finn. You smell like hell."

And the compliments keep rolling in. "Did you try the healing spray?"

Victor unties the rubber band around my bicep. "What for?"

"You know what for."

He sighs. "No. I have no reason to think it'll work on me, Finn."

"Why not?"

"Because I don't have a cut or a broken bone."

"Victor—"

His smile is grim as he removes the port. "There's nothing physically wrong with me. I'm just crazy. Perhaps I ought to go back with them to Wonderland. I'd fit right in."

"You are *not* crazy. Stop saying that."

His chair rolls back. "Fine. I have a mental illness. Scratch that—I have two." He clears his throat. "Victor Frankenstein Van Brunt has," and here he gets that clinical sound crap voice that sounds far too close to our childhood shrink for my comfort—"moderate to severe bipolar disorder coupled with borderline schizophrenia, which, when put together, makes him a giant fucking mess." He mock salutes. "Thanks, bio-dad."

Victor has been on special protocols and medicines from various Timelines more advanced than ours for years to combat these disorders. Therapy has helped, too, but my brother's demons always seem to come home to roost. Successful, witty, intelligent, loyal, and loving, he cannot seem to get past these genetic markers. Fear grips him at the very thought of passing such disorders on to future children, so he continues to muck up his relationship with Mary on a regular basis, thinking somehow it will be better in the long run than her pain over a potentially so-called screwed-up kid.

Reasoning with him does nothing. We just stay on him about his protocols and keep hoping that someday, he realizes he is enough. He is not his illness.

I stand up and go over to my brother and hug the crap out of him. He doesn't even question me. He just hugs me back. And then I take his advice and go take that nap.

THE PRINCESS & THE UNICORN

ALICE

I DREAM OF STARS.

When I open my eyes, soft morning light filters through the window in the room. I'm . . . apparently on my stomach, despite never being one much for sleeping in such a position. My face is squished against a fluffy pillow and fuzzy blankets are pulled up to my shoulders.

Asleep next to me, in a chair, is Jace.

I blink several times, shifting on the bed. And—shifting! I can move! And move enough, because now I am aware of a horrid crick in my neck from the position I'm in. All my rustling about wakes the White King of Wonderland. He scoots his chair closer, and strokes a familiar hand through my hair.

"Hallo, Alice," he murmurs. "How do you feel?"

"Like bloody hell," I whisper. I can talk! Callou, callay!

"I can only imagine." His hand drifts away, back to his lap. "It should not last long, though."

"A few hours at the most," comes another voice—a dear one, one I feared I would never hear again.

"Cheshire!"

Soft padding across the mattress brings the King's advisor into sight. He appears fine, thank goodness. His coat is thick and shiny, his eyes bright, his tongue just as rough as always as it flicks against my hand. "Good morning, Your Majesty."

And then, if that was not enough, a large spider I have known for years, one whose loyalty has meant much to me, lowers himself from the ceiling. "It does my heart good to see you awake, Your Majesty."

I fear I am dreaming. So many loved ones, long thought left behind, are here with me? "May I have help sitting up? This is a dreadfully uncomfortable position."

Jace has me out of the bed and into the chair he's vacated. "Do not lean back to far," the Cheshire-Cat warns. "You do not want to undo all that has been done."

"And what has been done?"

Once I am settled, Jace brings a chair from the other side of the bed round so he may face me. "That is a story I may start, but another must finish. Would you like to hear it?"

"Most assuredly. But first, are you truly sitting here with me right now?"

His smile is bittersweet. "Indeed."

"Are we in Wonderland?"

"We have journeyed to New York City. And this is part of my tale. But let me start at the beginning and go to where I may stop, and from there, as I said, you must find completion elsewhere."

I curl my fingers around the chair's arms, delighting in how achy they feel. The Cheshire jumps into my lap, shrinking to the right size. He promptly begins to groom himself, purring.

How achingly, wonderfully familiar this all feels.

"I had just returned to camp from a campaign to root out the Red King's personal guard." The King leans forward in his chair, his arms pressed against his thighs. "In much of the confusion of the last few months, he has, as I am sure you will be unsurprised to hear, become much more aggressive in capturing land for himself. Complaints of stolen property were coming in at an alarming rate. The White Queen and I decided his greed must be culled."

The Red King, being possibly the most materialistic person I have ever met, would be unsatisfied if the entire world was his.

"We were successful. Most of his guard were either killed or captured in our campaign, and with his strongest out of the way, it is assumed he will have a much more difficult time carrying out his wishes. But, rest was not to be enjoyed, as the Red Queen recently captured Frippleton."

"I cannot believe it." Frippleton is a border town between the Hearts and Whites lands. The Reds dared to move that far into enemy territory?

He holds up a hand. "My advisors and I were discussing what must be done to launch a campaign to take it back when I was given word a most unexpected visitor had arrived." Then, more softly, "You see, it was your Finn Van Brunt."

Finn *had* gone to Wonderland, just as I feared. I glance around the room, but Finn is not here. How could I, for even a moment, forgotten to search for him? Where is he? Why is he not here, too?

"He was bloody and dirty and in the company of the Hatter and Grimsdyke. He risked moving through a highly dangerous area to get to me. The Hatter informed my soldiers they were attacked on the journey, yet Finn was able to successfully best them in combat."

"The Hatter is a coward," Grymsdyke says from his perch on the bed. "Sir Finn and I did all the work." And then, more gruffly, "He did most of the work. I fear I failed him in that regard."

Finn's life was put in danger. This is unacceptable.

"Nonetheless, your Finn came, Alice, because he was desperate to save you."

My hands shake as I stroke the Cheshire's soft fur. "Where—"

"Your Majesty, it was determined that you were infected with a boojum."

My eyes fly down the Cheshire, a sickening dread spreading in the pit of my belly. "What?!"

"From what Finn told us, we determined it could be nothing else than a boojum," Jace continues. During the next several minutes, they tell me of how supplies were gathered once the determination was made and of how they were under siege twice during their journey to the rabbit hole. He tells me of how Finn refused to give up on me and was the one to set my poultice.

The lingering painful resignation and yet acceptance in Jace's eyes over this cuts me to the bone. And still, I cannot marvel at how large this man's heart is. He stood back and allowed Finn to be the one to seal the magic.

Love is so terribly, devastatingly cruel and wondrous all at the same time.

"There is so much I want to say," I whisper. "But for now, I offer up my deepest gratitude that you dear, beloved souls came in my time of need."

The King places his fist over his heart and lowers his head. The Cat rubs his head against my hand, purring. Grymsdyke lowers himself into a bow.

My voice cracks. "I have missed you all so much, yet . . ."

"He is down the hallway, in a place called the Lab," the Cheshire says. "His Majesty and the doctor forced him to rest, though he protested. He is a stubborn one. He even berated us all when he didn't feel we were answering him as quickly as he wished. I rather like this about him. He would make an excellent Wonderlander."

I let out a choke of a laugh.

"Let me fetch him for you," Jace says, but I hold a trembling hand up.

"I will go there. It will do me good to stretch my legs after a few days of not being able to do so." And then, more quietly, "You will not leave yet?"

A ghost of a smile curves a mouth I know as well as I do my own. "Not yet. Soon, though. There is Frippleton to take care of."

The Cheshire jumps off me so the King may help me to my feet. So much of me yearns to pull him into my arms, to bury my nose in the crook of his neck.

I let his hand go instead.

The trio accompanies me down the empty hallway, afraid, I think, of me falling face first. But my legs, as weak as they may feel, are strong. My footsteps are sure and steady.

Inside the lab, I find Victor dozing whilst sitting on a stool. His face rests on arms crossed upon a table.

"We will go speak to Finn's father," the White King whispers closer to my ear. "There is much to discuss before our departure."

I nod. Jace and the Cat leave; Grymsdyke remains. He scuttles across the room, toward a door in the back. His coarse whisper beckons, "Here, Your Majesty."

Sure enough, upon a small bed crammed up against a wall, lays Finn. He's on his side, his hands curled into fists, and he's breathing deeply. He's also filthy—blood, mud, and sweat cake his skin, hair, and coat.

My heart aches, it is so full right now. *He did not give up on me.*

I crawl onto the bed next to him, shrugging one of his heavy arms around me. I then slip an arm beneath his coat to curve around his warm body. I press my forehead against his chest and breathe him in. I don't smell dirt or violence. All I smell is love.

Finn went to Wonderland on his own. He risked potential death from my spiders and then fought his way to reach my former lover. He begged help of someone other men whose hearts are not so large or wise would abhor and envy, and he brought the same man back to the Institute to aid in my healing.

He completed an ancient yet rare blood magic ritual to save me from a creature unseen and nearly forgotten in Wonderlandian history. Does he know that he did so? Is he aware of what his actions symbolize? His intent? Does he realize that one of the reasons boojums were so devastating was that it took not only royal blood for the infestation cure, but that from only the purest of true love?

Jace knew this, and yet he came anyway. He stood by and provided Finn the means to work this ancient magic even though he could have completed it all on his own.

The arm around me tightens, and a tiny sob I refuse to free chokes my throat. A kiss is pressed against the top of my head. The knot in my throat intensifies. I clutch at Finn's shirt, not wanting to ever let go. Each beat of my heart reminds me how much I love this man. Each beat of his, heard as I press my face against his warm chest, reminds me of how much he loves me.

I am so very, very lucky.

His voice is husky. Sleepy. "Are you in any pain?"

"No," I whisper in return. All I feel right now is love. Immense, incandescent, overwhelming true love.

"Obviously you can move?"

Because of him. Because of his love. "Yes."

"We're going to find her," he says, and this only further illuminates what I already know. *He knows my heart.*

I press a kiss against his dirty chest. "I know." *We* will, my partner and I. "And you? How do you fare?"

"I'm fine."

"I meant . . ." I trace a finger to hover over his heart. The events of St. Petersburg are not so far away.

I feel rather than see the shake of his head. He is not ready to talk about it. It is okay, though. I will be here when and if he does.

Gentle fingers tug through my messy hair as we lay together in silence. I am content here. The world around us grows more complex, more terrifying, yet here in this tiny room in Mary's lab, lying upon a bed with Finn, I am content.

And Finn thinks I know nothing about *once upon a time . . .*

Once upon a time, I planned of a life with a wonderful man. We had so many beautiful dreams together. When the prophecies tore us apart, I feared I would never love again. I did not want to, to be honest. How could I, when I'd already found true love?

"Would you like to hear a Wonderlandian fairy tale?" I ask Finn.

He kisses the top of my head again. "Yes."

"Once upon a time, in the mists of ages past, there were more Courts within the lands, more than just the Diamond, White, Red, and Hearts. There were also those of the Black and Spades. The Spades Court was magnificent and admired throughout the land. The King was fair, the Queen generous, and their people prospered. For many years, no babe was born to them, although it was their greatest wish. It wasn't until a trip to the Sage was made that their hopes would come to fruition. A sacrifice was offered to the land, and within a year, a princess' birth delighted all far and wide.

"The Princess was beloved by both her parents and those who lived under Spades banners. She grew up precocious and intelligent, charming even those Monarchs of the other Courts. Conveniently, the Black Court had a prince a few years older than the Spades Princess. He was

handsome and wise, and as the years passed and the two grew, they fell in love.

"This was not a problem for Wonderland, as there was no guarantee either the Spades Princess or the Black Prince would ever be chosen to rule after their parents' deaths. Chances were against them—it was, and still is, exceedingly rare for heirs to assume crowns. Even still, such children retain the right to their titles after birth and become part of the nobility of the land. So, when it was announced that the Spades Princess and the Black Prince wished to wed, there was much celebration rather than fear.

"Two days before the ceremony, the Black Prince disappeared. Nobody knew where he had gone or why. Contingencies from both Spades and Black Courts searched high and low for him. Two days after the wedding date, his body was found near a riverbank in Hearts land. The Prince's heart had been cut out of his chest and replaced with a stone shaped as a Spade.

"The Black Court was in an uproar. The Spades Princess was inconsolable. Her love had been taken from her, and his heart was forever gone. In its place was a symbol of her parents' Court, which many saw as a declaration of war. Accusations flew. Both the Spades and Hearts Courts denied any responsibility of abduction or murder. The land lamented, the people raged. Joy turned to bitterness.

"Riddled by grief, the Black Monarchs demanded the heart of the Spades Princess as payment. Unwilling to allow her people to be ravaged by the cost of war, and despite the pleadings of her sovereigns, the Princess agreed as long as her sacrifice would ensure the fighting would end. The truth was, though, not so altruistic. She had lost her will to live now that her love was gone forevermore.

"On the journey to the Black Court, the princess met a Unicorn in the forest. It was having tea and invited her to join. She did, and during the course of their afternoon, she told him her sad tale. 'My lover is dead,' she cried. 'My life means nothing without him. What do I care if my heart is removed?'

"'That is a very stupid thing to say, let alone believe,' the Unicorn told her.

"'You have obviously never been in love,' she argued.

"'I have many times before, and if I am lucky, many times after to-

216

day,' the Unicorn replied. 'I am in love with this tea, for example. I am in love with how the sky turns lilac before it storms. I am in love with the smell of roses when they dance under the full moon and I am in love with sugar cubes.'

" "Those are things, not people,' the Princess exclaimed. 'It is not the same!'

" 'When I was a young colt, I was in love with a beautiful filly. She chose to mate with an idiot, and when I was eighteen, I fell in love with a Turtle. Her family objected to our pairing, saying a Uniurtle would only serve to embarrass them come the holidays, and she chose them. When I was twenty-three, I fell in love with another Unicorn. She was beautiful and sweet but as the years passed, we grew apart, as some must do. She now lives on White lands and has found love again. As I still love her deeply, I rejoice in knowing she is happy.'

" 'It cannot have been true love,' the Princess insisted. 'If it was, life would lose its meaning.'

" 'It is the best kind of true love,' the Unicorn countered. 'True love does not have limits or restrictions. True love allows a person to love deeply and unconditionally. True love does not ask you to let go of life. True love encourages you to love even more, Princess. True love encourages you to live.'

"The Princess would not listen, though. She finished her tea and thanked him for his hospitality. She finished her journey to the Black Court and presented herself to their vengeance.

"Her heart was carved out and replaced with a blackened rock. It took four days for her body to reach the Spades Court. In the end, the Spades Princess and the Black Prince did not lay together in death. His body was interned in Black land forevermore, hers within Spades territory. Many years later, a rogue Gryphon confessed to the Prince's death. He thought he was doing the Prince a favor by giving a heart in the shape of the Prince's beloved's Court. He was apologetic and remorseful and more than a bit confused by anatomy. The Unicorn fell in love again, when he was forty-eight and silver haired. It was with a Sheep who cared very little about what others thought of such unions. Their life was a wonderful one, filled with much love and happiness. When death came to claim them many years later, there were no regrets."

Finn says nothing. His warm hand still strokes my hair, his steady heartbeat still thumps below my cheek.

I hope he knows what I have just told him.

Beyond the room, Victor is saying, "Mary would love to meet you. Shall we go find her?" And then the lab lights turn off and a door shuts.

I shift on the bed until I'm level with Finn. There is dirt smudged on his face, a nasty, crusty cut across his ear. He is the most beautiful thing in the world to me.

True love encourages you to live.

Thank goodness for true love.

My lips find his. Our kiss is soft and beautiful. Eventually, it grows hungrier. I'm pushing off his coat when he murmurs, "Your back."

My back is perfect, thanks to him. "I guess this means I'll have to be on top. Which really isn't asking too much, as it is my preference anyway."

He helps with the coat and then with all the rest of our clothes. He's gentle when sliding the ridiculous medical gown I've been forced to wear off. Fingers trace my spine, down to the bandage at its base.

I kiss him again. Kiss his mouth and his neck and his chest. He kisses me, too, his hands writing our love story all over my body. When our bodies join together, moving in the best of rhythms, it's languidly delicious. We take our time. I stare down in his blue-gray eyes and he stares up in mine.

My heart is impossibly full.

COINCIDENCES

FINN

S EVERAL HOURS LATER, AFTER another nap and a long, shared shower, Alice and I make our way to the conference room. It's hard to believe just yesterday she was paralyzed. There's no shakiness, no weakness. There's only the strong, confident Alice she's always been.

When we arrive, there's already a crowd gathered. The White King and Cheshire-Cat, now nearly as large as a pony, are present. The Five of Diamonds waits in the hallway, his pike at full attention. My father glances up from the laptop he and Marianne are hunched over. "It's good to see you on your feet again, Ms. Reeve."

She smiles wryly. "It is good to be upon them. I'm sure you can contest that those infernal wheelchairs are dreadful."

"Indeed they are. Worse yet when they are unneeded, and children keep forcing them upon you."

"I don't see what the problem is." Mary does her best to keep a straight face. "You two were pushed around and totally pampered like royalty."

Grymsdyke, dangling from a massive web he's built in a corner, says, "The Queen of Diamonds *is* royalty and thus should always be treated as such."

Several people warily glance up at the spider. More than a few seem puzzled by his ardently stated fact, but the majority are basically terrified in general there's a talking spider with massive fangs hanging out in the conference room.

Mary smiles brightly. "Grymsdyke and I have been getting to know one another. He's delightfully droll. Victor could learn a thing or two from him."

Victor sighs heavily.

"I am much encouraged by your visage," the White King is saying to Alice. "The Cheshire was insistent that you would recuperate quickly, but one never knows with these things."

She waves her hand dismissively. "Now that I have had time to reflect upon it, I am greatly troubled by the use of a boojum. I must admit I'd thought them to be little more than superstition meant to frighten children keen for thrills and chills."

He smiles wanly. "You are not alone in such thinking."

"This brings us to the point of how Hearts obtained a boojum," the Cat interjects. It hops onto a chair. "And more importantly, how she was able to pass it off to someone outside of Wonderland. And most importantly, why there is no tea here at the table."

The room goes quiet as all ears turn toward him. Brom sends word for tea to be brought up.

"Until the Queen of Diamonds returned from exile recently, none knew of any existence other than our own and that of Her Majesty's beyond the rabbit holes and looking glasses. During my tenure in the Hearts dungeon, there was no indication of her knowledge of this." To the White King and Alice, he adds, "She was obsessively focused on the war. Anyone in her Court who voiced anything to the contrary of her beliefs or spoke of other matters was immediately executed or imprisoned. Songs were sung, plays enacted. Paintings were commissioned, highlighting desired results of her campaigns."

The White King sits in the chair next to his advisor. "And yet, we know it must be Hearts who supplied the boojum. The description matches perfectly, and who other than she or someone from Wonderland could supply the beastie?" He looks to the crowd joining him at the table. "Unless snarks are indigenous to other Timelines?"

"Well, parasites are common in most," Victor offers. "And other creatures that are similar. For example, we have these worms that I think act a bit like the boojum. Leeches subsist on blood. Tapeworms feed on raw meat and blood. But I have never seen anything like a boojum before." He shudders. "That face." To the group, "It had a face. Like, a legitimate *face.*"

My blood boils at the thought of that thing being in Alice.

"I look forward to dissecting it," Mary says cheerfully. "It's currently in my freezer."

Brom strokes his short beard. "I must admit, the more we uncover in our quest toward the perpetrators behind the Timeline deletions, the more complex the web grows." His eyes meet mine. "Victor and I questioned Todd extensively during your absence, and he is unfortunately still sleeping off the vast amounts of serum pumped into his system."

Victor tugs on his collar. Coughs.

"He had no concrete answers to give about his association with the Queen of Hearts, other than to say they had met on a pair of separate occasions and spoke of nothing except Ms. Reeve. Additionally, he has no solid answers to give on any matter. He has never met the person assigning which catalysts he was to obtain or which ones to destroy. He presented a series of names we are in the process of researching and claimed the voice he occasionally spoke to on the telephone changed depending on the day. All communiqués were either typewritten or simply torn pages from books or newspapers."

I rub at my hair, frustrated. "What about Wendy? Was there any legit connection there?"

"Todd had no answer when it came to dealings with Ms. Darling. That said, he did claim he'd been in touch with someone who bore a striking resemblance to the perpetrator in our security footage."

"What does Wen has to say about this?"

My father purses his lips. "Ms. Darling has said nothing at all since her seizure."

"She's fine, though," Victor interjects. "As far as I can tell, nothing's physically wrong with her right now."

I ask my father, "Are we really thinking that . . . *guy,* for lack of a better word, was Peter Pan?"

It's the A.D. who answers. He's sitting next to Brom, taking notes on a tablet while a recorder lies on the table between them. "It has to be, right? Wen wouldn't betray us for just anyone."

"Mr. Dawkins, there is no concrete proof that the person in the security footage was Peter Pan. In all our dealings with 1904BAR-PW, no Society member has ever successfully made contact with this person. We have not even been able to breach Neverland." To Alice, he offers a rueful smile. "I'm afraid it was much like your Wonderland. Unlike Wonderland, though, 1904BAR-PW's catalyst was not located within Neverland. Once we obtained it, we had no need to breech Neverland's borders."

"I am curious. How many years did the Society attempt to locate Wonderland?" the Cat asks.

"Several," Brom admits. "Eventually, we shifted our focus to finding someone who had been to Wonderland yet now resided in the world beyond. Ms. Reeve was always our first choice. I believe we searched for her for . . ." His eyes flick to me. "Two years. Had we known, of course, that she wasn't even in England and still in Wonderland, it would have saved us many frustrating trips and searches."

"You mean it would have saved Finn many frustrating searches." Victor elbows me. "Poor sod. You had him and Sara in their so-called free time traipsing all over the bloody country in their search. There was one point I thought he would rip somebody's head off if they ever said Alice's name in his presence. She was like a ghost or urban legend to the Society."

Sometimes, my brother doesn't know when to shut his damn mouth.

Alice touches my arm. "You searched for me for years?"

"I already told you this." I did, didn't I?

She says more softly, "Yes, but you *searched* for me."

I love her, truly love her, but this makes not a lick of sense.

"Nonetheless, the point I was making was, we have no idea if it was Peter Pan who Wendy was communicating with, let alone if he even exists anymore." Brom taps his fingers against the desk. "Unfortunately, the video has no sound, so we cannot confirm this, but we must not rule out the possibility that the person in question hypnotized Ms. Darling into offering up our secrets."

I snap my fingers. "The pipes."

"But then, how do we connect the possibility of Peter Pan to Sweeney Todd?" Brom continues. "And to a Sweeney Todd who was supposedly hanged?" He swipes a finger across the table. "And from there to the Queen of Hearts—a person who, by all accounts, knows nothing of Timelines and yet was seen by someone outside of Wonderland? Unfortunately, Todd has provided us no answers to any of these questions. Rosemary and Jenkins know even less than he. Incidentally, I had Rosemary moved to her own room in the containment ward, next to Jenkins.' I don't want any of them to communicate with the others."

"Would the Queen of Hearts have edited from Wonderland?" Marianne muses. This is the first she's spoken so far. "From the reports I have perused on the matter, it is believed none can edit directly from that land but must instead rely upon travel to England or Wales first."

Taking in the group in the conference room, I notice a face is missing—the one that actually might have the answer to Marianne's question. "Where is the Librarian?"

"She has," Brom says carefully, "gone to acquire a piece for our collections."

He might as well have dropped a bomb on the Society members sitting at the table. The Librarian has, in the entire time I've known her, never left the Institute. Going outside is stepping onto a patio or the rare trip to the roof. In the winter, she pulls out those Seasonal Affective Disorder machines, and for years, we all laughed about it because how was winter any different for her than any other season? Her entire life is lived out within these walls. She does not know how to drive. I highly doubt she's ever been in a car. I asked her about it once, and her answer came with a straight face. "Why would anyone entrust their life to a steel trap such as an automobile?"

"What do you mean, she's gone to acquire something?" the A.D. asks.

"My words were not unclear, Mr. Dawkins," Brom says evenly. "She had an errand to run. She is doing so."

"Outside of the Institute?" an agent named Holgrave asks from farther on down the table.

"Logic would indicate so."

Henry Flemming asks, sounding just as dumbfounded as the rest of us, "How did she leave?"

"As I was not with her when she left, I cannot answer that, Mr. Flemming. Nor did she see fit to explain it to me."

"When did she leave?" Holgrave presses.

"While I was interrogating Todd."

This makes no sense. The Librarian has just left? "What books?" I ask my father.

"That I do not know either."

"What do you mean, you don't know? Didn't she run them by you?"

He gives me a meaningful look, one that leaves me edgy. He didn't say she was going to get a book. He said she was going to acquire *something*.

"Did she go to meet Pfeifer?"

Alice's head snaps up; her eyes narrow. "Do you mean Lygari?" And then, before anyone can say anything, "You questioned Todd about his estate. You asked him about Bücherei."

"What is Bücherei?" The Cat's eyes focus on Alice. "And who is this person who apparently has two very different names? And where is the tea? How can any of us be expected to elaborate upon strategy without a proper cup of tea?"

As if on cue, the door bursts open with a man hauling in a cart filled with teapots and cups.

The Cat sniffs; its nose wrinkles. "This world," it says, "is barbaric. I'm sorry, but there it is. From what I can tell, you're trying to serve us jabberwocky urine."

Neither Alice nor the White King even blink at this. The King himself is side-eyeing the tea that's hastily being poured for them.

"You will get used to it. I did, and I am fine. As for Lygari, he is a book collector," Alice tells the Cat, but my father is giving me a look that tells me, quite clearly, that I need to keep my mouth shut. "Finn and I were sent to purchase several volumes a number of weeks back. Bücherei translates to library, and it is a fitting nomenclature, as the estate in actuality is an enormous library filled with artifacts belonging to authors. It was most unpleasant." She turns to me. "Why would the

Librarian go see him? We were there so recently."

It's my turn to glare at my father. He didn't tell her, did he?

And . . . he is utterly unapologetic.

Screw his wishes for silence. "Right after we got back from St. Petersburg, I was sent back to collect a catalyst from him. You were asleep and I was given no choice."

Her eyebrows lift up in surprise. "Lygari collects items associated with authors, not Timelines. He made sure to elaborate upon that in vivid detail."

The Cat murmurs quietly as it peers into its cup, "Yes. I was right. This is urine. How you all function is beyond me."

Brom sends another message out, requesting more tea. I tell Alice, "According to the Librarian, he also had a catalyst from a book of fairy tales."

A V forms between her eyes. "We discussed this before. While there were multiple references to fairy tales, he had none showcased in his exhibits."

"I know. And the book they claimed it was from—"

Someone down the table murmurs quietly, "Claimed?"

"—Is one that doesn't even have a legit origin text for us to pinpoint. Or, at least, one that's easy to pinpoint. It's never been one we've gone after before, simply because we can't even prove the Timeline exists."

My father says nothing during this. He simply tents his hands and listens.

"Were you successful?"

The A.D. snorts. I say carefully, "No. When we got there, the library wasn't there anymore."

Her eyes widen. "What do you mean the library wasn't there?"

"It wasn't there," the A.D. bursts out. "There was no bloody library. None of any of the fancy stuff you and Finn reported. All that was there was an empty house."

"*What?*" Alice turns back to me.

In a way, her confused outrage is comforting, like it means I'm not as crazy as feared. Like my memory of the night is right. "From the outside, it looks the same. Same design. Same hedge maze. But inside . . ." I turn to face her. "Do you remember how the library stretched all three stories up? And filled most of the house? How there were those massive, carved doors, and that the floor was tiled with scenes from stories?"

There's no hesitation. "The ceiling had frescos with eyes that followed us everywhere."

"It wasn't there. None of that was there. There—there were floors to the house. Three stories worth of floors. There was an indoor swimming pool where he had that damn Twain table, one that connects to another outside. There was carpet. The ceilings were just ceilings. There was a kitchen. Bathrooms. Alice, it was a *house.*"

Her acceptance of this isn't any easier than mine. "We were there for close to an hour and toured the entire space. What you are telling me is impossible."

"Your Majesty," the Cat says from his perch, "you of all people know the impossible is quite possible. Except, perhaps, the creation of proper strategy tea in this Institute of yours."

"In Wonderland, yes. Here?" She waves a hand around. "Not so much." To me, she says, "We need to go back there."

The A.D. smacks the table. "I'm telling you, there's nothing there!"

"There was," I correct, "one thing."

Her eyes narrow as they take me in, almost as if she's bracing herself.

"I found a photograph."

She whips to face my father. "You showed one to Todd. You asked him about it. He said . . . He claimed Rosemary took it."

That's news to me.

Alice touches my arm, brings back my attention. "What was the photograph of?"

I take a deep breath. Even now, just thinking about it is creepy. "Us. It was of us, the first time we ever went to the coffee shop down the street."

It's rare to ever see Alice rattled. Nothing fazes her. But her mouth drops open now, just a little. Her eyes go wide. She says quietly, "There was a photograph of the two of us in Lygari's home? One taken prior to any introduction to the gentleman?"

I nod. "It was where the Carroll exhibit was."

"He had photographs of Carroll's," she whispers. "Dozens of pictures of little girls. He—he had a picture of the real Alice."

"You are the real Alice."

"Is anyone real?" the Cat murmurs.

"I . . . Mary and I met him at that dance club. He told me his name was Lygari. He said—" She shakes her head, more pissed than confused. "He had on a ring. A blue ring. I saw him again, at the Public Library. He asked me to coffee. He has two names. Why does he have two names? He said . . . He said, 'Many of us do.' What does that mean?" She blinks before refocusing. And then, in a low, cold voice, "He had a photograph of us, Finn. Taken by Rosemary. Lygari knows Rosemary. We must assume he knows Todd and possibly Jenkins as well."

"Let us question Rosemary and Jenkins, as well and—"

Alice cuts my father off mid-sentence. "Lygari is a patron of the New York Public Library." She snaps her fingers. "Mary, what day is it?"

Mary rattles off the date, but before she finishes, her eyes widen. In perfect unison, the ladies exclaim, "Tonight is the library fundraiser gala!"

Victor tosses his pencil at me. Mouths, "Told you."

Asshole.

"The Caterpillar used to tell me that coincidences are not coincidental at all." Alice looks at her Wonderlandian friends, flashing a grim smile. "He was quite insistent about that."

The Cat sniffs. "For a pompous thing, he was usually right."

"It is settled," Alice says firmly. "We will go to the gala tonight and search for Lygari. I suspect more than one of us has questions for him. Perhaps it's time we have a chat."

A GALA

ALICE

AN HOUR AFTER THE meeting ends, I visit the flat Jace and the Cheshire-Cat are residing in during their stay. While matters in Wonderland require their attention, both insisted on remaining at least one more day to ensure my recovery has taken. Jace and Finn are to create more poultices together in the morning before his departure, so that I will have enough to last throughout the week.

And then there is the matter of how he is giving us his blood for protection. I do not know how to properly show this wonderful man just how much gratitude I have for him.

"Does it really take a week's worth of applications to ensure the boojum's influence is gone?"

My former lover's smile is wry. He is dressed in some of Finn's clothes, and it is entirely jarring to see him so out of time in a flannel shirt and jeans. "I have no idea, to be honest. But it is best not to take chances."

For a moment, neither of us speaks. The Cheshire-Cat is in another room, napping in front of a sunny window. Grymsdyke is . . . well, I am not quite sure. Exploring the Institute, most likely. Finn is conferring with his father, and Mary is undoubtedly ensuring I have a dress proper enough for the evening.

I allow myself to touch Jace. Just a hand upon his arm, but I allow myself this anyway. "Thank you."

The smile on his beloved face turns bittersweet. "I will always come to your aid if you need me. Always."

I do not ask him why he stood back and allowed Finn to enact the blood magic. Truthfully, there is no need, as I already know the answer. *True love does not have limits or restrictions. True love allows a person to love deeply and unconditionally. True love does not ask you to let go of life. True love encourages you to live.*

Instead, I walk over to the window and pull back the curtain. He comes to stand with me, and we watch the taxis and cars far below zoom down the streets, honking, and the helicopter in the sky blocks away, and the people in their races to get everywhere and anywhere.

"New York is not as I imagined it to be."

My head tilts toward him. "No?"

"It is so busy." He sounds sad, even. "So vast and yet so small all at once." A hand presses against the cold pane. "The sky is lost amongst such giants."

He speaks my own heart's secrets. "Do you remember that day in the Field of Daydreams?"

He chuckles, and dozens upon dozens of warm, happy memories flood me at such a beloved sound. "Of course. It is a favorite of all my favorite days, I think."

"Mine, as well."

"The sky," he says softly, "was more of an ocean than a sky that day. The waves were gentle, the crests foamy. We were happy that day."

We were, indeed. He and I had ridden out by ourselves, much to the consternation of our Grand Advisors. We lay beneath that ocean and talked for hours. The grass was velvety, the flowers sweet with their songs. We did not get too many days like that, lazy, warm days built upon feelings rather than experiences, nor many more visits to the Field of Daydreams in the year that followed. But that day was a picturesque one. It was sublime.

"The sky is not the same here," I tell him. "It is just sky and nothing more."

"Do you miss Wonderland?"

I focus on the scene before us rather than his face. "Desperately."

"It misses you."

Gone unsaid, by the both of us, is how much we miss the other.

"Have you—"

"Yes," he says softly. "Last week. The White Queen and I had an official treaty signing and ceremony announcing our joint resolve. It was, what we thought, a shot straight at Hearts' psyche, but now I wonder if she was even in Wonderland to know of the alliance."

"I am sure you still had Red's wrath."

He chuckles again. "Yes. Apparently she had effigies of the both of us thrown to the bandersnatches during games meant to mark the occasion."

My smile fades. "It is a sad state of affairs for Wonderland for Monarchs to have to sign treaties with their counterparts to ensure alliances."

"It is, indeed." He blows out a hard breath. "And still, I would not turn my back to the White Queen, Alice. Her knives are sharp."

"Nor would I."

"She is in love, you know."

My eyebrows lift up.

"He is, from what my spies tell me, of the Red Court."

"No!"

An easy grin stretches across his face. "Yes. The Knave, if I'm not mistaken. Perhaps not exactly love, but it is assuredly lust. I find this to be most amusing."

"I would have thought she would have pressured you into a more permanent alliance by now."

"It was suggested," he says carefully.

I would not hesitate to lay wagers upon it was more than suggested. The White Queen has long coveted her counterpart. I cannot blame her, though.

"I wish them well, then."

"Shall I tell her you said that?"

It is my turn to laugh. "I would delight in seeing her face at such news." More soberly, "Does she know you are here?"

"No. I left word I was on a secret campaign and that I would return shortly." His nearly colorless eyes track back to the glass. "We are set to hold a joint meeting in four days' time. It will be good for our troops, I think. The war has left many disheartened and disillusioned."

"Jace . . ."

It is his turn to put a hand on me. A gentle one, with fingers curling around my forearm. "You must not worry about such things."

The truth is whispered. "I cannot help but do so."

"I know. And yet, I would ask of you to not anyway. It does neither of us any good, our worries about the other. Now. I believe you must get ready for tonight's party, do you not?" His smile is warm and reminds me of happier days together. "You have a man to hunt."

"I do not have a good feeling, Jace. This Lygari man is . . ." I shake my head. "He leaves me uneasy."

"I ask of you to trust those instincts, then. They have never steered you or I wrong." He lifts my hand and presses a kiss against my inner wrist. "Perhaps in the morning you and your Finn can take me to this coffee shop everyone keeps talking about so that I may finally have my initiation into this world."

Only to shortly leave it behind.

I head back to my flat and find several dresses already laid out upon my bed. Say what you will, in this moment I truly appreciate Mary's meddling, as the last thing I want to do is dig through my closet with great frustration.

After sunset, we arrive at our destination. The New York Public Library is beautiful tonight. The domed room we are in, the Celeste Bartos Forum, is practically dripping splendor. Warm, yellow lights mixed together in elaborate wreaths and hangings leave the atmosphere enchanting.

I am in a beautiful golden gown with the most handsome man in the room on my arm. When he first saw me in it, he couldn't even speak.

I rather like this gown.

According to Mary, the Society has long been associated with the New York Public Library. There are those in its employ who know of the Society and of Timelines, often supplying books and research to the Librarian and various agents over the years. Society members in New York often become patrons of the museum, as their interests overlap. As we got ready for the evening's events, she told me that the Van Brunts have been very loyal with their patronage, starting with Katrina. At one point, Finn and Victor's mother actually volunteered at the public library on a regular basis. Now, they come to the fundraising gala every year that she delighted in attending, and donate vast amounts of money or books in her name.

Finn and I mingle with other guests, drinking champagne and nibbling on canapés. Our eyes are constantly surveying the room for Lygari. Mary and Victor are also present, doing the same. Van Brunt is in deep conversation with a woman I do not recognize, and I tease Finn it appears she is flirting shamelessly with his father.

The A.D. is outside in a van filled with screens and computers. Henry Flemming is with him, alongside Marianne Brandon. We are all fitted with tiny earpieces in case we find Lygari.

"This isn't the date I envisioned," Finn murmurs in my ear.

I offer him a meaningful smile over my glass of champagne. "I thought I made myself clear that I do not require dates." I lay my hand against his face. "You and I . . . We are beyond such things. Courting is meant to endear lovers to one another. I am already hopelessly attached to you, Finn Van Brunt."

He kisses the palm of my hand just as one of the fundraising chairs comes over to where we're standing. She's brought with her the deputy mayor of New York, and it turns out both know Finn. I listen to them chat about various library issues without adding much, using the time to continue my surveillance whilst offering small, noncommittal sounds to indicate my participation in the subject.

Nearby, the librarian named Bianca Jones gives me a pair of thumb's up and makes a heart shape with her fingers.

I quickly look away.

I'm just about to return my full attention to the conversation when . . . There. Over by a stack of books, a slim flute with golden bubbles in her chubby fingers, stands a woman I did not believe I would ever lay eyes upon again and yet fervently prayed to do just so.

I came for Lygari and found a quarry much, much more desirable.

I stare at her, eyes narrowed for nearly a minute, before I'm roused by a gentle squeeze of warm hand against waist.

My focus shifts back to Finn. Concern reflects in his eyes; expectation, too, as if he knows I have found prey. I allow a reassuring smile, as this is not the moment to inform him I am planning the assassination of one of Wonderland's foulest plagues at an elegant party. "Did I miss something whilst woolgathering?"

It's clear he doesn't buy my attempts at lightheartedness, but Finn has enough manners to not question me further in front of acquaintances. The chair, however, says, "I apologize for going on and on about fundraising, Ms. Reeve. I realize that it's not the most entertaining topic at such a gala, not when there are other much more exciting things to do."

"Do not be silly." I offer up another smile, even while, out of the corner of an eye, I observe the Queen of Hearts sip her champagne. She thinks to catch me off-guard, does she? Does she have another boojum ready at the quick? "Fundraising for this magnificent library alongside literacy efforts is of utmost importance and I am keen to do my part in ensuring success. I apologize, though, as I must excuse myself momentarily."

Finn's eyebrows lift up in a silent question, but I merely lay a hand upon his cheek for a brief moment prior to stepping away. Guilt over leaving him in the dark is only momentary. Hearts and I have business with one another.

I weave my way through the richly decorated tables and crowds of well-dressed patrons, my eyes never leaving her familiar form. Enrobed in a bright red and black silk dress, her dark hair piled high upon her head, she appears exactly as I remember her: striking and haughty with more than a touch of malice coloring every movement.

She watches my approach as well, her full lips curving slightly upward as she holds her glass aloft in silent yet insulting salute.

The Queen of Hearts, in modern-day New York City. In the New York Public Library, no less—and no doubt to finish what she so foolishly started.

When I stop several feet away from her, she says, "Diamonds." Her dismay at my still-beating heart is obvious.

As I always have been, I am more than happy to thwart her plans.

"Hearts."

Viciousness and spite make her red lips practically stretch across her face as she delights in taking me in with great exaggeration. "My, my. You've gone native, haven't you?"

Petty retorts that touch upon her inability to dress in any other hue than red or black, shades both patently unflattering to her skin tone, tickle the tip of my tongue, but I know better than to engage. I remain silent. She's here for a reason—granted, the reason is most likely the extraction of my head, but still. I've long learned that it best suits my needs to discern her movements and wishes before taking any action of my own.

"Tell me, Diamonds. Have you gone so soft in your exile that you require a bodyguard?" She inclines her head in the direction I came from, back toward Finn whilst tsking loudly. But then she taps her long chin with one of those bizarrely chubby fingers of hers. "If one of my soldiers touched me the way yours just did, I would have his hand as payment."

She appears to be alone. None of the nearby men or women are any that I recognize—not that that means much, as the Queen of Hearts burns through employees at an alarming rate, thanks to her infamous temper. Yet still, I highly doubt this woman would attend unaccompanied. Her ego and inflated sense of importance would never allow such a thing.

"I wonder," she continues over the rim of her glass, "what White would think of your mingling with the help." She lowers the flute, her eyes going deceptively wide and sympathetic. "But then again, with the White monarchs unified under a joint banner, perhaps he doesn't have time to ruminate on such unsavory reminders of the past in the first place."

Her baiting has always been as terrible as her fashion. I offer an exaggerated yawn against the back of a hand. "You've come across time and space for that?" It's my turn to tsk. "Or was it to ensure your boojum did its job?"

"Oh, poppet. I do delight in finding you still just as bratty as before. When I heard you'd languished within the walls of an . . . What do they call them here? An asylum? I feared you were yet another Dumpty." Her mock sympathy returns. "No matter what, no matter if it's deserved or not, Queens of Wonderland must be afforded better than that."

And yet, she thought it best for a fellow queen to have a boojum implanted at the base of her spine, one who slowly drained both mobility and life away from its host?

"It must be a terrible disappointment, knowing there is absolutely nothing you can do to remove me from the Queens' Council." *Or kill me.* I mimic her spiteful smile. "That, even in my absence, my rule and sovereignty in Wonderland is valid until the day of my last breath."

"That's the thing, poppet," she coos. "Your last breath is not protected, is it?"

"How amusing it is," I counter, "that you are here, in New York, at a gala for a house of literacy for the sole purpose of confronting an exiled colleague instead of being back at home, fulfilling your duties as a monarch on the battlefield."

For all of her—what does Mary call it? *Trash talk?* For all of her petty words, I will admit it appears the Queen of Hearts has matured a bit toward resisting such taunts. "Have no fear over my duties, Diamonds. I am, as I ever was, vigilant in those things I must do to ensure Wonderland's prosperity."

Her dress is voluminous, leaving plenty of places to hide weaponry. At least I can reassure myself that her wicked battle-axe is not upon her person, though. There is not enough silk in any world to hide such a monstrosity.

No matter. I have bested this woman before with my hands. I can do it again. Besides, I've got a nice pair of small blades strapped to my thighs beneath my gown.

"The other queens and I convened recently," she says casually, "and we were most distraught at how our people suffer. It appears your absence has afforded Wonderland precious little relief."

Finally, one of her jabs lands true and strong.

"Perhaps it is *you* who has gone soft in *my* absence," I say flatly. "You foolishly jabber on like the Duchess. If you're here for a fight, let us fight. Or are you resigned now to others doing your dirty work for you?" I tsk once more. "What would your armies think of that—the mighty Queen of Hearts, enlisting a filthy commoner and non-native to carry out what she is unable to do?"

The gurgling sound that emerges from between her clinched lips is sweet music to my ears.

"Then again, if all you want to do is act like a mimsy and chatter on with toothless threats and innuendos, I have better uses for my evening."

One of my jabs lands true and strong, as well. Her eyes narrow, her fingers curl tighter around the glass until the skin turns white. And then, just as the veins in her eyes turn blood red, the glass between her fingers shatters. Champagne soaks her silk.

I afford her a falsely sympathetic, sweeping glance of her newly ruined dress. Somebody nearby gasps; another person attempts to pass her a linen napkin.

Fury mottles her skin as she barks for him to leave her person alone. And then she rages incoherently for a good twenty seconds, her face now the exact shade of her dress.

I'm reminded of one of the many skirmishes between us, one in the halls of the Red Queen's palace. It'd been after one of our monthly Queens' Council meetings, and she and her axe devastated several statues and cracked the floor after her ridiculous arguments had fallen upon deaf ears. Red had done as she always did, shouting for guards and uselessly lamenting over insignificant things such as broken marble, while White had slipped away like the slithery *tove* she is to whereabouts unknown. It'd been up to me to put this beast of a woman in her place, and I came away with a nasty scar upon my belly for my efforts. Nonetheless, I'd bested her, and now that her recent villainy is so fresh in my mind, I have little doubts upon doing it once more. "Shall I save you the efforts toward screaming for my head?"

She's nearly choking, so she's apoplectic.

I slowly run a finger across my throat. "Do you best, Hearts."

For a moment, it appears as if she'll fall prey to my baiting. But alas, just as her wound-free hand shifts toward the opposite sleeve, a level head emerges. She sucks in a deep breath, blowing it out of quivering nostrils.

So. A weapon lies within one of her sleeves.

"Are you not going to inquire as to why I am here?"

She'd like that, wouldn't she? Her eagerness to lord her explanations over me is nearly tangible.

Words allow lies, the Caterpillar used to say.

"Why should I ask when I already know?"

But then she reaches behind her to reclaim a small clutch from a nearby table, all so she might extract a square of silk out to press against her bleeding hand.

Cold, bitter rage frosts my heart as I stare at the receptacle.

Darkish, mottled green in color, with just a hint of shimmery blue, her clutch is as familiar to me as the skin on my own body.

My hands shake. Fury tints my vision. Not only did she sever the head from my Grand Advisor and place it on a stake outside her palace, but she harvested his beautiful skin to fashion a handbag.

The hag's mouth twitches into a larger grin. "It's a pretty thing, isn't it?" She snaps the golden closures shut and holds the bag aloft between us. "A favorite of mine."

There are shards of glass still littering the ground beneath her feet. It would take little effort to claim a piece, only slightly more to drag it across her undeserving flesh.

"Diamonds, I'm disappointed in you," she says amiably. "To think you would even consider causing mayhem within these learned walls . . ."

For a moment, I'm taken aback by her silence. The Queen of Hearts, out of steam during one of her infamous monologues? But then she says, her voice low, "It appears I'm not the only one who allows filthy commoners to fight their battles."

"Is that what I am?" Finn asks from right behind me. "A filthy commoner?"

Hearts looks at me, not him. And it's an expectant look, as if she's daring me to prove her right.

"The thing is," Finn continues quietly, "the Queen of Diamonds doesn't require me to fight her battles. She's more than capable of fighting them herself."

Hearts says nothing. She doesn't move. But slowly, oh so slowly, the smile across her face spreads until it nearly eclipses her other features.

It's an uneasy smile, one that sounds alarms. I itch to glance around to find Victor. Locate Mary, or Van Brunt. Because I've seen this smile before.

Nothing good has ever followed this smile. Violence has, though. Immense amounts of violence.

"Hello, poppet," she clucks, but she is not speaking to me. "Aren't you a delicious tart?"

Finn comes to stand next to me. Upon my back, in a gesture meant to look loving, he taps and slides his finger. Victor and Mary, to the left at eleven o'clock. Van Brunt, to the right at four o'clock. HQ notified.

The meaning is not lost on me. There is someone else who ought to be here, someone else who has a stake in this confrontation.

Someone else I hope is en route immediately.

"Tell me," Hearts continues, "does it bother you, Finn Van Brunt, that you are nothing more than a consolation prize?"

He laughs at her—not so much in the shared shock we surely both feel at her expanded knowledge of his person, though. This laugh I know. This laugh is all about scorn. "Imagine my surprise," he says to her, "to find out that the infamous Queen of Hearts is so desperate that she has to resort to stereotypical tropes in efforts to throw her opponents off-guard." He shakes his head. "Sorry, *poppet,* but I don't play those school-yard games. Or didn't your informant tell you that? If you want to get under my skin, you're going to have to do better than that."

Hints of anger flare in her dark irises, but then, without warning, that nefarious smile of hers reemerges.

"What a darling plaything you have here," she says to me. Before I can counter, she turns to him. "In the spirit of our meeting, let me issue you this friendly warning. Collateral damage is a messy yet unfortunately unavoidable casualty in battle. You may want to choose whether or not you want to be in the midst of this one. You see, Diamonds is not your monarch, nor is she your equal. Her loyalty and affections will never truly lie with you. How could they? That's the thing about Wonderlandian monarchs, even those who are mistakes. Our constitutions are different from yours. Our blood and psyches requires something more. Diamonds' priorities, even here," she offers an exaggerated glance around us, "even now, even in exile, are the same as they ever were. And they will be so until she dies."

For his part, Finn simply looks bored.

"In the end," she says in a horribly kind voice, "when you look around wondering how it all came down so quickly, I hope you remember that I tried to warn you." She brushes back a stray dark strand and tilts her head. "If, in fact, you're still standing. Rest assured, though, sweet tart. My fight is not with you. As for others . . ." Her shrug is infuriatingly charming. "Others and their plans are their own."

The unease in the pit of my stomach grows exponentially, but my words are controlled. "Todd has been neutralized."

She is unbothered by this. And it's then that I understand he truly was nothing but that *filthy commoner* to her, a disposable one that had nothing to do with her end game.

Todd, for so long, has been of great importance to the Society. Todd and Rosemary, Jenkins, even, were the villains. Their crimes were atrocious. Their captures were bittersweet victories.

I know better now. Todd and his cohorts were the small fish in the pond. And the Queen of Hearts? I have a feeling she's not much better. Her fight is with me. I would lay down my crown that she has no interest in Timelines.

No—someone else does, though. Someone . . . who is using her.

Part of me insists I walk away now. That my goal is to find this person—or persons, if our guesses prove to be incorrect—and wield justice so many innocents so richly deserve and yet can never witness. But there's something that stops my feet from uprooting, something that holds me back.

The painfully ironic scene of a small rectangle still clutched within a bloody hand.

The Caterpillar would call me a fool. A sentimental fool, to be exact. But this sentimental fool cannot stand by and allow a bitch like Hearts hold onto such a thing.

If she wants a fight, a fight is what she'll get.

"You're right about one thing," I say coolly yet calmly. "My loyalty to my subjects is unwavering. I will always put matters concerning them above my own."

She doesn't miss a beat. "Are we back to this, then?" She fans herself with the clutch before pressing a loving kiss against it. "Are you really ready to come at me in such a place, during such an event? All by yourself?"

Finn's fingers tap against my lower back again as she offers Finn what I'm certain she feels is apologetic yet insulting in nature. And then, almost as if it were out of a storybook, or a modern movie, an achingly familiar voice says, "She will not be alone."

The Queen of Hearts' mouth closes; her head snaps to the left. Approaching us, still wearing the flannel shirt and jeans from before, is the White King of Wonderland.

I try not to take pleasure in how her face drains of color. Nor do I try to stare too long at how beautiful yet alien Jace continues looks in such garb. He is here, in New York, confronting the Queen of Hearts once more alongside me, and the surreality of the situations is nearly too much to bear.

Was he in the van with the others? He must have been. How else could he have come to our sides so quickly?

The slow dragline of vision between my past and my present leaves the Queen of Hearts in rare speechlessness. I, however, say quietly, "If you expect to exit this building tonight on legs that still function, you will permanently relinquish your barbaric trophy to my care."

Her lips thin, her eyes narrow. She is calculating her odds. But, in the end, she does what is asked. She knows better than to face two Wonderlandian monarchs at once.

Her bloody hand stretches the short distance between us, flipping up to offer the remnants of my advisor. As if he can read my mind, Finn takes it from her, tucking it into his coat. He then presses a finger against his ear. "QH extraction, T-minus five minutes."

Her whisper is strangled. "You are stupider than I previous assumed if you think—"

"Here is what I know, not think." The White King closes in on her. "The King of Hearts has already agreed to testify against you. The White Queen and I are in agreement of your crimes. The Queen of Diamonds will submit written testimony in our favor. That makes an even majority, Hearts. Imagine what they will say when I tell them of your use of a boojum, especially against another Monarch, exiled or no. The accords are still in effect, Hearts. The penalty for any who use them—Monarchs included—is death."

And then she does something that wipes clean our shared confidence. Faced with her imminent future, she smiles that horrendous, smug smile of hers, the one that triggers every last alarm inside me.

"Finn," I say, "Jace, we need—"

The room goes black. All the lights wink out, leaving nearly two hundred patrons voicing their loud displeasure in the heavy ink of stillness. A crash of glass sounds, and I'm immediately lunging forward.

Only, the Queen of Hearts is no longer before me.

Finn has his cell phone out, the flashlight function aimed at the empty space I'm groping. There are tables there, and shards from an empty champagne flute lined with red lipstick, but no villainess queen.

To say my heart plummets out of my chest would not be a mild exaggeration.

"She can't have gone far," Jace is saying. He's already scouting the area, his eyes squinting as he peers into the darkness. Around us, hushed chatter ratchets up to annoyance as yet another glass shatters in the distance. More cell phones are extracted; more lights are shot to form pale beams crisscrossing the room. But there is no red and black dress, no dark hair piled high like a teetering mountain.

"Shit!" Finn's finger presses against his ear. "Marianne, the Queen of Hearts disappeared during a convenient blackout. Get the lights on in this place and figure out just who in the hell is behind this. I want a team looking for her—she can't have gone far."

I don't hear her answer, but I can only imagine the string of polite yet angry words frothing out of her mouth, as many are banging on the back of my lips.

The lights reappear, bringing with them a collective heave of relief amongst the revelers. Victor and Mary materialize in the crowd. "No sign of her," Victor says to us. "Mary and I will check the back entrance. You three head to the front. Dad will—"

"There." Jace points toward one of the doorways. "She is there."

A woman in a gray dress is sent sprawling as the Queen of Hearts shoves her out of her path through the main entrance.

Victor informs Van Brunt of our shared directions. We fight our way through the crowd best we can, but there are many within the library's walls tonight. People stare as we rush past, some indigently so. Elegant people in a sophisticated setting do not appreciate such behavior, even though one of their own was recently attacked. Once out of the hall, a flash of red turns down another corner; a scream follows.

It ought to be noted it is difficult to sprint in modern shoes.

The lot of us round the corner just in time to see a glowing doorway appear at the end of yet another hall. A security guard is on the ground, blood squirting from his neck. Floating there, book and pen in hand, is a young man dressed in green and brown. Standing next to him, impossibly, is Sweeney Todd.

How—?!

As Victor and Jace sprint faster toward the doorway, Finn pulls out his gun and shoots.

The Queen of Hearts roars when his bullet strikes her shoulder. She stumbles through the glowing doorway, disappearing out of view. I send a blade whistling through the hallway.

The floating man hits a nearby wall and slides to the ground. His eyes are wide in shock as he peers down at the blade jutting from a bleeding shoulder.

The man-boy's book and pen on the ground, the doorway winks out of existence. Todd has a book out, though, and a pen to write in a new destination. Finn is running, so am I. "Don't let the bastard get away!" Mary shouts, and Jace and Victor are so close.

The doorway opens. Todd grabs his cohort and yanks him through the door.

Jace and Victor fly through behind him, Mary close on their heels. Finn and I barely are through when it disappears behind us.

CHAOS

FINN

HAVE NO IDEA where we are. It's . . . somewhere in the past. And
. . . also somewhere in Asia. Japan I think. Maybe early Twentieth
Century? We're running through a street and there are people everywhere. Cats, too. Like, *lots* of cats. Cats that look like they're shrewd
and assessing. Todd and the Pan guy are ahead of us though, the crowd
giving them a good head start. How in the hell is Todd here? The last I
saw, he was strapped to his bed in the medical wing of the Institute, still
heavily drugged from all the truth serum Victor and Brom used on him.
But the man ahead of me doesn't look like he's been heavily sedated.
Batshit crazy, yes, but not sedated.

If Todd is here and not there . . .

The Pan guy lifts off the ground and floats, and the women and
children around us scream bloody murder. People scatter, terrified, and

the closer I get, the more I see why.

The Pan guy is brandishing a wicked, curved knife with a glowing purple blade. Alice's dagger, though, is ripped out of his shoulder and thrown to the side.

My gun is out, but I can't risk the collateral damage. Todd is already causing enough all on his own, sending children and innocents flying as he slashes his way through the crowd with his switchblades. Pan, because I don't know what else to call the bastard, is hacking away at people, too—only his movements are far clumsier thanks to Alice's ministrations. We catch a break, though—the street we're on narrows down on a dead end, buffered by a wall.

Or so I think, because all of a sudden, an explosion lights up the sky.

I'm flying back at least a good ten feet, it's so strong. My breath is wicked clean from my chest, the pain from pavement slamming against my ribcage is so intense. Hot rubble rains down, smoke fills the air.

Alice.

I push myself up, wincing as pain sluices through me as I shout her name. All around me, screaming and sobbing weigh the air. I can't— where is she? Victor? Mary? The White King? Anarchy reigns in this moment. The smoke is thick, the panic even thicker. I do my best to help people up and check to see if they're okay, but my God.

So many people are hurt.

"Finn!"

I stumble through the chaos and find her comforting an elderly man who is clutching an unresponsive woman. It's a sucker punch to see, and one that fills me with so much rage I can barely handle it.

The wall, the one that was going to block Todd and Pan in, is now gone.

As soon as Alice lets go of the man, my arms are around her; hers wrap around me tightly.

"I'm okay," she tells me. "Just banged up. Nothing to worry about. You?"

Compared to some of these people, I'm doing damn good.

We find Victor about ten feet away, kneeling over a young child so he can check her pulse. My brother's jacket has been torn, his shirt, too, down to bare, bloody skin of his shoulder. The White King is nearby, doing his best to carefully help up an old woman. Alice squeezes my arm, retrieves her dagger, and then jogs over to him.

I search for Mary.

As the smoke begins to dissipate, I find Victor's love sitting next to a little boy who is sobbing. Her face is dirty and bloody from several scratches down her cheek. She's got tears in her eyes, too.

"Did Todd do this?"

"I don't know." I kneel down before them. "I think so. Him or Pan."

Just as she sucks in an outraged breath, a woman runs over and snatches the boy up. She says something to us, something I think is along the lines of thank you. Gratitude and sadness fight for space in the mother's eyes.

Everyone is in shock and pissed to all hell. And yet, we know we don't have time to waste. We have to find Todd and Pan before they edit elsewhere.

Shit. A thought occurs to me. I dig into the inside pocket of my dress coat, praying I was smart enough to bring my Institute book and pen. "Does anybody else have their pens on them?"

Mary and Alice shake their heads. Victor claims yes, digs into his own pockets, and then admits sheepishly that he thinks he left them on his dresser while he was getting ready.

The five of us have a single pen between us.

"Speaking of," the White King says, "I am fully cognizant that this is a difficult request at a moment such as this, but it is best for me to return to Wonderland immediately. The Queen of Diamonds and I are in agreement—the most assured bet is that Hearts will go back to Wonderland to hide, if that wasn't already her destination at the party. I will hunt her on that front. That way, we can divide and conquer these villains. It is obvious they are in league with one another."

"You'll need someone to edit you into 1865/71CAR-AWLG," I say.

"I'll do it." Mary squares her shoulders. "Of the lot of us, you know I'm weakest in a fight. You three go track these sonofabitches down. I'll lead the White King back and then figure out what in the hell happened at the Institute that allowed his escape." She turns to the King. "Your Five of Diamonds is still there, and Alice's assassin. Plus, the Institute was filled with trained agents and a wicked security system that Marianne has completely overhauled. How did he get away?" To the rest of us, "Is Rosemary gone? Jenkins? Is—"

She's so worked up she can't even finish except to unleash a string of shouted cuss words that have people all around us staring. None of us have answers to her questions, though.

We're able to find a nearby alley that is surprisingly empty. I write them to the floor all our apartments are on; Mary is going to need her pen to send the White King home. As the door flashes open, Alice turns to her former lover.

"Stay safe."

He places a fist over his heart. She matches the motion. And then he gives me a look that both says, *"You stay safe, too,"* as well as, *"Keep her safe or else."*

Mary and Victor hug briefly. And then Mary and the White King are through the door. Our remaining trio jogs down to the end of the street, to where the wall once sat, only to find an empty field in one direction and a row of houses in another.

"Shite!" Victor grabs at his hair as he looks around. "I bet they're long gone, those bloody bastards. Should—"

A blood-curdling scream erupts from one of the houses.

Alice rips off her heels and then we're all off, toward the homes. Another scream that ends abruptly sets our destination. We're inside the house quickly, both my and Victor's guns out.

A pair of children huddle behind a chair, their eyes filled with tears. A woman in a kimono lies dead next to them. The boy lifts a shaky finger and points toward the back of the house. And then we're off again.

The house empties into another alley. A new scream rings out and we're heading toward the left. Finally, up ahead, I spot Pan. He's flying erratically, but more importantly, he's injured more than just with the hole in his shoulder. The children playing in the alleyway scatter in fear as he hacks away at them, shouting unintelligible things.

"He's gone mad!" Victor shouts.

Within reach, I launch myself at Pan. He and I smack into a wall with a nasty crunch, but it does nothing to slow the bastard down. Sharp, blackened teeth snap at me while he growls like a feral dog. Even worse, he fights like one.

What the hell?

I have no handcuffs. Nothing to hold him back. My best bet is to knock his ass out and haul him back to the Institute. He's a beast for something so small, though. I'll give him that. His teeth tear at my shirt and arms, all the while he bucks like a bronco.

"I see Todd!"

Not taking my eyes off the wild child, I yell at my brother and Alice to go. The indignity of not being able to subdue Pan quickly is getting to me. Eventually, I land a good punch in his jaw that leaves him howling, but he manages to kick me squarely in the nuts.

Which, you know, hurts like a *motherfucker.*

I reel back, hunched over in pain. I am going to kill this man-boy if it's the last thing I do. Pan growls again, and the next thing I know, he's got a hold on his weird, glowing blade. I swing out an arm, but it's too late.

He slides it straight into my body, through my side.

I—I—

I'm down on the ground. And then Pan is, too, and Alice is standing above us, wielding a broken piece of wood.

"Finn!" She's on her knees next to me. "Are you all right?" And then, once she gets a better look, "That little pissant stabbed you!" She's so outraged she kicks his prone body.

"It's—" I pull my hand away. Excruciating, is what I ought to say. Instead, I tell her, "I'm fine. I don't think it hit anything."

Pan gurgles and lifts his head. Alice takes my gun from me and slams the butt down against the back of his head. The boy slumps back to the ground.

"You—" I gasp as she presses her hands down upon the wound. "You should get this asshole back to the Institute."

She looks at me like I'm insane. "Do not be ridiculous. I am not leaving you, Finn. If anyone should get back to the Institute, it's you."

Victor shouts something from farther on down the alley. People have spilled out of their houses and are watching the fight go down between my brother and Todd. Victor is good in a fight—one of the best—but I am not going to leave him alone to face Todd.

"I'm fine. Please. Take this sack of shit back and Victor and I will be right behind you. Help Mary figure out what happened. I have a bad feeling about all of this."

"Me, too."

"*Go.*"

She digs her feet in, but Pan makes the choice for me. A hand grapples clumsily for his nearby sword.

"Son of a jabberwocky! What does it take to bring this fiend down?" She snatches his sword and uses the hilt to strike across the base of his skull once, twice. Then her daggers are out and she's shoved them both into his sides.

The little man-boy squeals and then shudders.

Victor shouts my name.

"Alice, please. You need to go put that poultice on, too. We can't risk any lingering boojum infection taking over."

She takes a deep breath, no doubt ready to argue. But then she kisses me swiftly. "Fine." A finger juts out toward me. "If you do not follow within a quarter of an hour, I will come back."

"Of course." Nearly out of time, I flip to the first page in my Institute book and write her in to the lobby. The door opens before us. Alice grabs hold of Pan's leg and drags him forward. "A quarter of an hour, Finn."

I give her a small salute. And that's when the second explosion happens.

As I hit the wall behind me, my pen goes flying past Alice into the Institute. The door vanishes right as Todd rushes past me, Victor hot on his heels.

"He has grenades!" my brother shouts.

I push off the wall and push past the pain. I'm off after them.

BRØKEN GLASS

ALICE

"**H**ELLO, ALICE. HAVE YOU found the right rabbit hole yet?"
The door and all of the chaos I've just left behind vanish as I toss the fiend who attacked Finn across the lobby floor. Standing behind us, wearing a crisp tuxedo much more suited to a fine event such as the gala rather than the lobby of the Institute, is Gabriel Lygari. Or Gabriel Pfeifer, considering. He's holding something small in his well-manicured hands. Lovingly, like it's precious to him.

In between us lies Finn's editing pen. *Bloody hell.*

Mary appears, but from her angle on the stairs, she cannot see Lygari. "Alice! Thank God. I can't seem to find anybody. I've just gotten back from 1865/71CAR-AWLG. Where are Victor and Finn?"

My teeth clench together. "We have a visitor."

By this point, she now has an excellent view of Lygari. Shock and then anger fill her face. "How in the hell did you get in here?"

It is an excellent question.

Lygari smiles, his teeth white and yet still tombstone-like all at once. "Some of us are more familiar with rabbit holes than others. Isn't that right, Alice?"

The pull of Finn's pen between us is a siren. Finn and Victor are—I have no idea. Somewhere far away, chasing after Todd. They have no pen to edit back with. And now, here stands a man just earlier tonight we were hunting. There is no surprise at my appearance via a magical door, no awe or terror over things that cannot be easily explained. "I have no idea what you are talking about," I say coolly, "but I concur with my friend. How is it you found your way into this building?"

His head tilts to the side; his bright eyes almost appear regretful as he looks at the battered man-child bearing both my blades at my feet. "Sometimes, sacrifices must be made in order for an objective to be met."

Silent alarms ring throughout me. Where is everyone? One of our quarries has appeared within our walls, and no one is to be found? A surreptitious glance around proves that we three are the only ones within the elaborate, large lobby. "What are—"

He extends the object until it settles within his palm, leaving my words lost between us. It is a postcard with an Asian script, featuring a series of cats.

Prickles of unease send nearly every hair on the back of my neck standing straight up. There were so many cats on the streets I just ran upon. So many. *Please, for all that is good in all the Timelines, do not let that be what I think it is.*

Mary immediately pulls out her cell phone and punches at the screen. Near-paralyzing dread fills my belly. This man with two names has hidden a library and altered the shape of his house. What more is he capable of?

"Are you ready for the next move, Alice?"

I reach for my daggers, but remember I have none on my person, as they're in the Pan-boy's belly. I am weaponless: no gun, no dagger, no nothing. Lygari must be stopped, though. If what he holds is, in fact, a catalyst, then—

Lygari tsks again and then calmly tears off a corner of the picture-postcard in his hands. The piece flutters to the floor. But to both my and Mary's amazement, before it touches the gleaming wood, the bit turns to ash.

"What in the bloody hell!" Mary's whisper is like the crack of a shot, though.

Bloody hell indeed.

Fast as a wink, my hands wrap around a nearby statue of a Greek Muse. It's black and thin and has protruding edges that will do nicely. But Gabe merely laughs—throaty and amused, warm as honey in tea. "Go ahead," he murmurs, another piece of the picture-postcard falling to the floor in soft whispers of gray and black. "Let's see if you can strike me before I finish what I've started."

Mary's scream is deafening as she sounds an alarm. I swing the statue toward Lygari right as he drops the remaining shredded pieces of the picture-postcard to the floor and grinds them to dust beneath his feet.

No!

An explosion, white and cold and terrifying, sends Mary and me sprawling across the room and into panes of stained glass. Ribbons of colored knives slice through my skin, leaving me dazed as I blink through the smoldering remnants of a once beautiful lobby.

Gabriel Lygari murmurs, his voice gentle against the ringing in my ears, "It pains me to do that, you know. But it was time." And then he pulls a musical pipe out of the inside of his coat and plays a few dissonant yet beautiful notes.

Everything is liquid. I feel like I did for years in Wonderland, drugged. *Has he drugged us?*

I struggle to push myself up, but cry out when my hands land upon the spiky jags beneath me. I cannot focus through my injuries. How can that be? Years of training . . . *Why can't I focus?* Mary, for her part, does not move from where she lays bleeding nearby. *Get up, Alice. You've been in worse situations than this before.*

Haven't I?

Haven't I?

He lowers his pipe. "Nowhere is safe," the man I regretfully once allowed to press his lips against my neck in a darkened nightclub says. "And no one. Not if I don't want them to be." He smiles again, his teeth much too bright in the haze enveloping me. "Not even you. Not even those from the Society who think they can halt what needs to be done. I wanted you to know this tonight. It's best to stay out of my way unless I seek you out first."

"Wha—" Words, garbled. Boys and girls of varying ages, dressed in brown jerkins, dance about me. They lift up the Pan-creature who stabbed Finn and carry him across the room. *What magic is this?*

"*The Adventures of Huckleberry Finn* and *Frankenstein*," he continues softly, "were filled with irresponsible characters. Even those who originated from those Timelines resented their stories, did they not?"

My bones and muscles are useless, even as his words sink in like rusty nails driven in by hammers.

Glass crunches beneath Lygari's feet as he turns away; a mournful melody trails his steps. A glowing doorway appears before him, books and shelves, glass cases filled with familiar items fill the distance.

Bücherei.

Colors swirl around me, light and bright and dark and heavy. Rage percolates, though. Rage and more sorrow than I thought ever possible.

The children trail him through the doorway, swaying to the tune as they haul the Pan-boy's body. Music swells and then falls, and then the doorway disappears.

Clarity strikes me fast and hard in the new silence. Despite the pain, I am able to push myself up. Crawl on bleeding knees over to Mary. Fingers fumble against her neck. She's alive. Thank God, she is alive, even though there are new gashes on her head bleeding profusely.

The wreckage of the lobby swarms with bodies. Nobody can seem to remember much of the evening, to be honest, but one thing is for sure. A catalyst has been destroyed within the Institute's walls for the first time. They've seen enough of these events to know their markers.

A catalyst has been destroyed.

Breathing becomes laboriously difficult.

So many people asking what happened. So many people wondering why they feel like they've been asleep for a century. So many people scared, because time is missing for them.

Van Brunt finds me once I'm upon my feet, and the look in his eyes—the questions, the fear, the assumptions—are nearly too much to bear.

He asks me about my failures anyway. "What happened?" he barks.

"Where are Finn and Victor? Who did this, Ms. Reeve?"

"They—" I swallow. I must focus, if I am to get through the coming minutes. I must focus, if I am to do what must be done. "They stayed behind to capture Todd. I came ahead with—" And yet, my prisoner is gone. "I must get the doorway opened quickly. Finn was stabbed, and I don't think it best he continue for much longer."

Van Brunt swears softly before he snatches up the Muse statue I'd attempted to use as a weapon earlier. It hurls it across the room in a burst of shouted anger. The hole in the wall it leaves behind is not so small.

"Gabriel Lygari was here in the lobby. How did he get past your security measures?"

His attention reverts to me, his eyes glassy. "Lygari? You mean Pfeifer? The rare book collector we were hunting at the gala? *He* was here?"

"The very one."

The Librarian appears, somber as she surveys our surroundings. When did she return? "What did the catalyst look like, Alice?"

I tell her, doing my best to remain calm and failing all at once, "It was a picture-postcard. It was . . . Japanese, maybe. It had cats on it and appeared old."

Her eyes close. The room around us falls silent. Van Brunt's fingers curl into fists when he takes in her sorrow.

I ask what I fear anyway. I ask, "What Timeline was that a catalyst for?" When neither answers me, I shout the question anew.

"1905/06Sōs-IAAC," the Librarian tells me, and for the first time in a long time, I do not think she is playing word games with me. "It is for a book about a cat that takes place in Japan in the early Twentieth Century called *I Am A Cat.*"

No. *No.* I stumble backward, my balance lost.

"Ms. Reeve," Van Brunt says flatly. "What Timeline are my boys in?"

I shake my head. They—they could be anywhere. We were in Japan, yes, and there were cats, but . . . but it does not necessarily mean 1905/06Sōs-IAAC. It could—it could be any Timeline. There are thousands of books written about Japan at this time. There—

My name is said. Hands take hold of me, but I shake them off. Van Brunt asks me again, but I simply shout my denial.

I would know if Finn was dead. I would sense it, wouldn't I? My footing would no longer be on firm ground. Gravity would abandon me and I would once more be adrift.

Marianne weeps openly. Flemming and Holgrave are pale and shaken. Mary is still blissfully unaware of how our world has just been so very horribly altered, and the A.D. is shrill in his insistences about how they need to get her to a hospital immediately.

"You must go, too." Van Brunt's words are hollow. "You're in bad shape, Ms. Reeve."

These words mean nothing to me. I fight for logic. Fight for clarity. "Lygari went through a doorway, into a library." I turn to the Librarian. "It must be Bücherei. It must be."

"You are going nowhere except for the hospital," Van Brunt is saying. Sirens in the distance grow with each passing second. "There is no time to root through Ms. Lennox's medical supplies from various Timelines. We first must ensure all are safe and accounted for." A tiny catch in his voice sounds. "The local doctors will take care of you, Ms. Reeve."

"No." Anxiety crawls up my throat. It's the only word that makes any sense right now. "*No.*"

"Ms. Reeve—"

"Whatever you are insinuating—you, of all people, should know better than to say it, let alone think it."

Van Brunt is undeterred. "Ms. Reeve—"

I refuse to allow him to vocalize such a cowardly belief. "You are wrong. Know this now. I will never give up on finding him. *Never.*"

Van Brunt simply stares at me.

"Lygari had a magical pipe," I say coldly. "It is time for us to determine who is capable of altering reality with a musical instrument, and then go after him with all our might. Did you not all claim that the flying boy had pipes with him, as well? It is not a coincidence."

Yet he does not address this. Instead, Van Brunt asks brusquely, "Did my sons have their pens with them?"

Strength, do not fail me now. My knees wobble once more, but I remain strong as I reach down into the rubble. Finn's pen is miraculously in one piece and yet it is still here, with me and not with him.

I have to force the words out. "Victor forgot his upstairs."

Van Brunt does not query me as to why Finn's is here at the Institute rather than with him wherever he currently is. But he does not have to, not when it does not matter in the least. Because, without their pens, he is reminding me that Finn and Victor had no way out of 1905/06Sōs-IAAC.

I cannot accept this.

I cannot.

More importantly, *I will not.*

The urge to pluck at my hair finally proves irresistible. One by one, tiny golden strands float down as I begin formulating my plan. Lygari will be stopped. He will pay for what he's done. Todd will, too. He will never have the chance to exit this building again alive. I will find Finn— and Victor. They will be fine.

He will be fine. Our story is not done.

I will save him as he saved me.

"She's in shock."

I blink and the room slowly comes back into focus. There are medical personnel here, examining Mary. There are medical personnel strapping something to my bicep and inspecting the cuts zigzagging up and down forearms. I am sitting, and Van Brunt is no longer standing with me but over where Mary is being placed onto a gurney.

The Librarian is here, though. She reaches a slim hand out and strokes my bloody head as one of the men in a blue uniform flashes a light in my eyes. And then, before I am placed within the waiting beast of a machine outside alongside a still-sleeping Mary, she leans in and kisses my cheek.

She whispers, regret and pain and sorrow lining her beautiful face, "I am so sorry, Alice. More than you can imagine. I failed. Remember to trust your instincts."

The door shuts behind her. A siren blares above us. I glance at Mary and think savagely: *I always do.*

EPILOGUE

London

"FINN! HE'S EDITING!"

Sure enough, Todd is scribbling in a book, all the while hacking his way through the growing yet terrified crowd. People are screaming and it's chaos once more, but there isn't time to calm them all down. Victor and I take off after him, pushing our way through the alley.

I can't let him edit out. Not after what he's done.

I also can't shoot him. There are too many innocents in the way. I can't risk hitting anyone—I'm a damn good shot, but even I don't think I can target him in this crowd, both of us being jostled around by terrified civilians trying to get to safety.

An explosion goes off right behind us, one that feels different from the rest. I nearly fall, it's so strong, but dammit, he's got his door open.

"Don't let him get through!" I bark at Victor.

Another explosion sounds. Bright lights fill the sky; a loud buzzing drowns out any further sound. The earth shakes below us. People are dropping all around us, hands frantically pressed against their ears to stem the pain. Cats howl, their plaintive cries nearly matching the din.

I think my ears are bleeding, it's so bad.

In the confusion, my brother leaps forward, his long arms stretching just far enough to grab a corner of the asshole's shirt. And then I'm right there with them, hurling ourselves through the doorway and onto the hard, wet, dirty cobblestone street of a deserted alley that reeks of piss and trash. The doorway winks away, and as there are no longer any crowds to stop me, my gun is out.

Fuck it. The time for talking is done. I give no warning. I shoot the asshole in the shoulder. He roars, dropping his book and pen into a puddle that looks more yellow than anything else. But rather than stopping him like I'd hoped, his rage propels him toward us. Instead of a book, he now wields a dagger pulled from his boots. *What the hell? Where did he get that?*

"Gonna slice you pretty boys up, nice and neat!"

His words are garbled. My ears still hum from the buzzing of the last Timeline.

"Finn, my gun—I lost it in the fight!" I think Victor interjects, and that only solidifies my decision.

I shoot again, right in his knee. And then in the other knee, so I know he's in pain. Thank God for silencers.

He screams and then wobbles, but goddammit, Todd keeps coming at us. What the fuck are these people taking? Are they all high on meth or something? Between blackened teeth, he hisses, "My hands were all over her body. Did your pretty little girl tell you that? Did she tell you how she liked it?"

Oh. Hell. *No.*

My shot runs clean through the middle of Todd's forehead. He drops to the ground, blood from his arm and legs puddling beneath him as his crazed eyes stare up into the gray, cloud-covered sky. As if on cue, it begins to rain.

Hearing becomes easier and yet still painful.

I shoot the fucker again, just to be sure. This time, I aim directly for his heart. The body spasms as my bullet strikes true. *That one is for*

Alice, because he tried to take my heart from me.

"May I?"

I pass Victor my gun. He shoots Todd directly in the nuts.

"That's," he says quietly, "for our mother, you sonofabitch."

We both stare down at his body, neither of us feeling a single shred of remorse. I can only hope he was lying to me in the end, because the thought of Todd touching Alice in any way makes me want to physically rip him apart with my bare hands. "Too bad you didn't do that when he was still alive."

Victor laughs quietly, but there's no humor there. He passes me my gun so I can slip it into the holster beneath my coat. When fingers brush against my side, I wince. Shit. With all the adrenaline of the last chase, I'd almost forgotten about how Pan stabbed me. "You lost your gun?"

He sighs. "Yeah. The arsehole managed to land a good kick." More sheepishly, "He got me right in the bollocks."

"If it's any consolation, Pan landed the same kick on me."

He claps me on the shoulder. "I'm afraid it's not the best of days for men and their bollocks, is it?"

God, I love my brother.

His fingers tighten on my shoulder. "Let's get back to the Institute. I want to know how this one got out."

I rub at my hair. "Yeah. About that . . . I lost my pen in the second explosion."

His hand drops to his side.

I take a deep breath. "It went through the doorway, after Alice hauled Pan back."

"Bloody. Fucking. *Hell.* Could this day get any worse?"

I wipe bloody fingers against my pants before Victor notices. "Do you think their pens are DNA coded? Todd had one on him."

We both glance toward the foul-smelling puddle the pen and book now lay in. And . . . yes. The day most certainly could get worse, because the pen is blackened and smoking, a piece of it missing. DNA coding is the least of our worries.

I let out a huge sigh.

"Well, at least we can figure out where we are," Victor says. "And go from there. Between us, we ought to know who most of the liaisons are. All we have to do is go find this one's."

"If we even have a liaison to this Timeline."

He nudges my arm. "A little optimism hurts no one. Besides, the ladies are going to be hot on our trail. Like Mary or Alice ever gave up on anything."

I squat down next to the soggy book and glance at the pages. We're in London, by the looks of it. And . . . Hot damn. Maybe we do have a bit of luck left.

"Do you know where we are?" Victor asks.

I stand up, wincing once more as pain dulled by adrenaline now surges forward. "I most certainly do. We're in 1905BUR-LP."

My brother's eyes widen comically. "Are you funning me?"

I shake my head and we both laugh. And then I flinch again as my side spasms.

Doctor he is, my brother is practically breathing on top of me. "What the hell, Finn? When did this happen? We need to get you somewhere where I can clean you up. Is this a stab wound? Did Pan get you with that weird glowing blade?" He doesn't let me answer, though. "Does it feel like it hit anything important?"

Whether or not it did, I shake my head. First things first.

"Right then. You hold on a second so I can hide this bugger."

Victor moves toward the body. I debate slumping against a nearby wall, but fear I may not be able to push myself up when it comes time to leave. "Search his pockets?"

"I swear, brother. You act as if this were my first rodeo."

Victor works carefully, shoving Todd's body behind a bunch of broken wooden crates. His pockets, regretfully, are empty save one blank scrap of paper. Victor keeps it anyway. And then he collects the remaining pieces of the pen so that Wendy—no, Marianne, can examine them if and when we can get back to the Institute.

He also takes the book, wrapping both in stray newspaper littering the street and tucking them inside his coat. The action is followed by a brief shudder—shit, I would, too, if a urine-soaked book and smoldering pen were inside my coat—but there's no way we can leave that book out for just anybody to find.

"Let's go find Sara," he tells me. And then we make our way out of the alley and onto the streets.

BY THE TIME WE make our way through the London streets, the rain is coming down so hard that it's almost impossible to see ten feet in front of us. We're both soaked and doing our damn best to not chatter, but London in the winter isn't exactly the warmest of places.

Finn is worrying me. He's pale, his lips nearly white, and he's shaking. I damn well know it has nothing to do with the temperature, either. I keep trying to get him to let me look at where Pan stabbed him, but Finn's having none of that. *We need to get to Sara's,* he insists. *We need to get back to the Institute. I've got a bad feeling about all this. Todd shouldn't have been able to get out.*

Pardon me if my bloody priority is making sure my brother is okay first.

We have no money though, no way to go anywhere safe for me to examine him. He's got a point. It's not like I can pull him into a pub and rip off his shirt. Police would be called. We'd have to answer questions about why we're dressed as we are and still looking like we've lived through several bombings and why Finn has not only a futuristic-looking gun on him but also a hole in his side.

I cannot believe we landed in Sara Crewe's Timeline—and in the past, to boot. Only, she's not Sara Crewe anymore, is she? She's Sara Carrisford. But honestly, what are the chances? Why here? Did Todd know that Sara and Finn once worked together? Or that Sara worked with the Society? Was this honestly a random choice?

Questions such as these leave me bloody nervous. Alice was right. All these coincidences don't feel coincidental at all.

There is no way my father would have allowed Todd to leave. Thinking about this leaves me in a panic. I sent Mary back early.

God, please make sure Mary is okay.

Everything in my brain races too fast. Anxiety builds up in my chest. I've been rotten at taking my meds lately, and wouldn't that be just the best? Me, having a full break with reality here in Sara's London, especially when my brother needs me most?

"Why do you think we landed in 1905BUR-LP?" I ask shortly after we ask a drenched newspaper boy directions. We're moving in the right direction, thank God.

Finn doesn't answer right away. In fact, all he does is offer up some kind of worrisome grunt before stumbling, and that only solidifies my resolve to get to Sara's house as quickly as possible. It takes us nearly half an hour before we finally arrive, and when we do, I'm left doing a double take.

Sara's home is large and gray, its walls stretching a good distance on either side of a fancy door and elaborate columns. I knew she was well off—hell, everyone at the Institute gossiped like crazy when she left us to move back home and marry her (my Mary put it best, as she often does) *sugar daddy.* A good several dozen years older than herself, the senior Carrisford had practically raised Sara in lieu of her father, his former, now-deceased partner.

It was nasty as all fuck, is what it was. Mary told Sara this straight to her face; Wendy backed her up. The rest of us cringed whenever we were faced with the situation. But Finn . . . Finn had her back the whole time, even though he knew she was making a horrible decision. He didn't say anything when she basically spat in all our faces that we were nothing to her, and that the Society better keep their distance now that she was going off to be a good little wife and lady.

And now here we are, going to see the May-December romance in full bloom, aren't we? And I can't very well object, as 1) I need a place to examine my brother's wounds, and 2) we need to get home as fast as bloody possible to make sure everyone is okay. I can only hope that Sara won't slam the door in our faces.

I knock several times before the door finally opens. And just as it does, Finn topples backward, off the steps. I lunge and grab him just in time to see the butler staring down his nose at me.

Right bloody prick.

The door begins to swing shut. I kick out a boot and force it back open.

"Excuse me!" The sod is indignant, like we're some kind of stray dogs covered in fleas or something. "You can't just—"

"We need to see your mistress," I say firmly. "Now."

He sniffs. "The lady isn't at home."

I drag Finn along with me as I step forward. "Then we will wait until she is."

The butler sputters, and I'm just having no more of his prattle. I whip out my brother's gun and aim it right at the arsehole. "I can guarantee that if Mrs. Carrisford knew you were keeping us out here like this, she'd break your kneecaps."

All right. That might be a tad of a stretch. Sara wasn't exactly the strongest of fighters—she was a quiet little thing, whose shot was better than any kind of punch she could throw. But my threat must be enough, because the butler's eyes go wide and then narrow before he steps to the side and lets us in. The moment the door shuts behind us, Finn slumps straight to the ground.

Shite!

He's burning up, his pulse is weak. "Help me take him to the kitchen," I order the butler, but then I hear my name called.

Upon the stairs, dressed in bubblegum pink like a *frou-frou* doll is none other than my brother's former partner.

"Victor?" Sara says again, like she can't believe I'm inside her house, dripping like that wet dog the butler fears I am, all over her shiny, pretty tiled floors. And then, "Is that . . ." Her hand goes over her mouth. "Finn!"

She bolts down the stairs and practically knocks the butler away. "What happened?! What are you two doing here? Is he—" She yanks open his coat before I can and then gasps at the bloom of red that stains half his shirt. "He's been stabbed! You might have opened with that, Victor!"

So much for saying we all *better stay away or else,* thank goodness.

The butler garbles, "Ma'am, these men—"

But she cuts him off. "Groverley, help us get Mr. Van Brunt to the guest room."

"Kitchen," I correct. "I need to examine him."

She nods grimly. "Listen to Dr. Frankenstein. Let us get our guest to the kitchen immediately." Raising her voice, she yells, "Mrs. Groverley! We need towels and hot water. A needle and thread!"

"But . . . ma'am!"

Her already high-pitched voice ups a whole octave. *"Now, Groverley!"*

Finn moans softly when we pick him up, but he does not open his eyes. Bloody hell. We wind our way through the house, bursting through the kitchen. The cook and the kitchen maid both squeak in surprise, and then blanch when Sara swipes every last bit of food and cutlery straight off the island. Groverley and I slide Finn upon it, and I curse silently that I didn't have time to bleach the surface. Sara's got Finn's shirt spread open, and we both go still when we peer down at his skin.

Mottled purple and red streaks form a hellishly large, vivid starburst around the wound.

"What . . ." She swallows hard. Turns as pale as he is. "What causes something like that?" And then, with fright, "What have you two done?"

I don't know what to tell her. Or to say. Or, fuck, *do*—because I have no idea. Not one bloody idea. What do I tell her? *Peter bloody Pan did this with a glowing sword?* I get down to business, though. The cut . . . It didn't hit any major organs. And it's gone clean through his side, a perfect open hole in his body. Christ. What am I going to do? I'm in Nineteenth-Century England. It's not like I've got a ton of medical options at my fingertips. Or, hell, antibiotics, which he desperately needs. Does Sara even have a thermometer?

My emotions scatter. I realize I've missed my latest dose of protocol. And now I'm scared shitless I'm not going to be able to focus enough to save my brother.

As the housekeeper bustles in with strips of cloth and a whole sewing box of needles, I lean down and say my brother's name. I say it even louder, not caring that I sound like I'm about to start yelling my bloody head off. When he doesn't answer me, I press my fingers against his throat. His breathing is shallow, his pulse even weaker.

I peel back one of his eyelids, and then, in horror, the other. The cook drops the pan of water she was bringing to us and shrieks.

Finn's eyes are completely black.

A BIBLIOGRAPHY

Curious as to who was featured or mentioned within
The Hidden Library?
Here's a list of some of the people and the books they came from.

Abraham Van Brunt (AKA Brom Bones); Katrina (Van Tassel) Van Brunt
Featured in the short story *The Legend of Sleepy Hollow*, found within *The Sketch Book of Geoffrey Crayon, Gent.* by Washington Irving

Alice (Reeve) Liddel; the White King; the Mad Hatter; Grimsdyke; the Caterpillar; the Cheshire-Cat; the Queen of Hearts; various other Wonderlandian animals & peoples
Both from and loosely based upon *Alice's Adventures in Wonderland* by Lewis Carroll
Through the Looking-Glass, and What Alice Found There by Lewis Carroll
The Hunting of the Snark by Lewis Carroll

Anne (Elliot) Wentworth
Persuasion by Jane Austen

Cat(s)
I Am A Cat by Natsume Sōseki

Catherine (Morland) Tilney
Northanger Abbey by Jane Austen

The Earnshaw and Linton Families; Heathcliff; Nellie Dean; Joseph
Wuthering Heights by Emily Brontë

Elizabeth (Bennett) Darcy
Pride and Prejudice by Jane Austen

Emma Knightley
Emma by Jane Austen

Gwendolyn Peterson (AKA Wendy Darling); Peter Pan
Based loosely upon *Peter and Wendy* by J. M. Barrie

Henry Fleming
Red Badge of Courage by Stephen Crane

Dr. Heidegger
Featured in the short story *Dr. Heidegger's Experiment,* found within *Twice Told Tales* by Nathaniel Hawthorne

Mr. Holgrave
House of the Seven Gables by Nathaniel Hawthorne

Huckleberry Finn; Tom Sawyer; Becky (Thatcher) Sawyer; Judge Thatcher; Jim; The Widow Douglas; various other St. Petersburg residents
Both from and loosely based upon *The Adventures of Tom Sawyer* by Mark Twain
Adventures of Huckleberry Finn by Mark Twain
Tom Sawyer Abroad by Mark Twain
Tom Sawyer, Detective by Mark Twain

Jack Dawkins (AKA The Artful Dodger)
Oliver Twist by Charles Dickens

Marianne (Dashwood) Brandon; Elinor (Dashwood) Ferras; Colonel Brandon
Sense and Sensibility by Jane Austen

Mary Lennox
The Secret Garden by Frances Hodgson Burnett

Professor Otto Lindenbrock
Journey to the Center of the Earth by Jules Verne
Sara (Crewe) Carrisford
A Little Princess by Frances Hodgson Burnett

Sherlock Holmes; Dr. Watson
A Study in Scarlet by Sir Arthur Conan Doyle
The Sign of the Four by Sir Arthur Conan Doyle
The Hound of the Baskervilles by Sir Arthur Conan Doyle
The Valley of Fear by Sir Arthur Conan Doyle

Sweeney Patrick Todd; Rosemary Nellie Lovett
Based loosely upon *A String of Pearls: A Romance,* most likely
written by James Malcolm Rymer and Thomas Peckett Prest

Victor Frankenstein Jr.
Based loosely upon *Frankenstein; or, The Modern Prometheus* by
Mary Shelley

ACKNOWLEDGEMENTS

Much gratitude is sent out to the following people who helped make this book the best it could be: my editor Kristina Circelli, my publicist KP Simmon, my assistant Tricia Santos, Victoria Alday for designing another gorgeous cover, and my formatter Stacey Blake. Further appreciation is sent to Bridget Donelson and Nicole Friedrich for proofreading.

Jessica Mangicaro, Andrea Johnston, Vilma Gonzalez, and Tricia, I am deeply grateful for all the time, feedback, and love you've given these characters and their stories.

To the fab members of my street team, the Lyons Pride, I adore you all and am forever grateful for your support. (in no particular order) Ana, Tricia, Kathryn, Vilma, Megan, Jessica, Amy, Christina Marie, LeAnn, Rebecca, Kiersten, Meredith, Maria, Ivey, Whitney, Daniela, Caitlin, Tracy, Sarah, Enrica, Ethan, Leigha, Nicole, Cynthia, Heather, Cherisse, Autumn, JL, Bridget, Lindy, Gina, Brandi, Jessica, and all the rest . . . you guys rock.

As always, no book of mine can ever be written without the love and support from my family. To my husband and children, all the love and gratitude to you guys for putting up with me sitting in front of the computer for hours upon end. And to my parents, I am eternally grateful for your support. Thanks for installing a deep love of books and reading into me at an early age.

All the thanks to you, too, sweet reader.

ALSO BY HEATHER LYONS

"Each of us here has a story, but it may not be the one you think you know . . ."

"The most unique, fascinating, wondrous book I've read in a very long time!
I was glued to every page."
-Shelly Crane, New York Times bestselling author of Significance and Wide Awake

From the author of the Fate series and The Deep End of the Sea comes a fantastical romantic adventure that has Alice tumbling down the strangest rabbit hole yet.

After years in Wonderland, Alice has returned to England as an adult, desperate to reclaim sanity and control over her life. An enigmatic gentleman with an intriguing job offer too tempting to resist changes her plans for a calm existence, though. Soon, she's whisked to New York and initiated into the Collectors' Society, a secret organization whose members confirm that famous stories are anything but straightforward and that what she knows about the world is only a fraction of the truth.

It's there she discovers villains are afoot—ones who want to shelve the lives of countless beings. Assigned to work with the mysterious and alluring Finn, Alice and the rest of the Collectors' Society race against a doomsday clock in order to prevent further destruction . . . but will they make it before all their endings are erased?

An enthralling mythological romance two thousand years in the making . . .

What if all the legends you've learned were wrong?

Brutally attacked by one god and unfairly cursed by another she faithfully served, Medusa has spent the last two thousand years living out her punishment on an enchanted isle in the Aegean Sea. A far cry from the monster legends depict, she's spent her time educating herself, gardening, and desperately trying to frighten away adventure seekers who occasionally end up, much to her dismay, as statues when they manage to catch her off guard. As time marches on without her, Medusa wishes for nothing more than to be given a second chance at a life stolen away at far too young an age.

But then comes a day when Hermes, one of the few friends she still has and the only deity she trusts, petitions the rest of the gods and goddesses to reverse the curse. Thus begins a journey toward healing and redemption, of reclaiming a life after tragedy, and of just how powerful friendship and love can be—because sometimes, you have to sink in the deep end of the sea before you can rise back up again

"Love, love, love this book! Such a fun and exciting premise. Full of teenage angst and heartache with a big helping of magic and enchantment. Can't wait to read the rest of this awesome series! Not to mention . . . TWO hot boys to swoon over."–*Elizabeth Lee, author of Where There's Smoke*

Chloe Lilywhite struggles with all the normal problems of a typical seventeen-year-old high school student. Only, Chloe isn't a normal teenage girl. She's a Magical, part of a secret race of beings who influence the universe. More importantly, she's a Creator, which means Fate mapped out her destiny long ago, from her college choice, to where she will live, to even her job. While her friends and relatives relish their future roles, Chloe resents the lack of say in her life, especially when she learns she's to be guarded against a vengeful group of beings bent on wiping out her kind. Their number one target? Chloe, of course.

That's nothing compared to the boy trouble she's gotten herself into. Because a guy she's literally dreamed of and loved her entire life, one she never knew truly existed, shows up in her math class, and with him comes a twin brother she finds herself inexplicably drawn to.

Chloe's once unyielding path now has a lot more choices than she ever thought possible.

Follow Chloe's story in the rest of the Fate series books . . .

"Heather Lyons' writing is an addiction . . . and like all addictions. I. Need. More."
—*#1 New York Times Best Selling Author Rachel Van Dyken*

"Enthralling fantasy with romance that will leave you breathless, the Fate Series is a must read!"—*Alyssa Rose Ivy, author of the Crescent Chronicles*

ABOUT THE AUTHOR

photo @Regina Wamba of Mae I Design and Photography

Heather Lyons is known for writing epic, heartfelt love stories often with a fantastical twist. From Young Adult to New Adult to Adult novels—one commonality in all her books is the touching, and sometimes heart-wrenching, romance. In addition to writing, she's also been an archaeologist and a teacher. She and her husband and children live in sunny Southern California and are currently working their way through every cupcakery she can find.

Website: www.heatherlyons.net
Facebook: http://www.facebook.com/heatherlyonsbooks
Twitter: http://www.twitter.com/hymheather
Goodreads: http://www.goodreads.com/author/show/6552446.Heather_Lyons
Stay up to date with Heather by subscribing to her newsletter: http://eepurl.com/2Lkij

www.ingramcontent.com/pod-product-compliance
Lightning Source LLC
Chambersburg PA
CBHW060900250626
47159CB00008B/2820